Rave reviews for Brynn Kelly's
Edge of Truth

"*Edge of Truth* has it all—danger, desire, and heart-pounding action. Brynn Kelly captures you on page one and doesn't let go!"
—Laura Griffin, *New York Times* bestselling author

"Brynn Kelly will capture your heart and leave you breathless in this passionate, harrowing novel of romantic suspense. A must-read!"
—Brenda Novak, *New York Times* bestselling author

"Dark and deep—a twisting romantic suspense that will grab you and never let go."
—Cynthia Eden, *New York Times* bestselling author

"*Edge of Truth* is a breathtaking romantic thriller. The characters are so real they leap off the page, the love story is hot and the action never lets up. I couldn't put it down."
—Karen Robards, *New York Times* bestselling author

"Kelly is rapidly demonstrating that she is highly skilled at developing intricate stories that are packed with intrigue and jeopardy, while also rich with human emotion. This book is a nonstop thrill ride.... Kelly is proving to be a gift to the romantic suspense genre!"

—*RT Book Reviews*, Top Pick!

Praise for Brynn Kelly's
Deception Island

A *Booklist* Top 10 Romance Debut of 2016!

"Intense and exciting...romantic suspense at its best!"
 —Carla Neggers, *New York Times* bestselling author

"Smoldering chemistry, cunning twists and a whole lot of heart. Brynn Kelly delivers everything I love in a romance."
—Heather Graham, *New York Times* bestselling author

"Kidnappings and pirates and romance—oh my! *Deception Island* is a keeper."
 —Cindy Gerard, *New York Times* bestselling author

"The perfect book...one you'll never forget."
 —Sharon Sala, *New York Times* bestselling author

"Brynn Kelly pens a raw, dark, emotional novel of danger and intrigue that will keep readers turning the pages."
 —Kat Martin, *New York Times* bestselling author

"*Deception Island* is nothing short of brilliant. I love this book and am salivating for more!"
 —Lena Diaz, award-winning author

BRYNN KELLY

A RISK WORTH TAKING

HQN™

HQN™

ISBN-13: 978-1-335-49829-8

Recycling programs for this product may not exist in your area.

A Risk Worth Taking

www.HQNBooks.com

Printed in U.S.A.

**Also available from Brynn Kelly
and HQN Books**

A RISK WORTH TAKING

CHAPTER ONE

Tuscany

A DOZEN TINY spiders tiptoed up Samira Desta's nape. She planted a placeholder finger on her file of evidence and blinked as her focus adjusted over the rolling red and gold fields, their folds in charcoal shadow like an unshaken quilt. Cypress trees: check. Cows: check. Paranoia: check. She rubbed her neck. Nothing there, of course. Not a Sangiovese grape out of place in paradise.

The buzz of a motor curled in on the breeze, echoing off the hills. Her breath stalled. Vehicle? Helicopter? Drone strike? What did a drone strike even sound like?

She tsked. A droning, presumably. And by the time you noticed it, would it be too late, like seeing a tsunami or hearing the rumble of an earthquake?

A red motor scooter bobbed up over a distant rise and ducked away under the next, appeared again, disappeared, appeared…rising and falling from view like a surfer in a swell. The rider wore a high-vis jacket. *Il postino.* Samira exhaled. *Stand down, Sherlock.*

Or could it be a mercenary masquerading as a postal worker? That would be a great cover.

Yes, she was losing it. Too much time alone.

Low morning sun bathed the courtyard but the air channeling down the neighbor's vines was cool around the edges, sending leaves rattling and scratching across the terra-cotta tiles. From the speakers inside the rented cottage, Carole King and her piano were working through their problems. "It's Going to Take Some Time."

No kidding, Carole.

Coffee fumes wove into the decaying earthy scent of fall. *Autunno*, here. The world didn't get more breathtaking but the beauty didn't hit Samira in her chest as it might once have. One day, when all this was over, maybe that little skip would return.

With a sigh she tightened her ponytail and returned to the document. The letters seemed to float off the page and rearrange, like they were trying to edit themselves. Ah, who was she kidding? She'd memorized every word of her evidence for the special counsel investigating Senator Tristan Hyland's terrorist links. No matter how often she revised, it got no stronger than circumstantial and hearsay. And no wonder people weren't believing it. A wildly popular war hero orders a terror attack in Los Angeles that kills thousands, for political and financial gain? Preposterous. He could still wriggle out, proclaim it was a conspiracy to end his presidential ambitions— if Samira even got to testify before suffering a conveniently fatal accident, like her fiancé had.

Note to self: Google the sound of a drone strike.

Or would that send an alert to a gray-faced analyst in a monitoring center in some industrial park in America? A company with an ominously banal name—Tactical Security Associates or Virtual Monitoring Solutions. *She wants to hear a drone strike? We'll give her a drone strike.*

No, she really wasn't winning the concentration battle. She heaved the document shut, the echoing slap sending a cow thundering across a neighboring field. Scraping the chair backward, she pressed her knuckles into the middle of her back and arched. For many months it'd felt like a bubble of air was trapped there. She'd writhed and wriggled, twisted and stretched, bent backward over innumerable sofas and chairs in a blur of rented cottages and apartments, but the satisfying pop just wouldn't come. If Latif were alive he'd gather her in his arms and yank her tight around the ribs. Just the right spot, just the right angle, just the right pressure. Her back would crack, the tension would release, she'd take a deep breath, they'd kiss…

She gave up on the back crack. Wishful thinking. The bubble had been wedged there since she'd read the newsflash about "collateral damage" in a drone strike in Somalia and known by the snap in her heart what it meant.

Nineteen months since his death. Thirteen months since she'd become a witness in the case against Hyland and disappeared underground on a self-imposed protection program. Thirteen months of fleeing from hiding place to hiding place, living under a series of assumed names, rarely reaching more length or depth in her conversations than *"un cappuccino, per favore," "un café crème, s'il vous plaît," "ich möchte etwas kaffee."* Her Continental grand tour, from Africa to France, then Switzerland, Slovakia, Croatia… She traced a finger around the lip of the coffee cup. Where had she gone after that? The Milan apartment? The former monastery near Barcelona? All private, secluded rentals that didn't require ID. Cash up front to cover a couple of months' rent for a "writing retreat." All the time with that bubble lodged in her spine, that prickly sensation of being watched. She shuddered.

Still, she had no right to complain—about anything. How much would Latif love to come back for this one day, as hollow as it was? Sunshine, countryside, starlings… It would all be pretty cool to a dead person.

She shook a twig off her foot and hunkered into her scarf. *La couleur de minuit.* A memory triggered—crunching through leaves alongside the River Loire, the scarf around her neck, hand in hand with a man she shouldn't have been hand in hand with. But his palm was dry and warm and rough, and his voice was deep and mellow, and her grief was raw, and his kiss was…

A man who shouldn't return to her thoughts as often as he did. Like right now, virtually pulling up a chair alongside her and nuzzling her nape, murmuring phrases that hadn't been covered by her French tutors, his Scottish lilt blending with his throaty French *R*.

She tugged the scarf free and twisted its smooth cotton length through one loose fist, silver threads flashing in the deep violet. Memory or fantasy? She'd been living in her head so long…

Either way, it was unfair to force Latif's fading ghost to compete with the all-too-vivid memory of Jamie. And futile. Both were entombed in her past and would stay there. She hadn't replaced Latif with Jamie. Jamie had been a…what? Fling? Escape? Lapse of judgment? All of the above? It might as well have happened in her imagination, except for the scarf he'd bought her from the market below the Château de Langeais and the voice in her head, and the very real confusion twisting beneath her ribs. If it wasn't grief over Latif, it was guilt over what she'd felt for Jamie. Still felt.

Was that really a year ago?

Her phone alarm trilled through the Bluetooth speakers. The *A-Team* theme. She caught the phone as it vibrated off the wrought iron table, and swiped it silent, her heart skipping. The music restarted. The scooter had

turned onto her road—a dead end she shared with a boutique family vineyard and an organic farm—triggering
the first of her motion sensors. She threaded the scarf
around her neck and knotted it. The engine tapered from
a hum to a chug as it neared her long driveway. Probably
nothing, but she gathered up the file and the coffee cup.

The scooter disappeared behind a strip of strutting
cypresses, its engine slowing, the sound sharpening as
it turned. Samira's pocket jumped. The second alarm—
MacGyver. The scooter was in her driveway. With a few
more swipes, she muted the alarm and Carole, midclimax
of "It's Too Late." She grabbed her backpack from where
it leaned against a whitewashed wall just inside the French
doors—packed, always packed. She hadn't left as much
as a toothbrush out in a year. The scooter whined as it
climbed the gravel drive. Breath catching, she drew the
doors closed from the outside, coaxing them flat with
her fingernails, and stole behind the fat trunk of an oak
across the courtyard.

Probably just mail for a previous tenant, but the fewer
locals she encountered, the better. The only people who
could feasibly mail her anything—and only through a
trusted, off-the-radar intermediary—were her parents
and the journalist who'd broken the story a year ago about
Hyland's connection to the LA attacks, Tess Newell. Her
friend Tess Newell. Because she was seriously short of
those. And they knew not to contact her unless it was
vital. Too many ways to tip off the enemy.

She leaned against the trunk, tracking the scooter's
progress by its noise as it rolled into the turning bay and
idled. Over the fence, several white cows stopped chewing and stared at Samira. She made a face but they didn't
get the hint. Footsteps crunched. A knock on the thin
door frame, rattling the glass inserts. A pause. Another

rap. More footsteps. The hiss of the rider reclaiming the seat, and then the scooter decrescendoed down the drive. Samira waited several minutes then pushed off the trunk, strands of her hair pinching as they caught on the bark. A white stamped envelope lay beside the door.

The alarms triggered in the opposite order as the scooter resumed its rounds. Oh, for a life that simple. Deliver the mail in the morning, idle away the afternoon and evening eating *panzanella* and drinking Chianti…

Huh. Was any life really like that, or was this a case of greener grass in the other field—or whatever that English saying was? Her English was getting rusty. Heck, her native Amharic was rusty. Even her Italian wasn't getting a workout.

The letter was addressed to her—at least, to one of her aliases. She scraped her teeth over one side of her lower lip as she crouched over the plain business envelope. Typewritten label, Helsinki postmark. Her shoulders settled. The trusted friend of her mother who was acting as her emergency contact—a retired former diplomat who had no sympathy for Samira's enemies but was comfortably off their radar. Samira sent the woman a breezy postcard in a fake name every time she changed address. Laughably old school, but the irony of the twenty-first century was that every government, agency and criminal organization was too busy tracking electronic communication to bother with opening people's mail. If it didn't require a cryptographic exchange, who gave a damn?

Samira perched on a courtyard chair and tore open the envelope. Inside was another envelope, plain and brown. Inside that, like a nest of matryoshka dolls, a thick postcard and an unaddressed and unsigned note in her mother's handwriting, in Italian, for good measure. *Always thinking of you. Kisses.* It would have killed her mother to leave it at that but Hyland would be a fool not to have her parents under surveillance, even at the Ethiopian Embassy in Ottawa, and their diplomatic protection went only so far. Her mother would have had an aide drop it in a distant mailbox. Sudbury, according to the postmark. Samira had been there once—it had to be a five-hour drive from Ottawa. She ran her thumb over the familiar looped handwriting, the bonded paper thick and rough.

The postcard showed a gleaming Arc de Triomphe. Who did she know in Paris? She flipped it. It was also unsigned, the handwriting unfamiliar, addressed to her mother at the embassy.

Hey, Janis, it began. Samira frowned. She hadn't used that avatar since grad student days at Brown. Three scrawled lines followed. *I have a gift that will change your life. Just what Jagger was looking for. Can't wait to see your face when I give it to you. A good excuse for you to visit—soon! Luv, Vespa.*

Samira tapped the edge of the postcard on the table. *Vespa* was the avatar of Charlotte Liu, her English university roommate from Brown—the Latin name for her favorite British football team. Jagger was Latif. The aliases they'd used playing "Cosmos" during all the late nights they should have spent studying.

It could only be Charlotte. No one else knew those names. Samira's mother must have guessed the postcard was for Samira, that it was important enough to forward.

When had she last heard from Charlotte? Not since Latif had turned whistle-blower and the two of them had dropped off the earth, but Charlotte had to know he was dead—she worked for Britain's biggest spy agency. Why contact Samira now? And why the secrecy?

The oxygen seemed to thin. Only one "gift" would change Samira's life for the better—the elusive evidence that would secure Hyland's prosecution. Then he'd have nothing to gain from her death—the cat would be out of the cage. Box. Crate. Whatever. *Just what Jagger was looking for.* The additional evidence Latif was chasing when he died? If anyone could get access to damning evidence, a GCHQ surveillance analyst could, but she'd have to be very careful how she shared it.

The card was postmarked in Paris two months ago. The white envelope was stamped a week later in Helsinki. It'd probably spent the seven weeks since stacked in some postal holding center in Italy. Charlotte could have delivered it on foot in that time—though when she'd mailed it Samira had been holed up in... Denmark? Had Charlotte crossed the Channel from London just to post it, assuming that Samira's parents would know her whereabouts?

Whatever she'd found, it had to be big. Charlotte could be jeopardizing her job—and her life—and she was as cautious as Samira. Latif had been the risk-taker of their geeky trio.

Samira rubbed her thumb over the glossy Paris street and leaned back. The scooter was out of sight, its engine a faint hum. Suddenly that view looked a whole lot less suffocating. *Can't wait to see your face when I give it to you. A good excuse for you to visit...* Meaning, Samira had to collect it in person from Charlotte's London flat. But going to London meant crossing a border—with an untested fake passport. Having it as a precaution for an emergency was one thing. Using it to break into Fortress Britain?

Could Samira get Tess to collect the "gift," seeing as Samira would only be handing it along, assuming it was the evidence they needed? Charlotte would know who Tess was, after all the coverage about her scoop on Hyland. Tess would know what to do. She was in contact with the special counsel investigating Hyland, she had the media at her bidding, she was a folk hero in certain circles in the United States—and public enemy number one in others—and she had ten times Samira's courage. Like that was hard.

Not forgetting that Tess had a bulletproof French Foreign Legion boyfriend backed up by a squad of Legionnaire friends who'd do anything for each other. Like escort a stranger into hiding. And look after her a little too well.

Guilt poked Samira in the ribs.

Calm down, Conscience. It'd been an error of judgment at a stressful time that'd rightfully ended, abruptly and awkwardly.

So why had she thought about him every day since?

She hissed in a breath through her teeth. Because she had too much time to think.

Anyway. Small steps, and none of them involved Jamie… Jamie… Hell, she didn't even know his surname. The others had just called him "Doc."

Anyway. First, she had to break comms silence and contact Tess. Tess would come up with a plan that bypassed Samira, hopefully. She fished her Italy guidebook from her backpack—because pages read in a book couldn't be tracked like pages on the web—and chose an internet café in Perugia, a two-hour drive in the opposite direction from the last one she'd used to contact Tess. Though they were communicating rarely and via a secure, coded system, they'd defaulted to extreme precautions after Samira's carelessness had revealed Latif's location to Hyland.

She pulled out her wallet and counted her shrinking pile of euros. The last of the money she'd saved for her wedding and a deposit on an apartment in San Francisco. A long-dead dream from a long-dead life.

From a distant field, a bull bellowed. She flinched. At least a lengthy drive would give her a break from the hell that was paradise.

BY THE TIME Samira returned, the hillside glowed amber in midafternoon sun. She parked her little white Fiat, as usual, between an overgrown olive grove and a derelict barn beside the neighbor's vineyard, tucked back from the main road. It meant a cross-country hike through a steep field to the cottage, but better that than being stuck in her dead-end driveway when the shit spun in the—when the fan turned the sh—

Whatever.

She locked the car and pushed through the olive branches. At least paranoia gave her something to do with her many spare hours.

From the ridge, the cottage looked as lifeless as she'd left it. Such peace and beauty, yet the thought of locking herself away for another night… In the field the cows' great heads nudged the scorched grass. They bolted if she as much as sneezed, so if they were calm, she was calm. They wouldn't appreciate it when she got to the cottage and fired up the four Js on the speakers—Janis, Joni and the two Joans. You could bring the culture to the cow… She screwed up her face. No, that wasn't nearly the expression.

She checked the motion-sensor data on her phone's security app. With one bar of Wi-Fi coverage from the cottage, it took its time loading. Several cars had passed along the road in her absence but none had entered the driveway and there'd been no movement in or around the cottage. She tapped the phone, tempted to check for a reply from Tess, but…no. The phone was only to control her security system—and play her music, because otherwise she'd go insane. No network connection, no calls, no data, no browsing.

She squeezed through the rickety wire fence, the sunshine a balm on her nape. After sending the message to Tess, she'd waited at the internet café as long as she could without raising eyebrows but there'd been no reply. She'd checked a couple of media sites, via an incognito connection. Hyland was still proclaiming his innocence. "Why the heck would I be involved in a ludicrous plot to kill American citizens in order to orchestrate a war? This is an outrageous conspiracy that robbed me of the chance to lead the country I love, and continues to haunt me and my daughter, who stands with me through this difficult time. Patriotic Americans everywhere should be alarmed about this threat to our democracy. I am confident that the special counsel will find no evidence of wrongdoing on my part, justice will be served to those who slander me and I will be free to continue doing what I've spent my entire adult life doing, as a marine, a CIA agent and now a senator—serving and protecting this great nation."

Creep. As Samira followed the fence line, a rhino-sized cow jerked its head up and eyed her, freezing, as if she wouldn't notice it if it didn't move. One by one its sisters followed until half a dozen black-lashed brown eyes tracked her progress. *"Va tutto bene,"* she said, quiet and warm. *"Non aver paura."* Right—because Tuscan cows were more likely to understand *It's all right, don't be scared* in Italian? The rhino's head twitched and a smaller cow sprang sideways, but for a change they didn't bolt en masse. Maybe they were getting used to her. Which had to be Fate's way of warning her it was time to move on.

WELL AFTER DARK, Samira jerked awake. The *A-Team* theme tune was squeaking out of her phone. She swiped it off, her chest tight. Definitely engine noise, but low. She swallowed. A car in the night was unusual but not unheard of.

Another alarm. The *A-Team* again. A second car on the road. She silenced it, shot out of bed, slipped on her waiting boots and coat and grabbed her backpack. Two cars on her little road at this hour? One hell of a coinciden—

The alarm shrilled again, followed immediately by the *MacGyver* tune. Shit. Three vehicles, one already on the driveway. Working on feel, she pulled up the bedcover, restored the pillows, scattered cushions over top and let herself out of the cottage, as she'd practiced a dozen times, keeping out of scope of her sensor lights. *MacGyver* started over. Multiple engines purred. Modern, expensive cars—two on the driveway now.

By the next repeat of *MacGyver*, she was ankle deep in pasture, cows scattering before her. The cold whipped her bare legs. Her heart thumped with the shock of being slingshot out of warmth and sleep. With fumbling fingers, she set the phone to vibrate, blinking fast to force her eyes to adjust. Damn, she should have practiced her evacuation at night. The first engine muted. A car door clicked open. Her breath skittered as she stumbled uphill, looking over her shoulder. Her security lights burst on, flooding the courtyard and driveway, and setting her phone shaking again. A big black SUV had pulled up in the turning bay, headlights doused.

Four darkly clad figures silently fanned out, their arms locked straight and pointed downward. Handguns. An identical vehicle pulled up alongside, leaving one more engine approaching. More people spilled out. Her phone kept vibrating. Or was that just her hand?

A crack, a smash—wood, and glass. Hooves thundered, shaking the earth, the cows' glow-in-the-dark flanks flashing past. Hell, they wouldn't stampede her, would they? Between their flying bodies she made out the figures of two men down at the French doors, looking like they were pulling up from a shoulder charge. White-blond hair gleamed from one guy's head. He braced for another go. She upped her pace but her foot shot into a hole. Her ankle buckled, pain flashing through it, and she sprawled onto the grass, her cry muffled by a crash as the door gave. She pushed herself up and tested the ankle. Just a strain. Cold dew coated her leg. *Focus on what's right in front. Small steps.* If she didn't capitalize on her scant head start, she was—what? Dead? Despite her efforts to make the cottage look deserted and as pristine as if a cleaner had just left, the goons might feel her body heat in the small bedroom. If they pulled back the covers, they'd discover the sheets were warm…

Her chest pinched. The world tipped, and she planted her feet wide. No. Not now. She squeezed her eyes tight. *Don't do this to me, Brain. I know we're in danger. Small steps, okay? One foot. Another foot. Another.*

Fighting for every breath, she reached the fence to the olive grove, squeezed between the wires and scraped through the trees. Below, they'd switched on one set of headlights, aimed outward. Another set clicked on, directed into the field she'd just left. The cows bolted again.

Yep, use those lights, people. They'd be blind to any-thing outside the reach of the beams.

She pitched forward, groping in her coat pocket for the Fiat key. It rasped as it went in the lock. She eased the door open. The interior light flicked on. Shit. She scrabbled to disable it, panting. She threw the backpack on the passenger seat and her butt on the driver's seat. Her hand shook as she jabbed the key at the ignition. *Come on, come on.* After a few wild misses, it slid in.

She froze. Oh God, she couldn't start the car—they'd hear it. She covered her nose and mouth with both hands, which only amplified her struggling, squeak-ing breath. Her airways felt like they were narrowing. No. *Why screw this up for yourself?* Her assailants had to be fanning out. They'd find her in minutes. Her phone was still vibrating. She snatched it from her pocket and switched off the alarm. She was *well* alarmed.

She stilled, staring at the screen. She forced her trem-bling hands to navigate the unlock pattern. The Blue-tooth signal was faint but it might be just enough. Lights zigzagged across her vision as she scrolled her playlist.

"I Knew You Were Waiting."

"She Works Hard for the Money."

"Because the Night."

No, no, no, no.

Oh. She paused, scrolled back up a few tracks. Yes.

Swiping quickly, she hooked into the cottage speakers, slid them to full volume and pressed Play. From down-hill, a snare drum hammered. She tapped along on the steering wheel—eight quick counts—and shakily started the engine as the drum and bass guitar joined, followed by the rhythm.

She automatically went for the headlights, stopping herself a second short of stupidity, and navigated out of the rutted driveway and onto the road, eyes open so wide they hurt. Joan Jett launched into her lyrics, echoed by half a dozen ghostly Joans glancing off the surrounding hills, half a second off the beat. The connection would cut out at the end of the track. Two minutes and fifty-five seconds. One song. One chance.

"I Love Rock 'n' Roll," the hillsides sang.

"So do I, Joan," Samira muttered. "But now what do we do?"

After a couple of minutes of driving, the tinny phone speaker kicked in, as the next song on the playlist uploaded. Out of range. The cottage would have silenced. Advantage over. Was it enough? She was in the next valley, so the car sound would be difficult to pinpoint. No movement or lights in the rear-vision mirror, and her preplanned escape route had enough twists and turns they couldn't easily track her. First chance she got, she'd contact Tess, nail down a new plan.

"Time Has Come Today," squeaked out of the phone.

Indeed. Time to come out of hiding and end this, whether she liked it or not—and she definitely did not. But Hyland had just made her decision for her.

"Yes, Joan," Samira said, swinging into a side road. "The time has come."

CHAPTER TWO

London

IT WASN'T PARANOIA. Samira *was* being followed. A tall, brittle man with crisp blond hair fading to white. Jeans, a brown leather jacket, a burgundy overnight bag. The guy who'd shoulder-charged the French doors the night before last?

In Paris that morning he'd been one of the few other patrons at the café two blocks from the Gare du Nord, apparently engrossed in the weekend *Le Monde*. At the station, she'd bought her ticket to London minutes before the cutoff for the 8:13 a.m. train—but as she'd crossed the concourse she'd glanced back to see him scurrying into the Eurostar ticket office. If he had time to read the newspaper and drink a *café latte*, why wait until the last moment? She should have kept walking, waited for the next train, aborted the whole lunatic mission. Midway through the Channel tunnel, he'd strolled into her carriage and slipped into a vacant aisle seat three rows behind. He'd hung back as the train emptied at St Pancras and lingered among the seats, tapping on a phone. She'd ducked into the bathroom, willing him to disappear, hissing to her sunken-eyed mirror image that she was being irrational. More than one man in Europe had white-blond hair. When she emerged, he was still there.

Now he was trailing her down the travellator to border control. Coincidence? She dragged her tongue over her teeth. She didn't do coincidences anymore.

She looked around for a clock. Tess and Flynn should be waiting at Pancras Square near the station, after landing at Heathrow overnight, as they'd hurriedly planned. Very soon, if the passport worked, Samira could sponge off their confidence. Just having people to talk to would be a novelty, if she was even capable of carrying a conversation.

After the hushed voices and hum of the train, the station boomed with white noise that filled the air like a gas, curving up to its soaring glass dome and sweeping back down. Pearly light hung in the air. As she pulled up at the back of the immigration queue, she adjusted the plastic shopping bag on her shoulder. Inside, the polystyrene-wrapped champagne bottles whispered and clunked. Somewhere among the thick-coated passengers a newborn baby yelled, long beyond the reach of comfort, its shuddering mews swelling, ebbing, swelling, ebbing. Her blood pressure was playing that song, too.

She tightened her scarf and pulled her necklace over top of it, fingering the small gold cross. The queue was moving slower than she'd bargained for. There blew the theory that fooling UK border control at the Gare du Nord was enough, that the check at this end would be cursory. She shuffled to her right. Ahead, at a counter hung with a sagging string of red tinsel, a blue-shirted officer studied a passenger's passport and ticket. Did they suspect something or were these checks standard? She'd only ever entered Britain with her parents, through diplomatic checkpoints.

Not that she always got a free pass into the United States, either, despite her green card. Carrying alcohol was a ruse Latif had adopted for their many flights in and out of JFK, when foreign students with names and faces like his had begun to draw suspicion.

They see the whiskey and figure you're not some extremist jihadist, he'd once said at duty-free, picking up a bottle of Jim Beam he'd later donated to Charlotte.

She'd laughed. *Or they conclude it's an elaborate ruse to make you look less like a jihadist and pin you down for a cavity search.*

She'd called him paranoid.

She shut her eyes tight until the burn eased. Not paranoid enough, in the end. Really, she needed to stop reliving their every conversation. And if she wasn't doing that, she was having imaginary new ones. Sometimes imaginary arguments, sometimes aloud, pausing for his answers as they ran through her head. Day by day his image faded but his voice still curled through her.

Great, so she had two voices in her head—Latif's and Jamie's. *Way* too much time alone.

She pulled down the edge of the champagne bag to better reveal its contents. Doubling down on the paranoia because today it was her friend—and racial profiling wasn't.

On the pretense of cricking her neck, which really did need a crick after a night sleeping in her car, she glanced over her shoulder. The blond man was two people behind. She swallowed past a prickly lump in her throat. Subterfuge was way beyond her comfort zone. Sure, she'd done shady things—hacked into secure systems, cracked passwords, unleashed harmless viruses— but only from behind a keyboard and monitor and only to prove she could or to test her clients' systems. It was Latif who'd got off on this spy stuff, Latif who'd dragged her into this world of shadows, Latif who'd got killed and left her to finish this.

She spun her backpack to her front and removed the passport. Her hand trembled. Pretending to be engrossed in fiddling with a zip, she shuffled forward with the crowd.

Here she was in strolling distance of Regent's Park but not yet officially in the country. No-man's-land. In front, a toddler peeped over his mother's shoulder, eyeing Samira through thick black curls. She gave what she hoped was an indulgent smile. The tot ducked. After a few seconds he peeped one hazel eye up. She winked and the boy buried his face, wrapping fat arms around his mother's neck. The game continued until they moved off—and didn't do a thing to settle Samira's nerves. From somewhere the newborn was still wailing. Samira's breath was getting shorter. Her chest stung.

Not now. Not ever but not now. But when did a panic attack ever come at a convenient time? She forced a deep inhalation.

"Next!" An officer beckoned Samira—young, light brown hair tied back, expression set to don't-fuck-with-me. "Ticket and passport."

The woman flattened Samira's passport at the photo page, wincing. "This is a very old passport. Not machine-readable."

Heat rolled up Samira's face. "Yes, I need to get a new one soon." She'd checked it was legally valid for entry, despite its looming expiry date. The forger had sworn that everything about the passport was legit except the photo, which had been swapped for hers, and that it hadn't been reported stolen. Its owner had sold it to him and he'd repurposed it for Samira—for a gagging price.

The woman made a ticking noise. "What is the purpose of your visit?"

"A wedding, of a university friend." Samira had been confidently faking an Italian accent all morning but suddenly she felt like a bad actor.

"Where is this wedding?"

"In Cornwall."

"Where in Cornwall?"

Samira frowned. "Ah, it's in…" She riffled through her backpack and pulled out a gilt-edged invitation on heavy matte card, created yesterday at a self-serve print shop on the outskirts of Paris. "Mousehole?" She held out the card, deliberately mispronouncing the town's name. According to the forger, the passport's former owner—real owner—had never visited Britain.

The woman smirked. "*Mow-zul.* Wait here." She left her post, with Samira's documents. Damn. Why?

Behind Samira, a man groaned. One thing she wished she hadn't double-checked: using a fake passport at the border could get her ten years in prison or—once they figured out her real identity—deportation, probably to Ethiopia, though she'd spent only a few years of her life there. Either way, assassins would be waiting. And questions would be asked of her parents. The Ivy League–educated daughter of career diplomats busted for identity fraud? She pulled a water bottle from her bag and worked a sip down her throat. Maybe she should have taken the risk with her real passport.

No. It could have taken weeks to get a visa, raising too many flags in too many systems and giving her enemies ample notice to arrange a welcoming party. And she'd already lost time with the postcard delay. This plan was imperfect but it was the best she had. In risk versus risk, risk had won out.

The woman approached a man in the same blue uniform, who was surveying the queue with his arms crossed. He bent his head to one side to catch her words, his pale forehead creasing. Both faces turned to Samira. *Here we go.* She forced her expression to neutral, channeling the psychology journal article she'd read online yesterday. "The Physical Manifestations of Guilt." She'd converted it into a list of takeaways and memorized them—because she was that much of a geek—then set fire to her list in a Dumpster in a deserted alley, followed by every page of her evidence. Tess had a copy, for what it was (not) worth.

Look unconcerned but not wide-eyed. Not flustered but not cocky. And, most challenging of all: *don't try too hard.*

The man sauntered toward Samira, unfolding his arms. A master of the neutral face she'd practiced in her car mirror. Her vision swam until he looked like he'd turned to jelly and was dancing. She tightened her hand around the liquor bag, as if that'd keep her upright. *Hold it together.* She'd made it this far. Now it was either freedom and a chance at reclaiming her life, or prison. Or worse.

"Good morning, ma'am. If you wouldn't mind coming with me a minute…" He spoke quietly, stepping aside to let her by as if it were the gentlemanly thing to do.

They can't see the nerves in your belly, so don't let them show in your face.

He led her to a high metal table and leaned an elbow back on it, as if settling in for a leisurely chat-up at a bar. Deliberately keeping this low-key, for now?

"Dove vive, Signorina…" He peered at the passport,

clicking and unclicking a cheap ballpoint. *"...Moretti?"* he asked. A confident Italian speaker but not a native one.

"Certaldo," she replied. *"In una piccola città vicino Firenze."* Bravo, Samira. Six weeks in Tuscany had been just long enough to take her Italian from rough back to smooth, though it might not fool a real *Italiano*.

"I know it," he said. *"È una bellissima città."* Click. Unclick. Click. Unclick.

"Sì," she said, forcing a proud smile. "The most beautiful place in Italy."

"Big call." *Click. Unclick. "Che lavoro fa?"*

"I have my own web design company." She reached for her side pocket, where she'd slipped her freshly printed fake business cards—and froze. Not yet. *Be accommodating but not too forthcoming.* She'd loaded herself with layers of deception, to be revealed gradually and only as necessary.

Click. Unclick. Click. Unclick.

She'd even found a genuine wedding she could claim to be attending, harvesting the details from a bride's blog. Everyday people put too much on the web—people who thought they had nothing to hide, who thought the world had only benign intentions. People who weren't being hunted by one of the world's most powerful people.

Not if I catch you first, Senator.

The officer pulled out a cell phone, held it where they could both see it and typed into the browser her fake name and "web design." Her breath stalled.

"This one?" he asked, pointing to the top hit.

She nodded, not trusting her voice. The SEO had worked but any second he'd notice the search had netted suspiciously few results—because the site was less than twenty-four hours old.

He clicked the link and the site loaded. "It's in English."

"Awo." She bit her lip. She'd used the Ethiopian word for *yes*. Old habits… "Pardon me," she said, patting her upper chest, as if she'd hiccuped. *"Si,* that version is. Most of my clients are in English-speaking countries. I also have an Italian site." She pointed to the green, white and red flag icon in a corner of the home page. She'd be almost disappointed if he didn't open it, after the effort it'd taken to translate.

He studied her as if he could see right through to her Ethiopian DNA sequence. "How much do you charge for a simple e-commerce site?"

"Scusi, signore?" Damn. She had no idea of the going rates.

"My wife and I are thinking about setting up an online…" The other officer signaled him and he raised a pointer finger—*one minute.* The ambient noise crescendoed, as though it'd been silenced for their conversation and someone had just pressed the unmute button. "Never mind." He handed back Samira's documents. "When you return to Certaldo I suggest you update your passport. You'd be surprised how much ID fraud we're seeing these days. Desperate people out there." He swept a hand toward the thinning queue. "Hence the extra checks."

He moved on to his next target, leaving Samira's *"Grazie"* hanging—and her way clear to the exit. She zipped the documents into her bag and let her chest fill. It'd gone almost concave. She walked—not too fast—boots clicking on the floor, heartbeat thumping along in her ears in double time.

There was something to be said for paranoia. But her delay had given the blond man time to clear the checkpoint. Leaning on a white column ahead, bag at his feet, he swiped at his phone. He caught her eye and quickly looked away. Too quickly? Dear God. She skirted behind a tribe of tracksuit-clad teenagers—some lanky, overgrown sports team—and strode toward the border control exit. The border itself, technically. Once she left the station, once she found Tess, her nerves would settle. She took note of the area's security cameras then angled herself away, bunching her hair around her face. She pulled a beanie from her bag and tugged it down to her eyebrows. Facial recognition software wasn't as easily fooled as human eyes. She slipped on the Audrey Hepburn–style sunglasses she'd picked up in Paris.

Tension fell from her shoulders as she emerged into a soaring atrium—an arcade, with shimmering glass shopfronts over Victorian brick arches. A massive Christmas tree circled up to the dome, so laden with ornaments she could almost hear it groan. She adjusted her backpack. Her shoulders were beginning to ache under its weight, coupled with the champagne. She'd used precious euros to buy a dress, coat and heels at a Parisian outlet store, suitable for a fall wedding, and had gift wrapped some of her spare tech gear. It seemed absurd now to have spent all that money. Or maybe the knowledge that she had proof to back up her ruse had warded off the panic attack. Either way, what was done was done. Very soon, she and Tess would be toasting their breakthrough with the champagne.

She walked faster. Every step got her closer to Tess, Charlotte's flat and the evidence. A sign ahead pointed to the overland trains. Wait—that wasn't the right exit. She needed to find the pedestrian tunnel linking St Pancras to the square Tess was waiting in. This was the opposite direction. She stopped and looked around as if she were waiting for someone, picturing the station map she'd studied online. Discordant piano chords plinked out a toe-curling tune. Which way was she supposed to have turned out of border control? The blond guy emerged from the crowd, looked up at the signs and headed toward a taxi rank, without a glance her way.

She closed her eyes a second. She never used to be paranoid. She used to trust that the world was a good place, that nothing bad would happen to a thoroughly ordinary woman. She used to have complete faith in the digital age, in its promise to connect cultures and minds, blur borders between the developing and developed worlds, make information and education accessible for all. She clicked her tongue. At some point the limitless possibilities had become limitless threats. Emails, phone calls, databases, servers, web searches... nothing was private, nothing was truly secure, everything could be traced and hacked in an ever-accelerating spiral of cat and mouse between the security analysts and the hackers—in her case, sometimes one and the same person. Once, she'd been contracted to infiltrate a system she'd previously been hired to secure, and that remained the only one that'd eluded her. She still didn't know whether to be proud of that or embarrassed.

She blew out a breath. One step at a time. First, find the tunnel. After hours enclosed in a capsule, the thought of fresh air and freedom tugged her toward daylight like a magnet was clamped to her chest. Freedom would come when this was done. Freedom from danger and— just maybe, just a little—freedom from grief and guilt?

A large man in a navy suit pushed past. She snapped out a hand to catch the champagne, and patted her bag's zip pocket, checking for the outline of her wallet—the fictional Italian *signorina*'s wallet, rounded out by a

fake driver's license and fake credit card, and the re-
mainder of Samira's real euros. Getting pickpocketed
would be a disaster.

Ignoring her clenching stomach muscles, she followed the signs toward the far end of the long station,
white columns marching along beside her. The blond
guy couldn't be the one from the cottage. Her enemy
couldn't know she was here. Nothing would go wrong.
She'd passed the biggest challenge—getting into Britain. Maybe the evidence would be damning enough
that she wouldn't need to testify. She could wait out the
storm at a cozy flat in an English seaside village where
she didn't see a threat in every shaking leaf or heavy
footfall. Then maybe she'd be able to breathe without
forcing every inhalation. Since Latif's death, her every
breath had seemed like a conscious effort, as if it were
her instinct to die, not live. She'd had the sense she was
viewing the world from afar, hardly feeling the ground
under her feet.

With the exception of that one day—and night—
last fall...

Which she shouldn't be thinking about.

And today was real. Stomach-curlingly real. Despite the fear, it was empowering to do something that
wasn't sitting around lurching between anger and sorrow and frustration and regret. She would finish the
mission Latif died for. If she died, too, so be it, so long
as she avenged his death and made his sacrifice worth
something.

She passed a TV on the wall of a café, tuned to a
news channel, just as it flicked to...something familiar. Someone. She backtracked. Tess. Tess was on the
screen, walking between two black-uniformed cops.
Handcuffed. Samira's throat dried. *Whistle-blowing*

reporter arrested, read the scroll at the bottom. Then, *Sen. Tristan Hyland cleared.*

Feet operating automatically, she stepped inside the café, hardly able to absorb the words. The special counsel had announced there was insufficient evidence to prosecute Hyland, and had instead charged Tess with obstruction of justice for her sworn testimony. She'd been hauled off a plane on the tarmac at Dulles Airport in Washington, DC, "caught trying to flee the country," according to the voice-over. The picture changed. Tess's Legionnaire boyfriend, Flynn, surged through a churn of journalists, his face thunderous. "How the [bleep] do you think I feel?" he mumbled. "This is bullshit."

Samira pulled her scarf away from her throat.

A family bustled into the café, speaking loud German, drowning out the news report. Suddenly another familiar face was staring out from the TV. Shit. Shit. Samira's green-card photo—she looked so young. *Warrant issued for arrest of Newell accomplice.*

Samira yanked her beanie lower. The senator appeared on the screen, speaking to reporters in front of a plane. His daughter, Laura, rested a hand on his shoulder, almost protectively. As the German family retreated into the back of the café, his words became audible.

"…would like to thank the many loyal Americans who've supported us through these baseless and incredibly hurtful allegations. It's been a long and tough road but we always had faith that the truth would prevail and the real villains would be exposed—those people in the media and my political opposition who would manufacture lies to destroy me, my family and my career, solely for ratings and profit and political point scoring." He eyeballed the TV camera, as if he could see Samira standing there. "Today, the scales of justice rebalanced. For that I am grateful, if not surprised. God bless you, America."

Applause.

Samira clenched her fists as the senator hushed the cheers and listened to a question. It was inaudible but a smile relaxed his face. Laura wiped away tears—real tears, going by the smudges in her heavy black makeup. The audio faded out and the network's presenters began speaking over the footage, lamenting the millions "squandered on this witch hunt" and predicting Hyland would revive his presidential ambitions. The senator adjusted his tie and rolled his shoulders, drawing attention to his broad frame. His shirtsleeves were rolled up, revealing tanned, muscular forearms and his Marines tattoo. He laughed, like he was sharing a joke with the reporters.

How the hell had Tess and Latif ever thought they could take him on and win? The darling of American politics, with his boyish grin and blue eyes and square face and thick salt-and-pepper hair and insane popularity—JFK and Reagan rolled into one physically and politically attractive package. When he wasn't being declared the sitter for America's next president, he was being hailed the country's most eligible bachelor. The next silver fox-in-chief. Heck, Samira had once thought him hot. Latif had teased her about it but she wasn't alone. A meme cult had grown out of his good looks. And the senator knew just what he was doing when he brought his chic environmental crusader of a daughter to press conferences and functions—a reminder that he was a grieving widower and devoted father, and there was an opening for a future First Lady.

Teflon Tristan. When Tess and Latif had uncovered evidence that the military contractor he'd founded had orchestrated the LA terror attack, Hyland had argued it'd gone bad long after he'd sold it—successfully, it now appeared. Somehow he'd swum clear of the maelstrom that'd dragged down his former pals. But Latif, who'd worked for the contractor, had sworn that Hyland had still been calling the shots at the time of the attack, desperate to save the foundering company from liquidation and legal scrutiny by securing more war contracts. Latif had died searching for evidence to skewer his former boss.

The screen switched to the presenters, who moved on to another story. Eyes on the white tiled floor, Samira walked out robotically, hollow from her stomach to her toes. She no longer had anyone to meet. At a newsstand she picked up the *Guardian*. Nothing yet about Tess— or Samira. But on page three, a story about Hyland announcing a UK visit. Shit, he was coming here? She scanned the story. The secretary of state had fallen ill overnight, so Hyland was on his way to Edinburgh for a NATO meeting, and to observe a joint military exercise in Scotland.

It couldn't be a coincidence. Was he coming to supervise Samira's capture and extradition? He always kept a private security team around him and Laura— was this an excuse to bring them to Britain? Had he known Samira was heading to London when she fled Tuscany? Did he know about Charlotte? What the hell did any of this mean?

Below the main story, another article zeroed in on controversy that Laura was traveling with him, having hurriedly arranged a book signing in Edinburgh for her memoir, which reportedly painted her father as a saint. A quote from the minority House leader: "This is yet another clear case of the Hylands profiting from the senator's—"

"No free reads," belted a voice from the stand.

Samira jumped, nearly ripping the paper. She shut it abruptly and tossed it back on the pile.

Tess wasn't in London, wasn't waiting in the square with Flynn. And Samira was officially a wanted woman. Thank God she'd turned down the special counsel's offer of witness protection in the United States, or they'd have her now, too. Thank God she hadn't used her own passport. Thank God she no longer looked like the naive, optimistic ingenue in her green-card photo. But the UK probably had a swift extradition agreement with the United States—if she survived long enough to fight a legal battle. What now?

Small steps. First, get out of the station. Fresh air. She needed fresh air. She slipped out of the atrium into a brick-walled space with a low industrial ceiling. Where was the damn tunnel to the square? Icy fingers from an invisible draft brushed her cheeks. Her camel coat was so thick it could stand up by itself, but the dry cold rushed into her lungs, chilling her from the inside.

Behind her, a man shouted. Indecipherable but panicked. She straightened, her spine prickling. Border guards, coming for her? More shouts. A clunk. Clattering. Hissing. Ahead, people began turning. People began *running*.

She swiveled, wheezing. Blue smoke gushed and fizzed from dozens of tin cans rolling along the floor. This was no arrest. It was an ambush. Urgent beeping bounced around the room. The smoke billowed, boiling across the low ceiling and pouring back down like a dozen waterfalls, lit by a strobing white emergency light. Screams, shouts. Shadowy figures darted through the thickening mist. Someone slammed into her arm, knocking her sideways. Her shoulder struck the floor first, then the side of her skull. The champagne bag swung out and smashed behind her. Coughing, she pushed to her feet. Bitter chemicals stung the back of her throat. Tear gas? She stumbled across the floor, her feet swallowed by a blue snowdrift. An alarm wailed. Dark smudges shunted her like a pin in a bowling alley.

"Attention, please." A male voice, over a loudspeaker. "Due to a reported emergency, would all passengers leave the station immediately?"

Sure—if she could figure out where the exit was. She staggered like a zombie, one arm flailing in front of her. Wasn't tear gas supposed to burn? Her hand scraped something rough. A brick wall. She swiveled and leaned back on it. She had to return to the atrium. If she just walked straight…or was it left…?

But if the smoke was cover for Hyland's people to capture her, wouldn't they be waiting for her to stumble out? Should she head for the Tube, try her luck in the maze of tunnels?

Yes. She pulled up her scarf, breathing into it as she inched along the wall, panic clamping her chest. Her arm fell through space. A doorway? Smoke cocooned her. Her head spun like she'd been spit from a carousel. A clonk, nearby, and a man's head and shoulders loomed out of the fog, a green-and-yellow jacket zipped to his chin, his face hidden under a gas mask and beanie. She sidestepped but he caught her arms, kicked her legs out from under her and lifted.

She bucked but he was too strong, too solid. Her backpack was snatched away. Her spine hit something soft and flat—a gurney? A second man, in matching jacket and gas mask, leaned over the other side. A white patch was stamped on his chest pocket: AMBULANCE.

Her lungs pinched. She wrenched away but the first guy trapped her upper arms. Something yanked her stomach into the gurney. A strap. One by one her wrists and ankles were pinned, too. A creature from the deep catching her in its tentacles. The trolley began to roll. The first guy shoved a hat over her beanie and a mask over her face. They were sedating her? She lashed her head side to side but he pushed the mask's straps on. A few tugs and her head was locked down like the rest of her, the arms of her sunglasses digging into her temples. She resisted inhaling until her chest rebelled and sucked in a desperate breath. It came out again as a Darth Vader wheeze. The world narrowed to the visor in front of her eyes—blue smoke, the men's bent heads. The first guy laid a hand on her belly. A warning.

She didn't flake out—it wasn't a sedation mask; it was a gas mask like those the men wore. The blue haze dissolved into white light. Columns, brickwork and glinting glass sheets flashed by. Back in the atrium. The alarm sharpened, the dome swelling the panicked uproar. Anxious faces rushed past, people swerved out of the speeding gurney's path.

Samira shouted for help but the mask muffled her. She was being kidnapped in front of hundreds of people and all she could do was squeak.

CHAPTER THREE

SAMIRA JAMMED HER fingernails into her palms—about the only body part she could move. Would they kill her straightaway or interrogate her first? She wouldn't give up Charlotte or further incriminate Tess, if that was what they were after. She'd be as fearless as Latif was. *You hear me, Samira? Fearless.*

The gurney spun ninety degrees. The wheels on one side lifted, lurching her stomach into weightlessness. Shops and cafés rushed by. Her kidnappers kept their heads bowed as they plowed through the panicked foot traffic and rattled under an arch into a cloudy gray world. A redbrick facade rose up, curving in the visor's distortion. They were taking her out a side entrance? A firefighter flashed past, in a yellow helmet. She cried out. He didn't even slow. The gurney rattled and bumped over rougher ground, jolting her vision. Beside her, blue lights flashed against a red blur—a fire truck. Her breath hissed in fast pants, the mask heating. The sharp scent of warming rubber curled up her nose, itching the back of her throat. A siren screamed and waned, screamed and waned, louder and louder. Voices faded. The world took a dive.

The gurney slowed and the second paramedic—or whatever he really was—jogged out of her field of vision. She strained her head as far as the restraints and mask allowed. Where had he gone? Diagonal red and yellow stripes, flashing blue lights—the rear double doors of an ambulance, its number plate coated in mud, though the chassis gleamed.

This was well planned. Who would stop two para-medics loading a prone woman into an ambulance? She shouted but it came out a whimper. The double doors swung open. The men lifted the gurney and it clattered into the back of the vehicle, the first guy jumping in alongside. A bump, and the rear doors slammed, one by one. The driver's door opened and shut, and be-neath her the ambulance shuddered and rumbled. Her breath rasped like an asthmatic's. Her arms tingled. Black spots dotted her vision.

No. Fight it off. Or let it go. Or whatever the hell she was supposed to do. The solution always seemed so logical when she wasn't having an attack.

A siren bleeped and the ambulance moved. The guy guarding her fiddled with something beside her ear, his head angled to look out the rear window. Pressure lifted from her forehead, leaving a floating sensation.

"Bravo Victor Control, Bravo Victor Control, Bravo Victor niner-one, over." The driver, speaking into a radio, in a northern English accent. Wait—was this a real ambulance? Tess had warned her that Hyland's con-spiracy had sucked people in from everywhere—but the London Ambulance Service?

As the ambulance rolled out, the guy guarding her drew away her mask, knocking her sunglasses off with it. She gasped cold air and went to scream. His hand clamped over her mouth, rough and dry.

On the radio, a reply crackled back. "Bravo Vic-tor niner-one, Bravo Victor Control. Go ahead. Over."

Her lungs caved. No need for torture—she was suf-focating herself. She retched, her body shaking against

the bonds like she was having a fit. Bravery? Who was
she kidding? With his free hand, her assailant pulled
his mask and beanie off and drew in a breath. Close-
cropped brown hair glistened with sweat.

Jamie.

The blue strobe illuminated uneasy cobalt eyes as
he bent over her, releasing her mouth and sweeping his
hand down her arm to push up her coat sleeve.

Jamie.

He encircled her wrist with his fingers for a few moments, then deftly released her hands from the bonds.
"Samira, you're having a panic attack. We'll get through
it together, okay? Just like before."

Before. Yes, last year, when they were escaping from
Ethiopia.

"You want nitroglycerin?" the driver called. "I have
tablets."

"No need," Jamie replied, his gaze pinning hers. He
laid a hand on her upper chest, and another on her belly,
over her coat. "Breathe out, Samira, every last puff of
air."

She widened her eyes. She didn't *have* any air—that
was the problem.

He patted her belly. "Okay, now let this fill, nice
and slow." He patted her upper chest. "Keep this still."

Sure. Like breathing was that easy. She scraped in a
breath, hyperaware of the slight pressure of his hands.

"Now, let it out, slowly—all of it, until there's nothing left. I'll breathe with you."

She concentrated on his eyes—the flecks of brown
in the blue, the creases in the corners, the way they angled down like teardrops—and focused on matching
his breaths, calm and even, pushing his hand away with
her belly, then letting it drop. Jamie? Here?

What did it matter how? Just—*thank God*. Pressure lifted from her chest. Her vision cleared. She sank back on the gurney, letting go of effort, crisp oxygen swirling in her mouth.

He touched the back of his hand to her cheek. "Okay now?"

"Yes and no." Mostly, she felt like an idiot.

"They were onto you," he said, quietly, his focus darting from window to window as he unstrapped her head. "I had to create a diversion, extract you before they could figure out what was happening. I'd forgotten about your panic attacks."

Her stomach flipped in time with the rises and falls of his accent, taking her mind back to their last morning together, when she'd told him to leave—and he'd wasted no time or breath complying.

It hardly mattered now. "Was this Tess's idea? She's been arrested—I saw it on TV."

"It was Flynn's. We had to move quickly. Tess was tipped off that Hyland's mercenaries were planning to have St Pancras surrounded. But then she got arrested, so we had no way of contacting you. I flew straight here from France. One of the other guys in my unit flew to Paris but he got held up and you'd already left—Texas, you remember him?"

"*Awo*—I mean, yes, the American… So, the smoke—that was you?"

"It was the best plan I could come up with at short notice. We use smoke grenades on exercises, for cover, so…"

"But won't the police—?"

"As far as the authorities are concerned, the grenades will be dismissed as a prank by a couple of student protesters who escaped without detection behind a rather convenient smoke screen. A harmless gag, except for one poor tourist who had to be treated for... breathing problems."

She patted her head, and pulled off the "hat" Jamie had forced on her—a brown wig. Hearing his voice again was unnerving after it'd been trapped in her head for so long. "I think that's called a self-fulfilling prophecy. You couldn't have warned me?"

"No time, and no channel. I couldn't just walk in and lead you out, with them watching. We used the masks for disguises and parked the ambulance in a security camera black spot." He unzipped his jacket and tossed it on the front passenger seat. Underneath he wore a short-sleeved green shirt with epaulets, a coat of arms on the chest pocket. A real paramedic uniform? A tendril of a tattoo curled out from under a sleeve. Her pulse seemed to glitch as her memory filled in the rest of the mark. "It'll take Hyland's goons a while to put all that together, no matter what resources they have."

She swallowed. "They have access to *all* the resources, according to Tess. Has something gone wrong, I mean, apart from the arrest? Charlotte...?"

"Is that your London contact? I don't know." He moved to the straps on her feet and began releasing them. Deciphering his thick accent was taking concentration, though just the timbre of it rolled through her chest and eased her breathing. "All I know is that I was the only one who could get here this quickly, so I was it." It sounded like an apology, like he assumed he was the last man she'd want to see again. How wrong he was. "Flynn was sparing on details and obviously we're needing to keep this operation contained, so..."

"This *operation*?" she said. "You're making it sound even more terrifying."

"Oh no, this is commonplace. We're just couriers, yeah? Here to collect and deliver. Operation UPS. Angelito and Holly are trying to get away from some unpronounceable town in Eastern Europe but that'll take a while. And Texas is waiting for a seat to come free on the Eurostar."

Angelito. Flynn and Jamie's *capitaine*, who'd helped her escape Ethiopia. "Holly…?"

"Angelito's girlfriend."

"She can be trusted?"

"She could come in pretty handy." His brow creased. "I've been wondering how you were, where you were. Tess and Flynn assured me you were safe but wouldn't say more."

She inwardly winced. Was that censure in his voice? He'd made her promise to keep in touch. She'd crossed her fingers behind her back.

Call if you need me, he'd said, scrawling down his number as he'd stepped onto his train in a French town she could no longer name, to return to his base on Corsica. *If you want me. I'll come straightaway.*

So many times she'd nearly relented, even once picking up a pay phone and dialing all but the last digit.

"They didn't know where I was—it was safer for everyone that way," she said. "I moved around a lot. And Hyland still caught up with me." More than a year of being careful and it had very nearly been for nothing. "At least I assume the ambush in Tuscany was his doing?"

"Yes. You did well to get away."

She sat up, blinking rapidly. "Does Hyland know why I'm in London, where I'm headed?"

"We're certainly hoping not. But then, until a few hours ago we hadn't expected all this, either. You might need to fill me in on the details of what we're going to be doing. We're picking up something?"

She liked the sound of "we." But if Hyland's thugs had her in their sights, what about Charlotte? "*Awo*, from Putney. I mean, yes. You might as well know everything." She gave him a breathless rundown. God, there was a lot to explain—Tuscany, Charlotte, the postcard…

"Wow," Jamie said, when she'd finished. "I hope this 'gift' will exonerate Tess and bring down Hyland."

"So do I, but I honestly don't know. This could all be for nothing."

"Flynn seems to think it's the only chance we have."

"Dear God, don't say that."

The ambulance swerved. She grabbed the sides of the gurney. Jamie caught a yellow metal handhold.

"The ambulance," she said. "How did you—?"

"Called in a…favor from a…friend." He glanced at the driver, who was still on the radio. One hell of a favor. She caught the words *assessing*, *respiratory* and *SOB*.

"Did he just call you a son of a bitch?" she said.

A grin flickered across Jamie's face. "SOB. Shortness of breath. But probably the other thing, too."

"This is a real ambulance?"

"On a real callout. I used to be a paramedic in London, in another lifetime. Somebody—" His voice deepened with mock conspiracy, his pupils melodramatically shifting left and right. "*Somebody* called nine-nine-nine on a burner phone to report that a woman had stopped breathing at St Pancras. By…chance, this was the closest ambulance. A lone officer, as far as Ambulance Control was concerned, returning the vehicle to his station after a repair." The ambulance slowed. "A happy coincidence all around, wouldn't you say?"

"We're going to a hospital? Jamie, that's not a good idea. If anyone saw paramedics take me from the station, they'll assume that's where we're headed. And there'll be security cameras. My photo is—"

"Everywhere, I know. You're an overnight sensation. But that photo does you no justice. And don't worry—the patient is about to have a remarkable recovery and refuse transportation." Jamie grinned, wrinkling the suntanned skin beside his eyes. God, that was a beautiful sight.

The siren bleeped and the driver accelerated.

"Recovery?" She rested a hand on her chest and swiveled, her legs dangling over the side of the gurney. Her backpack was by her feet. "I don't know if we can be sure of that yet."

"Happy to perform any medical procedure you need. Cutting people open is my favorite pastime."

She smiled up at him. It was a relief to smile for real. To talk to someone. To not be alone. To be with…him. "You *are* joking, yes?"

He shrugged, his eyes not leaving hers.

Of course he was joking. He was ninety-five percent tease and flirt. It was the five percent that intrigued her, those flashes of frustration or concern that broke through the facade, like a solitary boom of thunder from a clear sky that left you wondering if you'd imagined it. "I didn't know you were a paramedic."

His eyebrows angled up. "To be fair, you don't really know me at all."

Ouch. "I…guess not."

She *did* know for sure that he'd hold eye contact as long as she was game, like it was a challenge—or he was drilling into her mind and amused by what he found.

Deliberately, she turned toward the windscreen. *You don't really know me at all.* The exact words she'd thrown at him that fall morning after he'd offered to stay. *I know you want me to,* he'd said. Coincidence, or did he remember that hideous conversation as clearly as she did?

The driver navigated onto a narrow street flanked by stone-and-brick buildings with sash windows and brave balcony gardens, all shrouded in a gaseous gray light. Near-leafless trees stretched up like clawed skeleton hands. Her breath had shallowed out. With everything that was going on, with everything she was processing, she didn't need the kind of confusion that came from looking a charming, magnetic man in the eye for too long.

A branch scraped the ambulance roof. She shivered. Winter had set in prematurely here. Even after all her years living in North America and Europe—through most of her childhood, her teens, her college and university years, her twenties—the sight of bare-limbed trees chilled her. From the corner of her eye, she registered Jamie unbuttoning his uniform shirt.

More reason to look elsewhere. In the last year she'd assured herself that her memory was exaggerating the connection she'd felt with him. Right now, her mind and her belly and even her skin weren't so sure.

He was right—despite one fateful week, ending with one fateful night, and one hideous morning—she knew very little about him. He was Scottish, a medic in the French Foreign Legion and in his early thirties, a little older than she was. And now she knew he'd been a paramedic, which wasn't hugely revealing—in Ethiopia she'd watched him stitch a head wound with the precision of a master tailor. Maybe he was one of those friendly people you thought you knew when you really didn't, a flirt you thought singled you out when he treated every woman like the only one in the room. As a medic and soldier, he was paid to be protective and observant. He was probably assessing her mental health when he looked into her soul like that—with good cause.

Her peripheral vision reported that he was down to a khaki tank. *Don't look.* She caught a fresh scent, somewhere between mint and pine, weighed down with something spicier, like cinnamon. Had he smelled that way in France? Something tweaked low in her belly, like her body remembered even if her mind didn't.

She shook her head slightly. She had bigger things to think about. Like mercenaries. *Mercenaries.* Wow. She was trained to deal with virtual problems, not real ones. If Jamie hadn't got to her first...

"Mate," called the driver, looking in his side mirror. "Know anyone who drives a white Peugeot hatchback? I'm taking back streets, as you said, but he's making every turn we are—and he just followed us through a red."

Sure enough, a car was hugging their rear, with two people in the front—including a wiry blond man, talking on a cell phone.

"Oh no," Samira whispered.

"You recognize them?"

"The passenger—he was on my train. And there was a guy with hair like that in Tuscany the other night but I didn't get a close look. He seemed to be following me at the station. I told myself I was imagining it."

"Looks like your instinct was right." Jamie pulled out a chunky gray handgun. A holster was strapped to his side, over his tank.

"Oh my God. Where did you get that?" He couldn't have flown into London with it.

He clicked something into place. "An acquaintance. Get down." He raised his voice. "We need to lose him, Andy."

The driver swore. "You're still as much of a shit magnet as ever, I see." He flicked a switch and the siren wailed. "Hold tight."

Jamie stooped to read a street sign. Samira followed his gaze. King's Cross Road. "Keep away from the markets. We get caught up in those and we'll be stuck tight, siren or no."

"Mate, you're talking to the guy who *didn't* run off and join the fucking Foreign Legion. I know every road cone this side of the Thames. I'll loop round, head east."

Jamie hauled a backpack from a cubbyhole and pulled something out of the front pocket. A phone.

Gripping the gurney with one hand, Samira caught his forearm. "We can't make any calls. Tess said—"

"Tess is the world's most paranoid woman. It's a brand-new phone and I'm not making a call, just doing some Googling. I have an idea of how we could lose them." He glanced at the car. "Besides, I think Hyland's already onto us."

The ambulance swung onto another street. She slid sideways, into air. With his spare arm, Jamie caught her around the waist and steered her onto a fold-down seat. The sight of his bare arms made her shiver all over again. Why was she the one breaking out in goose bumps?

"You might want to buckle up, Samira," he said.

He swayed to the narrow gap between the front seats and spoke to the driver, swiping the phone. She dived for the seat belt. Between the siren, the straining engine and the thick accents, she couldn't follow the conversation. Something about bridges and gates.

Behind them the blond man was still on his phone, his gaze fixed on the back of the ambulance as if he could see her through the one-way glass. Calling reinforcements? How many thugs did Hyland have in London? The Peugeot driver wore a cap low and a scarf high, with sunglasses bridging the gap. The car stuck to the ambulance like a water-skier behind a boat, skidding left and right as they weaved. The man nestled the phone between his shoulder and his ear and made swift hand movements in his lap. He lifted something, its black outline obvious for a second before it disappeared behind the dash.

"Jamie, they have a gun."

"They what?" yelled the driver. The ambulance lurched sideways. "Shit."

Jamie swiveled. "Flat on the floor, Samira."

Gladly. She unclipped, and crawled onto the gray vinyl, Jamie crouching beside her, gun aimed down. His London acquaintances evidently occupied different social circles from her family's. Through the windows, the tops of stripped trees and squat buildings flashed by—red brick, black brick, blackened stone, dirty concrete, steel and glass. The ambulance turned, tossing her against a row of cupboards. With one hand, she clung to the track anchoring the gurney. She cradled her other arm over her head—like that would stop a bullet. The ambulance jolted left and right, braking and accelerating like it was tossing in the surf. She swallowed nausea. At least there was no panic attack.

Don't say "panic attack."

The London she knew was a sedate place—dim lamps in hushed private libraries, leather back seats in purring black embassy cars, silver calligraphy on heavy card. Until now, her scariest experience was getting separated from her father in Madame Tussauds when she was eight.

Jamie checked his watch. "Eleven minutes," he called to the driver.

"Until what?" Her words dissolved in the noise.

"GPS says there's congestion on the one-way loop from Whitechapel," the driver yelled. "If we approach from there, they should get neatly stuck."

"Good," said Jamie, planting a hand on Samira's back as the ambulance swerved again. "Time it right and we can squeeze in just before the gates close."

Gates? He was planning to hole up somewhere?

"And if we arrive a minute later we'll be trapped," the driver shouted.

"Well, don't get there late."

"What's to stop them slipping in behind us?"

"Selfish bastard London drivers. Who's going to let them through?" Jamie winked at Samira—like she had any idea what they were talking about.

"You're assuming those same bastards will part for an ambulance."

Doubt flicked across Jamie's face, and vanished.

"Mate, can't you just call in an air strike or tank assault or something?" said the driver.

"That's plan B."

The floor shuddered as the ambulance picked up speed. They were on a wider road, passing the blurred tops of trucks and double-decker buses. The siren wailed and waned. If the driver switched it off, it would surely continue in Samira's head.

Jamie popped up to check the windows then knelt

again. He thrust his phone at Samira. "Keep an eye on this. Tell me when you see the traffic stop."

She juggled it, struggling to focus on the screen while avoiding sliding into Jamie. A live webcam was trained on Tower Bridge, its castle-like twin towers straddling a gray river. Cars and trucks stuttered across it as the stream buffered.

Outside, the gray light dimmed to charcoal—they'd driven into a tunnel, an underpass maybe. Fighting nausea, she pulled up to a sitting position, bracing her back against cupboards and her feet on the gurney, focusing on the traffic on the little screen. Everyday people going to everyday Sunday places—markets, churches, Christmas shopping, visiting a friend to collect evidence that would take down the future American president… Jamie crept between her and the blond's gun. Had he deliberately given her a menial task to keep her from panicking?

The driver leaned on his horn. "I can't lose this bastard. He's careering like a maniac at Le Mans."

"She," Jamie corrected.

"What?"

"The driver's a woman."

"Whatever. Still a maniac."

"That's because she's following you and you're the worst driver in London." Jamie dropped to a whisper and leaned toward Samira. "He's the best, really. Totally mental."

If Jamie's humor was meant to keep her from freaking out, it wasn't working—though at least her lungs were no longer panicking. Just her brain.

"I heard you, you know," the driver called.

"They're not firing at us," she said to Jamie, sounding like a child needing reassurance.

"They'll be waiting to corner us, waiting for reinforcements. If they create too much chaos we could slip away into it. Their job is to keep eyes on us while their team regroups and closes in—but don't worry," he added, quickly. "We'll slip away, very soon."

She tapped a fingernail on the screen. "Traffic's stopped in one direction."

"A couple of minutes," Jamie called, rising a little to look out the windscreen.

"It'll be tight," the driver shouted. "Hold on!"

A stout cruise ship appeared on the screen, downstream of the bridge. Samira frowned. Tower Bridge… it was a drawbridge, yes? "Jamie, I think the bridge is about to lift."

"That's the general idea."

She blinked twice. "You're planning to jump it?"

"Now, there's a plan."

"Oh God," she said. "All traffic's stopped now."

The driver slowed, honking and bleeping the siren. Her limited vision told her they were nudging through traffic across to the right-hand side of the road—the wrong side, here. The driver floored it. The engine whined like it was gunning for takeoff. What the hell? Through the windscreen, the crown of the nearest bridge tower came into view. Her quads burned with the effort of bracing against the gurney. To their right was a beige stone wall, studded with…arrow slits. Above it rose spires, circular towers, a Union Jack. The Tower of London. She'd been there once, with her mother. A very different trip.

"The gate's closing," the driver yelled. Underneath the wailing siren, another alarm sounded, high-pitched and wavering.

"Keep going," Jamie said. "We have to get past. The Peugeot's through the traffic but fifty meters behind."

"It's still closing!"

"They'll open it," Jamie called. Samira caught a slight movement at his side. He'd crossed his fingers.

"James? A few seconds and I won't be able to stop in time."

"Keep going," Jamie said. "Trust me."

The driver tooted again. "The Peugeot's gaining." Sure enough, the engine behind them was straining to a new pitch. More horns sounded.

Samira pulled herself onto the flip-down seat. She couldn't not watch. Ahead, on the bridge, under a stone archway, a pair of pale blue gates spanned the road. The left-hand one was closed, traffic queued before it. The other was at a forty-five-degree angle and drifting shut. The ambulance wail morphed into a panicked shrill squeal. She hugged the back of the seat.

"Hold tight," said the driver. "This'll be close."

Her eyes burned but she couldn't blink. Behind, the Peugeot was keeping pace. Jamie crouched, clinging to a handhold, muscles tight from his hands to his neck. Shouts filtered in from outside, over the alarms and horns and engines. The tourists were getting a show. The ambulance lurched sideways. The driver yelled. Jamie's gaze flicked to hers, as steady and calm as his jaw was tense. This was one time she wouldn't break eye contact. He winked. *Winked.*

A thump. Her stomach lurched. A metal-on-metal screech—the side of the ambulance scraping against... the gate? But they were through. Behind them, the gate had stalled, almost closed. The Peugeot gunned it, its driver hunched. The gate lurched then swung shut. She winced, bracing for a crunch. The car fishtailed and pulled up sideways in a screech of brakes, smoke puffing from its wheels, maybe an inch short of crashing. The blond man whacked the back of his driver's head, who spun toward him, evidently shouting, her arms flailing.

Samira leaned back in her seat. Blue and white cables streaked past the windows, then another stone archway like the yawning ribs of a whale, then the Thames, its concrete waters rippling around the prow of the cruise ship, which looked three times bigger than it had on the screen. On they sped, still with the alarm wailing, passing the second tower, more cables, another archway, a line of traffic... The exit gate was open. Tourists crowded against a barrier, a dozen phone cameras trained on the ambulance. A woman in a high-vis raincoat holding a walkie-talkie shook her head pointedly at the driver.

Jamie eased to standing. "They might have to dock that wee scrape from your pay."

"Fuck you, James." The driver flicked a switch and the siren stopped.

The silence washed through Samira's head. She swallowed, trying to equalize.

"Can't believe you're still getting me in the shit," the driver continued. "Thought I was well rid of you."

Jamie grinned, meeting Samira's eye and shrugging, as if he'd been given an embarrassing compliment. "Have you seen the bridge lift before, Samira? It's an awesome sight." He nodded at the view behind.

The road they'd just driven along was angling up, obscuring their view of the Peugeot on the far side of the bridge. The towers stood like rooks on a chessboard, closing in to protect their king. Was that her—the king on the chessboard, the defenseless target, able only to shuffle while the enemy swooped from all angles? What did that make Jamie? Certainly not a bishop. Too lithe for a rook, and he was no pawn. Which left a knight. Yes, the most agile of the pieces. He moved always with a liquid athleticism, at once at ease and on guard, both blasé about the possibility of a threat and capable of sidestepping it with a microsecond's notice.

"We got away," Samira said, breathlessly.

"Not quite yet. We bought ourselves a seven-minute lead but we'll have to use it wisely."

Her stomach dropped. "Only seven?"

"Should be enough. The streets are quieter this side of the Thames, on a Sunday. Once we get some miles between us and grab a black cab—out of view of the CCTV cameras—we'll be gold. And my friend here will be on his way, indistinguishable from all the other ambulances working central London. As far as our enemy is concerned, we'll have donned invisibility cloaks."

She swallowed. "I'm glad you're coming with me."

He fished in his backpack and pulled out a pale green sweater. "Why not? Could be fun. And the Legion is nipping my hide about my unused leave, so…"

"This is not my thing, this James Bond stuff."

"To be fair, it's not mine either. I'm a medic."

"You're a soldier, too."

"Sure, but I try to do as little fighting as possible. I prefer fixing people to shooting them. Sometimes these days I end up doing both. Just making work for myself because that's the secret to job satisfaction, right—digging holes and filling them in?"

She couldn't help smiling. He really was her polar opposite. Still, a man composed enough to make jokes while fleeing bad guys was a man she wanted on her team.

"James," she said, trying the name on for size.

As he shrugged the sweater on, a frown crossed his face. It was gone by the time his head emerged from the neckline. The joker in him, the charmer, the flirt—that part was a Jamie. But the hidden part that made his eyes look twice the age of the rest of him—that shouldered too many secrets for a Jamie. That was the James. Serious and aloof, with shifting depths.

"I haven't heard you being called anything but Doc." He hadn't told her his real name until they'd kissed, that day by the river—and even then it didn't come with a surname.

"It's been a long time since I got called anything else."

"What does your family call you?"

That flash of darkness. "All sorts of interesting names, I imagine."

"But what do they call you to your face?"

"Probably the same things they'd call me behind my back, which is why I'm not game to find out."

She couldn't imagine anyone disliking him. She mentally replayed their first meeting in Ethiopia—when he'd arrived with his commando team to rescue Flynn from terrorists, and ended up rescuing Samira—their escape to Europe, their week in France. Had he told her nothing about his family? She would have remembered. "You're not in contact with them?"

The side of his mouth twitched—and not in jest. "Haven't seen them for three years."

A dull thudding beat the sky above. His forehead creased.

"Ah, James?" The driver leaned forward, squinting up through the windscreen. "You know any good reason for a military helicopter to be circling us?"

Jamie swore under his breath.

"I'm thinking we might need your plan B after all, mate," the driver said.

By the look on Jamie's face, Samira guessed he didn't have one.

CHAPTER FOUR

JAMIE SCRAMBLED ONTO the front passenger seat and peered up. The helo was an MH-6 Little Bird—not here for sightseeing. Shite. Must have been on standby. Hired from a local military contractor? Hyland had to be desperate to throw that kind of resource at Samira.

He clapped a hand on Andy's shoulder. "Change of plans. Go straight to Saint Jude's A&E, on blue. Make it look like a real emergency."

"It will be unless you take your hand off me." Andy flicked on the siren.

"And radio into the hospital. See if anybody I'd know is on duty."

"You mean someone you have dirt on?"

"Preferably."

"Great. So I just casually ask, 'Oh, and is there anyone there who's been fucked over by James Armstrong?' and see how many dozens of hands go up?"

Shut it, Andy. Not in front of her. "Maybe a touch more subtle." He gave Andy's shoulder a double pat and pushed back between the seats. Andy got on the radio, the siren wailing.

Jamie had been gone five years. Most of his med school and hospital friends—not that they would use the word *friends* anymore, if they ever had—would have moved on, moved up. Even if they hadn't forgiven him, they'd surely have forgotten.

Samira was staring at the roof of the ambulance as if she had X-ray vision. *"On blue?"* She lowered her wide brown eyes to meet his gaze.

"Lights on, top speed."

She clicked her seat belt on. "You're planning to out-run a helicopter?"

"Just the vehicles they'll be directing. When you're the bug about to go under the boot, best you can do is slip between the floorboards. Even they wouldn't risk opening fire on a London Ambulance, not this close to Westminster, no matter how deep their contacts go here. They'll want to keep it relatively low-key. We can play that to our advantage." If the enemy knew the city, the Peugeot would already be backtracking to London Bridge to cross the Thames rather than waiting for the drawbridge.

"Vehicles. There are more than one?"

The ambulance swerved. He clutched an overhead handrail.

"Jamie, don't think you have to keep anything from me, because of the…because of earlier. It's the surprises that throw me."

Her knuckles blanched where they gripped the seat belt. But she was right. She was tougher than her panic attacks might suggest. "I counted three cars when I was setting up to pull you out. We should assume there are more." He made a point of keeping his tone casual and confident, like he had it all under control. And he did so far. More or less.

"I thought we were avoiding the hospital?"

"Just passing through. The place is a maze. We'll lose them there and come up with another plan to get to your friend's place." He dropped volume and nodded toward Andy, who was straining to decipher the voice at the other end of the radio. "To the authorities, to Hyland, this all has to look authentic for Andy's sake, like a real response to a nine-nine-nine call, like you just cleverly hoodwinked the system."

"So he's an innocent pawn?"

"A pawn, aye. Innocent, no." Even so, Jamie wouldn't leave his former crewmate in the shit again. Last time it'd been merely a lucky escape from unemployment—or worse. "As long as we keep ahead of the ground troops between here and the hospital, we'll be fine."

She nodded, buying his attempt at reassurance. He sure was good at sounding confident when really he had no idea. Maybe all that medical training was useful for something.

He checked his watch. The wave of Saturday night drunks and pill-poppers would have passed through the emergency department and the advance guard of sports injuries would be limping in. Not peak time but there'd be a few ambulances coming and going. If they timed it right, the chopper wouldn't know which Merc to follow out of the ambulance bay—or know if Samira was still in it.

"Harriet Davies is the consultant on," Andy said, ending his call. "You remember her?"

Jamie smiled. "Perfect."

"Ah, shit, not her, too. Is there anyone you didn't fuck over?"

Samira's eyebrows shot up.

"He's joking," Jamie whispered.

They drove on, the engine alternating between a whine and a roar as Andy slowed and accelerated. Jamie watched for enemy vehicles as the landmarks flashed by, so familiar he could be stuck in a dream about his past—a Tesco's supermarket, a redbrick church, squat terraced houses and dreary office blocks, graffitied rail bridges, the Shard jutting up like a great glass splinter. Still the same South London in the same grimy brick and concrete. But he no longer belonged.

Samira clutched the sides of her seat, evidently concentrating on regulating her breathing. In for four, out for four, in for four, out for four. For one all-too-short day—and night—he'd glimpsed the woman underneath that tight self-control, that reserve. Her speech was so precise she always seemed to be mentally scanning a dictionary. She held herself so straight—neck long, chin level—she might have been brought up under a ballet instructor's whip. The kind of well-brought-up woman his mother would have approved of.

Huh. These days he was the man mothers warned their daughters about.

"We're coming up to Waterloo," Andy called. "We could try to lose them in the railway underpasses?"

Jamie narrowed his eyes, picturing the snaking street layout. "No, keep going. We wouldn't be able to stay undercover long enough to fool them—we're not exactly stealth in this thing." From above, the ambulance roof was a high-vis yellow target. "If anything, it'll just delay us while their ground forces catch up."

Andy tsked. "Ground forces," he muttered.

"We're close enough to the hospital now—head straight there."

"Yes, sir, Sergeant Major, sir!" Andy blasted the horn. "Do you have sergeant majors in your weirdo army, Jamie?"

"We just call them arseholes. You should join up— you'd fit right in."

Jamie opened his rucksack. "Here," he said, pull-

ing out a black cap and passing it to Samira. "Keep it
pulled d—"

"Down low, I get it," she said, putting the wig back
on and ramming the cap over top. She arranged the hair
to frame her face.

He grabbed another cap from his bag and yanked
it on. Tess had them all paranoid about who could be
watching any CCTV feeds, legally or not. And no city
did security cameras like London. Paranoia capital of
the world.

But then, Samira would know more than most about
surveillance, given her job. Former job. What had she
called it? A forward-deployed infrastructure security
engineer. *It means I get paid to set up the most secure systems in the world and then get paid to hack
into them. I have to constantly keep ten steps ahead
of myself.*

Aye, he'd always had a thing for the smartest woman
in the room. They made his brain light up, among
other parts, they made life interesting, they got him
in trouble—good trouble and bad trouble. Next time
he ran away to join a mercenary force he'd check first
that it was unisex. Not that five years ago he'd had the
luxury of options.

Samira retrieved her mirrored sunglasses from the
floor and jammed them on under her cap.

"Are those sunglasses or hubcaps?" he said, shrugging on his bomber jacket. He left it unzipped for
quicker access to his Glock.

A laugh, white teeth against plum lips and brown
skin. He could almost feel a click in his brain as the
reward center—the *nucleus accumbens*—lit up and
the dopamine released. The rat getting the cheese. He

frowned. Weird. That feeling—the warm, sweet buzz in his veins. It was the sensation he used to get when…

"You're looking at me strangely," she said, dabbing her nose and chin as if expecting to find the remains of breakfast.

He directed his gaze out the window, swallowing. The evidence might not pass peer review, but there it was, clear as an fMRI scan. The day he and Samira had given in to their insane attraction had left its mark on his brain, laid down a pathway of memories that were right this second tugging at him to seek that pleasure again, promising that if he just drew her to him and…

Resist.

"We're nearly there," he said, blinking rapidly. "Let's swap rucksacks. Mine's lighter."

They rolled into the ambulance bay and pulled up alongside two other identical Mercs. Andy was home free. Now for Samira. The sooner Jamie got her to safety and left town, the better for all involved. Giving in to impulse was not something he did, not anymore.

"Cheers, pal," Jamie called as he reached for the door handle.

"My pleasure," Andy replied, sounding like he'd stepped in dog shit. "And do me a favor, James?"

"A favor? Thought we were even and you wanted to keep it that way."

"Never contact me again."

"Ah, still so fickle, Andy." He pulled Samira's rucksack on. "Okay, Samira. Stick close and let me do the talking."

A glint of white on the road alongside drew his eye. His hand froze on the handle. The Peugeot, slowing, the blond guy looking from Merc to Merc. Shite.

"Jamie?" Samira had followed his gaze. Her breath

shuddered. Crap. A panic attack now could be the death of them both.

The car rolled past and pulled up on the roadside, the passenger door swinging open before the wheels stopped. The angles of the parked Mercs would protect them from view but only for a few seconds.

Jamie pushed open the rear door and grabbed her hand. It was icy. "Out. Quick." He slammed the door behind them and drew her to his side, his right hand hovering over his weapon. They skirted the bonnet of another Merc, dodged a paramedic holding a crying, struggling toddler and scooted in through the first of a double set of mirrored glass doors. They backpedaled a second while the second set opened. Behind them the blond goon's head bobbed across the forecourt. Andy drove straight at him, forcing him to lurch backward, briefly cutting him off. They were definitely even.

Inside, the waiting room had been upgraded to something resembling a posh airport lounge. In the middle was a circular reception desk in a bubble of light. Jamie adjusted his path, scanning the faces of the staff.

"Jamie," Samira whispered, tightening the straps of the rucksack on her back, "there's a woman staring swords right at you."

So there was. A tall, trim figure in a white shirt, a tablet in her hands, leaning back against the reception desk, looking noticeably less accommodating than the junior doctor he remembered. As they approached, he glanced behind. Beyond the mirrored glass, Blondie was checking the back of an ambulance.

"Looking well, Harriet," he said.

"That's because you're no longer around." Her gaze dropped to where his hand joined Samira's and then rose to Samira's face. What was that—*pity*? Whatever happened to jealousy? She clutched the tablet like it was a ballistic chest plate. "I assume you want something."

"I need to borrow your security pass, just for five minutes. And quite quickly."

She raised thin eyebrows. "And that doesn't sound at all dodgy."

"We're passing straight through—I won't touch a thing, I promise. There's a guy following us. We have to lose him."

"Is he a cop?"

"No."

"What did you do to him? Maybe I should let him catch up."

"Harriet…" He sharpened his tone. She needed to think he still posed a threat.

"You know I could lose my job? I've only just recovered from the last time we—" She glanced at Samira. "Traded favors."

"Only if somebody finds out. And you know I don't share secrets."

Her mouth tightened, a pucker of smoker's fissures. They both knew he had her at "secrets." Blondie was nearing the automatic doors.

"Seriously, we're in a bit of a hurry," he said. "I don't have time to explain."

"Good. I don't want to hear it."

She exhaled in disgust and swiveled. They followed her around the circular desk until they were shielded from view of the entrance. He squeezed Samira's hand, which hadn't defrosted one degree. Harriet swiped at a security check and pushed a door open, ushering them into a deserted hallway—leading to the acute ward, if that hadn't changed. The door swished closed and the lock clicked. He pulled Samira away from a window set into the door.

Harriet hugged the tablet again. "Did you ever stop running, James, this whole time?"

"Nope. That's why I'm so square-jawed and fit."

"Oh, please don't think I'm going to go all weak-kneed from one smile. I'm immune to you. I've developed antibodies against the virus that is James Armstrong. We're even now, right?"

He held out his palm. "Card."

"Which gate are you heading to?"

"We'll go out the west staff entrance to the Thames Path."

She yanked her lanyard over her ponytail and shoved it into his hand. "I can't believe I'm doing this. Straight through. Keep it out of sight. Don't talk to anyone."

He closed his fingers around it. "Didn't plan to."

"Mariya's charge nurse in the Princess Alice wing today. Leave it with her—*no one else*. I take it you remember her."

Mariya. His luck was holding. "I do, as a matter of fact."

"Don't let the bosses see you, and for God's sake, restrain yourself from operating on anyone on your way through. We can all do without your 'help.'"

"Ah, you know me so well, Harriet."

"To my eternal regret." She drummed trimmed fingernails on the back of the tablet. "This makes us even, right?"

"Guess so."

"Good. I look forward to never seeing you again."

"Nice catching up, Harriet. And you might want to call the cops to pick up the tall blond guy who has just walked into the A&E. Blue jeans, brown leather jacket. He has a gun."

She swore, raising a palm, dismissively. "Oh God. It never ends with you, does it?"

"I'm serious, about the guy."

"Just. Go."

The department's renovations evidently hadn't progressed further than the waiting area. A two-star hotel with a gleaming false advertisement of a lobby. He pulled Samira into a dingy corridor toward radiology, the hospital layout coming back to him like a blueprint overlaid onto his vision. His life had forged a new path but the corridors hadn't. Still the same industrial-strength disinfectants failing to mask the stench of urine and decay. No number of interior-design consultants could disguise that. Still the same artificial lighting, so white it made even the healthy look gray and sick. Hell, it probably *made* people sick. And no matter what chirpy color hospitals painted their walls, how did it always end up some shade of mucus?

Beside him, Samira looked like an incognito movie star on a surprise visit to cheer up sick children. He realized he was still holding her hand. Ah, well, couldn't hurt. Physical contact—proven to produce oxytocin, lower blood pressure and reduce stress and anxiety. Ergo, ward off panic attacks.

And just you keep kidding yourself it's for her benefit.

At the double doors into the back of cardiology, he scanned Harriet's card over the reader. The light went red and it bleeped. Damn. He'd assumed she'd have access everywhere. They must have tightened security. He'd have to reconfigure his route.

The doors opened and a tall bald guy in a short-sleeved white shirt and bow tie strode out, speaking to a staff nurse in a Belfast accent. Crap. Jamie spun to the handwashing station and bent over it as they passed. Samira took the hint and blocked the side view. That smarmy idiot had made consultant? God help the good people of South London. And the only excuse for a bow tie on a Sunday was if you'd got lucky at a black-tie do the night before.

Jamie caught the door before it closed, and ushered Samira through, reluctantly dropping her hand. Best to look like colleagues catching up with paperwork on their day off.

"You know this place well," Samira said, quietly. "From when you were a paramedic?"

"Aye," he said, a mite too eagerly, "that's why I brought us here."

Their enemy couldn't watch every exit from the ever-spreading octopus of a complex. And the exit he planned to use was so obscure that only the longest-serving staff smokers knew about it—or, in his case, those who wanted to come and go without being observed or clocked. The sooner they got away, the less chance of being surrounded. Once out, they'd catch the first black cab or bus they saw. Melt into London.

It'd be quicker if they could cut through the court-yard to the Princess Alice wing, rather than navigate the horseshoe of corridors and departments encircling it, but they needed air cover. Back at St Pancras he'd got a reasonable look at the ground enemy. Four men, three women, including Blondie and his driver. He'd committed their faces to memory—though an amped-up mercenary should be easy to spot among the glassy-eyed zombies who haunted the hospital on a Sunday morning. Then again, Samira stood out, too, in style alone.

She looked healthier than when his train had pulled

out of the Gare de Blois, leaving her standing motionless on a deserted platform, staring after his carriage. In his mind's eye, she'd been there ever since—until he'd spotted her at St Pancras. A little curvier, her face less gaunt, her hair longer. Perhaps grief had started to release its stranglehold.

In that week they'd spent together, unwrapping her had become a game—one he'd taken too far too fast, and paid the price. Every now and then he'd succeeded in drawing out a piece of the real Samira. Like a rat in a lab, he'd learned to steer the conversation to subjects that would engage or amuse her or—when that didn't work—enrage her. When he'd played it right and lit her up, he'd lit up, too—and not much accomplished that these days. Boy, had she lit up. Her eyes sparked, her spine straightened, breath quickened, voice sharpened. Even her skin seemed to change, turning mahogany like a flame was warming it from beneath. Watching that was the reward for his persistence. He'd like to see that side of her again. Maybe he should have sucked up his pride and tried harder to convince her to let him stay. A year together in hiding. Nothing to do but—

Stop. Nothing to do but hit on a grieving woman under the pretense of protecting her? Nothing to do but give her a chance to get to know and loathe the real him? To give in to his impulses and let them control him? She'd made the right call, for both of them.

The best he could do for her now was help to complete her whistle-blower fiancé's mission. Seeing her find peace would be his only reward.

At the cardiology reception desk, a nurse was handing a form to a bear of a man clutching a brown paper bag. "Do you not have anyone who could pick you up?"

she said. Her lilac scrubs marked her as an agency nurse, not a permanent employee.

"The ferry's fine," the bear replied. "Pretty much door to door. And no bloody traffic."

"You've just had a heart attack. You really should have someone to—"

"Will the NHS pay for a black cab?"

"No, that's not in—"

"Thought not."

Another security door loomed, into neurology. Would Harriet have access there?

"Yes, that was the fascinating thing," Jamie said to Samira in an imperious public-school English accent. He gave the nurse a cursory nod as they passed, and hovered Harriet's card over the sensor. "The MRI clearly showed an isodense intramedullary spinal cord tumor at C3 but it'd been misdiagnosed as a glioma, would you believe?" Red light on the sensor. Damn.

"Excuse me," he said to the nurse in his best impatient-yet-condescendingly-polite consultant tone. "Terribly sorry, but would you mind…?" He gestured to the card reader, shrugging in a would-you-believe-it's-*still*-not-working way, and turned back to Samira. "Bloody thing. I did ask Charlie to order me a new card. What was I saying…?"

"The glioma…" Samira said, her head bowed as if deep in concentration. Or prayer. Heck, he'd take any help they could get.

In his peripheral vision, he registered the nurse scrambling to the door, still arguing over her shoulder with the patient. With a bomber jacket and rucksack, Jamie didn't look doctorish, but perhaps he could pull off aging consultant trying to pass for cool young hipster. "Ah, yes, so naturally I recommended we use immunostaining to rule out a neuronal tumor, and you can imagine Caroline's reaction…"

He kept up the monologue as the nurse scanned her card and opened the door. He walked through with a distracted nod of thanks, Samira murmuring in sympathy with his fictitious neurological predicament. The door clunked shut. He trailed off a few meters down the corridor.

"Nearly there," he said to Samira. "You holding up?"

"Awo," she said, looking at him with more respect than he deserved—the way people used to look at him back when he wore scrubs and a stethoscope. He'd got off on that look a little too much. But, hey, if his bullshit made Samira confident, he wasn't about to burst her bubble.

Ahead, at a nurse's station, a woman in pale blue scrubs leaned over a clipboard. From a patient bay to his left a TV droned. Few patients would be unlucky enough to remain under observation over the weekend. His chest tightened in the same cocktail of nerves and adrenaline he'd felt the first time he'd walked in here as a senior house officer on his first rotation, knowing that people were relying on him to get out of here alive. He, Jamie Armstrong, who'd been playing schoolboy rugby not that long before.

Really, he should be living that Irish numbskull's life by now. Wife and little kids. Heavily mortgaged semi-detached Victorian villa in Ealing. Sweaty-palmed first-year doctors gazing at him with fear and adoration. He could send money to his sister and her kids, rather than emptying his military pay packet into the crevasse of his mother's private nursing-home upkeep. His dad might still be alive if he'd been there to recognize the danger signs instead of ankle-deep in mud or dust in Mali or

Afghanistan or Guyana. Or maybe the old man's heart wouldn't have given out in the first place.

Not now, Dad.

They strode silently through the east and north wings, the circuitous route zapping his nerves. Finally, he pushed open the doors into the west wing. A curvy blonde in red scrubs looked up from the reception desk, her green eyes widening.

He nodded. "Mariya."

"Doctor Armstr... I mean—"

"James," he said, quickly.

"What are you doing h—?"

"Give this to Harriet, would you?" He slapped the pass on the counter. "And only Harriet. You didn't see me."

Mariya screwed up her face. "Does...this mean we're square?"

"You're returning an ID pass. As favors go, it's not a biggie."

"I'll have to walk to the other side of the building."

He pointed to a fitness monitor on her wrist. "It'll keep up your steps. Besides, that hardly makes up for..." In his peripheral vision he caught Samira tipping her head, assessing the conversation. "Whatever. We're square."

"And I won't ever have to see—?"

"No, you won't," he snapped.

Did she *have* to look so relieved?

He opened an unassuming side door onto the smoker's porch, ignoring the ALARM WILL SOUND sign. He'd been gone only five years—it probably hadn't been fixed. By the smell of it, the staff still weren't respecting the smoke-free rules. Same broken brick to hold the door open while they sucked in the very poison they lectured patients about. He shoved it into position, in case their exit was compromised. Drizzle tapped on the mildewed corrugated plastic awning.

"Where next?" Samira said.

"See that wee gate in the wall, across the car park? It leads to the Thames Path. Easily the most obscure of the hospital's exits." Over the solid stone, the broad gray river rolled south. Across it, the houses of parliament and Big Ben were coated in a hazy gold film. Once on the Thames Path they could cross to Westminster. Or, better still, follow the current south to Lambeth Bridge, to avoid doubling back past the hospital walls.

"Do you think they'll be watching it?"

"Anything's possible, but they'll prioritize the other twenty or so exits. They wouldn't have a big resource out there, at any rate. Come here. Your hair is showing."

He tucked a black lock under her wig and pulled down her cap. Under the sunglasses, about the only visible parts of her were her chin and nose, already pinking up in the cold air. He resisted the urge to touch.

"Perfect," he said.

"Peerrrfect," she repeated, to herself.

"Are you mimicking my accent, Samira?"

She bit one corner of her lip. "Sorry, it's just…"

"Indecipherable, I know. Sometimes even I have trouble understanding myself. I wonder if we could… *borrow* another coat for you. The enemy will have seen you in that one. Or maybe you could take it off? What do you have on underneath?"

"A black dress. I have another coat, in my backpack. It's thinner, but…"

A thumping noise. "Shite, the chopper." He pushed her back inside. "Change the coat, just in case…" He raised his voice. "You have a brolly, Mariya?"

"Course I do," she said, in an are-you-*still*-here voice.

"Can I borrow it?"

"Borrow, as in...?"

"As in, I probably won't be passing back this way but I'll think of you every time it rains."

"I thought we were square."

"I'm unsquaring us." He held out a hand. "Come on. It's just a fucking umbrella."

"Fine." She whacked it into his palm. "Whatever. I'll just catch pneumonia."

"A small price, Mariya. Lovely catching up." He nodded sharply and turned. "Wow." Samira was belting a bright blue coat that wrapped up her curves like a Christmas present. *But not one with your name on it.*

"I can change my footwear, too," she said.

"Sure."

She unzipped her boots and slid on a pair of heels to match the coat, over her black stockings. He imagined himself slipping the shoes off in the nearest hotel bedroom. Rolling the stockings down, slowly. Running his hands back up her legs to—

"Jamie?"

"Sorry, what?"

She'd been speaking? Mariya caught his eye, raising her eyebrows. Samira retied her purple scarf with a convoluted series of twists, then pulled on cream leather gloves.

The scarf—it was the one he'd bought her, the one that made her eyes breathtaking. *"La couleur de minuit,"* he murmured, clenching the umbrella in both hands so as not to reach out and touch the fabric.

"The color of midnight," she whispered, her mouth softening. Just the way it had that day beside the river in the moment his self-control had deserted him.

He cleared his throat. "They'll have seen your rucksack. We'll pack your things into mine," he said, loosening the straps to expand his pack. "There's plenty of room."

A few minutes later they stepped outside. He tucked in a label jutting from her coat collar. On her nape, above the scarf, a sliver of skin goose pimpled. *Don't go doing that to me now.* He opened the umbrella.

"Jesus, I've seen dinner plates bigger than this," he said, looking up. "Can you hold it while I keep an eye out?" He swung her to his left, anchored his arm around her waist and pulled their hips flush, gratified by her tiny gasp. "We'll walk to that gate, nice and smooth."

They set off, awkwardly, given their height difference, Jamie hunching to fit under the umbrella. It always took a while for a couple to settle into a stride. Not that he remembered what it was like to be in a relationship where you strolled arm in arm. And not that he and Samira were a couple or ever would be—he'd broken enough hearts attempting a regular life, and hers was scarred enough already. Even through her coat he could feel her suppleness, his fingers moving as her hips swayed. Wasn't often he missed relationships…

He pushed open the gate into a northwesterly blast and ushered Samira out. The bear with the paper bag lumbered past, head bent against the drizzle, breath labored, face as gray as the pavement. A jogger approached from the other direction. The path was otherwise deserted. As the gate locked behind them, Jamie coaxed Samira around to head south. They were channeled in by the wall but a canopy of trees still clinging to amber leaves provided air cover, and the shower gave them an excuse to huddle close and walk fast. A cluster of tourists in raincoats rounded a bend, some taking photos of Westminster. He clutched her tighter, skirting to one side of them. Fat drops of rain unleashed, blurring everything into gray.

A stout dark-haired man pushed through the tourists, scanning from person to person, hand inside his coat. Shit. One of the goons who'd been waiting for Samira's train. He'd paid no heed to Jamie at the station but he'd know Samira's face.

Jamie angled her to face him, planted a hand on each of her cheeks and drew her close, laughing as if she'd whispered something suggestive. As he sensed the enemy glancing their way, he lowered his head and did the only logical thing. He kissed her.

She went rigid.

Don't pull away. Trust me. Between his hands and his lips, he was covering the only identifiable part of her. All the guy would see was a brunette in heels and a blue coat.

She took the hint and relaxed against him, pulling the umbrella low over their heads and sliding her free hand under his bomber jacket to the side of his waist. He bore down to stop from flinching. Oh man, he shouldn't be getting a full-body reaction from that but there it was, as strong as a year ago—the nerves firing from his lips to his toes and back up...

The tourists passed and he released her lips, keeping his hands in place and touching his forehead to hers while taking a read from the corner of his eye— and catching his breath because...*damn.* The goon had moved away with the group, toward Westminster Bridge. The bear was lumbering the other way. Jamie dropped his hands.

"Oh my God," Samira breathed.

"I'm sorry. There was a guy, from the station. It was the only thing I could think of."

"*Eshi.* I mean, don't apolog—" She touched her lips with two fingers. He yearned to do the same. "It's fine."

Fine.

Fine.

Fine wasn't the reaction he normally shot for when he kissed a woman. Goddamn, those lips were just as smooth as he remembered. And insistent. And he'd remembered her a lot since—

Movement, to the south. The bear had tripped and was falling like a tree. No, not a trip—he was clutching his chest. He landed with a smack, his arm bouncing lifelessly on flagstones.

"Shite," Jamie said, taking a step. The goon had turned, watching. "Samira, I can't not…"

"Of course. Go."

"Come with me."

Jamie sprinted to the guy and shoved two fingers to his throat. Rain peppered his gray face. No carotid pulse. Fuck. Not breathing, either. He laid the guy flat, unzipped his coat and pulled it aside. His sternum was still.

"Has he been shot?" Samira said as she caught up.

"No. He's a heart patient. Went down clutching his chest, grimacing. Has to be a heart attack."

"CPR?" Samira said, holding the umbrella over them, her voice tight.

"I can go one better."

"What do you mean?"

"A precordial thump. Jump-start his heart. Not standard hospital procedure but the indications…" Jamie clenched his right fist and held it above the guy's chest, mentally measuring the gap. Twenty centimeters, right? "Okay," he whispered to himself. "Go." He smacked the side of his fist onto the guy's lower sternum then snatched it away. The guy jumped, twitched—and lurched up, eyes wide, like a dead man coming out of the grave. Which he pretty much was. He scraped in a breath and clutched Jamie's arm.

"Fuck," Jamie said. "I've always wanted to do that."

Shite, now what? They couldn't get him back into the hospital through a locked gate. They couldn't leave him. They'd have to wait for a passerby they could send for help.

"Jamie, that thug," Samira murmured. "He's coming."

He was coming, all right, and at a fair clip. No gun drawn but his eyes were narrowed at Samira. Crap. It'd confirm his suspicions if Jamie and Samira took off. And a shoot-out was best avoided. The priority was to get Samira out of there. Then deal with the goon. Then the bear. Triage, basically.

"Quick, Sa—s—sweetheart," he shouted. "You'll have to go for help. This guy needs a resus team, quick. I'll boost you over the wall." He lowered his voice. "Go straight to Mariya. Hide somewhere near her desk and I'll come for you when I've sorted out this goon."

Before she had time to think, he pulled her to the wall and linked his hands in front of him, ready for her foot. Rain sluiced his face. He blinked hard. Behind him, the bear groaned.

"Now, sweetheart!" he shouted. "Go!"

Samira puffed out her cheeks and put the ball of her shoe into his hand. "I don't know how to do this— jump like this."

"It's easy. I'll hoist you to the top. Just be careful jumping down—bend your knees. One, two, three."

He heaved, and she caught the edge of the wall and pulled herself up. One of her heels fell, and Jamie caught the shoe before it took out his eye. She slipped the other shoe off and disappeared, grunting as she landed on the other side. It felt wrong to let her out of sight, even for a minute.

He swiveled, hand hovering by his holster. The goon had gone. Shit. The bear hoisted himself to a sitting position.

"What happened to that guy who was running for us?" Jamie said. "Did you see?"

"Nah, sorry. Bloody hell. What just…? Did I…? Are you a doctor?"

"Your heart stopped." Jamie ran to the low wall separating the path from the river and looked over. Stones, rubbish, water… The goon had to have gone after Samira.

Gunfire rang out—muffled potshots from a pistol, over the wall. Then the echoing whine of an approaching helicopter.

Shit. Samira.

CHAPTER FIVE

THE HELICOPTER SWUNG out over the wall, to the north. Gunfire popped. Beside Jamie, the glass dome of a streetlamp smashed. Bullets plinked along flagstones. He sprinted for the hospital wall, sheltered from view by the spindly canopy.

"Sorry," he yelled to the bear. "I gotta draw their fire away."

"Might be an idea," the guy said, shakily. He had to be wondering what alternative world he'd been resurrected into. *Just keep breathing, pal.*

"I'll send help. Just…take it easy, relax."

"Relax. Sure."

The shooters weren't door gunners, just guys with assault rifles. Not as precise.

More ground fire, over the wall. An alarm wailed, echoed by another, farther off.

Jamie found a foothold and launched over the wall, under tree cover. As he landed, he skidded on wet leaves. No sign of Samira or the gunman. He'd royally fucked that up. Once in a while the first idea wasn't the best idea… The smokers' door was banging in the breeze. *Don't latch. Don't latch.* He peered up through the branches. He'd have to cross open ground but better that than the chopper spraying the trees and taking out the bear.

He launched into a sprint, pumping his arms, dodging cars, breathing hard. Gunfire plinked into steel, punched asphalt. As he bounded up the concrete steps, a gust swept the door. It latched. Shit. He hammered on it, turned, flattened, drawing his weapon—not that a Glock would take out a helicopter. The chopper veered toward him. He released the slide. A dozen alarms and sirens clashed.

The door fell away behind him. He stumbled back.

"Fuck me." Mariya stood, hands on hips. "Is that a gun?"

Gunfire hammered the porch, tearing through the awning. Jamie pulled the door shut and shoved Mariya farther inside.

She shook him off. "Are you a good guy here or—?"

"Where's Sa—?" he said. "Where's my friend?"

"She ran down the corridor." Mariya pointed. "Some guy followed her. He fired a fucking gun. I called security but they're not here yet."

Shit. Without an access card Samira would have run into a dead end. Jamie grabbed Harriet's pass from the counter and looped it around his neck.

"Get out of sight and stay down," he ordered. "Away from windows."

"You just can't help yourself, can you?" Mariya called as he rounded the corner of her desk and scoped out the corridor. Long and empty. At the far end, one of the double doors into Occupational Therapy hung open. He ran silently along the wall, gun down, pulse cranking, checking the empty bays either side. At the double doors, the security panel had been shot to pieces. A crackly voice sounded over the hospital loudspeaker. "The hospital is on full lockdown. Proceed directly to a refuge, as indicated by staff. Do not enter or leave the premises. This is not a drill."

From ahead, a man's voice trickled in over the recording and the alarms. A one-sided conversation, though Jamie couldn't make out the words. On the phone?

He peeped between the doors. Nobody in view. Occupational Therapy would be empty on a Sunday. He took a longer look. The admin station was in an alcove halfway down the narrow wing, opposite a deserted waiting room. The guy had to be in there. With Samira? Jamie edged through the doors.

"...no idea where the fuck I am," the guy was saying, in an American accent. "Place is a fucking maze. There are treadmills and shit in here—some hospital gym? I'm looking out a window at a courtyard with a tree in it... Yeah, I know that's not very fucking helpful. Can't you track me from the GPS on the phone or some shit?"

A window blind rattled. Jamie quietly lowered the rucksack to the floor.

"Why don't I just shoot her and then the problem's solved?"

Jamie's forehead prickled. As he inched closer, he heard—or imagined—Samira's breath wheezing in time with the ebb of the siren. He ran his gaze around the ceiling. No security cameras. He couldn't count on help being forthcoming—and even if it was, Jamie could well end up taking a bullet.

"Hang on, man. She's having a fucking fit or something."

A clatter. Gasping.

"Lady, this better not be some trick... Nah, serious, man, she's going purple. She ain't breathing. What do I do? Well, someone's gotta make a decision here! Where's Fitz?"

Jamie exhaled and inhaled, like he was trying to do it for Samira. She would be fine. Terrified, of course, but nobody died from a panic attack. He pictured the goon's position from his voice—looking down at Samira on the floor, facing the window? Gun in right hand, phone in the other? Doubly distracted.

"If Fitz is gonna interrogate her he better get here quick... No, I don't fucking know CPR. Hang on. I gotta put the phone down a sec."

Jamie launched around the corner. The guy looked up, fumbling to adjust his grip on a pistol. Jamie leaped, shoved the gun aside, wheeled and smacked his elbow into the guy's forehead. The goon staggered back but gathered control of his weapon, swiveled and aimed it at Jamie's forehead. *Not so smooth,* caporal.

Something blue flew across the alcove and clocked the side of the goon's head. The impact rippled through him. He tipped sideways into a desk and crumpled onto the floor. What the fuck? A hand weight rolled off the desk and thudded onto the guy's side.

"Oh my God, is he alive?" Samira's voice, to Jamie's right, barely audible over the alarms. She was kneeling in a corner, gray-faced, eyes huge. Over the loudspeaker, the recorded message repeated.

Jamie kicked the guy's weapon across the floor. "You threw that weight?"

"It was sitting right there. It looked like he was going to... I didn't think. Is he...? Did I...?"

Jamie checked the guy's vitals. "Little groggy but okay. What happened to your panic attack? Were you faking?"

"No. But then I saw you and then the weight, and somehow I pushed through it."

A tinny voice sounded. *Merde.* Jamie held a finger to his lips, and located the goon's phone on an office chair. Still on. He picked it up, settling his breath.

"Nah, I'm okay. I'm fine," he shouted, in his best imitation of the guy's accent, muffling his voice with his hand. "Just some fucking security guard. Knocked him out cold. Listen, there's some paperwork sitting here, says I'm in the…" Jamie stared at a concrete courtyard. What was on the far side of the building? "The…gynecology outpatient clinic. Shit, someone's coming. I gotta go. You better get here, quick."

Jamie hung up. The goon groaned. Jamie retrieved his rucksack, and drew out a syringe and vial from his white box of goodies.

"What is that?" Samira said, grabbing her sunglasses from the floor beside her.

"A sedative. Keep him in a happy place a while longer." The guy wouldn't be able to give much of a description of Jamie, especially with a concussion, but the longer they kept him quiet, the better.

"Where did you get it?"

"Would you believe a prescription?"

"No."

He laughed.

"Let me guess," she said. "You have a contact?"

"Traditional weapons are a little harder to come by here and a few people owed me—"

"Favors. I'm beginning to see a pattern."

Not that this favor had come cheaply. Andy had charged him top dollar. But at short notice, with limited access to real firepower, Jamie needed every advantage he could think of. And if there was one weapon he knew how to wield…

After injecting the guy, Jamie tucked him into a bed in a private room in the evacuated orthopedics ward next door. Samira relieved him of a clip of pounds in his pocket.

"I wish they'd shut off that fucking siren," Jamie said as they left the room, closing the door. "We'd better get out of here before security arrives—or this guy's buddies. I'm afraid we've lost your shoes, Cinderella. You might want to put your boots back on."

"I have an idea how we can get away," Samira said a minute later, as she zipped up the boots.

"All ears."

She led him back to Occupational Therapy. "There," she said, pointing to a display box fixed to a wall. Inside, two dozen keys hung on nails. A sign read *OT Pool Cars. Sign the log BEFORE you take a key. Return with a FULL TANK. NO exceptions.*

"Crumbs, Samira! Are you suggesting we steal a car?"

"Just…borrow." She stepped back, abruptly. "You're right. What am I thinking? It's a terrible idea."

He caught her shoulders. "It's a great idea. You're more easily corruptible than I'd thought."

The box was locked but he found the key in a drawer. They tidied up the nurse's station. He took the logbook and buried it in a paper recycling bin two wards north.

Now for the staff car park. As they approached a blind corner in the corridor, Samira grabbed his arm. Footsteps. He pushed her through a door into a bathroom and drew his weapon. The footsteps passed.

"Good timing," he said. "I'm needing to use the facilities."

As they emerged, they nearly collided with a trio of local police, packing Glocks.

"Shit, you gave me a hell of a fright," Jamie chided in his best Scouse, tucking his weapon into the back of his waistband and pulling his jacket over top, hoping it looked like he was adjusting his jeans after a bathroom break. He leaned slightly to make Harriet's ID spin facedown on his chest. Hopefully they were searching for a chubby guy with black hair, from the description Mariya would have given. "Know where we're supposed to be going for this bloody lockdown? I skived off to the pub in the last drill."

They listened intently to the bobbies' directions, and set off accordingly, Jamie loudly grumbling that this was the last time he was coming in on his day off. When they were clear, they doubled back and crept through corridors and tunnels to the parking building, skirting security cameras wherever possible, hunkering into their clothing when not. He might be a rat in a maze, but this was his maze.

They found the car in its allotted space. "There she is," Jamie said. "Saint Jude's finest piece-of-shit hatchback."

He tipped his rucksack into the car's boot, nudging aside a collapsed wheelchair. Samira checked the car for a GPS unit or tracker.

"You're giving the NHS credit for a bigger budget than they have," Jamie said.

"Can't be too careful when you're committing a felony."

"It's just a regular old crime, over here."

"That makes me feel so much better."

Samira hid in the footwell of the rear seat, covered in her brown coat. Jamie wrapped himself up in a football scarf and the cap.

At the hospital gates, a barrier arm guarded the exit. A parking attendant leaned out of her station. "We're on lockdown. No one in or out."

"It's an emergency." Jamie went with a Welsh accent.

The woman frowned. "That's an OT car. What even is an OT emergency?"

"You can ask me that when it's *your* grandmother who can't get off the loo because her grab rail came off in her hand."

The attendant blinked, like she was seeing a mind picture, then shrugged and lifted the barrier.

Outside the gates, they crept into a traffic jam. Rain peppered the roof. The windows fogged up. No sign of the helicopter—it'd probably scarpered after failing to take down Jamie, before local forces could scramble to respond. This close to Whitehall and Buckingham Palace, the police wouldn't take chances.

"What's happening?" Samira hissed.

Jamie rubbed the windscreen. The wipers beat like a crazed metronome. "Not a lot. Who'd be a getaway car driver in London?"

"Oh my God, Jamie. We just stole a car."

"Technically, I stole it—though you did force me into it. But don't worry. We'll return it clean and with a full tank."

As they crawled onto Westminster Bridge, a familiar blond head snaked around the umbrellas bobbing along the pavement. Wisely leaving the sinking ship, ready to regroup. Jamie would have to drive right past him, but with a dozen cops in view, the goon would be keeping his head even lower than Jamie's.

Police were waving traffic by with barely a glance. He'd bet they had no idea what they were looking for but figured it wasn't an NHS hatchback going two miles an hour.

Jamie hung a left after Big Ben and the traffic eased up. Union Jacks sagged from the towers of Westminster and the Abbey. He had to fight the urge to drive on the right-hand side, after so many years on the Continent.

When they'd passed through the main tourist area into the neoclassical stone of Millbank, he gave Samira the all clear to climb into the front seat. She slid her sunglasses back on and adjusted her wig. Not that anybody on the streets had their heads up. And the dreich day and foggy windows would mess with CCTV.

"So, Putney, right?" he said.

"You know how to get there?"

"Aye. Got an address?"

She recited it from memory. "I just hope Charlotte's there. I had no safe way of telling her I was on my way. I don't even know what we're collecting. This could all be for nothing."

"Ah, it's been fun so far. But you'd better hold your breath—we're passing MI5." He jerked his head to a stately building to their right, no doubt ablaze with activity beneath its imperial facade, given the morning's alert. "Look at it, sitting there all fat and self-important while an enemy of the American people passes right by."

"Is this you trying to make me feel less anxious?"

"Not working?"

"Not working."

"Stick with me. We'll be okay."

Right. Because nobody who stuck with him ever came unstuck?

She doesn't need to know.

Then again, she'd had intimate experience of coming unstuck in his company. Shite, they were going to be alone in a car for maybe half an hour. She wouldn't want to talk about what'd happened between them, would she?

As they left the spooks behind and veered back to

the Thames, she swore and pulled something from her coat pocket. The goon's phone.

"I'd forgotten about this," she said.

"We'll chuck it in the river. You know how Tess is about phones being traced."

She lifted the phone to the gauzy light coming through her window and tilted it left to right, like she was looking for a way in. "Believe me, I'm the same."

"You've caught her paranoid tendencies?"

"You could say we contracted them from the same source."

"Get rid of it, Samira. The guy said something about GPS tracking."

She squinted at it. "This won't take a second."

"What won't?"

"It might be useful to find out what this guy knows, where he's been. If they can GPS-track it, so can I."

"How long will that take?"

"A minute or two. I'll download a backup app and sync everything to the cloud—GPS data, phone calls, texts… I can sift through it later."

"Just you do that. It's not password-protected, then?"

"Looks like a swipe pattern," she said, pulling off a glove. "Which is only effective if you wipe the screen after each use." She flicked a fingertip in a Z shape and the screen lit up. "You see?"

Oh, he did see. Nothing sexier than a smart brain. And the longer she used it for techie stuff, the less time for awkward after-the-morning-after conversations. With luck, they'd get through the next few hours with no chance to even reference their…liaison. Just so long as he didn't go kissing her again. Self-control wasn't his strong point but he could at least manage that, dopamine or not.

Right?

CHAPTER SIX

"NO TEXTS OR EMAILS," Samira said, swiping and tapping too fast for Jamie to get a fix on the screen. "No stored numbers. These guys are careful."

A white bakery van stopped in front of them, and the driver climbed out and opened up the back. Jamie leaned on the horn. Samira jumped.

"Sorry," he said. "This woman's decided to use Grosvenor Road as a loading zone." He veered around it. "Bloody London drivers."

"Jamie, if we're going to judge on stereotypes you'd be grumpy and pasty and miserly and I'd be a kid with a bloated stomach and flies in my eyes."

"Too long in this country and I'll be back to pasty and grumpy quick smart, don't you worry. And on my income, I can't be anything but miserly." Humor. Yes. Humor was good. You couldn't laugh and panic at the same time.

"I've forgotten what an income is."

He peered out the windscreen. "How long until you've finished with that phone? I have an idea."

"I'm done. I've uploaded the GPS data but I won't be able to throw it into a mapping tool until I get to a computer."

He lowered his window. "Give it here."

She wiped her prints off it. As a double-decker sightseeing bus passed the other way, he tossed it onto the open top level. Rain had driven the tourists downstairs.

"That should have the mercenaries driving in loops around central London."

"Nicely done," she said, wonder in her voice. He liked hearing wonder in a woman's voice. He'd missed hearing wonder in a woman's voice. He'd missed *her* silky voice, best heard murmuring sweet groans into his—

"How long until Putney?" she said.

"Uh. Twenty minutes. We'll park a few blocks from your friend's apartment and walk. Just a precaution," he added, as her shoulders tensed. "Ninety-nine percent of precautions are unnecessary. It's the one in a hundred that turns out to be necessary that makes the other ninety-nine worth it. But you don't need any lessons in caution now, do you?"

He resisted pointing out MI6 headquarters across the river, a cross between a Disney castle and a tiered wedding cake.

"So…you came here because there was no one else available…?"

Shite. "Uh, well, I know the territory, so I was the obvious choice." And the fact that Samira was the one at risk? Well, Jamie hadn't needed time to stop and weigh things up. Some would call that his downfall. That and dopamine. "And it sounded like a bit of fun."

"Huh."

What did she want to hear? That he hadn't stopped thinking about her in thirteen long months? In France she'd made it excruciatingly clear she wanted him gone, stat. And his conscious brain had told him she was dead right, for both their sakes. Other parts of him, on the other hand…

He stole a sideways glance at her. Whatever her reason for pushing him away, he'd swear indifference wasn't it.

"A bit of fun," she echoed. "Kidnapping a woman from a train station, hijacking an ambulance, trespassing through a hospital, impersonating a doctor, lying to police, stealing a car, drugging a man."

"Ah, but you're forgetting the time I saved a man's life while under fire using a rare and controversial technique, outran a helicopter assault, engaged in hand-to-hand combat to rescue said woman, outwitted the entire Met Police force and escaped under the noses of MI5 and MI6."

"MI6?" she said, looking around.

"Oh, we left them way behind."

"I'm not sure if you're brave or reckless."

He smiled. "Definitely reckless. You, on the other hand, are brave."

"Hardly. I'm only doing this because I have no choice."

He shrugged. "So am I."

"What do you mean you don't have a choice?"

"Well, I wasn't going to let you walk into the hands of those bastards, was I? And with guys like Flynn and Angelito—when they say they need you, you don't say no, regardless of the cost."

Samira was silent a minute. She pulled her glove back on. "You shouldn't have come."

And there it was. What had he expected? *Jamie, you have to leave*, she'd said that morning in France, pushing away the croissants he'd bought from the boulangerie while she'd slept in. *This was a mistake.*

"Samira, look, it'll take—what?—half a day to get

this evidence off to Tess? Then you'll never have to see me again, if that's what you want."

"No, I didn't mean it like that."

Well, that was something. "Then what did you mean?"

"I mean, it's dangerous to be here with me."

His eyes widened. *Tell me about it.*

"No, I don't mean that, either."

Shite, how did she follow *that* train of thought?

"I'm not very good at explaining myself. I mean, I'm relieved you're here. But being around me makes you a target."

"I know that. I'm good with that." Her gaze practically itched the side of his face.

"Did I ever tell you how my fiancé died?"

Whoa. He hadn't seen that coming. "I don't believe so, no." Come to think of it, she hadn't mentioned the guy at all in France.

"He died in a US drone strike in Somalia after I called his cell phone," she said, quiet and precise. "That's how Hyland's goons tracked him down—they'd been waiting for him to break cover."

"A *military* strike? How'd Hyland get away with that?"

"Tess reckons he arranged for the US to get intel that a terrorist leader was hiding out where Latif was staying, and then pressured the president to deal with it. Latif was collateral damage, officially. Of course, by then Latif had given enough information to Tess to bring down Hyland's former company and his cronies, but the senator slipped the noose. We think Latif had been hunting evidence that could bring Hyland down, too. And now Hyland wants me gone, thinking I know too much. Which, unfortunately, I don't."

"Oh Jesus. I knew some of that but not all. I'm sorry.

And we think Charlotte now has this evidence? She works for GCHQ, right? Why wouldn't she just tell her bosses?"

"Maybe she did. Or maybe she doesn't know who to trust. Governments are loath to intrude on other governments' dirty secrets. And everyone has secrets." She sat straighter. "Anyway, my point is that if I'm a target, you're a target. And I already lost one…"

He looked at her, but she was facing the other way. One…?

"I don't think I could handle losing another…" She rubbed her hands down her thighs.

Ah. So there it was—confirmation. She'd pushed him away last year not because she *wasn't* into him but because she *was* into him. And, hey, he'd left quite enough broken hearts in the rubble of his former life. Which, all put together, made them perfectly wrong for each other.

"Oh God," she said, planting a palm on her forehead. "That sounds selfish, doesn't it? What I mean is… I don't want you to die for *your* sake. Not just for mine."

"Sweet of you," he said. "And you're worried you might get me killed?"

"Awo."

"Awo," he repeated, mimicking the way she sucked in the word, like a breathy gasp.

"Sorry, it means *yes*. I got back into the habit of saying it when I was in hiding in Ethiopia last year."

"I remember it. I like it—it's catching. And what's that other word you use, for *okay, no problem*."

"Eshi."

"Eshi," he echoed. "And so…you're worried the same thing might happen to me?"

"Awo."

He waited, but she volunteered no more. "I appreciate your sweet concern but I'm here because I want to be. And I'm not leaving until this is done and you're safe. *Eshi?*"

"*Eshi.*"

"But you're welcome to not want me to die, for purely selfish reasons."

She laughed. They fell silent, Samira frowning at the long wash of the Thames. Battersea loomed from the gloom like a redbrick battleship.

"Jamie," she began, after a time, "there's something I don't understand... Well, there are many things, but... all those people—the paramedic, the doctor, the nurse. They didn't think much of you."

Yikes. *Everyone has secrets.*

"I'm very widely misunderstood." This was his invitation to come clean. But that'd mean seeing the respect die in her eyes. And he liked those eyes—the way her pupils flicked to one corner when she was thinking, the way they studied him from under thick jet-black lashes, the way the scarf made them sexy and smoky, somehow. Aye, he liked them a little too much. He could keep the disappointment from them for another few...what? Hours? Days? How long would it take to retrieve this evidence and figure out a way to deliver it to the United States? Then he would return to his futureless job and those eyes would once more be a pleasant memory to get him through deployments.

"The women," she ventured, "they are ex-girlfriends?"

"Hell no." If only hearts were all he'd messed with. "We were all young and wild together, that was all."

"You were a doctor there, weren't you? Not a paramedic."

He tightened his grip on the steering wheel.

"That nurse… Maria…"

"Mariya."

"She called you 'Doctor.' And you knew your way around…"

Would it matter in the end how much she knew? "I was a paramedic first, while in med school. Doctor later."

She turned in her seat. "Wow, really?"

Impressed. Ah, he missed that reaction. "Yeah, I pretty much didn't sleep in my twenties."

"Neither did I, but I wasn't saving lives. You never mentioned that."

"Didn't I?" he said, lightly.

That awe in her voice… He might not technically be lying but he was still a fraud. The ego boost he'd once got from telling people he was a doctor had long ago been replaced by the weight of expectation of the obvious next question. *Why did you leave?* The best thing about the Legion? If you didn't volunteer information, people knew better than to ask. He'd told only his immediate commanding officers the whole wretched story, including Angelito and Flynn. They had to know the risk he posed, his triggers, the warning signs.

The other good thing about the Legion was that you quickly learned to deflect flak.

"What were you doing instead of sleeping?" he said. "Or shouldn't I ask?"

"Spending more time on computers than was healthy."

"Wild."

"For a brief, beautiful period, I was the world champion of 'Cosmos,' back when it was at its height. And when I say brief, I mean it lasted about three minutes one night, around four a.m. Eastern Standard Time. I considered adding it to my résumé." She leaned back in her seat, more relaxed than he'd seen her all day.

"'Cosmos'? That's old school."

"It's addictive, that's what it is. Well, all games are, aren't they? That's the point. Gaming, social media, sugar… So much to get addicted to these days."

Jesus, did she have to come straight back to that? "Indeed. We're breeding a generation of addicts, all looking for a lazy buzz. Half the recruits to the Legion sign up because they think it'll be all 'Soldier of Fortune.'"

"With no consequences?"

"No consequences, no tics, no fucking tinea—and an undo button. Luckily they're the ones who don't get through selection."

"So paramedic, doctor…soldier? That's an unusual career path."

"Oh, I don't know. All fueled by adrenaline, all about reacting quickly to a bad situation before it gets worse. And I'm a medic, so…"

"Was it so bad, working at the hospital?"

"No. I liked it."

"But something went wrong."

He coasted to a stop at a red light, behind a moped. How were they talking about him again? "I got bored. Wanted to try something new."

"No."

"No?" Shite. Most people shook their heads and left it at that.

"Med school is what—five years, minimum? Plus clinical experience. That's a lot of effort to walk away from."

Like he needed the reminder.

"And you were good at it." A statement, not a question.

"Now, why would you think that? You just heard

three of my former colleagues tell me to piss off forever."

"*Awo*, but that was personal—which I also don't understand. You seem so..."

He raised his eyebrows. He'd learned to give her time to finish her sentences. She liked to process things, as if she were thinking in Amharic and translating it to English before she spoke, like when he first started speaking French, before he started thinking in French, too. But she'd probably been speaking English her whole life. Maybe she just wasn't comfortable thinking aloud. Or was too wise to.

"...so..." she said.

Patience.

"...nice."

"Really? After all that? Ouch."

She laughed. "There's nothing at all wrong with being nice. But I've seen you in action. The way you helped me through that panic attack, the way you saved that guy's life, the way you took on that goon... You're calm, you're efficient, you're..."

She pressed her gloved hands to her cheeks. He could swear her skin was turning that delicious mahogany.

"I bet you had a good rapport with your patients," she continued. "That alone..."

The moped ahead moved off, forcing him to take his gaze from her.

She cleared her throat. "A good rapport alone gives people faith, and faith is a powerful thing. And you are obviously intelligent. You were good at it, weren't you?"

He shrugged.

"You're allowed to admit it. You were a good doctor, a good paramedic and now you're a good medic. Yes?"

"I guess."

Her turn to wait for *him* to continue. She'd be disappointed. Aye, he could be good—the best—but only under the right circumstances, with the right artificial help.

"So why did you really walk away from it—the hospital?"

"Maybe I was just walking to something else."

"Maybe," she said, evidently not feeling it.

His chest felt weighted. He'd rather be flirting. Or dodging real bullets.

"I'm sorry. I didn't mean to... It's a painful topic, yes?"

He swung the steering wheel, turning onto the approach to Putney Bridge. Not too much more of this. "Yes."

"So now you're a doctor who carries a gun."

A reprieve, of sorts. "Aye, more hypocritical than Hippocratic."

"Have you shot many pe—? I'm sorry—is that a bad question to ask a soldier? It's just... I can't see you doing that."

"It's what everybody wants to know and never asks. I've been fortunate that I've not had many situations where I've had to fire, and I've only served five years. Mostly we *protect* people—against raiders, terrorists, militias... Our enemies tend to be cowards who don't attack platoons of armed, trained soldiers. Usually they just wait until we're ordered to leave, which they know will happen sooner or later, wait until those people are vulnerable again."

"That must be gutting."

"It is."

"How long will you remain there?"

"I've just re-upped for another five years."

"You don't sound happy about it."

He shrugged. Happiness was no longer something he sought. Escape and distraction were enough. When he'd lost his job and flown to Paris to enlist, five years had seemed an eternity, but it'd passed quickly. As would the next five, and the five after that, and the five after that, until real life had passed him by. What had he imagined, back when he'd walked through the gates at Fort de Nugent outside Paris? That after five years he'd slide back into normal life, without boundaries and rules and officers and his commando team? Leaving the Legion should be like leaving prison, with day release, then parole, then probation. If anything, the thought of free will made him more anxious now than when he'd enlisted—all that choice and personal responsibility. In the Legion, somebody always had his back—was paid to have his back. And he was answerable to his commanding officer not just one shift at a time but 24/7. In real life who would stop him from stepping on a land mine—real or figurative? And if anybody tried, would he heed the warning?

He slowed as they crossed the bridge and entered the thicker traffic of the high street. Samira had stilled, studying him but giving him space to think, as he had for her. Or perhaps she was just reading his mind again.

"Do you miss it?" she said, eventually. "The hospital?"

"With friends like those?"

She sighed. "Must be exhausting to always have to find a joke to suit the occasion."

"Sometimes I'm so funny I have to go and have a lie down."

She groaned, quietly. "Those people—there was respect there, too. They did what you asked, even though they seemed a little…reluctant."

Reluctant? An understatement. And it was less about respect and more about fear that he'd spill some very damning secrets, which was far more than Samira needed to know. He turned off the high street into a lane flanked by brick terraced houses. "Ah, that's my curse. People always seem to follow my lead when usually they shouldn't."

"I can see why they follow you."

"You can?"

"You seem so together, so competent."

"People quickly learn they've followed the wrong guy, often to their lasting regret. I have a knack for dragging people into trouble. Consider yourself warned."

"What kind of trouble did you drag those people into—Mariya and the others?"

"Nothing I didn't also get them out of."

"Is that why they all owed you favors—because you got them out of the trouble you dragged them into?"

Holy freaking hell. And this was why he didn't talk about his past. One sucking great black hole of trouble, especially with a perceptive woman like Samira. He shouldn't have taken her into the hospital. Those were favors he'd never intended to call upon.

Deflect. "We're nearly there." At least the conversation seemed to have settled her anxiety. He'd put up with a lot of discomfort for that. He checked his mirrors and surroundings for the thousandth time since they'd left Westminster.

"Well," she said, "this time you were the one dragged in. And I was dragged in myself. So we're blameless, yes?"

"Totally." Letting him off the hook, at last.

"Do you miss being a doctor?"

And right back on. He blew out a breath. Did he miss it? He tried never to think about the past. It only opened the door to regret—a door he'd bolted and padlocked and welded and parked an articulated lorry against.

She was so violently twisting her scarf in her gloved hands it was in danger of ripping. Best he kept talking, kept her mind off what they were doing and who was hunting them. He could take the hit to his pride.

"I miss some things," he conceded. "I liked the uneasy energy of the ambulance shift, knowing that every time a job came in you could be thrown into anything from a stroke to a chain-saw accident. I liked the way that sparked up my brain and I liked the adrenaline. I could literally feel it in my heart and my veins. That's why I gravitated to emergency medicine, before going into neurology. Every time those automatic doors open you can be thrown into a challenge with life-or-death consequences."

She shuddered. "My idea of hell. I can't even *think* on my feet, let alone operate on someone."

"Oh, I loved it. That's what I miss—the mental challenge, the speed." *Jesus, don't say "speed."* "You're cycling through ailments and procedures in your head, trying to remember the textbooks, the practicals, that one time you assisted on a procedure kind of like the one you're wrist-deep in, while the consultants are yelling at you, trying to catch you out, and the monitors are beeping, and there's this patient in front of you who could well die if you make the wrong decision." Just the thought made his stomach flip.

"You're really not selling it to me." She shuffled in her seat. "You must get adrenaline from your current job."

"Yeah, but the buzzes don't come very often. I'm a grunt who follows orders, and mostly it's exercises and uneventful patrols. It's not often you can do anything really impressive."

"Impressive," she repeated, as if she'd never heard the word and was trying it out. "Interesting choice of word."

"How so?"

"You didn't say *rewarding*, or *satisfying*. You said *impressive*. Like you're doing it to get approval."

Shite, she might claim not to think quickly but she sure thought deeply. "Maybe that's it," he said.

Approval, huh? *You're such a fuckin' show-off*, his sister had said nearly every day of their childhood. Luckily, these days he had less to show off about and nobody to show off to. Knowing cool stuff about weapons when you hung out with commandos didn't get as much attention as wearing scrubs and answering to "Doctor." Especially female attention.

"You must get to impress your colleagues, with your medical experience."

"I'm mostly just dishing out diarrhea pills and hangover remedies. And if somebody catches a bullet there's often not a lot you can do. Last year, right before I met you, I lost a teammate. All those years as a paramedic, in the hospital, in the field, and there was nothing I could do but hold on to him and tell him everything was fine while…" He rubbed a hand over his face. "How about you?" he said, quickly. "Do you miss your job?"

"Do I miss my job?" she said, rolling the thought around. "I miss living a normal, inconsequential life. I miss not being scared. I miss being free to be who I am and do what I want, though I'm not even sure who that person is anymore or what I want to do. But I'd like to find out." She pursed her lips. "Take a right here. All this will be over very soon."

Her tone kicked him in the chest. She was clinging to hope. It'd better be waiting for them.

They did a circuit of the neighborhood and parked a block away. It consisted mainly of renovated terraced houses with little rectangular gardens out back. An elderly man strode past, hands in pockets, tinny music squeaking from his earphones, and a few cars drove by but few others were about—nobody sitting in parked cars, no suspicious vans.

Charlotte's address was on the ground floor of a brick Victorian mansion that'd been carved up into flats, and none too sympathetically, with mismatched doors and window frames and cheap wall panels. They crossed a rain-slicked concrete courtyard and Jamie lifted a knocker beside an opaque glass door. The dull thud reverberated through his cold hand. Nothing. Samira retied her scarf. Through the bubbled glass, he could make out a pile of mail on the floor below the letter slot. He knocked again, tried the doorknob. Deadlocked.

"Does she live alone?" he said.

"Awo."

"Think she'd mind if we waited inside?"

"How are we supposed to—?"

He pulled a little leather case from his pocket and unzipped it.

"You're breaking us in with a manicure set?"

"Not your average manicure set." He slid out one of the lock-picking tools disguised among the scissors and tweezers and clippers. "A birthday gift from Holly. A joke present. I think."

"You know how to use it?"

"I watched a video online."

A few minutes later they stood in an impeccable living room that doubled as a kitchen and laundry, so small that a modest television filled almost an entire wall. Jamie sneaked up a wrought iron staircase to a bedroom with a closet-sized bathroom and a tiny barred window overlooking the road. In the neighboring flat a man and woman were talking. If they'd been speaking English, Jamie could have joined the conversation without raising his voice. The mansion had evidently been broken up before laws about soundproofing—and fire exits.

Back downstairs, Samira was studying an envelope on the kitchen counter, a few words written on it in blue ink.

"What's that?" he said, joining her.

"'To whom it may concern,'" she read.

"It might concern us."

"Why would you leave a note saying that in your own house, unless…?" Her voice wavered. She went to pull off a glove. He touched her hand.

"Leave them on. Just a precaution."

She nodded, tiny wrinkles webbing out from her pursed lips. The envelope wasn't sealed. She pulled out a twice-folded sheet of thick notepaper. It trembled as she read.

She looked up at him, wide-eyed.

"A suicide note."

CHAPTER SEVEN

SAMIRA FELT JAMIE'S hands grip her shoulders as she read the note aloud. "'I'm sorry, I'm in over my head and I can't bear to live like this anymore. You won't find my body—no one should have to deal with that. Charlotte Liu.' It's dated three days ago. Three days." By the time Samira had left Tuscany it was already too late.

"Do you think it's legit?"

"I don't know. Why would she have asked me to come here and not waited for me? But…the postcard was delayed. She couldn't have been sure I'd receive it. Could she have given up? Maybe there was no evidence, maybe it was just a call for help for a woman who was planning to…"

"Is it her handwriting?" Jamie's voice remained calm.

"Honestly, I can't remember ever seeing her handwriting. We texted or messaged." She pictured the postcard, with its looped *I*s and old-fashioned lowercase *S*s. "But I think it's the same writing as the postcard. Oh God, not Charlotte, too."

Jamie slid his hands to her upper arms. "It seems too much of a coincidence that she would kill herself right now. She had a raison d'être. Maybe she's just gone into hiding."

Samira looked up, blinking. A child's drawing was taped to the fridge—purple house, rolling green hills, yellow field dotted with red poppies, blue sky... As she stared, it blurred. "*Awo*, maybe that's it."

Jamie squeezed her arms and released her, then opened a drawer in the kitchen cabinet, followed by another. "Let's look around, see if we can figure anything out, see if we can find this evidence. You've been here before—does anything look out of place?"

"It's been a couple of years but it looks much the same down here." She starting flicking through notices and bills on a pinboard. Two years. Before Latif died, before her life imploded, before Jamie. She'd come to London with her parents for the funeral of a duke. While they'd paid diplomatic calls one afternoon, she'd begged off to play "Cosmos" with Charlotte. They'd giggled like they were back at university.

"I'm not seeing any handwriting," Jamie said.

"She'd do everything on a screen—shopping lists, to-do lists, diary... I'll be surprised if we even find a pen."

Jamie slid the last drawer closed. "There's some printer paper here but otherwise no stationery at all. So where's the pen she wrote the note with?"

Samira examined the top of the note. "And this— it's not printer paper. It was ripped from a pad. Where's the pad? Where's the packet of envelopes? You don't just buy one envelope—you can't. And why a note on paper, anyway, left where no one would find it for who knows how long? This is Charlotte. She'd be more likely to post on social media."

"Maybe she has. Unless she didn't want anybody to find it for a day or so."

"So she'd schedule it in advance."

"You can do that?"

"Really? Where have you been the last...?"

He raised his eyebrows.

"Oh. Don't answer that. We need to check her social med—"

A door slammed. She froze, tension trickling up her chest. Footsteps, voices. Jamie flattened against the wall beside the front window and peered out. "Just the neighbors leaving," he whispered.

Upstairs, Samira found a box with a few highlighters and pens—colored, sparkly, for birthday cards, maybe—but nothing that matched the ink on the note. No notepaper. No envelopes. No thick dossier of evidence.

The staircase clanged as Jamie climbed it. "This woman sure is a minimalist. I guess you'd have to be, to live in a shoebox."

He got down on hands and knees and peered under the bed. "Did she play baseball?"

"No. Why?"

He drew out an aluminum bat and stood, swinging it. "Shite, it's a heavy beast. She went to university with you, right? Could it be a souvenir from the States?"

"Unlikely. The only sport she follows is English football." She nodded at a yellow shirt with a black collar hanging from a hook. "She's mad for it."

He ran a hand down the bat. "No scratches, no scuffs, no dirt. Never been used. Is she a hefty kind of a lass?"

"She's tiny. Why?"

"Because it's almost as if she's gone into a sports shop and bought the heaviest thing she could find."

Thunder cracked, followed almost immediately by pelting rain.

"For protection?" Samira said. "But if she went into hiding, why not take it with her? Too big?"

He ducked into the bathroom, chewing his lip. "Her toothbrush is here. Also something you'd take if you were going into hiding—if you had enough time to pack. Can you see anything else interesting?"

Samira pointed to two monitors on a tiny desk in a corner. Behind them was a rectangle traced in dust, like a box had been removed recently. "It's not so much what's here but what's not. Where are her laptops? Last I was here, she had two—a Mac for work, a PC for gaming. And two phones—one for work, one personal. Plus her tower workstation, her iPad, her Android tablet, her Kindle… She has every device known to man, and none of them are here. Not even the Xbox. No flash drives, no hard drives, no server, no modem that I can see. And no chargers, either. That's a lot of luggage. If you were committing suicide, why take all of that? And why would you need the chargers?"

"Why, indeed?"

"Whereas if you were Hyland and you'd discovered Charlotte was harvesting information, wouldn't you want her devices?" She thudded the knuckles of one hand into her other palm. "Hang on. She had security—cameras, alarms…"

She ran downstairs, the staircase wobbling. "The alarm sensor was there." She pointed to a corner of the ceiling. "It must have been ripped down—look." Flecks of plaster and paint lay on the otherwise pristine floorboards below.

"There was no security camera on the doorstep," he said, reaching the bottom of the stairs. "I checked."

"She definitely had one."

"Well, then. I think suicide is the least likely of the possibilities, don't you?"

"I'm not sure how much of a relief that is. Going into hiding also seems unlikely. But what's the alternative—

that Hyland had her killed and this is a cover-up? I'd rather not believe that, either."

"Maybe she staged the suicide to hide from Hyland? And took her gear to keep it from him."

"If so, the notepaper and pen and envelopes would be here, wouldn't they? And the bat wouldn't." She stared unseeing at the drawing on the fridge. "What do we do—call the police, anonymously? Someone should be looking for her. How about her family? They should be told—or maybe they already know something. Perhaps we could ask them?"

"At any rate, we should probably ge—"

A clunk. Frowning, he drew his finger to his lips and crept to the window.

"We need to go," he half whispered, half mouthed.

A silhouette darkened the front door. Even through the glass she recognized the blond hair. God.

"Up," he mouthed, pointing.

She widened her eyes. What good would that do?

He gestured again, urgently.

"The window is barred," she whispered.

"I know. Go! Quick!"

Shaking her head, she ran, cringing as her boots clanged on each step. Jamie followed her into the bedroom and picked up the baseball bat. He reached underneath his jacket and pulled out a gun.

"Here," he said, pulling back the top of the weapon and releasing it with a clunk. He handed it to her.

"You don't expect me to use that?" she hissed.

He tapped along the internal wall, behind the bedhead. It made a hollow sound. "Ever used a camera?"

"Of course, but—"

"It's pretty much the same." He stepped back and

raised the bat. Thunder rumbled. "Point and shoot—but not at me. Camera shy, you know."

Downstairs, a sliding noise—a key in a lock. They had a key? What did that mean for the theories of what had become of her?

The front door squealed open. Jamie charged at an internal wall. It caved but held. Shouts, downstairs. He swung again and light appeared through a crack. A clatter. A boot on the bottom stair. She swiveled, gun shaking in her hands, as Jamie again raised the bat. With her gloves on she couldn't even be sure where the trigger was. Should she take them off? How much force would it need? If she twitched, would it go off? She'd fired plenty of guns in games but hadn't touched a real one. A smash, behind her. She jumped and the gun exploded, knocking her back, an echoing crack popping her hearing. She dropped the weapon and it skidded to a halt at the top of the staircase. Shit.

She equalized her ears. It sounded like she was underwater. The footsteps seemed to have stalled. Urgent voices, downstairs. Jamie kicked down a sheet of plywood, making a portal into the neighbor's living room. Next thing she was being shoved through, his hand on her back.

"The gun!" she whispered. She couldn't even hear herself.

"Leave it."

The staircase clanged. She ran ahead through the living room and started down a flight of stairs, her surroundings narrowing to sage wallpaper and framed photos. At least three voices behind them—two men and a woman. Multiple feet. A gunshot cracked. Samira's throat closed. At the bottom of the stairs, an opaque glass door opened into a yard of overgrown grass, enclosed by a high brick wall. God, her sense of direction was skewed—she'd expected to be back at the road.

Jamie leaped onto a rusty grill beside a crumbling part of the wall, looked over the top and held out a hand to her, his eyes narrowed against the driving rain. As he launched her over the wall she caught a glimpse of movement at the door they'd come through. The blond guy. She landed on a spiky bush. Another gunshot—or was it thunder?—and Jamie thudded onto a lawn beside her, on his feet, knees bent, still holding the bat. He pulled her up.

They were in another yard, smaller, backing onto a terraced brick house. A muffled scream. Inside, behind a glass sliding door, a woman leaped off a sofa and stared, hand over her mouth. Jamie pretty much threw Samira over the next wall into an identical yard, and then another wall, another yard, another wall, another yard, like some recurring nightmare. Footsteps and shouts seemed to close in from all directions. She tried to picture the block they'd walked around. Did the terraces go all the way to the end of the street? Were there any gaps between them?

In yard number six—or five or seven or twenty—Jamie strode to the house. "Fuck this," he muttered. Unlike the others they'd passed, this was unrenovated, with an old-fashioned door on one side, leading into a kitchen. A window revealed a living room. He pulled out his lock picker.

"What if someone's home?" she whispered, catching up.

He pointed through the window. A crucifix, on a wall above a fireplace. "I'm taking a stab they're at church."

He made quick work of the door. Once they were inside and Jamie confirmed no one was home, she allowed herself to release a full breath. A siren wailed. Oh God, police?

"The cops won't be sure what they're looking for," Jamie said, as she followed him along a hallway to the front of the house. "Like at the hospital. We just need to not look suspicious."

"That woman in the house—she got a good look at us."

Jamie strode into a living room, pressed his back against a wall next to a bay window and peered out into the street, rubbing his left shoulder like he'd injured it— which was highly likely given his spontaneous demolition job. Thunder cracked. "A police presence might help. Hyland's goons won't want the hassle of being arrested any more than we do."

She flattened against the wall beside him. "You say that like it's a parking ticket, not breaking and entering and vandalism and prowling and— Oh my God, I fired a gun." Her hands still trembled.

"Which stalled them just long enough for us to get away. It was smart."

"It was a mistake. And I lost your gun."

"It wasn't my gun. It was the goon's, from the hospital." He pulled his hand from his shoulder. It was coated in blood. His jacket sleeve was shredded.

"Jamie. You've been shot."

"Just a flesh wound. A ricochet, I think."

A siren crescendoed and cut out. Several more approached.

"Sounds like they're surrounding the block," she said.

"Aye. We'd better get out before they bring in the ARVs. If they'd had reports of shots fired, they won't muck around."

"ARVs?"

"Armed response vehicles. And they'll bring dogs."

"So we're just going to stroll to our stolen government car?"

He grinned. "That's the plan."

"With a baseball bat and a gunshot wound?"

"Maybe not with the baseball bat. Wait here a sec." He left the room and returned a few minutes later with a khaki scarf and no bat. "That kid's going to get a surprise when she next cleans out her wardrobe." He checked the street again. "How do you feel about reverting to your natural hair color?"

"What?"

He walked into the hallway beside the front door and pulled a couple of overcoats from pegs. "The woman would have seen a nondescript white guy in a cap and bomber jacket, and a brunette in a blue coat."

Jamie was far from nondescript but she took his point, pulling off her wig and cap and finger-combing her black hair. She took a red raincoat from him and buttoned it over top of her blue one. He stripped to his tank and knotted the scarf around his upper arm, using his teeth to pull it tight. Once dressed, he shrugged into a charcoal overcoat, wincing as he eased it over his shoulder.

He adjusted the coat lapels. He looked a little bulky but passable. "Now, do we look like the type of louts who would jump over walls and frighten law-abiding citizens?"

"I don't think I've ever looked like that."

"Well, don't look so terrified, then."

"I am terrified. And you have cap hair." She reached up and mussed it. His head was warm and damp, the short hair surprisingly soft.

Frowning, he pulled a twig from her hair. Their faces were so close she could feel the heat from his skin. Or was that just her skin? Either way, it was altogether too intimate. He grabbed her waist, spinning her so they were nestled side by side, looking into a hall mirror. "You see? A perfectly ordinary couple out for a stroll."

Peerrrfectly. "I look like I haven't slept for two days."

"So we're a perfectly ordinary couple on honeymoon."

A laugh escaped her throat. If only.

No. Not *if only.*

He grabbed a multicolored golf umbrella from beside the front door. "A baseball bat in exchange for two coats and an umbrella. Doesn't seem fair, but then, we are trying to save the free world." He found her waist again. "Ready, darling?"

"No."

"Try looking at me like you're in love. That's, like, the opposite of terrified."

She swallowed, her face warming. "The idea of being in love again is pretty terrifying."

The corners of his mouth flicked into a sexy uptick. "See, that's better already." He planted a quick kiss on her lips. She gasped. He blinked, like it'd taken him by surprise, too.

"Aye," he said, sounding winded. "That worked. That's what I'm going to do every time you get that guilt-ridden-slash-terrified look on your face." He scooted to the window and peeked out, then returned. "After you," he said, opening the door.

As they stepped out he unfurled the umbrella. He winced, and swapped it into his right hand.

"You're in pain," she said.

"Nothing serious. We need to prioritize getting away."

They kept a steady pace, the umbrella pulled low against the drizzle, his arm strong around her waist. Her heart pounded—because of the goons or the police or Jamie? She felt a magnetic pull to him, right under her ribs. And having him flush against her hip made her feel…grounded. Safe. How ironic was that, given the circumstances?

She counted four police officers in high-vis yellow jackets, going door to door. As they passed a brick terrace, an officer jogged down the concrete steps from its front door.

"Excuse me?" the woman said. "Ma'am? Sir?"

Jamie tightened his grip around Samira. A *let me do the talking* grip.

"Something going on?" Jamie said, in an English accent, nodding at the nearest police car. "I heard the sirens."

"We've had reports of shots fired, of intruders running through the backs of these properties."

"Gunshots? Here? You're joking? Jesus, I heard thunder but…gunshots?"

"Have you seen anything out of the ordinary?"

"Nothing at all, sorry. Hope you get to the bottom of it."

The officer rejoined her partner and they tried another door. A woman answered—the woman who'd seen them. Samira pulled the umbrella lower.

"What if she gives a description of us?" she whispered. "What if she spots us?"

"Walk faster." Sweat had popped across Jamie's brow. She reached up and wiped it with her raincoat sleeve, which just smeared it.

"Now you're the one who looks terrified," she said.

"Maybe you'd better kiss me." The joke couldn't hide his graying complexion. "I think the adrenaline ran out."

She wasn't sure how he managed to navigate them to the car—with all the parallel rows of terraced houses, she couldn't be sure which street they were in—but they made it, just as the sun broke through the clouds.

"They let themselves in with a key," Samira said, as he unlocked the doors. "What does that mean?"

He was silent a beat too long. "Shall we try her mobile phone? It's not like we're stealth anymore—they seem to know why we're here."

"I don't know her number."

"How about her work number? Maybe she's just sitting in the office and has no idea about any of this." He pulled his phone from a pocket.

"Oh, how I wish that were feasible."

"Worth a try though, right?"

"Of course. She does work shifts, so she could be there on a Sunday. But we shouldn't use that phone—we should protect your number. Does London still have phone booths?"

They drove stiltingly through a few suburbs and parked outside a strip of shops—nail salon, dry cleaner, fish-and-chips shop… Sharp chemicals failed to kill the heavy, stale stench of grease.

"Do you even know how to use one of these?" Jamie said as they approached a fat red phone box.

"I have a master's degree in management of secure information systems. I should be able to figure it out."

He pulled open the door and stopped short. "I don't think even that's going to help here."

No phone. Just shelves of dog-eared books.

"It's a…library?"

"How about the offy?" Jamie pointed at a shop win-

dow papered with posters. A handwritten sign read Internet Café.

"What did you call it?"

"The offy—off-license. A corner store—you know,
next to the chippy and across from the greasy spoon
and the bookies'."

"O-kay."

The "café" consisted of a desktop computer in a
dingy corner of the store, squeezed between a pay phone
and a milk fridge. Worth the risk. Even if they triggered
an XKeyscore selector, they'd be well away before anyone caught up.

She pushed her sunglasses onto her head and lifted
the phone. "Now, how does this thing work?"

"Well," he said. "That's the handset. And those buttons, they're the numbers. You dial the number you
want, and—"

"I meant, what kind of calling card do we need?"

He dug into his pocket. "This kind," he said, pulling out some change.

"Seriously?"

"They're called coins. Like arcade tokens but you
can use them to buy all sorts of stuff."

Samira rolled her eyes as she plucked the money
from his palm.

"I know, right?" he said. "Whatever will they think
of next?"

Charlotte's office line went to voice mail, killing
the illogical hope that'd crept into Samira's chest.
While Jamie wandered about the shop picking up supplies, Samira set up a new email address for "Janis"
and emailed a cryptically banal message to Charlotte's
work and personal addresses. No out-of-office message
bounced back.

"I wonder if I can risk logging in to Facebook," Samira said, as Jamie perched on the desk beside her, chewing on a stick of salami.

"What are you worried about?"

"Our location being tracked."

"How precisely can they track it? And how quickly? Safe to say Hyland and his goons know you're in the general vicinity."

"Good point. I'll be quick, anyway."

She felt a pang of loneliness as she logged in. *Sorry, Facebook, I need a trial separation*, she'd written in her last post, nearly two years ago, so her friends wouldn't call the authorities when she stopped obsessively posting and commenting. *It's not you—it's me. I still love you. I just need some time away to reassess our relationship, and find myself.*

Charlotte's page had been updated three days earlier—a selfie of her holding the artwork now stuck to her fridge, her blond hair tied back. "Look what my friend's little boy drew for me! Sooo cute!" The same message was copied to her other social-media sites. Before that, she'd posted several times a day without fail, mostly about gaming. Never anything to do with her work, of course.

Samira rapped her fingernails on the desk. "No suicide note. No tributes from friends. But if she's disappeared from the internet, she's disappeared from the world. This *is* her world. I could risk a call to her father, pretend to be an old friend from university just arrived in London, trying to track her down. Which is pretty much what I am. As far as I know, he still lives in the town Charles Dickens came from. What's it called?"

"Ask me any question at all about mucus and vomit. Literature, not so much."

She did a web search. A jumbo jet roared overhead—

the fourth since she'd sat down—they had to be near Heathrow. "Rochester, that's right." Another search revealed his phone number. "I don't get why people put their details in the phone book. Anyone can find you."

"That's kind of the point. This might surprise you but to regular people the world's a benign place where people don't hide in the shadows ready to ambush you."

"How quaint. That's my ambition in life—to be an ordinary person living an ordinary life again."

"Nothing about you is ordinary, Samira."

"I used to be incredibly ordinary, before this."

A pause. "I very much doubt that." He spoke in that dead serious tone that never failed to make her breath catch.

"Oh, believe it," she said, moving to the phone, cursing her warming cheeks. "I'm still that ordinary person. It's the circumstances that got weird."

Charlotte's father hadn't heard from her in a week but didn't sound worried. Charlotte wouldn't be impressed to discover how readily he gave her cell phone number to a stranger. When Samira tried it, it rang out.

"So what now?" she said, plunking into the passenger seat of the car. "This was supposed to be all over once I made it to Charlotte's." She'd imagined herself and Tess leaving Putney in separate directions, Tess to save the day and Samira to hide until it was all over. She was only supposed to be the middleman—middle *woman*. "I guess we should ditch the car."

"I doubt it'll be discovered missing until the therapists arrive at work tomorrow. And then they'll have to check security footage, talk to the guards…"

"Oh my God, the cops will begin to put it together—the shutdown at the hospital, the train station… They'll put out an alert on the car, Hyland's people will see it, they'll trace us—"

"Samira!"

She flinched and stared at him. He was as pale as the moon.

"You're in pain," she said. "Your arm…"

"Sorry, I didn't mean to shout." He swore under his breath. "It'll take them a while to stitch things together—if they ever do. In the meantime, we should at least get out of London, out of CCTV Central."

"We have to figure out what happened to Charlotte."

"And find a Boots."

"You want to buy shoes?"

"A chemist. Pharmacy. Drugstore."

"Oh." Her gaze fell onto his arm, not that anything beneath the stolen coat was visible. "Shouldn't we go to a doctor? A hospital?"

"For a bullet wound? Not if we want to avoid attention—they'd have to call the police. Anyway, it's not that bad—a ricochet or shrapnel or something."

"If it wasn't that bad you wouldn't be looking like you'd rolled in chalk. Should I drive?"

"That's okay. I can… Shit, Samira, get down."

Before she could react, his hand was on the back of her neck, pushing her face to her knees. He ducked, too. Her pulse rocketed.

"Oh my God, what?" she said.

"The Peugeot, coming our way."

"Are you sure? How the hell did they find us?"

"I swear they didn't follow us here." After a few minutes he eased back up, checking the road and the mirrors. "They've gone past."

"Could they have tracked us through traffic cameras?"

"Then why didn't they recognize the car just now,

and stop?" He slapped the steering wheel. "Could it have been the phone call to Charlotte's mobile? It rang out. The number would have come up. And if they have Charlotte's phone, they could have—?"

"I used a prefix that disables caller ID—and they'd be searching the store by now. Has to be something else."

He started the engine. "I'm not sticking around to find out."

They drove west, avoiding the main arterials, until the indistinguishable suburbs became towns separated by fields. To give herself something to focus on, Samira repacked the spilled contents of the backpack. Charlotte's postcard had been crushed in the bottom of the bag.

"This is definitely the same handwriting as the note," she said, pulling it out. "But I can't be sure either was written by Charlotte."

She smoothed her hand over a dog-eared corner. Her finger struck something sharp. She frowned, examining it. Her cheeks went cold. A wire, sticking out of the corner.

"Shit!" She yanked off her gloves and tore into the card with shaking fingers.

"What is it?"

The postcard had a false front stuck to it. She ripped it off. Underneath was an identical Parisian scene. The two postcards had been glued together. Between the layers was a microchip connected to a wafer-thin battery and an antenna running the width of the postcard.

"A tracking device. Oh my God, they'll be tracking us right now."

"How pinpoint could it be?"

"Only to a few blocks but this is next-level stuff."

The postcard trembled in her hand. "This is how they found me in Italy. How they knew I was traveling across France, heading for the Gare du Nord, how they knew we were at that internet café, and at Charlotte's. Maybe the postcard was just an attempt to track me down. Have they been waiting for a chance to pounce, this whole time? Oh my God, maybe there's no evidence at all. Maybe they forced her to write it. Or could they have intercepted it after she posted it, in which case there *is* evidence? Were they watching her? Shit—maybe she's working for them. Or maybe they were watching my parents, and that's when they intercepted it?"

"Whoa, whoa. I can't answer any of it but I know that we need to—"

"Get rid of it." She lowered the window, nodding, her finger so shaky it slipped off the button.

"Wait."

"Wait?"

"Don't toss it. I have a better idea." He U-turned the car, backtracked a few blocks and pulled into a fifteen-minute car park outside an orange-brick train station.

"We're taking a train?" she said.

"Give me the device. I'll be back in a few minutes. Stay down."

He left, with the postcard. Halfway across the parking lot he swiveled, jogged back, opened her door and threw the car key on her lap. "Just in case."

"In case of what?"

"Parking wardens." He winked and left.

She let her head fall back. This was not her life. She'd dropped through a wormhole into someone else's world, someone else's skin. An alternative reality game. *No consequences, no tics, no tinea, and an undo button.* Jamie dissolved into the gloom inside an arched entranceway. *Back in a few minutes.* As in three minutes, or ten? What was he doing?

A white car caught her eye, cruising past like a shark—the Peugeot, pulling up into the station's drop-off zone. Samira slunk in her seat, trying to shrink. If only. The blond guy got out, along with the woman, both of them adjusting something under the waist of their jackets. They headed for the station entrance, the woman swiping at a phone.

Oh God. Samira had no way to warn Jamie.

CHAPTER EIGHT

IF SAMIRA BLASTED the horn she'd draw attention to herself. What would she do in a computer game if this happened? Use a stun gun? A concealment spell?

An alarm sounded—train doors, about to close. Would they drag Jamie out? Did he have his gun? Would there be a shoot-out? Had he got away, in the train? Was she on her own now? She really didn't want to be on her own. Crap, she sucked at reality. Too many possibilities, too many options, unknowns, consequences. She was always so kick-ass behind a screen. The train whined. Moving off.

She stared at the clock on the dash. Two minutes passed. Three. Four. Her stomach churned. Should she creep out and try to warn Jamie? Or would she mess up his plan if she showed up? What *was* his plan? Was it already too late to do anything? At what point should she drive away? Oh God, oh God, oh God.

Breathe.

Nearby, a car door opened, then another. A man's voice, urgent but indecipherable. A woman replied. An engine started, and moved off. Another couple of minutes and she'd dare to look.

The driver's door swung open, rocking the car. She gasped. Jamie landed in the seat.

"Oh thank God."

"Key?" he said, holding out his hand, looking down at her with a half grin. "You okay down there?"

She sat up, gingerly. No sign of the Peugeot. "The blond guy and his driver...did you see them?"

"Aye. As far as they know, we're en route to Portsmouth. I planted the device on the train."

She reached for the seat belt. "That's a long trip. It has to buy us an hour or two."

"Try nine minutes."

"Nine?"

"That's how long it'll take them to get to the next station, search the train and realize we're not there."

"Oh God, you're right. Here's me thinking—"

"I was hoping to find an express train but of course it's a Sunday, off-peak, so nothing's in a hurry." He put the car into Reverse, and winced, his jaw tight.

"Your arm is getting bad, isn't it?"

"We can't stop now. Let's get to the next town—in the other direction—and find that Boots."

The rain had slicked a gloss onto everything—the road, cars, fields. Blue sky spread up from the horizon like an opening portal, rays of sun lighting the grassy hills below. Samira shuddered. All that time she thought she was escaping Hyland and he'd known exactly where she was and where she was headed. They had to have come close to capturing her in Paris. Just as well she hadn't slept soundly in her car—she'd moved it every hour or two, trying to find a place that felt safer. Sometimes insomnia and paranoia came in useful.

"So," Jamie said, "whatever has happened to Charlotte, we can assume Hyland's mob have at least some of her electronic equipment. Either they stole it after she left or when they took her."

"Yes. But whatever data she has, she'll have stored it

carefully. If they're trying to discover what dirt she has on Hyland, they won't find it without her…cooperation."

"Are you worried they'll find information about you?"

"We haven't been in touch for nearly two years, and I don't think there's much they don't already know. But the problem with my friendship with Charlotte is that so much of it could be traceable to anyone with the right access—and you wouldn't need her equipment. It's all text messages and emails and social media and direct messaging and gaming. Our enemies could know everything up until the point I went into hiding and went offline. And if that were the case, they'd also know I don't have a lot of other friends—real friends. So if they were going to choose someone to send that postcard to lure me out…" She twisted the ends of her scarf. "This is doing my head in."

"Let's cycle through the possibilities. We can assume she was alive three days ago, going by the selfie. We don't think it's a suicide but we do think she wrote the note, so either she ran or they captured her."

"Or she's working with them or they've killed her. And it's possible she didn't write the note *or* the postcard."

"What does your gut tell you?" he said, checking his driver's mirrors.

She looked behind them. Nothing but a truck they'd passed a few minutes ago. "I am a little hungry but I can wait."

"I mean, what does your instinct tell you, about what's happened to Charlotte?"

"Oh, you meant it metaphorically. Sorry, my brain's not really… I don't do the whole 'instinct' thing—unless you count paranoia. I'm more interested in facts and logic. Instinct leads to silly decisions."

"I disagree. I think instinct is our sixth sense. De-cisions made by instinct, adrenaline—they're usually pretty sound."

"Not for me, believe me. I can't put together a co-herent sentence unless I've had five minutes alone in a room to compose it."

"Don't sell yourself short. That right there was a lovely sentence."

"Only because you're…easy to talk to." *When you're not promising to kiss me.* "Anyway, my instinct would always have me running and hiding, which is usu-ally not the best way to deal with a problem." Except now. Now would be a great time to run and hide—if it weren't for Charlotte and Tess. "I admire people who can think on their feet, react quickly. Maybe that's why you have an instinct for these things and I don't."

"Your instinct got you out of that place in Italy, didn't it?"

"Not at all. That was planning and forethought. They tripped an alarm system I'd set up. If I'd left it to instinct, I'd be in the cell next to Tess right now—or worse."

He checked his mirrors again, which made her com-pulsively check behind, her nape prickling.

"But your instinct had you install those alarms," he said.

"No. That was logic and fear and thinking it through and too much time on my hands."

"Maybe you silence your instinct, you over-rationalize it. Our brains know a lot more than they let on to us. They pick up on nuances our conscious thoughts miss. We fool ourselves that sophisticated thought is superior—we're raised to believe the word of people wearing white coats over our own experience in our bodies. You know what I always found as a doctor? Occasionally a diagnosis would come out of the blue but ninety percent of people who claimed to be shocked could pinpoint when their symptoms began. They'd noticed something but they hadn't wanted it to be true, or they didn't want to make a fuss or appear silly, so they ignored their instinct. I'm always telling people to give themselves more credit." He made a ticking noise. "I mean, I used to tell people…"

She stared at his profile. Was that…regret? His five o'clock shadow—or whatever o'clock it was—was flecked with blond and white, and his brown hair was blonder near the temples. If he grew it, would he get a tousled, sun-kissed look? She could see him on a Mediterranean beach, blue water reflected in blue eyes. Holding a surfboard. Wet. A wetsuit stripped to the waist, just that tiny bit too low on his hips—

"You want to go and sit in a quiet room for five minutes and think about that, don't you?"

She snapped her gaze to the front. He was making intelligent conversation about psychology and she was imagining him half-naked on a beach. She shut her eyes tight and forced a hurried mental rewind. Instinct. He was talking about instinct.

"It's just…" she said. "I don't think my instinct will help us figure out what's become of Charlotte."

"Okay, so let's try something. Without thinking about it, answer this question straightaway. Is Charlotte alive?"

"How can the speed at which I answer produce a more accurate result?"

"Humor me. Is Charlotte alive?"

She chewed the inside of her cheek.

"No, don't think. Don't weigh up the pros and cons. Just answer—is Charlotte alive?"

"This is stup—"

"Don't think. Answer." Those eyes drilled into hers

like an interrogation lamp but his voice remained even. "There's an answer in your head, isn't there? It popped up straightaway, but now you're testing it, second-guessing it. Just tell me—what was that initial response?"

"That she's alive. But that's just…wishful thinking. There's no way my brain could have picked up on anything that would enable me to answer that question accurately."

"Maybe, maybe not."

"What medical school did you even go to?"

"One that taught me that science knows next to nothing about the human brain. Humor me, Samira. You know this woman well, right?"

"I used to."

"People don't ch…" He let out a harsh breath.

"Change?"

"Aye," he said, forcefully. "Assume she's still that woman. Quick-fire answers. Here we go… Is Charlotte working for Hyland?"

"Ah…"

"No thinking, Samira. What answer popped into your head?"

"That she's not working for Hyland but—"

"No buts, not yet. Plenty of time for buts later."

God, don't mention butts.

"Let your subconscious answer the questions," he continued. "The postcard—was it her handwriting?"

"Yes."

"Did she write the suicide note?" He checked his mirrors.

She snapped her head around, her pulse speeding up. Nothing. "Dear God, would you stop doing that!"

He looked at her, jaw dropped. "What am I doing?"

"Checking your mirrors all the time!"

"Was I? Just something I do when I drive, I guess. You want me to stop changing gear, too?"

She pressed a palm over her eyes. "I'm sorry. I just—"

"You're worried. That's okay. Your instinct is pricking, like a cat with raised hackles."

"It's not *that*. It's just…" She slapped her hand on her thigh.

"Who wrote the note, Samira?" he said, gently.

"Charlotte wrote it." She almost shouted. It felt like a pressure valve in her chest was blocked and about to explode. "And the postcard."

"What's she doing now?"

She threw up her hands. "How would I know?"

"You just pictured her, right? When I asked that, you pictured her. What was she doing in that picture?"

Samira thumbed the soft cotton of her scarf. "Alone in a room. Scared."

"What else is in this room?"

"Nothing. It's just a…bedroom."

"Any computer there?"

"No. She's hugging her knees. She has dark circles under her eyes, like her makeup's smudged."

"Interesting."

"It's really not. I'm not psychic, Jamie. I'm just a worrier, a pessimist. I've watched too much TV. This is stupid."

"If you were a pessimist, you'd be convinced she was dead. I'm not saying you're a psychic. I don't believe in that stuff but I believe we all could pay more attention to our brains." He slowed for a roundabout. They'd reached the industrial outskirts of a town. The rain had started up again, flat splatters on the windscreen. "Let's unpack all that. Why do you believe—not think, *believe*—that she hasn't committed suicide?"

"The information she had—like you said, she had something to live for. When she gets passionate about something, she doesn't let up. It doesn't fit. She wouldn't just give up like that."

"And why do you believe she's *not* working for Hyland?"

"Because I know her. But that's just naive, yes?"

"Not at all. It's rare that somebody we know and trust that deeply will…betray us. When people do betray us, we usually find that the warning signs have been there all along and we've simply ignored them because we haven't wanted to believe it." Again his tone seemed weighted with something. Sorrow? Regret? "You get that niggling feeling. Just like the patient getting the 'shock' diagnosis."

She stared at the wipers. Left, right, left, right, left, right… "And it's also because all her electronic equipment had gone—everything. If she was working for them, if they trusted her, why would they need to take her Xbox, her security cameras, her modem…?"

"Good—that's dead right."

Left, right, left, right. "Which also means she must have some evidence they're trying to pinpoint. The postcard couldn't have been just Hyland's trick to lure me out."

"And her handwriting?"

"I must have seen it somewhere, sometime—in a birthday card maybe. It just seems right. And, of course, the avatars she mentioned in her postcard—only the three of us would know those." She grimaced. "The two of us."

"The room you saw her in, where did that come from?"

"I have no idea."

"Let's break it down. The lack of computers…?"

"Hyland's men had been in her flat. She hasn't been on social media. If she'd given up on me coming to get the evidence, she would have found another way to release it. She wouldn't rest."

"And yet, in your mind picture, she was doing nothing."

"Oh my God, so she *has* been captured?" Samira stared at Jamie, then recoiled. "I can't believe I'm starting to believe this."

"So far it's totally believable, whether you're thinking logically or instinctively. Your instinct just got there a lot quicker and had to wait for logic to catch up."

She opened her mouth to argue but the words wouldn't come.

"Next question. Is there a niggle in your brain—is your brain trying to tell you something more? Do you have a feeling you're missing something?"

He turned onto a shopping street. What did they call it here—the high street? "Plenty of things. But I don't know what I don't know, do I?"

"Don't force it. Let it come when it's ready. Be open to it but don't go searching for it."

"You're sounding like a TV medium."

He laughed, deep and sexy. Which did things to her. Dear God, if she let instinct have its way…

He pulled into an angle park near a Boots. She'd swear she could smell the blood from his wound, sharp and iron-like.

"Won't be a sec," he said.

Even in the few minutes he was gone, anxiety constricted her chest. It hadn't taken her long to get used to having company. Turned out even she had a limit for being alone—and she'd always been fine by herself.

Preferred it, most of the time. The only child of diplomats didn't get much choice. In her first fifteen years she'd lived in six countries. Tough on a kid who took a long time to make friends. By the time she'd reached boarding school in Rome, then college in LA and university in Rhode Island, she'd thirsted for time alone like Charlotte had craved parties. If anyone should have been able to survive a year as a hermit...

But before the last year she'd always had a computer and, inside it, her constructed world—the virtual friends who felt closer than the people around her, the communities as tangible as concrete-and-timber villages. Even hiding behind an avatar she'd had a more defined identity online than off.

Without even her virtual world, enforced solitude had turned into less sanctuary and more punishment. Going to bed alone each night knowing you'd wake up alone, with no one to talk to tomorrow, or the next day, or the day after, virtually or in person... With nothing and no one to interrupt your thoughts they meandered to crazy places, like the swells of the Southern Ocean endlessly circling the globe without landmasses to temper them. And the currents and tides had inevitably led back to Jamie, to that night, to the week leading up to it, to harmless fantasies about where they might meet again.

Which no longer seemed harmless.

Jamie returned with a paper shopping bag, a newspaper and a polar blast. "There was a car park back there, overlooking a wood," he said, heaving the door shut. "On a day like today I don't think many people will be out hiking. We can park up while I sort this out."

The "wood" turned out to be a stand of amber and gold trees in the seam of a valley, flanked by green fields. Or were they "meadows" here? In the distance a squat stone farmhouse sat on a plateau, coated with a green creeper as if trying to camouflage itself. Tiny cattle dotted the hills behind. Like in Tuscany, her brain could appreciate the beauty but not her heart.

A thought pulled at her, again. What? *Is your brain trying to tell you something?* Her poor brain was being tugged in all directions. Her brain, her heart, her instinct, other parts...

No, *those* parts were all being pulled in one direction.

She turned to the back seat, where Jamie was spreading a medical arsenal onto the red raincoat—sealed packets of scissors, tweezers, wipes, pills, syringes, vials...

"You got all that from the drugstore?"

"I bought some supplies through Andy as well, via an old...contact. This is not all over-the-counter stuff."

"Is that legal?"

"Asks the woman with the stolen car and fake passport."

"*I* didn't steal the car."

"I don't think you can claim I kidnapped you, if that's your plan."

"Technically you did kidnap me. There were witnesses."

He laughed and went to pull off his torn sweater, having discarded his other layers. "Shite," he said, the sweater muffling his voice. "Can you come over into the back seat with me and help get this over my head?"

Come over into the back seat with me. Under different circumstances that would be very appealing.

After awkward maneuvers the sweater came free. The scarf ripped clear of the wound with a sucking tear, and blood bubbled up in its wake. He pressed the fabric back onto it, screwing up his face.

"It'll feel better once it's cleaned out," he growled. Was he trying to convince her, or himself? After a few deep inhalations, he pulled away the scarf, revealing a pulpy, bloody gash in the dip where his shoulder muscles met his arm muscles.

"Yikes," she said.

"It's nothing."

His tattoo was hazed with blood. Four words in a vintage cursive font. She remembered tracing the swirling letters, his skin goose pimpling under her finger. His skin had felt taut, a little dry. She'd kissed it...

"I think you might lose a few letters from your tattoo," she said.

"That'd be appropriate."

"*'Je ne regrette rien,'*" she read, haltingly. "'No regrets,' yes?"

He gave a rueful grin. "'I have no regrets.'"

"Lucky you."

"Wishful thinking. I should have gone with *'Karma est une salope.'*"

"Meaning?"

"'Karma's a bitch.'"

She laughed, which just seemed to set off the nerves in her stomach. What was she nervous about—their predicament, his wound or being in the back seat with a shirtless Jamie?

"Samira... I hope you don't have regrets about that day we...?" He spoke in a rush, as if he'd been holding the words back awhile.

Her stomach hollowed but she at least owed him the respect of an explanation. "Maybe I wasn't ready, mentally. At the time I thought I was, but afterward... It was...overwhelming, in a way I hadn't expected."

Was she ready now? How would she know? Not that he was asking.

"I hope…" he said, his eyes narrowing. "I hope you didn't feel pressured, by me. You were grieving. I shouldn't have started it, that day by the river."

Started it. By taking her hand, drawing her to him, cupping her cheeks…

"Oh, it started for me well before that," she said.

He smiled. A genuinely unguarded moment that made her want to melt into the seat. She knew exactly the moment it started—when she'd first seen him hiding out in the alleyway outside her grandmother's guesthouse. She didn't believe in love at first sight, but…

Love. Why had *that* word come to mind? It wasn't that, not then. Not now. It was…*intrigue* at first sight, a curiosity that kept growing. Was still growing. She'd grabbed his elbow, pulled him inside, hid him and Flynn as their enemy searched. *That* Jamie had been the dead serious one. The soldier. The protector. Within thirty minutes she'd met the joker, the medic, the loyal friend…

She was still meeting new Jamies. Which one had she first fallen for, and when?

She swallowed. "I'm a grown woman, Jamie. I was just as eager as…"

"You certainly were."

Her nerves bubbled into an abrupt laugh. "Well… it's history, so…"

"Aye," he said, with a swift nod. "History."

He grabbed the packet of alcohol wipes. She folded her legs underneath her, on the seat beside him. It was a relief to have at least broached the subject, but it felt less a resolution than a cease-fire. Like in France, he'd taken the out a little too easily, a little too quickly.

So maybe he hadn't been ready, either, for reasons that prowled the darker alcoves of his mind—and his past, as she was learning. Still wasn't ready.

While he concentrated on cleaning the wound, she let her gaze stray. What was that American term— "eye candy"? He was definitely eye candy. All muscle, no fat—but not puffed up like a bodybuilder. The shapely shoulders of a sprinter or swimmer, his smooth light skin interrupted by scars and freckles and hair and tan lines. She remembered running a finger from the side of his neck down to his knuckles—coarse on his throat where it bordered his stubble, smooth through the collarbone and in the dip below, a little rougher over the peeling skin of his shoulder, gliding down the swell of his bicep to the hair of his veined forearms. She'd bumped over the watch at his wrist and he'd captured her hand in his, warm and rough and dry and reassuring.

And that reassuring hand had just unwrapped a syringe.

"Jamie, you're not expecting me to inject you…?"

"I can manage it. A little local, because I'm a wimp."

He was a wimp? She turned back to the *other* scenery, trying to zone out the rustling noises. The windows were steaming up.

"Safe to look," he said, after a few minutes. "But I am going to need your help. Ever done any sewing?"

"What?" She swiveled. "I couldn't!"

"I can't stitch myself up."

"No, honestly, you don't want me anywhere near you with a needle."

"You'll be surprised what you can do. Easy as sewing on a button."

"Do that often, do you?"

"Buttons, hems, patches... My tailoring skills are in big demand in my team. You'd be surprised what price you can name for clothing repairs in the middle of the desert."

"Stop trying to make this sound everyday."

"I'm joking about the sewing," he said, chuckling, opening another packet. The tweezers. "I'll use suture strips. Stitches can wait."

"You bastard."

"You'll have to help me with those but it shouldn't be too bad—just like applying sticky tape. Once you've had a close look at a wound it's never as daunting as you first thought. And I'll also need your help to make sure I get everything out. Whatever's in there, my body's not happy about it. Every time I knock it, it does more damage." He nodded at a tube of hand sanitizer. "Use that, first."

They settled into silence as they worked. Like he'd said, it was easier once she was familiar with the wound, but her stomach refused to settle. Lucky she'd hardly eaten in the past twenty-four hours.

"God, this is really not my thing," she said, as she tugged out a particularly stubborn piece of metal, unleashing a rivulet of blood that he caught with balled-up gauze.

"It's not many people's thing. We're nearly done."

She rubbed the window with her elbow, smearing the green fields.

Wait—green fields, rolling hills...

"Shit," she said. The thought that'd been tugging at her brain... "Shit!"

"What?" He ducked to peer through the smudge in the condensation. "What's out there?"

"Nothing. It's what was on the fridge at Charlotte's, what was on her social media."

He frowned. "That kid's picture?"

"The date of that post—it was the same as the suicide note, yes?"

A vehicle engine approached. A blue strobe flashed, and a car pulled up alongside in a haze of white and blue and yellow.

"Oh God," Samira said. "The police."

CHAPTER NINE

SAMIRA THREW JAMIE'S coat over the medical supplies between them—the *stolen* coat, over the *illegal* supplies. Exhibits A and B. Or were they up to M and N by now?

"Maybe the car's been reported," she whispered.

A car door opened. A radio sounded and cut out.

"Let's hope it's too soon for that," Jamie said, shoving a syringe under the coat.

"What do we do now? This is not going to look good. They're going to ask questions. I wasn't brought up to lie to police."

He bit his lower lip. "We do what they expect two people to be doing in the back seat of a car with the windows steamed up." He reached over, grabbed her waist and effortlessly hoisted her over the charcoal coat and astride his lap, running his fingers up her outer thighs to hitch her dress.

"Oh my God."

He hurriedly unbuttoned her blue coat and slipped it off her shoulders. "You've got that terrified look again, Samira."

"I am terrified—not of you, of being caught."

"Well, for God's sake, play along."

He grabbed her bottom with both hands and slid her up his thighs until her knees hit the back of the seat, the apex of her stockings jammed into his jeans. Oh God, oh God. He threaded a hand through her hair.

"Now you're just looking grossed-out," he said.

"No! Not at all." He was usually good at reading her but *that* he'd got all wrong. "Just...surprised."

"This is nothing personal. Cover the wound with your hand." A shadow fell across the door. "Quick."

As she lowered her palm onto the gash he surged forward and planted his lips on hers. Her stomach flipped. He relaxed back on the seat, coaxing her with him. Like she needed coaxing. Oh God, his lips pulling gently at hers, his hands gripping her waist, the front of his jeans pressing into her... A groan escaped her throat. Nothing personal? Her mind and her body needed to resync.

A knock, on the window. She gasped, even though she'd expected it.

Jamie released her lips. He inhaled, blinking, and opened the door. Cold air blasted in. A gray-haired officer stood in the drizzle, wearing a heavy blue jacket. Her heart jackhammered.

"Jesus, aren't you two a bit old for that carry-on?" the cop said. "Usually it's teenagers I'm sending home from here." His gaze rested on her hand. Shit. Around it, Jamie's skin was noticeably red.

"None of my business at all but I do hope this man is at least your *husband*, ma'am," he said, his gaze drifting to her other hand, and nodding at her engagement ring. "If not, I'd suggest you find a venue that's not so public."

She exhaled. He was looking at her rings, not the wound.

"There's a woman lives over there..." He nodded toward a strip of houses across the road. "Who rings us every single bloody time someone parks up here, thinking someone's being raped. You're not being raped, are you, ma'am?"

"No, sir," Samira said, mimicking Jamie's Scottish

accent for some reason. "Not at all." She could still feel the look of terror on her face. She planted her free hand on Jamie's chest, to back up her story. How come he was always so warm? "Sorry. We were just…having some…time out from the kids."

"Believe me, I get that. But in future just…don't. You may not have better things to do with your time but I do." He scanned the interior of the car. "And in your work car. Ugh." He shook his head and pushed the door shut. Dismissed.

Jamie stared at her, looking as bemused as she felt. As the patrol car pulled out, he laughed, his chest shuddering. She pulled her hands off him.

"Shite, that was a good accent, Samira. You sounded terrifyingly like my aunt Morag." He stared straight ahead, into her cleavage. "Which is a little disconcerting, considering…"

She awkwardly shuffled back and climbed off his lap, his hands still on her waist, guiding her. The throb between her legs was so fierce she wouldn't be surprised to hear drumming.

"We're like Bonnie and Clyde," Jamie said as she climbed over the coat and plunked on the seat beyond.

"Bonnie and Clyde were gunned down by police."

"Killjoy."

"And I am about the least Bonnie-like woman you'll ever meet." She straightened. "How did he know it was a work car? There's no signage."

"I guess he ran the plates before he approached us."

"Oh no."

"It's a good sign—means the car hasn't been reported stolen yet or he wouldn't have just warned us about…" His words dissolved into a chuckle. She joined in but her laugh sounded as fake as her attraction was real. He cleared his throat, his gaze dropping down her body, then quickly back up. His pupils had swelled, making his eyes look darker. Wasn't that a sign of—?

Shit, her dress was hiked way up over her waist, her lacy underwear visible through her stockings.

"Like I told you," he said, lifting the overcoat off his supplies, "it'll take them a while to figure it out. We should get out of Dodge, though. At some point even the sluggish neurons of bureaucracy might connect."

She tugged her dress back into place. Holy cow, that kiss, that connection. And that time it hadn't even been for real.

"Are you okay?" Jamie said. "You look shaky."

"Eshi," she said, dismissively. "I'm just a little…um."

"Samira, if he'd known the car was stolen he'd have arrested us by now."

"Oh. Yes. Good."

If Jamie kissed like that when they were "history"…
Not going there.

He looked at his wound. "I'll have to sterilize this again." And suddenly he was back at Serious Jamie, like *that* didn't just happen. "You were saying something about the picture, before we got interrupted…?"

"Yes!" The picture. God. "In Charlotte's flat, I didn't find a black pen but I found colored pens—red, green, sparkly purple. And highlighters, in yellow, orange and blue. The same as in the picture."

"Maybe the kid who drew it came to her house, used her stationery." He tossed her the sanitizer. "In a minute I'm going to need help with these strips."

"It's not just that," she said, cleaning her hands while he opened another sealed packet—white suture strips on a paper backing, like small plasters. "The picture—it's not a random kid's drawing. It shows a scene from one of the worlds in 'Cosmos'—that's the game we were obsessed by, the game the three of us used to play."

"The game you aced at four in the morning."

"Last time I saw Charlotte, we played it. This world has rolling green hills and a blue sky and a yellow field with red flowers. Those fields and hills…" She gestured out the window. The smear where she'd wiped had faded into the film of water. "Well, not that you can see them now but they lit something in my brain. Only I didn't…"

"You didn't trust your instincts."

"Just now it all clicked."

"You think Charlotte drew the picture? A message for you?"

"Maybe. We didn't have a house in our game as it does in the picture but it's the kind of game where you can build things, like an early 'Minecraft.'"

"Ah, interesting. Hate to interrupt your very promising train of thought but I need your conscious and subconscious minds to work together for a bit. If I hold the wound closed, can you press the strips on? Start in the middle."

Applying the strips was quick and easy, even with her mind on the picture. Especially with her mind on the picture. As he dressed the wound, occasionally borrowing her hand to hold things in place, she downloaded "Cosmos" onto his phone, logged on and loaded the game she and Charlotte had last played on that giggly day before their lives imploded.

"Oh my God," she whispered, staring down at the screen.

"What's up?"

"This is weird. Last time I saw Charlotte, two years ago, we played this game. The three of us hadn't logged in for years, and I haven't logged in since. But now there are four players." She brought up the game history. "What the hell…? Latif played the day before he died. We were in hiding. We were supposed to be totally off-line while Tess fact-checked the documents he'd stolen. And he was playing 'Cosmos' with Charlotte—without telling me? Why take such a risk for a stupid game? And he added this fourth person—*Erebus*—a few months before that." She scrolled down. Jamie gathered the trash into a plastic bag and scooted along the back seat to watch over her shoulder. "The three of them have been playing it ever since. Charlotte was last on it three days ago and this person was on it…overnight." She stared at Jamie, her mouth dropping open.

"So…they've been playing a game. How is this significant?"

"They haven't been spending enough time on it to properly play—a minute or two here and there, look. It's not a quick round of 'Pac-Man.' It's the kind of game you only play if you have half an hour to spare, at least. *This* is how Latif was communicating—with Charlotte, and with this other person. I suspected he was still in touch with someone while we were in hiding but he denied it. I thought I was being paranoid."

"Your instinct was right."

"Why didn't he tell me? Why didn't he include me?"

Jamie retrieved his sweater from the footwell and pulled it on. "Perhaps he was protecting you. He didn't want you to freak out."

"Better freaking out about that than freaking out one night when you wake to find him gone, and freaking out again when you hear about civilian casualties in a drone attack and freaking out when his name is confirmed and…and…freaking out again when you see this." She jabbed a hand at the screen, her eyes stinging. "Despite what you might believe of me—what he believed—I don't need protecting from the truth."

"That's not what I meant. I—"

"The truth I can deal with. It's lies and deception I have a problem with—and people shooting at me. *That* you can protect me from, anytime you wish. But…" She exhaled shakily. Jamie put an arm around her shoulders and pulled her in. "Damn him. What was he up to?"

"This Erebus person…could it be Tess?"

"She would have mentioned it—and Erebus has been on the game since her arrest. And Tess was the one who'd warned us to stay offline. She was as surprised as me that Latif left our hiding place."

"Who else might he have been in contact with?"

"Oh my God. Tess said…" She tapped the phone with a fingernail. "That's *it*."

"What is?"

"Tess found out that just before Latif's death he'd been in contact with someone at Denniston Corp—the military contractor he used to work for, the one Hyland used to own, the one that went bust after Tess's story on its terrorism connections last year."

"Yes. The one Hyland's being investigated over— *was* being investigated over."

"Latif used to work there until he turned whistle-blower for Tess. She couldn't figure out who he was in contact with before he died or how but we know he was trying to track down more evidence—the evidence to bring down Hyland, for good. They must have been communicating on here. This contact, and Latif and Charlotte."

"Why Charlotte?"

Samira looked out the window—*at* the window. The glass was so foggy they could be parked in a cloud. "Maybe they needed her security expertise—though to be frank, I'm more experienced at this kind of stuff. Or maybe her access. Damn him." She clapped a hand to her mouth. "Oh God, that's the wrong thing to say about a dead person."

Jamie rubbed her shoulder. "When you say 'communicating'... How?"

"You can leave clues and notes for each other. It's a big part of the game—encrypting and hiding messages." The phone had switched to screen saver. She swiped it. "Charlotte's picture... I need to get into that world..."

"Then do it. Just...don't forget to breathe."

She forced herself to slowly inhale and exhale as the world loaded. She pointed to the screen—hills, fields, flowers, house. "Does that look familiar?"

"Honestly, I didn't look too closely at the picture."

"Charlotte added this house three days ago." She swiped the screen and flew through the door. "I hate playing this game on a phone. There, look."

He shuffled closer, his thigh touching hers. Against one wall sat a wooden treasure chest. A silver-haired man in a suit stood guard, flashing a big smile. "Does *he* look familiar?"

"Hyland? Is that the—what do you call it—*avatar* of Erebus?"

"No, he's a guardian of treasure. He's not a player in the game. Charlotte has created him."

"Treasure? As in a place to hide damning intel? Could she have hidden the documents inside?"

Samira frowned. "You can't upload files to the game but something must be in there that Charlotte wants me to find—and only me." She checked the page history again. "Erebus has been in here but hasn't opened the vault."

"*Something?* The something Charlotte brought you to London for?"

"Charlotte was last on here fourteen minutes before she posted the picture on social media."

"So maybe she knew Hyland's people were coming for her and quickly left a message."

"Then hurriedly drew the picture and posted it, to direct me here."

"Can we get into this treasure chest?"

She clicked on it. "It's asking for a username and password."

"The suspense is killing me."

"There's writing on it." She zoomed in. "Two strings of characters."

"The username and password?" Jamie said, hope lifting his voice.

"Possibly, but it's in a code we devised when we were at university. A simple keyword cipher. Each letter is swapped for another, basically."

"Was that for a paper?"

"Just for fun. Told you I was wild back then."

She decoded it and keyed in the solution. A metallic clunk, and the chest squealed open, revealing a basement. Samira's breath stalled as she dived in and did a three-sixty.

"It's empty," Jamie said. "Maybe she ran out of time."

"She had time enough to build the house and do some interior decoration. If she was in a hurry, we have to assume that everything in here is relevant. She's just being cautious."

"No kidding."

Samira zoomed in on a picture hanging on the wall— a mountain peeping above a cloud, in an elaborate gold frame. "The cloud—maybe these documents are on a cloud server. And the mountain…" She smiled as she figured it out. "Huh."

"Does that mean something?"

"What land is up in the clouds?"

"Is this a riddle? I love riddles."

"High lands. Hyland."

"Spoilsport. I would totally have got there."

"The frame—there's a secure cloud storage site called Gold Linings. Maybe Hyland has an account with them, with this username and password."

"Excellent. So we go to the site, log in, get these documents and problem solved."

"Not from across the Atlantic. It'll register as a suspicious log-in, send his people an alert, raise flags. We'd be locked out before we got anywhere. This site—it has top-shelf IDP. Every anomalous behavior detection you can think of—geographical, device, multifactor authentication…"

"I'll take your word for it."

A car pulled up next to them. Jamie wiped his window. A red SUV. Kids in the back.

"We'd better not stick around here, in case that cop comes back," Samira said.

"This Gold Linings," he said, as they reassumed their seats up front. "Is there any way through the security?"

"I worked on the development team," she said, clipping in as he started the engine and blasted the air con onto the windshield. "I can get around their device detection by spoofing the device headers."

"O-kay."

"It means I can mask the fact that we're logging on with an unrecognized device. But their geographical detection is infallible. Strong enough to keep even me out—and they'll have updated the security since I worked on it."

"Is there no way around it? Can you make it look like—I don't know—the log-in is coming from DC, or wherever he is?"

"Wherever he is," she repeated, slowly. "Oh my God. Hyland's coming here—to the UK, anyway. To Edinburgh, for a NATO meeting. Well, to catch me, probably, but that's his excuse. It was in the newspaper this morning."

As the windows cleared, Jamie reversed out and swung the car around. "I don't want you going anywhere near him."

"Neither do I. But we won't have to—well, not *too* near. We'll just need to try this log-in in Edinburgh after he arrives. As long as we're in the same city it shouldn't raise suspicions—unless the password is wrong."

She exited the house and dynamited it, with Hyland inside.

"Bet you enjoyed that."

"I did." She restored the field with its flowers. "I can't imagine anyone else would be able to crack all that but I'm not taking the chance, especially with someone lurking in the game. You see? That's about thinking through every possibility and not just relying on instinct."

"Which is all well and good when you have time for it, but not so much when people are shooting at you. And anyway, I would say this *is* you listening to your instinct."

She made a point of scoffing as she tapped and swiped. "And, in another feat of *forethought*, I'll set up an alert so it notifies me if Charlotte goes online." She gulped down a wave of car sickness, and forced herself to focus ahead, along a street of redbrick terraced houses. "So I guess we need to head north."

Jamie chewed his lower lip. "Are you sure it's a risk you want to take?"

"Says the man in the stolen government car with a cache of illegal drugs and a gun I'm guessing he doesn't have a license for."

"Not illegal drugs. Prescription drugs."

"That aren't prescribed to you."

"Point is, how do we get all the way to Scotland without being caught? You're a wanted woman and, as you so helpfully remind me, we're in a stolen car. There'll be hundreds of traffic cameras between here and Edinburgh. Look, there's one right there." He gestured at a yellow box on a pole. "As soon as this car's reported stolen we'll get a squad of police cars on our tail, and who knows who else?"

"But you said yourself it's not likely to be reported stolen until tomorrow." She sat straighter. "Or maybe could we take a train?"

"Know how many surveillance cameras they put in train stations? You're on too many radars for that."

"Jamie…where is all this coming from?"

"What do you mean? I thought you liked thinking things through."

"I do. But I'm the risk-averse one, not y—" She chewed on the corner of a fingernail. "I have an idea."

"An instinctive one, I hope."

"Strictly logical." She set the phone browser to invisible and did a web search. "One thing about Big Brother—whenever he's watching, you can be sure an army of anarchists and libertarians is staring right back." After a minute she showed him the screen, smiling. "You see? I have complete faith in other people's lack of faith in authority."

He glanced at it. "A map?"

"Showing all the fixed ANPR cameras in the UK. Thousands of them."

"ANPR?"

"Automatic number plate recognition."

"You're such a revolutionary, Samira."

"Believe me, I didn't used to be. And I don't like it. When all this is over, I shall go back to being the woman who drives a mile under the speed limit, takes out her trash a day early and overpays her taxes."

"You're an exemplary citizen. Give me a look at that map?" She held it in front of him. "This is a circuitous route. It's basically England to Scotland via Alaska. Is there no other way to make it look like we're in Edinburgh?"

"No." She drew away the phone. "It's the simplest way to end this." Hang on. Why was *she* the one trying to talk him into this? "Jamie, I'm sensing reluctance."

"No, it's just…it's a long way."

"You don't want to go to Scotland." She lowered her tone to teasing. "Worried about bumping into someone you know?"

"No more so than in London."

His voice and expression had gone grim. Thunder from a blue sky. She really had touched a nerve—but why?

"You're worried about something," she ventured.

"Not a care in the world."

Like hell. "Jamie," she said, gently, "none of this is what I want to do, either. I just want for everyone to be safe, and unfortunately, that's been left up to me."

He nodded, his expression remaining dark. What was going on under there? "And me."

"I…can't tell you how relieved I am that you're here with me. I can't do this without you—I *wouldn't* be doing it without you."

Silence. "So we drive to Scotland in a stolen car, evading police and killer goons," he said, eventually, a little too loud, a little too cheerfully. "Then break into the secure files of a leader of the free world, steal mysterious documents and transmit them across the world without being caught by web spy software—or anything or anyone else. What are we waiting for?"

Suddenly, he threw the car into a U-turn. The newspaper he'd bought slid off the dash onto her feet. She clutched her door handle, looking around breathlessly. No police. No Peugeot.

"What are you doing?" she said.

"Going to Scotland. We were heading south."

"Oh. Good… I guess."

"We must be the most reluctant defenders of truth and justice the world has ever seen."

She laughed. "I was secretly hoping you'd tell me my plan was terrible and we should just go and hide." Hiding out with Jamie. A cozy cottage somewhere, like in France. Nothing to do but…

No.

"It's a good plan. I just…" He shook his head, a movement so slight she could have imagined it. "It's a good plan."

As they drove, she picked up the newspaper and flicked through it. A later edition than the one she'd seen at St Pancras. "Oh my God, I'm on page three." She slapped the paper with the back of her hand. "Page three! How the hell is any of this happening?"

"What does it say?"

She sped-read, fighting nausea. "The authorities know I'm in the UK. The US wants to extradite me."

"They'll have to catch you first."

"There's some lobby group arguing that I'm a political asylum seeker. They're calling me a whistle-blower…literally talking about me in the same sentence as Snowden and Deep Throat. It wasn't me who blew that whistle."

"You would have though, if you'd come across the same information your fiancé had."

"No, I don't believe I would."

"I do."

He did? "If I hadn't been forced into this situation, I'd never have chosen it."

"You would have gotten that info out but maybe you would have been more care—" His eyebrows dived together. "I'm sorry. I didn't mean to suggest that your fiancé—"

"Don't apologize. You're right—he wasn't careful." She smoothed the newspaper. "But it wasn't just *his* carelessness that got him killed."

A pause. "You mean your phone call, the one they tracked?"

"He took a risk but he might have pulled it off if I hadn't gotten scared. My fear for his life had him killed. How ironic is that?"

"He knew what he was getting into. He knew the risks. I bet he'd be gutted to think you were blaming yourself."

Jamie covered her nearest hand with his and squeezed, filling her chest with something between warmth and an ache. Underneath their hands the newspaper rustled. Her eyes pricked. What was going on here? That night in France had been lust and desire, impulsive, to say the least. But this was attraction of a whole other kind. And was she ready for it?

She cleared her throat and shook out the paper, forcing him to release her. Ready? Her life was a mess. She was a mess. "I refuse to feel sorry for myself, not when I…" She stared ahead, sensing his gaze on her. "I will not feel sorry for myself. So please don't feel sorry for me, because that…" *Because that makes me want to melt into you and believe every word you say and take the comfort you offer—and so much more.* "I would never have chosen this situation," she repeated.

"Samira," Jamie said, in that gentle tone that did her in, every time. "There is no shame in fear. Fear is meant to keep you alive—like when you escaped Hyland in Italy. That's its purpose."

"I thought you said that was instinct?"

"There's no stronger instinct than fear. It's okay to listen to your fear—just don't let it make *all* your decisions for you."

"But my instinct always comes back to fear. It always tells me to cower. Like at the train station—my brain was telling me to go and help you but fear kept me in place."

"And your instinct was correct. You hid and I was fine."

"But my instinct is always going to be to hide, to run."

"And at the spur of the moment those are usually very wise decisions. It's when your conscious brain tells you to fear that you should question it. When you talk yourself into fear. When you tell yourself 'I'm a fearful person' so often that it influences your decisions— a self-fulfilling prophecy. I've seen the way you fire up at the thought of injustice. You would have found a way to blow the whistle. Maybe you would have done it in such a way that protected yourself—which is a good thing—but you would have done it."

She blinked. Wow. "You've really thought about this."

"Not really." He shifted in his seat. "I'm just thinking aloud. I make most things up as I go along and for some reason people tend to believe my bollocks, which is handy in the medical profession. And, hey, you've probably figured out that my big life decisions haven't always worked out so well. I'm the doc who tells you not to smoke, then dashes out for a fag between patients."

And the self-deprecating joker was back. Which was okay. She liked the joker. She liked all parts of him—the philosopher, the action man, the protector, the mystery man who lurked somewhere underneath and between. She liked altogether too much of him.

"I think you need to give *yourself* more credit," she said, her voice suddenly husky. "What's that saying about swallowing your own medicine?"

"Giving myself too much credit kind of created the fundamental problem that is *Caporal* James Armstrong. And I think the saying you're looking for is 'Practice what you preach.' In my experience it's far easier to preach."

He pulled to a halt at a red light and turned in his seat, fixing his gaze on her—that look that made her feel like the only woman in the world. His eyes narrowed, lines hatching in the creases. He reached a hand across—to her cheek, this time—and brushed something away. A second's pause, then he pushed his fingers through her hair and cradled the back of her head, coaxed her toward him and planted a kiss on her forehead. The ache in her chest started up again.

She went to pull away, then stopped. The fear, right now—it was in her conscious brain. Every other part of her brain—and body—wanted her to tip her head back, glide a hand to the back of his neck, touch her lips to his.

It's okay to listen to your fear—just don't let it make all your decisions for you.

Yes. Yes, this decision was all hers.

She tipped her head back. His frowning gaze held hers a second before dropping to her mouth. Like it was inevitable, like it'd happened between them a thousand times, he tilted his head and their lips met. Her fear vanished. In its wake she could feel her nerves firing up, trace their path to her brain as she softened into him, feel her heart pump faster, feel the blood quicken in her veins.

History?

Like hell.

CHAPTER TEN

A HORN BLASTED, behind them. Samira jumped, breaking contact, as Jamie scrambled for the gearshift. Not a police car, just a blue van. The traffic light was green. She pressed her hand against her chest, the heartbeats like seismic aftershocks. Wow. Wow, wow, wow.

Jamie accelerated, staring resolutely ahead, his breath as ragged as hers.

This thing between them—it no longer existed purely as a guilty secret. It had taken form again, like a bubble of gas around them. A thrilling, frightening, euphoric, suffocating drug.

She slid her hand up to her hot throat. And she couldn't let it continue. Her brain had enough to cope with—it couldn't be healthy to dump a heap more uncertainty into it.

"Jamie, you should know… I'm still not ready for… I can't go there." Was that even the reason? He might be good at making things up as he went along, but she needed to go away for an hour or two to process this. They'd kissed. For real. Not like on the Thames Path, on the street in Putney, the feint for the police officer, not even like France. This last one was barely more than a touch but every part of her knew it was real. It changed everything.

It changes nothing.

"I know you're not ready," he said. That catch in his

voice—it was the same one she'd heard in France after she'd insisted he leave. "I'm sorry. I shouldn't have—"

"*We* shouldn't have. It wasn't on you. I was just as… Let's forget about it." Forget about *that*? The sweet buzz in her chest, the promise of a future in that one light touch? In France she hadn't felt that promise. That was resolutely a one-night stand—not that she'd had a lot of experience in such things. She'd been a one-man woman for so long.

"Aye," he said.

She waited.

Aye? That was it? No passionate argument about letting instinct decide, about rejecting fear? Once again he'd relented altogether too easily. Just like in France. The speed at which he'd packed his few belongings that morning…

And she should be grateful he'd relented—then and now. Maybe in a few years, after she'd rebuilt her life, she'd be ready to share it with someone—someone less reluctant than Jamie—but first she had to put all of this behind her. Starting with *not* being on a wanted poster.

Yes, focus on that. Focus on the problems she could rationalize and take practical steps to overcome. Jamie did not fit that category.

She pulled the goon's money from her coat and counted it. "Jamie, how much cash do you have?"

"Uh…" He patted his jeans pocket. "About five hundred quid. Flynn advised me to carry cash rather than use a card." As he spoke, his voice recovered its usual energy. No doubt he was relieved to return to neutral subject matter, reset the clock. "Tess has turned us all into conspiracy theorists. What do you need?"

"A laptop. I ditched mine a year ago and I can't do this hack on a public computer." She grabbed his phone from the console between the seats and swiped it. "You really should put a PIN on this."

"Until now I had nothing to hide. Well, nothing that you'd find on a phone."

She found the address of the closest electronics store and directed him there. "You'd better go in alone," she said, as he found a park behind the building. She picked up his phone and typed a list of specifications into his notes app. "Here. And get a power bank. And a car charger. I'll pay you back when I can exchange my euros. When I'm no longer wanted on both sides of the Atlantic."

He laughed.

"I wasn't making a joke." She double-blinked. "Wow," she breathed.

"Samira?"

"I keep having these 'what the hell?' moments. Even after the crazy couple of years I've had, my life keeps getting crazier. It's like a permanent out-of-body experience. I really am a wanted woman."

He opened the car door, flashing a wry grin. "In more ways than one. Don't worry. We'll get you returned to your body soon."

In more ways than one. Spoken like his attraction to her was as reluctant as hers was.

While he was out, Samira installed a virtual tunnel and secure browser to his phone that would mask their web activity. Ten minutes later they were back on the road, Samira connecting the computer with the charging equipment. Once it had enough juice, she set up his phone as a hot spot, installed the same tunnel and browser on the laptop, and downloaded "Cosmos" onto it. No new activity. What was she expecting? That Charlotte had left her current GPS coordinates? A note to announce it was all a big prank?

Samira opened a web page. In the meantime, she'd have to pursue her own solution.

"What's that?" Jamie said, glancing at the screen.

"The site I uploaded that goon's phone data to." She scrolled, a thrill rolling up her spine. This was more like it. Something she *could* control. "The connection was only a few days old. No texts or emails or browsing history but there are regular calls with several other cell phone numbers—most of them sequential to his number. The phones must have been bought together."

"Can you hack into them, or whatever it is you do?"

"Phone companies are notoriously hard to infiltrate if you're not the NSA or GCHQ or some other government spy agency," she said. "But I can download a GPS mapping analysis tool and input the historical GPS data."

"So we'll be able to see where he's been?"

"Which might or might not be any use.

"This is interesting," she said, after a few minutes. "He was in the vicinity of Charlotte's house three days ago. And then he traveled south—not long after Charlotte's social-media post."

"Could that be where they took her, assuming that's what happened?"

"Maybe. But he covered a big area. With nothing to triangulate against, the location data is too broad to be any use. We'd have to knock on doors in an entire London suburb." She worked her knuckles into her back and arched.

"Sore back?"

"Always."

After an unproductive few minutes she sighed, closed the screen and stared out the window. They were back in the countryside, flanked by green hedges. "That's about all I can do until we get closer to Hyland." She yawned. The buzz from the kiss and the drama had lifted, sucking her remaining energy away with it. Even pretending the kiss hadn't happened was exhausting—on top of pretending France hadn't happened.

"When's the last time you had a proper sleep?" Jamie said.

"I honestly can't remember." Yes, that was why her brain was so skittish. Lack of sleep was not conducive to rational thought—or resisting self-defeating impulses.

"It's a fair distance to Edinburgh without the motorways—seven hours or more if we're to avoid all those cameras." His eyes turned to hers, dull and sunken. His five o'clock shadow had tipped from sexy to haggard, though she still felt a pull in her belly under his gaze. Goddammit. "Get some sleep."

"You couldn't have slept much, either."

"More than you, I'm guessing, and I'm used to it. I can nap later, while you're doing your techie stuff." He jerked his head toward the back seat. "Go."

She nodded, and climbed into the back. This way they didn't have to talk about the rhino in the room. Awkward situations were best tackled by avoidance.

As she curled up on the seat, her camel coat balled under her head, Jamie switched on the car radio. He cycled through a few stations and settled on an old Muse song, tapping the rhythm on the steering wheel. Rain tapped on the roof, and the wipers swished. A wave of warmth and security washed over her—the comfort she'd known as a child traveling with her parents, alone with her imagination in the back seat as they murmured a conversation years above her comprehension, her mother's perfume blending with her father's cologne like they'd bought his-and-hers fragrances.

There was no separation between her parents' professional and personal lives but it worked. Their conversations had no borders—work, politics, family, diplomatic gossip. They knew and understood everything about each other. Sure, they argued, but it was more competitive than cutting—each trying to outwit the other with pithy dissections of global issues. They rarely disagreed on anything of substance. They were on the same side. Maybe she'd subconsciously sought that for herself when she'd started looking for love. An ally in every respect—someone she understood, who understood her. Less yin and yang, more yang and yang.

Was that why she'd gravitated to Latif? They were both geeks, both loners, both Ethiopian, both navigating American culture. He understood her because he was the same in so many ways. How could Jamie understand her when he was so different? Hypothetically speaking, of course, because the offer was not on the table. The only trait Latif had in common with Jamie was his embrace of risk—and that was the one thing that had terrified her, justifiably, as it turned out.

Maybe Latif's risk-taking and her aversion to it would have pulled them apart, eventually. What was that saying her grandmother was fond of? *Only a fool pairs an ox with an elephant*?

Only a fool paired a gregarious adrenaline-junkie soldier with a shy scaredy mouse. Hang on—not *mouse*. Cat? Maybe she did need sleep.

Somehow I have a knack for dragging people into trouble. Consider yourself warned.

Yet here she was, taking an almighty risk in kissing him, in letting herself get a thrill from his company, in being seduced by the safety and warmth of his protection. He had so many qualities she lacked. Maybe she was attracted to him for exactly the opposite reasons she'd been attracted to Latif. Yin and yang.

Stop it.

Jamie sang the chorus in a bassy undertone, the murmur mixing with the hum of the car under her cheek and the rumble of the tires on asphalt. Despite all that was or wasn't happening between them, his company was a relief. His jokes were a relief—had she laughed even once since France? She should enjoy that while it lasted and refuse to regret what could not be.

At least when she woke—if she slept at all—it would be to a sexy, solid and oh-so-tangible man who knew her real face and her real name, and genuinely cared what became of her, even if he was an elephant to her ox.

As Jamie headed north, detouring in wild arcs to avoid traffic cameras, night swallowed the feeble attempt at day. The local wore off and the dull ache in his shoulder grew to a scalding pain that surged with every inhalation. In the footwell of the passenger seat, the rucksack practically glowed. A red pulsing light of temptation. One fentanyl capsule, or maybe an oxy, just enough to take the edge off.

But it wouldn't end there, would it? Damn Andy for putting the fucking things in front of him.

No. Nobody to blame but himself. Like always. He'd only wanted the sedatives, since he was seriously short of firepower—and they'd indeed come in handy. He should have said no to the rest. Should have chucked them out. Still could. And would, soon as he got the chance.

He turned a sharp corner and the pain soared. He was

a fucking princess. Flynn had once let Jamie stitch up his scalp without giving more than a mumbled curse. Jamie had watched people die of gaping, sucking, pumping wounds—not many, thank God, and may he never see that again. The pain was probably psychosomatic, on account of his location. An internal GPS.

He adjusted the mirror. Even in sleep the dark, curled shape of Samira's body seemed tense.

Jamie, I'm not ready for... I can't go there.

He winced, and forced his focus back on the dark road. Aye, he was a prime jerk to make a move on her. It didn't take a psych consult to conclude she hadn't advanced far in the stages of grief. No matter how often he made her smile or laugh, he couldn't ward off her ghosts for long. He could pinpoint the moment of counterattack as they curled their fingers around her heart and pulled her back into the shadows. Her eyes would retreat into her skull, her jaw would tighten, her shoulders would slump. But she would come back to life when he said something that fired her up—and, wow, did she come to life when they kissed. The kiss of life.

Maybe that was his problem—*one* of his problems. After spending so long in the business of saving lives, he had an instinct to breathe life into somebody who was ailing—CPR of the soul.

In the back seat, she groaned. She sat up in the darkness and rolled her shoulders, arching.

"Morning, sunshine," he said.

"It's morning?"

"No. But we're basically in our own time zone, so it can be anything you want it to be."

"How's your arm?" she said, clambering to the front seat.

"Fine. Completely forgotten about it."

"You still look pale."

"It's because we've crossed into Scotland. I've gone all pasty and grumpy and miserly."

She twisted her torso one way and then the other. "Where are we?"

"We've just come through the Borders, closing in on Edinburgh."

"Wow. I slept a long time. Shall I drive?"

"I'll push through." Trying to sleep would just focus his attention on his arm. This would be over soon enough. How soon could they catch a flight to France?

Hang on. Would Samira's fake passport get her back to Europe, now she was officially wanted for extradition? Would Hyland have clued in the UK authorities on the method of her arrival, and thus her false identity? If Jamie couldn't get her out he'd have to stay with her—and he wouldn't take the easy way out this time, wouldn't let her push him away.

And was that prospect intriguing or terrifying?

Both.

Samira grunted as a new song came over the radio—a soul-shriveling a cappella group cover of "Born in the USA." "Ugh," she said, diving for the radio.

"I think the antenna is broken. There's not much of a choice."

She dug around in the rucksack and pulled out a cord and an iPhone.

"You have a phone?" he said. "I thought we didn't trust phones."

"It's not connected to a network. Really it's just an expensive iPod."

She plugged it in and a throaty voice wafted from the speaker. Dionne Warwick? Samira screwed up her face, and swiped past. He mentally sang through the lyrics until he reached the chorus. "I'll Never Love This Way Again." Ah. Clearly unsuitable for the situation.

Samira glanced his way as another familiar voice came on. Gloria Gaynor, "I Will Survive."

He grinned. "Appropriate."

"I thought so."

She picked up his phone and opened the browser. "The BBC's reporting that the senator has arrived in Edinburgh, with his daughter. They're staying at the Balfour Hotel. Do you know it?"

"One of the grand old ones, near the castle. How close to him do we need to get?"

"As close as we dare but we don't have to be in the same block."

She tapped and swiped some more. He slowed for a village. Stone church, headstones sprouting from a graveyard like crooked black teeth, ivy-coated inn, humpbacked stone bridge over a burn, faded sign advertising a Sunday farmers' market. The kind of market his mother had dragged the family to for the same fruit and veg they could buy at the local grocer.

The music cycled through "Because the Night" and "Gloria." He followed the green signs out of town. The countryside closed in around them again. Edinburgh had never felt this far away before—but then, he wouldn't usually choose the scenic route.

How had he ended up willingly returning to Scotland? After taking leave for his father's funeral three years ago, he'd vowed never to come back. By then his mother was floating into the oblivion of dementia. Six months later she was in a secure home and his sister knew just who to blame. And who was he to argue?

Whenever he was forced to use up his leave, he'd forgo the traditional Legion drunken blinder in favor of staying on base and schooling up on emergency and military medicine. Also mind-numbing but nowhere near as fun. Life on the level was so goddamn dull. Not that alcohol had ever been his thing. Too messy, too uncontrolled. All that liquid going in had to come out again, in none-too-pretty ways. He did envy his buddies that escape, that off switch, but the temptation to succumb to his own personal demon required vigilance.

"Laura's on social media asking for the best place to buy whiskey this evening, and for recommendations for a local designer to visit in the morning," Samira said. "She wants to buy a dress for her book signing."

"She doesn't know how to use Google?"

"Who needs it when you have millions of followers only too happy to do your Googling for you? She's getting a lot of replies. And she's only doing it to promote her event. If it was just about the whiskey she could just send a concier— Oh my God."

"What?"

"Look," she said, holding the phone up. A gray, grainy photo filled the small screen.

"Some kind of security footage?"

"You and me at the hospital. Police want us to 'help them with their enquiries.' It's pixelated—too pixelated for facial recognition, especially with the caps and my sunglasses—but it's definitely us."

Fuck.

"They're not linking us with the wanted woman but…"

A matter of time. Somebody would recognize him from that photo. He rubbed his cheek—shaving might help. How far would Harriet, Mariya and Andy go to protect him if the authorities started asking questions? They could at least honestly deny they knew what he was up to. He'd turn himself in if he got wind they were in trouble. But then what would become of Samira? And what of the Legion? He couldn't lose another job, another career.

"It doesn't change anything," he said, gripping the wheel tighter. "We get this evidence and everything we've done is justifiable."

She pressed a hand to her chest. "God, I hope you're right."

Really, he had no idea. Through the speakers, Tina Turner cranked up the chorus of "What's Love Got to Do with It?"

"What's up with the music?" he said, forcing lightness into his tone.

She slipped his phone back into the console. "You don't like it?"

"There are no songs by men in this mix. Don't get me wrong, they're good songs, but it's sexist, do you not think?"

"It's not sexist. It's…empowering." Her voice hit that exasperated edge. Distraction accomplished.

"Why is it that discriminating against women is sexist but discriminating against men is empowering?"

"Maybe because women are emerging from several millennia of being unempowered? Does it emasculate you, listening to such empowered women?"

"Not at all. I like empowered women. I love empowered women." *Especially when they're fired up.* "Do you harbor secret rock-star ambitions?"

She relaxed into her seat with a harrumph. "Would that mean I'd have to go out in crowds, and people would look at me?"

"I think so, yes."

"Then no, I'm pretty much the opposite of a rock star."

"You certainly are."

Her head flicked to face him. She'd turned that alluring mahogany. "Just what do you mean by that?"

"Oh, so *you* can say you're the opposite of a rock star but when I agree *I* get in trouble?"

A reluctant smile. "Believe me, I don't need any critic but myself."

"What I mean," he said quietly, "is that you're far too levelheaded."

"Just what every woman dreams of hearing. And if what we're doing here is your idea of levelheaded, you're a danger to society."

"Nothing at all wrong with levelheaded... They make you feel braver, these songs."

She blinked, frowning. The music hit dead air, and then an acoustic guitar started strumming, joined by an electric guitar. He figured it out as the singing began—4 Non Blondes.

"I guess. Charlotte got me hooked on women rockers at university. Joni Mitchell, Janis Joplin, Joan Osborne, Joan Jett—we called them the four Js... They got us through many a late night of cramming."

"Ah, hence Janis and Jagger... You don't strike me as the cramming type. More the one with a long-term revision plan. On spreadsheet."

"Spreadsheet? Pfft. I created a scheduling app." They laughed, hers a husky sound he hadn't heard nearly often enough. "I needed it because I spent too many hours gaming. The thing is," she said, drawing her feet up and resting them on the glove compartment, "I don't feel like a coward when I listen to these songs. These women are powerful, passionate, confident...all the things I'm not."

"For starters, I don't believe for a second that you're not those things. And anyway," he continued, raising his voice over her objection, "I imagine their cool-girl image covered up a lot of insecurities. Look what became of Janis. And there's plenty of heartache and vulnerability in those songs. That's what makes them so good. Not to mention, it doesn't get much braver than taking down one of the most powerful men in America."

"For a beautiful minute there I'd forgotten about that."

He mentally head-desked.

"Anyway, this is not about being brave," she continued. "It's about being forced to do what it takes to survive."

"That's what most bravery is."

"I disagree. I think bravery is about putting yourself in a situation like this just because it's the right thing to do or purely to help others—even when it's not in your own best interests. Like what you're doing."

His eyes widened. His motivations weren't nearly as pure as she gave him credit for. "Me? No. I only came because it sounded like fun."

"We have a very different idea of fun. Does this not scare you?"

"Right now, no. And you know why? Because I'm not thinking about it. Because I'm having a lovely drive with good company and good music and I'm not about to ruin it by thinking about what's going to happen next when there's nothing more I can do to prepare for it. Because I'm not talking myself into feeling fear. Later on, if the shit hits the fan—"

"Yes! That's what it is," she said, to herself.

"Huh?"

"Just something that was annoying me. Go on."

"If the shit hits the fan, maybe I'll be scared, but that'll be around the time the adrenaline strikes, so there'll be no room for fear."

"And in the meantime, denial is your defense against fear."

"Denial is my defense against most things. Whatever gets you through the day, I say." Right. Like that philosophy had never got him into strife.

"But shouldn't we be thinking through the possibilities of things going wrong?"

Ah, he should never have brought up the senator. "Like what?"

"Like we get arrested for stealing a car and demolishing half a London block and trespassing and breaking and entering and having an illegal weapon and illegal drugs and carrying a false passport and entering the country illegally—well, that last bit is just me—and I get extradited to America and locked up next to Tess and we're found guilty of some fictitious charge, on top of all the real ones, and jailed for twenty years and you lose your job and wind up with a criminal record and Hyland becomes the American president and appoints the most corrupt government in the history of—"

"Whoa. Stop. Wow. Jesus. Is this seriously what goes on in your head?"

"I've…been alone a lot lately."

"You must have burned a lot of calories just thinking about all that. How do you ever get to sleep at night?"

"Is this not normal? Is this not what you're thinking?"

"Normal? There's no such thing as normal and I'm most certainly not it, but before you dumped all that on me I was just grateful that it's not raining and that the traffic's mostly going the other way."

She shook her head.

"And now you're looking at me like *I'm* the crazy one. *Not* that I'm calling you crazy," he added, quickly. "Far be it from me…"

"No, this is me looking at you in awe. I wish I could feel that relaxed."

"Okay, so I'm thinking you're the kind of person who needs to work through every scenario of what could go wrong before you can have confidence that things won't go wrong."

"I guess."

"So, let's go back to the start of that train of thought. How will the authorities catch us?"

"I don't know—a hundred different ways."

"Give me a scenario. You're evidently good at scenarios."

"Okay. That cop in Putney puts out a description of us and someone links it to my wanted picture. Or the cop who caught us…you know."

Oh, he did know.

"Or they both do!" she said. "Shit."

"Well, the cop in Putney will have everybody chasing a couple from Essex, if she noticed us at all, which I doubt, and the cop who caught us you-know-whatting would have written you up as a Scot—if he'd written us up at all, and he didn't seem the type to want to burden himself with the paperwork. You're giving the system too much credit for intelligence."

"But what if—?"

"What if, what if…? Two words to drive anybody crazy. But, okay, it's all highly unlikely but let's take that scenario to its natural conclusion. How would they find us?"

"They…catch us speeding."

"I won't speed. What else?"

"Someone we meet recognizes me from the wanted photo or you from the security footage and calls the police."

"So we don't show our faces until this is over and you're exonerated and no longer wanted. Next?"

"The car. The hospital discovers it missing and a cop spots it."

"Samira, it's a white hatchback, like all the other white hatchbacks. You know how many are in the UK?" He swept a hand in front of them. "I can see one up ahead right now. Oh, and look, one's just passed us. It's basically an urban camo car. Every cop from Land's End to John O'Groats is not going to be checking the plate of every white hatchback they see—we'd have to be doing something suspicious for them to bother. And we're avoiding traffic cameras. Besides, we're operating on a pretty sound theory that the hospital won't discover the theft in a hurry. But just to keep you happy, we'll ditch the car and hide as soon as we've done this hack. What else?"

"The police are tracking us somehow. Or Hyland's goons are, like with the postcard. Or both."

"We've established the car doesn't have GPS but you're the technology expert. How would they be doing that?"

"I don't know."

"Well, then, neither will they. Anything else?"

He could almost hear her neurons connecting.

"Not yet," she said, eventually.

"Keep me posted. In the meantime, let's just enjoy the drive."

She sighed but let the conversation slide. Ahead, a hazy gray glow in the dark sky pinpointed the city but traffic remained light as they approached. A sleepy Sunday night. Scrubby trees and neglected hedgerows, a whitewashed pub, a petrol station, power pylons... What the fuck was he doing back here? He grew up wanting nothing more than to get out of Scotland, work in the thick of things in a big city hospital, do something important. Now he was a nobody *caporal* working in places where flushing toilets were the exception, and was slinking into Edinburgh under cover of darkness.

Hard to believe that a week ago he was bedded down beside a dirt road in Mali, heating up a cassoulet on a butane stove. When they were told they were bugging out and heading back to Corsica for a debrief and a few days of leave, he'd got the usual hollow feeling in his stomach. While the younger guys were debating the best place around the Med to get shit-faced and screwed, he was picturing the stash of journals in his locker. Even Angelito wasn't going to be around—and he could usually be relied on to have plans even duller than Jamie's. But he'd retired from the Legion and set off for some shithole in Eastern Europe to look for the sister he'd lost in childhood. And Flynn, of course, had taken a leave of absence to protect Tess while she prepared her evidence against Hyland. Turned out absence made the heart grow fonder even of that Patty and Selma duo.

Flynn's phone call couldn't have come at a better time, just as Jamie had been yawning over "A Modern Case Series of Resuscitative Endovascular Balloon Occlusion of the Aorta in an Out-of-Hospital, Combat Casualty Care Setting." Could Jamie fly to London to rescue Samira from a squad of murderous mercenaries? Hell yeah, and thank you, God.

"It's getting colder," Samira said, twisting to get her extra coat from the back seat. As she dragged it over, she bumped his arm. He hissed until the pain passed. Something was still stuck in there.

"Jamie, why don't you take some more painkillers?

They're right here." She pulled his bag of tricks from the rucksack and held it up.

"I've taken the maximum dose. Any more and I'll start vomiting, and we don't want to have to pay a cleaning fee for soiling our hire car."

"These packets of pills—they're not even opened."

Damn. "I was using another packet."

"I didn't see another packet."

"I took some before you woke."

She pulled the laptop up and opened it, the white light illuminating her face. "Oh okay."

He let out a slow leak of a breath. *Chill out, pal. Innocent question.* And the lies had flowed like blood from a scalp wound, just as they always had.

She hooked into his phone Wi-Fi, tapped away a bit, then pressed her hand to her chest. "We're in range. Let's find a place to stop."

"Oui, mademoiselle."

They crossed over the city bypass and pulled up at a golf course where they could feasibly be stopping to admire the lights of the skyline, which, granted, were more sky than lights from there—the castle gleaming white atop its hill, the clock tower and a couple of sharp gothic steeples jutting up against the black slash of the Firth of Forth, a yellow glow rising from Princes Street and the Royal Mile, as if they were rivers of fire. Another spot his mother would like. If he brought her here today, would she know this view? Would she know him?

Not now, Mum.

Sorry.

He pointed out the Balfour, squat and grandiose, its facade washed in a golden light that had to make it hard for its guests to sleep.

"Wow," said Samira, her arms tightly crossed, hands clutching opposite elbows. "He's right over there."

"And we're not going any closer," Jamie said. "We'll blast him sky-high from here, like a remote control. Virtually speaking." He lowered his window, admitting the city's distant hum. The air was icy and still. This time he'd keep a closer watch for cops—and anybody else they didn't want to meet.

After hooking the equipment back up and loading the cloud server site, Samira stretched her long fingers above the keyboard. She froze. A muffled throb of bass music started up, a block or two away.

"Something wrong?" he said.

"If this password's incorrect, the system will flag a failed log-in. That could ruin our chances, too. And they might guess it's us and track our location."

"So if that happens we'll get out of town and think of something else."

"There is nothing else." She laid her fingertips on the keyboard and raised them again like it was boiling hot. "I'll type with one finger."

She struck the keys slowly, the rhythmic tapping like a slow ticking clock. He instinctively regulated his breathing, as if one wheeze too many would blow her typing off course. She pressed Enter, her throat moving as she swallowed. A circular loading icon appeared on the screen, turning. His arm throbbed.

"This connection is twentieth-century slow," she whispered.

"It's nearly over, Samira."

"What if it's not the information we need? What if he's moved it or deleted it? What if it was all a trap to begin w—?"

"We'll find out soon enough. Whatever happens, we'll deal with it, okay?"

The screen blinked, and filled with file names. She turned to meet his gaze and inhaled, like she was sucking confidence from him.

"We're in."

CHAPTER ELEVEN

JAMIE HELD HIS breath as Samira scrolled down an endless page of folders and files.

"What is all that stuff?" he said.

"Briefing documents, meeting agendas, draft legis-
lation, contacts, itineraries—including the one for this
trip... Thousands of documents—tens of thousands.
And it all looks totally inane and legit." She brought a
hand up and planted her chin on her knuckles. "I have
no idea what I'm looking for. I don't know what Charlotte was pointing me to. God, we need Tess."

"We have time to sift through them. Hyland's in
Scotland for a while."

Her eyes flicked to a string of icons along the top of
the screen. "No, we don't have time."

"We don't?"

"This password automatically changes once a week.
It's set to change at eight o'clock tomorrow night. We'll
be logged out and we won't be able to get back in."

"You can't change that?"

She tapped on the laptop casing. "Not without sending an alert. And I can't disable the alerts without the
system sending an alert that they've been disabled."

"Sounds like a bind."

The tapping became frantic. "Or change the email
address the alerts are sent to without it sending a confirmation to the original address."

"Okay, *now* I might need painkillers."

Her fingers stilled. "I thought you said you'd already taken some."

"I said '…*more* painkillers.'"

"No, you didn't."

"I…meant to." *Idiot.*

"I really hadn't thought this through. I thought once we accessed this, the solution would be obvious. Right here in front of us, like a…a…" She hovered the mouse over a folder and stilled, staring.

"Samira? What is it?"

"This folder. It's password-protected. It's the only protected folder here."

He leaned over and read the folder name. "'*Trésor.*' French for 'treasure.' Pretentious git."

"Hence the treasure chest in the game? This could be it." She clicked the folder, and stared at a password box.

"Could you try the same password as earlier?" he said, hopefully.

"If you put a password-protected folder into secure storage, would you use the same password as the storage site?"

"I wish I had something to hide that was that important."

"And if we try it and fail, it'll be flagged." She flicked to the Settings page and opened a tab. She pointed at a partial email address, three-quarters of it replaced by asterisks. "This email address—it's not a government one. It's a private server. Has to belong to Hyland—a personal address."

"Can you break into it?"

"Possibly." She flicked back to the files. "His contact book is backed up on here." She opened it, and scrolled. "This email address for his daughter, Laura—it's a web-based email, easily hacked. I could send Hyland an email that looks like it's coming from her."

"How does that help?"

"Just watch." She smiled, catching her bottom lip between her teeth.

Oh, he was watching, all right—but not the screen. This was the confident, smart Samira who lay under the anxiety and the fear and the grief. Eyes bright and narrowed, fingers scurrying over the keyboard. Like he said, he had a weakness for empowered women. For ten minutes or so, she was so immersed she didn't notice him shamelessly staring.

"Is there any point in me asking what you're doing?" he said, eventually.

"I've created a virus—well, picked one up off the net that I made a couple of years ago, and updated it—and I'm about to send Hyland an email that looks like it's come from Laura's email address. See?"

Jamie leaned over. The email was titled "Whiskey." He read aloud the body of the message: "'This one's got your name on it, Pops. What do you think?' Is that all you're saying?"

She pasted in a hyperlink. "Yep."

"What's the link?"

"She's just posted a photo of a bottle of whiskey on her social-media sites, from a store in Edinburgh that's opened especially for her. According to his itinerary, he should be at the hotel."

"Pops?"

"There's some correspondence from her saved onto his cloud server—it seems to be what she calls him in private." Samira sent the message. "When he clicks on the link it'll take him to her real social-media post about the whiskey, which will look completely harmless. But it'll be routed via the virus site, and will embed a virus onto his email on the way through. The email server will probably catch it fairly quickly but it should give me access just long enough to change the password and the backup contact info, so I can lock him out while I run this folder password through a little decoding system I created a few years ago. I've just updated that, too. Meanwhile…" She changed screens. "I've managed to hack into an add-on on the cloud server's site to temporarily disable their flagging process. It was as far into the site I could get, but it buys us time for my little password robot to hammer away at this protected folder between now and tomorrow evening. So pretty straightforward, really."

"I'm needing a lie down."

"This would be a good time. It's a waiting game now—we wait until he opens his email and springs the virus, then wait for the robot to break into the *trésor*. Let's hope he checks his email more than once a week."

"I have no idea what you just said or did, but I'm sure it was pure dead brilliant."

"*If* it works."

"You know, you don't need your four Js to make you confident. You just need a computer."

She smiled, looking at the same time hyped and relaxed, like she'd been doing hard exercise. Or having sex.

Kill the thought, caporal.

"Maybe that's my problem," she said, relaxing back into the seat. "I've been without a computer for more than a year. If this works, I can stop living this awful offline life."

He looked through the windscreen at the cityscape, the lights liquefying as rain approached. "Just awful.

Though to be fair, I'd rather be staring at the waters of the Med."

"It *is* awful," she said. "I live solely in the real world."

"You poor thing."

"Okay, I guess you don't spend much time on social media. But before all this?" She gestured blindly, as if to indicate her entire recent experience. "The internet was my life. I know switching off is supposed to be healthy and good for your brain, but do you know how lonely it is when you've lived almost your entire adult life online? Everyone I know lives in here and I can't contact them." She ran her hands reverently around the edges of the laptop screen, as if it were her own *coffre au trésor*. "My life is right in front of me and I can't access it. Can you imagine?"

"Honestly, no. I can't say I have a single online friendship. But you have real friends, right? Like, people you actually see in person—or would, if all this hadn't happened."

Her brow wrinkled. "Well, there's Charlotte and a few other friends from college and university but we're scattered around the world, so they're online relationships now even if they didn't start that way. And I have a few old school and work friends but I've moved around a lot, all my life, so they've all turned into social-media friendships, too." The screen went black as the screen saver clicked in, plunging them into darkness. "This must sound very strange to you. A guy like you must have a lot of friends—real friends."

"I wish I was the guy you think I am. You met all my friends last year."

"The soldiers in your team?" She counted on her fingers. "Flynn. Your capit—capita—?"

"*Capitaine.* Angelito. *Former capitaine.* He's retired.

Flynn's supposed to be the new *capitaine* but he's taken unpaid leave to be with Tess. And a couple of others from my commando team."

"*Awo*, the guy from Texas, and… Okoye? Was that his name—the man from Nigeria?"

Rain tapped on the roof. Jamie closed the window. "Aye. And Thor, from… Come to think of it, I have no idea where he's from. Norway or Finland or somewhere. He doesn't talk about it. He doesn't really talk at all."

"Yet he's one of your closest friends… So that's—what?—five? Plus Tess."

"I don't think I can claim Tess just yet. I hardly know her. But there is Angelito's girlfriend. I guess if we're tallying up I could claim her. I don't think she has many friends either, so…"

"Holly."

"Aye. She lives on Corsica with him and his son."

"A son? I wouldn't have picked him for a family man. He seemed kind of…fierce."

"They've opened a sailing school for tourists," he said, unable to keep the incredulity from his tone. Angelito was the last guy to settle down into such a normal existence. "Believe me, he's changed a lot in the last couple of years, since Holly…appeared."

"*Appeared?* You make it sound like she was conjured."

"The story of how they met…it's a long one. I'll tell you someday—what I know of it."

She frowned briefly at his *someday*. Yeah, like they had a future where they would sit around and share long stories over red wine. And when they were done talking she'd plant herself astride his lap, like in the car, and nibble his lower lip, and he'd grip her waist and slide her in and—

"So," she said, "five friends."

He inhaled. "Pathetic, yeah?"

"It's about three more than me—and I *am* choosing to count Tess. You must have friends here, in the UK. Childhood, med school, the hospital…?"

"You've met some of my former…acquaintances, so I think you know the answer to that."

She looked up at him, her eyes jet-black. In the course of their conversation, he'd managed to scoot across so he was leaning over her, the gearstick jamming into his thigh. "I don't get it. You're so…easy to like."

And so are you. He should shift back into his seat, reclaim a few inches of distance. He didn't have the self-control, which was his basic lifelong problem. He should show her some respect by telling her enough of the truth to warn her off. "I've done some things I regret. I've hurt people."

"Is that what you're running from?"

"I told you, I'm not running *from* anything." It was true enough, of this moment. Right now he didn't feel like going anywhere—running, walking or…tap-dancing.

"You just like the adrenaline." Her gaze dropped to his lips.

"Aye." He sounded like he'd smoked a carton of cigarettes. He cleared his throat.

"And being an emergency doctor in a big London hospital was…boring."

"Yeah."

Oh man, the fresh smell of her hair. The curve of her lips. Her vulnerability. Her brain. He had it bad for this woman. He let his right hand drift over almost of its own volition—*almost*—to find hers, and threaded their fingers together. She squeezed. He leaned down, she stretched up and their lips met, feather-soft at first, then harder, desperate, like they both knew they were stealing the moment. He released her hand and pushed his fingers into her curls, cupping her jaw. Sweet yet simmering with promise and intent. How was this happening? Did he have so little restraint that he could go straight from a feeble attempt to talk her out of her undeserved respect for him, to this?

He broke the kiss, panting, and forced himself to shuffle back to his seat. "It's not just what I've done," he said, abruptly, "but what I am."

"Which is?" she whispered, looking resolutely at her lap.

Tell her. "The kind of guy a woman like you should stay well away from." *Coward.* Pain pulsed down his wounded arm.

"Maybe you're right," she said when their breath had settled, her voice leaden. "You make me want to forget what's happened—what's happening—and escape into something beautiful. Like in France. But I can't forget. I mustn't. And it's wrong to escape."

His chest pinged. "Was that one of the reasons you pushed me away, in France?"

"You didn't seem unwilling to go."

He screwed up his face. He still felt the sting of that morning like a slap on the face. But forcing himself to leave had been the right thing to do…hadn't it? "It's not wrong to move on, Samira."

She looked up at him, hope lighting her expression.

"When you find the right guy," he added, quickly. "You don't need to forget your fiancé in order to do that. But first we need to finish this and give you the freedom to seek that happiness again."

She nodded, twisting her ring around her finger.

Her engagement ring. He shuffled over and pulled her close—an innocent hug this time. She rested her head on his chest and he buried his face in her crown. He wanted so much more of her—he wanted to dig into that bottomless mind, to explore that supple body, to draw out the passion that hummed inside her—but she wasn't ready to give it and he wasn't about to take it. Their lives were both in limbo. Her limbo would be over soon but he'd chosen his path and had no alternative. She deserved security and permanence, a stable place to rebuild her confidence and her faith in the world. The last thing she needed was to get involved with a screwup who'd lost his way, who would break her heart before it healed.

The computer dinged and lit up. Her hair brushed his face as she turned. "He's sprung the trap."

As she got busy on the computer, Jamie leaned back on the seat and closed his eyes. He cradled his arm to relieve it from the pull of gravity, which eased the burn a little. *Je ne regrette rien.* Was there ever a bigger load of bollocks? It'd be entirely fitting if the scar from his wound somehow wiped out the *ne* and the *rien*, leaving *I regret*. Five years ago the tattoo had seemed like a brilliant idea but now it only reminded him how many regrets he had. He should've followed Flynn's lead and had the bloody thing scrawled across his back where he couldn't see it.

Hell, now he was having regrets about his no-regrets tattoo. And he was clocking up more regrets with every minute he spent with Samira. He rubbed condensation from the windscreen and stared straight ahead at the rain-smudged lights. As he stared, they blurred even more…

Samira shut the laptop with a snap, jerking him from a sleep he didn't know he was having.

"Well, that's another crime to add to the list," she said. "Several crimes. Would you believe he doesn't keep a single email on his server? They get automatically archived somewhere and then deleted. Who does that?"

"Somebody with a lot to hide." Jamie grabbed a bottle of water from the back seat and drank until his dry throat eased. "So now what?"

"We crack the password. But that could take days—well, it'll take until eight o'clock tomorrow night. If it doesn't work by then we're screwed. Again. And once I set it to go, we can't stop it, or we'll have to start over. We need stable internet."

"So we find a hotel or B and B?" Brother. Just the thought was giving his body the wrong idea. *It's not going to be a repeat of France.*

She twisted, stretching her back. "I'd rather not run the risk of someone recognizing us. And we'd have to show ID, a passport, a credit card…"

"A private rental? Something we can book over the internet without anyone seeing?"

"It's nine o'clock. They can take days to arrange. We'd be better off sleeping in the car—except no Wi-Fi."

"We could break into a holiday cottage."

"God, Jamie, we've already taken so many risks."

"So what's one more? I know a place. It shouldn't be too much of a risk at this time of year—it's not the most pleasant spot in November." Well, it was no longer a pleasant spot for him year-round but if he wanted to keep her safe… "Does it matter if we're no longer in Edinburgh?"

"No. I've disabled the location alert. Is this somewhere we won't be seen by anyone?"

"Aye." He picked up his phone and loaded a holiday

rentals website. "It shouldn't be hard to find. It's a cottage beside a little loch—the only dwelling in miles."

He found it on the third site he searched. *Character charmer beside a loch. A hidden secret, owned by the same family for fifty years.* The main photo, taken from the loch in spring, showed a stone cottage beside the water, shaded by a crab-apple tree fat with pink flowers. The next photo was of the loch under a domed blue sky, the forest and hills so perfectly reflected you could turn the photo upside down and not know it. "According to the calendar, it's not booked until Christmas."

"And the family won't know?"

"They're Londoners—well, they were, when I was a kid. My parents booked it almost every summer. They said they liked the isolation but I think it was mostly because it was the cheapest holiday accommodation in the Trossachs. It's an hour and a half drive from here, maybe two hours if we have to skirt cameras, though there won't be many along this route, not once we're away from Edinburgh."

"It says the mobile coverage is patchy. There's internet?"

He swiped down. "Wi-Fi—there, see?"

"Let's do it. I'll drive. You need to rest."

He pulled his seat belt on. "I'm fine."

"Your eyes are sunken and your skin is the color of concrete. I may not be a doctor but I'm not a fool. I hope you're not one of these stubborn men who refuses to take painkillers. My father does that, too."

"Ah, a real man doesn't feel pain." Really, he should throw the fucking drugs in the trash.

"Are they not what you need? We can risk buying more."

"The kind of painkillers you get at a Boots wouldn't do shite for this."

"Is that an admission you *are* in pain?"

"It's a commentary on how we've collectively set up a social system that is built to protect ourselves from our own stupidity. Speed limits, drug restrictions, warnings on cigarette packets… All to stop the lemmings falling off the cliff, yet still they find a way to fall."

She shook her head. "Every time," she said, under her breath.

"Every time what?"

"Every time I ask you a serious question, you turn it around or compensate with abstract notions or humor."

"I compensate for everything with humor. Otherwise I'd be the dourest guy around."

"The whattest guy?"

"Dourest."

She raised her eyebrows.

"D-O-U-R-E-S-T."

"Ah, *dourest.*"

"That's what I sai—"

She'd already got out of the car. She walked around the bonnet and opened his door. "Out! I'm driving. And how is it your accent is getting stronger and we haven't spoken to a single Scottish person?"

Was it? God help them if he regressed in any other way.

TWO HOURS LATER the drizzle had given way to fog so thick Samira could be driving a submarine. She cleared her throat, louder than necessary, but in the back seat Jamie just shuffled, mumbling. She'd been holding off waking him, though she *might* have been braking a little too hard and singing along to Blondie a little too loud, in the hope he'd wake without it looking like she was spooked. But now she was spooked enough not to care.

"Jamie. Jamie!"

He moaned and rubbed his face. "Where are we?"

"No idea. I swear this road is narrower than the car. Your phone reception ran out half an hour ago, so I lost GPS. I'm using a…a real map that was in the glove compartment. On a piece of paper. I have to keep refolding it. We don't seem to be getting anywhere but I'm reasonably confident we're moving." She tapped the speedometer, which hadn't passed twenty miles per hour in thirty minutes. "And I'm eighty percent sure we're headed to this loch and not Denmark, though at one intersection I had to get out of the car and walk right up to the sign before I could read it through the fog. At least any CCTV cameras will have a hard time making out our plates—and there are very few cars silly enough to be out on the roads. I've only almost crashed into three."

"Wow, have you been saving up all those words for…" He checked his watch. "Two hours?"

That was just the beginning of her wild thoughts. The novelty of having someone to share them with hadn't worn off—and Jamie wasn't just anybody. She hurriedly adjusted the rear-vision mirror. Since she couldn't see anything through the back window, she'd angled it to him, though in the dark her imagination had been forced to fill the gaps—his lanky body flopped over the seat, his broad chest filling and emptying. She'd imagined feeling it rise and fall against her cheek— the musky warmth of his sweater, the thud-thud of his heartbeat, his arm slung around her, his hand resting on her lower back…

Those hands. Strong and rough but dexterous. A

surgeon's hands but a soldier's, too. He would nuzzle her hair like earlier, urge her face up toward his, take her lips…

Concentrate on the road.

"Just don't drive us off a bridge," he said. "Tess will think it a Hyland conspiracy."

"Trying my hardest."

"Shall I drive? Not being stubborn and chauvinistic here but I know the roads."

She happily stopped the car and scooted across to the passenger seat as he dragged himself out the rear door and in the front.

"We're close," he said, after a few minutes of driving. "The loch's just down there." He pointed along one side of the road.

"How can you tell?"

"You can't see the lights of the big old country house on the shoreline?"

"Is this a Scottish thing—some superhero power to see through fog?"

"No, I can't see shit. There was an old mile marker back there—I used to look for them along here when I was a kid."

The shadow on his jaw had darkened along with the night. It'd be deliciously rough against her skin.

She cleared her throat. "When were you last here?"

"Long time ago. Once I went to university I was far too cool to holiday with my family."

Hiding behind humor again. But hiding what? Grief? Regret? He hadn't seen his family for three years, so nostalgia was unlikely. Oh, to hack into his brain and crack the password to that vault. Plenty of people showed a fraction of their true selves to the world—she knew that better than anyone—but the fraction Jamie showed was very different from the part he hid.

Latif wasn't like that. Nothing inside was different from the outside. Even his final act—slipping away in the night—was in keeping with his nature. She'd been horrified to wake up and find him gone, of course, but that'd been her fear all along.

And there she was, comparing Latif and Jamie again. Why was it when she thought of one, the other immediately came to mind, like a word association? The ghost of Latif reminding her she'd never find anyone who understood her like he had? The specter of Jamie teasing her with a future that couldn't be? It wasn't as if Jamie were offering to fill the hole Latif had left. She could picture the kind of woman Jamie would date—fun-loving, confident, uncomplicated...

Great, now she was envious of a woman she'd just this minute conjured from her imagination.

She sighed. "Is it always this foggy here?"

"I don't remember ever seeing fog here but I've only been in summer. Think of it as a security blanket."

"Was it a nice place to come, as a kid?"

"Aye."

"Do you miss those days?"

He glanced at her with narrowed eyes, like it was a trick question. "In some ways."

She waited for him to expand but he didn't. He was all chat-chat-chat when they were talking about her. Was this how people felt when they tried to extract information from her? Charlotte had once complained that speaking to Samira was like getting dirt from a stone.

Charlotte. Guilt stabbed Samira between the ribs. Here she was, kissing Jamie—and fantasizing about much,

much more—when Charlotte was missing, Tess was in jail, her own life and freedom were at risk, and Latif was, well, still dead. Jamie was just her…bodyguard.

And what a body.

Shut *up*.

CHAPTER TWELVE

JAMIE MANEUVERED THE car along a twisting lane so narrow Samira could reach out her window and pick ferns from the bank. She guessed the expanse of mist on the other side of the road marked the lake. The *loch*. Only a vowel's difference, the way she pronounced it, but it turned a body of fresh water into an ancient and mystic organism, somehow. Of course, in Jamie's accent, the *ch* came out as a sexy, throaty growl, calling to mind his French *R*.

Ugh, did she have to get turned on by everything the guy said or did?

Eventually he pulled into a rutted driveway, the headlights sweeping over a tiny stone cottage, blinds lowered in its two small front windows like it was sleeping—windows designed to keep out the cold rather than let in the sun. A skeletal tree leaned onto one side of it, branches clawing the stone. Jamie parked out back, next to a wooden shed and an overturned tin rowboat with a faded blue stripe circling its hull. If not for that sliver of color they could have driven into a black-and-white movie.

She shivered. "This doesn't look like the picture."

"No, it's not quite how I remembered it."

Jamie stepped out and mist seeped into the car, its cold fingers prickling her cheeks. She let herself out and shut her door, the thud deadened by the thick air.

Using his phone as a flashlight, Jamie dug around a loose chunk of stone at one corner of the cottage. After a minute he held something up. "They've been hiding the key in the same spot for decades. Technically it's not breaking in now, right?"

The fog was so thick she could scoop a cupful and drink it, if it didn't remain a wary meter out of reach. Hard to imagine a happy family on summer vacation. Hard to imagine summer at all, though the thought of a night here alone with Jamie heated her up from the inside.

He unlocked a wooden door and shoved it open with a scrape. She clunked up the two stone steps and he stood aside to usher her into a living room. As he followed, the gray-white glow of his phone created more shadows than light, black shapes rearing and diving behind the furniture—a wooden table, four chairs, a sofa, a candelabra above a blackened fireplace, a kitchenette. It smelled of earth and damp and soot and firewood. Someone had brightened it up with turquoise curtains tied back beside the blinds, a pale blue-and-pink tartan throw draped over the sofa, a thick red rug on a rippled flagstone floor that might have been molded by centuries of foot traffic. Jamie shoved the door shut and laid the keys on a windowsill above the kitchen sink. As he slipped past, he touched each side of her waist. She tensed.

Two internal doors gaped, one revealing a tiny bathroom, the other a bedroom not much larger, with a bed that could generously be called a double. The only bedroom.

Not that they'd be doing much sleeping…and definitely nothing else.

"I take it you don't have a big family," she said.

"My parents took the bed, my sister curled up on the couch, I had a camp bed—we had to push the table aside to fit it in." He lowered the backpack to the floor. "My mum would light the fire even in summer because she liked the pine smell and the ambience, so we'd sleep with the doors and windows open."

"I'm struggling to imagine warmth." But she could see the charm—feel it like a tug on her heart. It wasn't a place her parents would choose. They liked five-star hotels, vibrant cities, art, museums, restaurants. "Where are they now, your family?"

"Here. Scotland." He scooted past again, briefly touching her upper arms, opened a little box attached to a wall and flicked a switch. The fridge rattled and hummed.

"Scotland" was evidently all she'd get. "Will you visit them, once this is over?"

"Maybe," he said, in an unnaturally casual tone. She reached for a light switch but he caught her wrist.

"No lights," he said. "With few leaves on the trees, it'll be visible at the country house. I'd rather not risk a neighborly knock on the door. No one at all knows we're here and we need to keep it that way. Wow, you really are cold." He took both her hands in his and held all four to his chest, frowning at the fireplace. Just him being protective, being the carer, but her breath rushed in. "I'll find some firewood. The fog and darkness will hide the smoke." He squeezed her hands and slowly let them go, as if giving her time to regain control of them.

They brought in their few remaining belongings and Samira set up the computer on the table while Jamie headed out with the wood basket. From habit, she repacked everything else, using the laptop screen as a light. She was over occupying other people's vacation spaces, though at least this time she wasn't alone with the four Js. If only it were a real vacation—the kind where you left your toothbrush out, drank red wine, played cards, laughed, rested your cheek on your man's chest and listened to his heartbeat and felt his steady breath in your hair…

The door swung open and thumped against the wall. She jumped. Jamie swept in, heaving the basket, filling the room with the tang of freshly chopped pine. He kicked the door closed. Attraction smacked into her chest like a physical force. Primal instinct? Protector *and* provider. Shouldn't she be immune to that, as a woman of the twenty-first century?

"What's that?" he said, staring at a box on the table, wrapped in gold foil. Her "present" for the fake wedding—actually the boxed-up leftovers of her home security monitoring system.

She tore off the wrapping. "It's a motion-sensor camera. I thought I'd drive ten minutes up the road and install it. It'll send an alert to the app on my phone if anyone approaches. Just in case your instinct doesn't alert us first."

"Pure dead brilliant," he said.

He lowered the basket beside the fireplace and knelt. His palm shot to the dressing on his arm. He held it for a second and tentatively rolled his shoulder back. Why deny that he was in pain? Why refuse medication? He didn't seem the type to let masculine pride shape his decisions—but then, there were mysteries in him she couldn't decipher. She swallowed. She was salivating. Hunger—for *food*. She dived into the shopping bag on the table and found more protein bars, plus bananas, dark chocolate and cashews.

"Sorry," he said, turning his head. "I didn't factor in an evening meal. And whatever became of lunch?

How about I try my luck with the trout while you fish for dirt on a certain presidential candidate?"

"You're going fishing? It's nearly midnight."

"So the fish won't be expecting it. My brain is straddling three different time zones right now. It's fishing time in one of them, I'm sure. Chances of sleep are very low."

"Me, too. And I had an overnight sleep in the car, so…"

"If I can find only pike then I'm afraid we're going hungry. My dad used to force-feed them to us." He gave a melodramatic shudder.

She sat at the table, eating cashews and staring at Jamie's broad back as he ripped newspaper and laid the fire. He seemed to take up more than his share of the room. Had he always been that muscular or was it a soldier thing?

She forced herself to focus on the laptop. Good honest—*dishonest*—work would make her forget about the way her belly filled with warmth every time she looked at his crinkly eyes or his accent rolled over her or he brushed past smelling of mint or he kissed her…

Not that they'd be kissing again. Whatever his reasons for pulling away, they were deeply buried and none of her business. She would stop obsessing about him when she started obsessing about finding this information.

Besides, who could fail to be attracted to a sexy, caring doctor? And a doctor who was also a soldier—how many boxes did that tick? Her stomach filled with bees again. In a minute it'd start buzzing.

She sensed a change in the air. He was studying her, his head tilted, lit by the blazing paper and kindling.

"What is it?" she said, her cheeks warming.

"You were staring at a black screen. Penny for the complicated string of thoughts that's tying your brain in knots."

She hurriedly touched the mouse pad, lighting the screen. "Believe me, my brain feels less knotted than it has in a year." In some parallel universe, a girl like her talking to a guy like him might add: *because of you.* She might even walk right up and kiss him. But not this girl, not in this universe. "It's just good to have someone to talk to. Anyone at all. I should get started."

"Glad to provide you with a warm body," he said, deadpan.

He stood. She pictured him assessing her with a raised eyebrow, but pretended to be absorbed in techie things. The fire popped and crackled, releasing a fresh woodsy scent.

Anyone at all? Really, Samira? It was just as graceless as she'd handled their—what did you call it? A breakup? A separation? After only one night?

In her defense, she was out of practice at human interaction. Heck, she'd never been comfortable with it. She felt him watch her a minute longer, her throat drying. He was probably wondering how he'd got stranded with such an idiot.

"Right, that should take care of itself," he said, stepping back. "Toss on a log every now and then, would you? I'll see if I can catch us some dinner. Otherwise it's going to be porridge—and I hate porridge."

"That's not very patriotic."

"Thought we'd agreed not to do stereotypes."

She laughed. She'd left out witty. A sexy, caring, *witty* soldier-doctor. Who was hurting, deep down.

Yikes.

"Pull the curtains across the blinds and it'll be safe

enough to light these." He grabbed a box of candles from the mantel, laid it on the table and left, scraping the door shut behind him. She took a smoky breath. Had he invented the fishing excuse to get some space? Or was she projecting her own escape mechanisms onto him?

She set the password cracker running. As the shell screen began scrolling with attempts, she browsed through Hyland's files. The sounds of Jamie rattling around in the shed and dragging the boat abated, leaving a ticking clock, the crackling fire and her tapping. The rest of the world had tiptoed away, leaving the two of them alone on a tiny island. Safe. How weird was that—she felt safe, even as she was doing the riskiest hack of her life? Had to be the Jamie effect. Who could fail to feel safe in his company?

The files outside the vault seemed as banal as their titles suggested. Tess would probably find dozens of stories in them but without context they meant nothing to Samira. She did keyword searches for everything and everyone she could think of related to Denniston and the Los Angeles terror attacks, and came up blank.

After half an hour, a shiver up her spine reminded her to top up the fire—and set up the camera. Away from the glare of the screen her eyes struggled to compensate for the gloom. She wandered to the window and pulled up a blind. After a minute she could make out a small lawn but not the narrow road or the lake—loch—beyond. She pushed her knuckles into the center of her back. No crack, of course. Her back was one big dull ache. All that time sitting in cars and the train seemed to have compacted her vertebrae.

As she headed for the car with her camera the silence pressed around her, save an occasional lapping from the water and the swish of her boots on damp grass. The fog had an eerie, diffuse glow, perhaps lit by a moon far above. Was it a full moon? She couldn't remember. A jetty disappeared into the loch but she couldn't see the end of it, let alone make out Jamie.

He was still gone when she returned. She fell for the allure of a shower, though with the water pressure of a dripping tap, it just left her colder. As she hurriedly dressed in jeans and a shirt, footsteps crunched outside. She flinched, her heart jump-starting. *Just Jamie.* Through the kitchen window she watched him slap something onto an outdoor bench, his face ghostly, uplit by his phone. Deep lines etched between his eyes as he gutted the catch. After a minute he rubbed his forehead with the back of his hand and stared toward the loch, remaining still for a long time. A faraway look, though he couldn't possibly see more than a few meters. He looked tired, haunted, older—not the Jamie she knew.

But which Jamie did she know?

He doesn't want to be read, so stop trying to read him. She grabbed the candles and lit them in the fire, one by one. She planted three on the candelabra and three on a plate on the table.

The door opened and Jamie strode in, ducking under the frame, sweeping cold air ahead of him. "I have fish, *mo ghràidh*!"

"More what...?"

"*Mo ghràidh.* Gaelic for 'my...'" He frowned, as if trying to remember the translation. "'...friend.' Another day here and I'll be speaking fluent Gaelic. And I don't speak Gaelic." He locked the door, the bolt clunking home. "I used actual worms for bait, which is another law broken, on top of fishing without a license—seeing as you're keeping count. In for a penny..." He crossed to the kitchen counter in a single stride and lowered a tray on it, laid with two pale pink fillets.

"Seeing as I can barely understand you now, I don't know if it'll make much difference," she said.

"You have an indecipherable accent yourself sometimes, you know."

"I do know. It's all over the place—sometimes even my parents don't understand me. Wait until I get drunk—you won't understand a word. I'll be speaking any combination of English, Amharic, Italian, Arabic, in accents that don't even exist... Who knows—maybe I'll pick up Gaelic while I'm here?"

"I'd like to see you drunk one day. We'd communicate in the secret language of drunk people."

One day. Another reference to a future they wouldn't have.

"I don't remember the last time I was drunk," she said. "Latif didn't drink alcohol and I've been alone awhile. Getting drunk alone just sounds too sad."

"Well, you're not alone now," he said, suddenly contrite, as if her isolation had been his fault. He produced a bottle of red wine from a little pantry, opened it, glugged it into a glass and handed it to her. "You know, I get that you didn't want me to stay, in France, but I would happily have come and spent time with you, if you'd..."

If she'd kept her promise to keep him in the loop? "I know you would have. I'm just not sure that would have made things any easier. I've been a little...confused."

"I was meaning platonically, but..."

But we both know it wouldn't have worked out that way?

"You miss him," he continued. "I can see that."

"Awo." She sipped the wine. "For a long time, I couldn't see past blaming him or blaming myself. Now I mostly just miss having him around. Something funny

might happen or I'll have some random thought and my first instinct is to find him or text him and tell him—and even after all this time it takes a second to remember that I can't."

A hand rested on her shoulder, cold, even through her layers of clothing. She flinched.

"Sorry, didn't mean to give you a fright. How's the hacking going?"

Jamie. It was Jamie's hand, not…

So now you're believing in ghosts?

"The program seems to be doing its thing," she said, grateful for his change of subject. She'd been staring into nothing. Into a past that no longer existed. "But it could take many hours."

He slid the plate of candles to the middle of the table, flickering shadows across the ceiling. "This is just like the eighteenth century."

"*Just* like it, apart from the laptop in the corner that's hacking away at the password of the next leader of the free world."

"Apart from that." He returned to the kitchen and stuck his head in the pantry. "And electricity and plumbing."

"And modern medicine, which I still haven't seen you take."

He planted salt and pepper shakers on the table, something flashing in his expression and fading again. A sea creature skimming the surface but not breaking through before it dived back into the deep. "And a curious lack of marching Jacobites and marauding Englishmen. Actually, the eighteenth century would have been a shite time to live in Scotland."

"I like the twenty-first century just fine. Or I will, once I get to join it again. I've been stuck in 1999 for the last year."

"Ah, 1999. I envy 1999. I'd be happy to have a do-over of the twenty-first century."

"For you or the world?"

"Both."

"What would you have done differ—?"

"I smell like a dead fish," he said, clapping his hands together. "Would you mind heating up a frypan while I clean up, super quick?"

As the shower trickled in the next room, she found a pan and a tin of cooking oil. People must have stood in the same spot for centuries, preparing food. If she blocked out the glow from the laptop, she could imagine herself transported back in time, with a white-legged kilt-clad husband and countless wild children with shaggy hair. Cut off from the world. An introvert's paradise.

And now she was imagining Jamie dirtied up and wearing a kilt. A Jamie who was currently naked, only a few meters away. They were alone, in a small space, not fleeing, not disguised. Her stomach knotted. They could live here for weeks.

The shower shut off, and the curtain rattled. If she were more courageous, she'd push open the bathroom door, sidle up behind him and slip her hands under his towel. He would turn and catch her cheeks, angle her head up for a kiss…

She closed her eyes, welcoming the desire skating up from her toes to her belly. She could enjoy that feeling, even if she didn't act on it.

"Samira—are you okay?"

Her eyes snapped open. He was standing right beside her. *"Dehnanay."* She swallowed. "Fine."

"You were miles away." He was sensationally bare-chested, a towel wrapped around his waist, just as she'd pictured. Yep, he'd look good in a kilt.

"Just…thinking," she said.

"Don't be scared to share your thoughts with me."

Oh, not these thoughts.

"You don't need to carry all this weight alone, you know. Talking can help."

She nodded, abruptly. Lucky she didn't have the courage to say *How about a quickie on the dining table, just to get it out of my system?*

But maybe she *could* strike up the courage to speak her mind. "Indeed it can, Jamie."

He tipped his head, with a trace of a curious grin.

"We're a terrible couple of people to be stuck together, you and I," she said. "A woman who struggles to express her thoughts and a man who makes a determined effort to bury his."

"I don't bur—" His wet, clumped eyelashes flickered as he looked away. "I'd better get dressed."

He shut himself into the bedroom. She sat on the couch, swiveled her legs onto it and leaned backward over the arm. No crack. Goddamn.

The door opened. "Oh hel-lo," Jamie said, walking in, dressed as before. She lurched back up and stretched her neck side to side.

"You do that a lot," he said. "Stiff back?"

"*Awo.* I just can't seem to find the right stretch. The least of my problems."

"But easily solved. You want me to crack it for you? I'm pretty good at that."

Oh yes. And oh, no.

"Come here," he said, holding out his hand.

She stared at the hand. Saying no would be more awkward than saying yes, right? And the idea of getting that crack… She let him pull her up, and he wrapped his arms around her. Unsure what to do with her hands, she rested them on his arms. He pulled tight across her back. No crack.

"Samira, you've got to relax. You're as stiff as a corpse. Breathe in with me."

He filled his chest. She copied, her own breath shaky, her breasts pushing against him, creating the polar opposite of a relaxing effect.

"Now, exhale," he whispered.

Halfway through her exhalation, he pulled tight. A series of cracks ran up her back like corn popping.

"Oh my God," she said.

"Wow," he said, releasing her but not moving back. "That's been building awhile."

She slid her hands off his arms. "Thank you."

"Med school has to be good for something, right?"

She felt taller, lighter, at risk of floating away on the euphoria of relief…and something else. His Adam's apple moved, drawing her eye to his throat. His eyes darkened, he touched her elbow and his warm breath brushed her forehead.

No. Enough of this torture. She turned, abruptly. "I'd better…check on the computer."

"Aye," he said, with a start. "I'd better… The fire needs wood. And the trout…"

As he took over in the kitchen, she idly looked through Hyland's files, her chest slumping. She'd been so sure when she'd got onto the site at Edinburgh that she'd find the dirt Tess needed, and the world would magically return to its normal axis. What if the vault contained nothing either? But Charlotte's message… Perhaps Charlotte had tried to hack in but couldn't. But with the security alert she couldn't have got into Hyland's account at all from London—or Paris. So how did she even know the vault was there? From this Erebus person?

"Dinner's ready," Jamie said quietly, as if hesitant to interrupt her thoughts. "It's pretty simple."

She moved the electronic equipment to the sofa, put Jamie's cell phone on charge and returned to the dining chair, sipping wine as he set the table and sat across from her. His lanky frame made the chair look like a child's. She needed something else to focus on, something that wasn't the files or her attraction to Jamie.

She took a breath. "Tell me about your family, Jamie. What happened?"

His lips parted. Panic flashed through his eyes and vanished.

"And don't brush it off with a joke," she added.

He took a forkful of fish and chewed.

"I happened," he said, eventually, the words directed at the trout.

Silence.

"Tell me the story."

"You don't want to hear it."

"You'd be surprised how much I want to hear it. I'm guessing they weren't happy when you enlisted."

"Why would you say that?"

"Come on—their doctor son going off to fight another country's wars?"

He smoothed an index finger across an eyebrow, like he had a headache. A bird cried as it passed over the cottage.

"I can see how heavy those secrets are, Jamie. And believe me, I'm good at keeping secrets."

"I wouldn't know where to start."

"You're not making jokes anymore, so that's already a start."

"You don't like my jokes?"

"Spoke too soon."

"Aye," he said, eventually, chasing food around with his fork. "My folks weren't impressed." She could almost hear the emphatic period at the end of his words.

"Yes, and...?"

He smiled slightly, and a ticking noise escaped his throat. Recognizing defeat when he saw it? "I was their great hope. The idea that a child of theirs could grow up to be a doctor... They weren't wealthy, they weren't able to make much of their own lives, but they loved the idea that future generations of Armstrongs would have all the opportunities they didn't have, without the struggles to pay the bills."

"And you haven't talked to them in three years?"

He shook his head. "Nor the two before that. I send almost all my miserable pay packet home and get the occasional cranky one-line email from my sister, but... yeah."

"Was it your choice to break off communication or theirs?"

He swirled the water in the glass like it was wine. "Mutual, I guess. They didn't try to contact me, either."

"It's probably not too late."

"My father died, three years ago. Heart failure. I came back for the funeral—the only time I've returned since I signed up. Before now."

"I'm so sorry, Jamie."

"I literally broke his heart." His voice wavered. "Caused him so much stress. Not to mention, if I'd been there or was at least visiting regularly, I might have realized how bad his health was getting... He was a typical man of his generation—ignored the warning signs until it was too late."

"And your mother...?"

"Dementia. She's in a home. Another thing I should have been there to see, to help with, but it's all too late. I fucked everything up and there's no undo button."

She laid her fork on the table. "That's why it's so hard for you to be here."

A twitch in the muscles between his eyes. "I never said it was hard."

"Sometimes I catch a glimpse of your thoughts, when you're not looking, not hiding them."

His tongue played with his bottom teeth. "Like I say, under all the joking around I'm a pretty dour guy."

"The dourest," she said, in an exaggerated Scottish accent.

"What language are you up to now? Is this the wild woman who speaks in four languages?" He reached over and topped up her glass. Back to his usual level of superficial flirting but that was okay. Small steps. "Well," he said, lifting his water, "here's to 1999."

"To 1999." She clinked, smiling. "You're not drinking?"

"Wine isn't my thing."

"But we drank it in France."

"I had a sip or two but I mostly bought it for you. You don't want it?" he said, nodding at the bottle.

"A little late to ask, isn't it? I don't want all of it."

He smiled, pain still heavy in his eyes, and pushed the bottle across the table. "I'll let you fill your own glass."

She'd hardly tasted the wine, hardly noticed herself drinking or Jamie refilling it, but she felt it warming and relaxing her—not that she could blame the alcohol for every part that was heating up. She pushed her glass away. Tempting as that path was, she had to stay sharp.

"Do you not drink at all?" she said.

"Never."

"Because you might reveal something about yourself?"

His mouth twitched. "Because I like to be in control."

"Me, too. But I like to escape, as well."

He swirled his water again and watched it settle. "So when you say you can glimpse my thoughts…?"

Maybe it was the wine but she felt bold enough to answer truthfully. "Sometimes there's this flicker of something in your expression but it's gone so quickly that at first I wondered if I was imagining it. But I've seen it a lot now and I know I'm not."

He tilted his head, his eyes glinting in the firelight. "And here's me thinking I was the one being all clever and figuring *you* out."

"You've been trying to figure me out?"

"I have."

"And what have you figured out?"

"Ah." He laughed, rubbed his chin with a scratching sound and leaned back in his chair, his eyes locked on hers. "That would be giving away my advantage."

"What advantage?"

"Good question."

"Go on," she said, intrigue pulling at her. "I gave away my advantage."

"Well… I know that smart humor makes you smile— or laugh, if I'm lucky—but it has to be sophisticated, not dirty or cruel."

"Okay, I'll give you that one."

He righted his chair with a clatter and leaned in, as if he were reading her thoughts in her pupils. "Talk of faraway places makes your eyes sparkle. Injustice and bigotry make them narrow. The past makes them sad."

He spoke slowly, dropping his voice to a deep roll as mesmerizing as his narrowed eyes. "Even after the crap the world has dished you, you still passionately want to believe that it's a good place, full of good people who can be trusted. When something happens to throw that perception, it unsettles you. And right now you're feeling mightily unsettled. You want to be able to trust people but there are so few you're certain of."

She swallowed. All this time she'd been trying to dig under his facade, and he'd been tapping her mind like a brain scan. How much of it was the truth?

He didn't move, his gaze and voice keeping her locked in place. "I also know there's a battle constantly raging in you, like that permanent storm on Jupiter. You're terrified and you want to hide from all this but you also desperately want to protect your friends, and see justice done for your fiancé and secure your own safety."

"I…" Her throat dried. She broke eye contact and sipped the wine. She'd expected this to be one of his flippant exchanges.

"Your instinct is to hide from a world you don't always understand—I'm guessing that started way before all this. That's why you like to interact from behind a computer screen, why you claim to not have many friends, why you've survived a year alone in hiding when it'd drive other people mad. Fear has kept you alive this past year or two. But now you've got to push through that fear, come out of that protective shell— and you already have, to get this far—and that scares you even more. You're feeling like you've waded in too deep, you're unanchored."

The flames flickered in her wineglass. And she'd

thought a man like him could never understand a woman like her. Had anyone bothered to look that deep before?

Don't bring Latif into this.

He pushed his plate away and linked his hands on the table. "Am I right, Samira?"

A candle flared. Ghoulish shadows fluttered around the walls. "On almost everything, though some of these things I didn't know about myself. I'll have to have a think about them."

"Of course. That's another thing—you think very deeply but you like to take your time over it." As his voice quietened and lowered, it developed a velvety warmth, like the wine and the fire. "You said 'almost everything.' Did I get something wrong?"

"Only one thing." She forced herself to meet his gaze. "I don't feel unanchored."

A bemused half smile, half frown settled on his face.

"I hadn't realized it until you said it," she said. "But I don't, not now, not for the first time in more than a year. You make a very good anchor."

"Because I'm dull and stubborn and a dead weight?"

She laughed. "Because you make me laugh when it's the last thing I feel like doing but probably the very thing I need. And you take the time to understand me. And you make me feel confident and safe. I don't remember the last time I felt that—well, I do, but…" *But I'm not going to think about that, not with the situation re-created in another borrowed cottage, in another country.*

Too late.

His smile won out over the frown but it wasn't the cheeky grin he usually brushed her off with. It was wide and gentle and thoughtful and it made her chest ache. "Good. I'm glad. We'll get through this, Samira—but first you need to eat. I froze my arse off catching that trout."

Yes. She'd hardly touched her meal. They finished eating in silence but not the suffocating kind she'd become accustomed to. A silence interrupted by the presence of another person—a warm body but a buoyant presence, too, despite his self-proclaimed dourness—his clothes rubbing as he shifted in his seat, the clatter of more than one set of cutlery, and, if she held her own breath and listened carefully, his breath, calm and steady.

When she'd finished, she pushed out her chair and stood. She waited half a minute for him to chase his last mouthful around before collecting both plates. As she passed, she caught her foot on the rug and wobbled, juggling her armload.

"Whoa," he said, leaping up. He reached around from behind, scooped the plates from her arms and dumped them on the kitchen counter. "I'm sorry. I shouldn't have refilled your glass without you noticing. I wasn't thinking."

She turned. Her nose was inches from his collarbone. A soapy scent drifted from his neck. "Oh, it wasn't..." *The wine?* Then how was she supposed to explain her unsteadiness? This fluttery sensation in her chest, her belly—it was the same feeling she'd dismissed a year ago as a reaction to the stress. Was it still that?

"You know, Samira, your speech doesn't give much away but your eyes do." He touched her cheek with two fingers. Her mouth opened. "So does your skin." His fingers glided down her jaw, her neck, following her tiny gold cross to where it rested between her collarbones. "Your breath."

He stepped closer. With the counter behind her she

couldn't retreat. And she didn't want to. He traced his fingers back up her throat to her chin, coaxing her to meet his eyes. Crinkled and intent, like she knew they'd be.

"There's this thing between us," he croaked, "and it's not going away."

"There is," she said, the words forceful with relief. "But you say that like you want it to go away."

"Only because I don't want to hurt you. I don't want you having regrets afterward, like in France. God, I felt like such a jerk."

"No, I was the jerk. I handled it badly. Sometimes… I'm not good at expressing myself. That day…" She winced. "I may have been a little forthright."

He chuckled. "Aye, you were certainly that."

"Regret upon regret."

"Me, too."

She tilted her head, in a question.

"I regret leading you where you weren't ready to go," he said. "But I also hate myself for walking away. I should have gone AWOL and—"

"Thrown away your life for someone you'd just met?"

"Well, when you say it like that… But you didn't feel like just anyone. You still don't. And that's half the problem."

"I know what you mean."

The crinkles deepened. "Samira, you sound scared. You know I wouldn't deliberately do anything to hurt you. Which is why I can't—"

"I'm not scared of you. I'm scared of a lot of things but not you. I'm kind of scared of…"

He waited, smiling, like he had all night. The firelight picked up yellow flecks in his eyes. He'd given her the invitation. She just needed to lean forward a fraction, tiptoe and…

"I'm scared of the way I feel right now," she said hurriedly, clinging with both hands to the top of the counter behind her back. "I'm scared that it's not real. But worse than that, I'm scared it is real." She puffed out a breath. "That all sounded a lot more logical in my head. I've spent so much time alone… Is this crazy?"

"The whole situation's crazy but that's not your doing. There's one thing in all of this that makes complete sense to me. Possibly the only thing. And that's you and me. I know we're very different but if you're feeling even half what I'm feeling for you…"

"*Awo*. Possibly even double what you're feeling because…this…"

"But, Samira, it can only be temporary. I'll be returning to the Legion once all this is over, and…" He paused, swallowed. "I probably won't see you again."

"I understand. I'm not in a place to commit to anything either." *As much as I might want to.*

"This is not the wine talking?"

"It may be the wine that's allowing me to do the talking but, believe me, this is all my words, my feelings. You're right—I just want to run away and hide from all this and I can't and that's making me so… But maybe just for a little while, just for tonight, I can forget. It seems like a good idea, yes?"

He laughed. "*It seems like a good idea*… I love your thought process—the little I can understand of it."

Her lips throbbed. She didn't know lips could throb. *Just one tiptoe, Samira. He's waiting for you. He wants you and you want him and that's okay.*

He slid one hand to her hip. Oh God, just that touch. She was turning to jelly. She forced herself to release the counter. Had she ever wanted anything more, wanted anyone more?

Latif. Had she ever wanted Latif this much? She froze, her arms stuck by her sides. Maybe she just couldn't remember the early days of their relationship or she'd been too young to recognize the feelings beyond the pure physical reaction. Maybe it was normal to have such a strong attraction at the beginning of a relationship—the anticipation, the buildup. Maybe her body remembered Jamie, knew what was coming. And maybe it was normal that the attraction would one day wear off, that sex would settle into enjoyable but no longer mind-blowing, the connection would settle into comfort but no longer spark. No longer *this*. Was that why people cheated in relationships, to get this feeling—the breathlessness, the delicious bubbling in her belly, the aching heat between her legs?

It's not cheating when he's dead, Samira. You're not betraying him. You're moving on. Well, not even moving on because this thing with Jamie is going nowhere beyond this cottage.

"Shite, Samira, stop thinking."

"Sorry, I'm—"

A thump, outside. He clamped his hands on her upper arms, listening. Scuffling, footsteps. Oh God. He pulled away. His hand went for his hip—he was wearing his holster, in here? He snatched the fish knife from the kitchen counter, the blade glinting.

"Hide, Samira," he hissed. He strode to the backpack and pulled something out. He pressed his back against the stone wall beside the nearest window, pushed the curtain aside and peered out through the gap between window and blind.

Hide? Where? As he went window to window, she

crept into the bedroom. The bed went almost wall to wall. There was no closet but the stone walls were thick. She squeezed in behind the bed.

In the living room, a click, a scrape, a swish. Jamie was climbing out a window? Outside, multiple footfalls clomped on damp earth. Had her camera trap failed? Was it Hyland's goons? The police? What if they killed Jamie? Should she try to sneak out, too?

Her chest pinched. She pressed her hand to it. A few minutes ago she hadn't thought it possible for her heart to beat any faster.

Jamie, be okay.

Come back to me.

CHAPTER THIRTEEN

THE COLD FOLDED around Jamie. His breath puffed out in front of him. The noise had come from the northeast, near their car. He stole across the wet grass of the front yard and crouched beside an unruly line of shrubs that'd once been a hedge. All was still, as if the fog were clamping everything in place.

He laid the fishing knife on the grass and opened the first-aid box, wincing at the click. He quickly loaded a sedative into a syringe. The quieter the weapon, the more chance of taking down any goons one by one, without gunshots to give him away or attract police—assuming they weren't already here. The fog was perfect cover for a silent ambush.

Something stirred on the loch. Water swished and lapped at the stony beach. A bird? His shoulder hurt like fuck.

He began a creeping perimeter check. As he rounded the backyard, he caught movement and ducked into moon shadow beneath a tree canopy. Beside the car, a deer raised its head and froze. Its ears flicked.

A fucking deer. *Merde.*

He'd been a soldier too long, on edge too long. Hell, when had he not been on edge? The cold seeped from the grass into the bones of his feet. A duck called as it flew overhead, like a hyena's squawking laugh. Eventually, the doe ambled off.

Jamie stayed hidden, though the deer would have bolted if there were people out here. He itched to reassure Samira. He forced himself to wait. A panic attack was recoverable. Failing to detect a threat was not.

Ah, Samira. The longer he spent with her the more he liked her, the more he wanted her, the harder it was to pull back. So much going on behind those deep brown eyes. Not a person you could know on first sight—or even after years—but the kind who revealed herself slowly, each layer more alluring than the last, until you were buried deep.

There was indeed a thing between them but he remembered all too well where acting on it had got them. If he hadn't kissed her by the river, maybe he wouldn't have scared her off, maybe he could have been there for her in the past year. And if he hadn't been so eager to run when she'd pushed him away…?

Wait—if you had two one-night stands with the same woman, did they still count as one-night stands?

Just the kind of real-life dilemma he'd been merrily avoiding. He hadn't allowed himself to miss normal life. He'd kept his body busy with work or training, his mind full of tactics and strategies and medicine. But Samira—she reminded him of that other dimension, of the magic of exploring a deeper connection with a woman who lit you up. She reminded him that you could truly bond with somebody only if you took the risk of laying your soul bare.

And no way was he doing that. Which only made him feel like he was deceiving her, all over again.

Far away a stag roared, a pained bleat that echoed around the bald hills above the tree line. The loch and cottage had changed so little he could be on a trip back in time. Any minute his mother would throw open the door and bellow for him and Nicole, her voice echoing like the stag's. No dinner bell needed in the Armstrong family. They'd hear it wherever they were—launching themselves into the loch from the frayed rope swing, fighting epic battles in the ruins of the castle on the hill (or suffering through Regency balls, if it was Nicole's turn to choose the game), spying on the posh holiday-makers around the loch at the country house.

He and Nicole would take turns rowing out with their dad to help him fish—as kids they fought over who got to go, as teens they fought to stay behind. In those later years, they'd moan about having to go to the loch at all but for him that was just for appearances. Here, his parents stopped worrying about work and money, stopped talking about his exams and football development squads and piano recitals. He no longer needed to be the best to make them happy.

He'd sure freed himself from that pressure.

You said impressive. *Like you're doing it to get approval.*

Hell, maybe approval had been his first addiction, the first indication that something was wrong in his programming. Maybe his drug back then had been attention and acceptance, which had worsened as he got older, his gut heaving with that endless spiral of craving and risk and reward, churning up to tornado forces. And once a tornado had started, nothing known to science could stop it.

Shite. Reality and regret. Were there two bigger passion killers?

His head ached, like the cold was shrinking it. He rolled the syringe in his hand. How good would just a small dose be? A wee reprieve from the pain, the memories, the failures and betrayals.

Was that why he wanted Samira so badly? He wanted an anesthetic; she wanted an escape. She wanted to forget the immediate future; he wanted to forget the past. And he'd like to give her that reprieve as much as he'd like to take it. The idea of spending even one night peeling off her layers… He blew out a foggy breath and stood, rubbing his quads.

After one last check, he banged on the door. "Just a deer," he shouted. "Nothing to worry about."

Silence. Maybe she'd gone to sleep. That would solve the dilemma of what to do next. He could sleep in the car.

Quick scuffling footfalls, and the door opened.

"You were gone a long time," she said, stepping back into the shadows.

"Needed to be sure." He laid the syringe and gun and knife on the counter and bolted the door. Suddenly he had…butterflies in his stomach. *So* not manly. His body was going all-out fight-or-flight—adrenaline releasing, pulse soaring, blood racing to the limbs and brain and lungs. Digestion slowing, blood vessels constricting in his gut, his stomach's sensory nerves complaining about the shortage of blood and oxygen. As if *she* were a greater threat than the goons. He turned, rubbing his hands together. And in one sense, she was. "I'll stoke up the fire, will I?"

Fight or flight or see this through—what would it be?

As he worked, he sensed her standing behind him, as motionless as she'd been on the platform at the Gare de Blois. In the bathroom, he washed the soot from his hands. When he returned she was in the same spot, the fire and candles throwing a warm glow onto her skin and hair and dancing in her eyes. Dilated pupils—her autonomic nervous system firing up, just as his was.

"Jamie." Her voice wobbled. His butterflies turned into locusts. "I want this—us, tonight."

"You're sure?" Was *he* sure?

"This may be the only thing I am certain of right now. I'm just…" She slipped her hands in her rear jeans pockets and fixed him with a determined look, the same expression as when she'd stared at the computer screen. A woman who knew what she was seeking and just where to find it. Oh aye, *now* his blood was going to all the right places. "I just… I still feel…strange about doing this when La—"

She closed her mouth and inhaled fiercely through her nose. She was thinking about her fiancé.

And so what? She wasn't looking for a replacement, just a distraction. And Jamie could absolutely provide that. The fire crackled, its warmth building. Slowly, he walked to her, pulling up an inch short. She dropped her gaze. She had to be the one to cross the gap, this time. No doubts. She smelled fresh, like shampoo. Tentatively, she rested her hands either side of his waist. He could see the touch of her fingers on his jeans but couldn't feel it, it was that light. Their chests were heaving, like magnets trying to connect.

Cross the gap, Samira. Come to me.

He leaned in just enough to brush his lips against her silky hair. The fridge ticked and hummed. Her breath grazed his neck. Finally, her hands drifted underneath his jumper and glided up his sides. He braced for a cold touch but she circled warm palms over his pecs and around to his back, her touch growing more confident, drawing them closer but still not to the point of full body contact. In a second his dick was going to take the initiative and close the gap. *Patience.*

She stilled, her hands splayed across his back. His

shoulder throbbed. Long seconds ticked by—literally ticked, on a wall clock he hadn't noticed before. This was it—she was going to back out. *Flight wins.*

She drew her gaze up. He couldn't tell where her pupils ended and her irises began but he was pretty sure they were focused on his lips. She rose onto tiptoes, her palms pressing firm for balance. He closed his eyes and she touched her lips to his like an experiment, like she expected an electric shock.

Hell, there was electricity, all right. Finally, she leaned against him, while maintaining a touch on his lips so feathery, so tentative, it might dissolve if he as much as breathed. Enough waiting. He threaded his fingers into her hair either side of her head and deepened the kiss, ignoring the fire in his shoulder. Her mouth was as satiny against his tongue as her hair was against his skin, as her fingers were, skating across his back. Hot and yielding and holy fuck.

She tasted of the lemon salt he'd used on the fish and the velvety smoothness of the wine. She melded from give and take to give and give, her body pushing hard into his, while her groan told him all he needed to know about what was happening inside her, as it was him. Relief hit him like a hot shower, washing away his headache and the tightness in his stomach. She eased off her tiptoes and slid her hands to the sides of his waist, digging in slightly with her fingernails. Fuck. Her tongue flicked against his. Changing things up.

He coasted his hands down her neck, her collarbone, her ribs. As he explored the shape of her, she stroked up the middle of him, over his stomach and his chest, her fingers coming to rest around his neck, pressing into the skin. The kiss heated, his desire cranked. No doubts, anymore, from either of them.

He scooped his hands under her and hoisted. Her thighs gripped his waist, her heat grinding against him, and her arms encircled his neck, one skating over his wound. Fire tore down to his fingers. He gasped, waiting for the burn to pass.

She broke the kiss, jerking her arm away. "I'm sorry. I forgot."

"Seriously, it's fine." Or it would be, in a little while.

"I don't want to stop but...if you need to..."

"I don't give a fuck about my arm. I don't want to stop for anything. I want this, Samira, like you wouldn't believe."

Long eyelashes flickered shut, and open again. "I think I might believe."

He managed the few steps to the table and lowered her, taking some of the strain off his arm. Definitely a bullet fragment or shrapnel in there. Something to worry about later. She pushed up his jumper. He grabbed the bottom of it and pulled.

"Merde," he said, as his shoulder refused to lift.

"Let me." She skirted behind him and helped ease it off, followed by his T-shirt. Her lips pressed between his shoulder blades, warm and soft, as her arms closed around his chest. He spun, caught her and planted her on the table again, her hair falling, sexy and disheveled, to her shoulders.

"Fuck, I love the way you're looking at me right now," he said.

She locked her legs around his waist and drew him in tight, like she was giving his dick a preview. "How am I looking at you?"

"No fear. No doubt."

"That's because I don't feel any of those things. You're

good for me." She rubbed his arms, up and down, just shy of his wound. "I might have to keep you on."

He froze, a current shooting up his torso.

Her eyes widened. "Sorry, offhand comment. I know you can't... We can't..."

"I wish I could, Samira. I really do."

She bit her lip.

Don't ask me why, not now. She opened her mouth to speak but he sealed it with a kiss, which was a little jerky but not as bad as making promises he couldn't keep. This was an escape, nothing more, and he would lose himself in her as long and deeply as he could. He left her mouth and pressed kisses along her jawline to just below her ear. Under his lips her pulse throbbed, twice as fast as the clock ticked. With one hand he cupped her nape and dived in to kiss her throat, her hair falling over his face. She leaned her head to the side as he explored the satiny hollows with his lips and tongue. She tasted of wood smoke.

Aye, she was just the drug he needed—just so long as he ended things before he couldn't function without her.

SAMIRA GROANED AS Jamie nuzzled her throat, lighting fires down her neck, her breasts, her belly... But mostly the fire was concentrated in the spot the bulge of his jeans was pushing into. She tightened her legs around him and pressed her fingers into his back. His lean, muscular body was so different from hers. He was far broader than Latif, a body honed from serious training, not casual pavement running.

For God's sake, stop thinking about Latif. Focus on Jamie.

Jamie pulled away, eyes narrowed. "You okay?"

How the hell did he sense that?

"Yes. *Yes.* But I'm too hot. The fire, you…"

He smiled wickedly, which only hiked her temperature even more. She hadn't meant it like that but, yeah, he was hot in *every* sense… She went to unbutton her shirt.

"Let me," he said, throatily.

He trained his eyes on hers while his fingers flicked open one button, then the next, then the next, each flick ratcheting up the yearning between her legs. She wanted the pressure back. Oh God, she wanted much more. She gripped the edge of the table. She was panting like a sprinter and he wasn't even touching her. Just the nudge of his fingers on her blouse.

"Whoa," he said, stilling.

"What?" *Don't back out now.*

"This shirt. You were wearing it the last time we did this."

"Was I? You remember this?"

"You might be surprised what I remember."

"We hardly knew each other back then."

"To be fair, we've only been in each other's company another…twelve?…fifteen?…hours since."

She frowned. "It seems like so much more."

"It does."

She'd heard of people falling for someone this fast but she'd always been skeptical. It had to be just physical desire and wishful thinking, yes? But with Jamie— the way he made her feel… Oh God, she *was* falling for him. Falling in *love*?

No. That was a whole other thing. And it was illogical. This was some Neanderthal gratitude that he was protecting her, fused with a completely understandable physical desire—liquid fire racing through her body, pooling between her legs and throbbing there like a dance party. She exhaled, shakily.

He slipped his hands around her neck and pushed the shirt back. She freed the sleeves and let it fall behind her. With one finger he drew a line across her collarbone, bumping over her necklace, edging her bra strap down her shoulder, his pale irises glittering as he watched its progress. One finger—he was touching her with one finger and yet it was like he was touching all of her, and not nearly enough... Talk about illogical.

Give in, Samira. Stop trying to reason your way through it.

He traced the scalloped edge of her bra cup across the top of one breast, down her cleavage, across her other breast, and lowered the second strap. She swallowed and his gaze landed on her throat. He leaned in, tipped his head, kissed the dip at the base of her neck and ran his tongue down into her cleavage. She threw her head back with a gasp. Wow. She'd expected a quick tumble, a frantic, hurried release of this crazy tension. A few jokes. Not this. She wanted to hurry things up and slow things down, all at the same time.

His fingers found her bra clasp, fumbled, released it, his breath warm on her shoulder. She forced herself to sync with his breathing. In, out, in, out... He drew the bra off, watching the slow reveal with heavy-lidded eyes. As the support lifted away, her breasts fell, excruciatingly tight and heavy.

With a groan, he slid a hand around her neck and stepped in for a kiss, gentle but probing, coaxing her down until her spine was flat on the wood, his erection pushing into the apex of her thighs, at the edge of the tabletop. She planted her hands either side of his waist and slid them to his back, urging him closer, needing his weight on her.

But he pulled back slightly, releasing the kiss, and, with a suddenness that made her cry out, took a nipple into his mouth. His hands found the fly of her jeans. She was only vaguely aware of them loosening and being pulled away as he sucked, his tongue and teeth working together in a gentle insistence, drawing moans from the depths of her throat. He drew her panties aside and thrust his fingers into her.

"Holy shit." She bucked with the delicious shock. But, wow, she liked that pace. Slow, slow, slow…and then, boom.

He switched breasts, starting the journey of arousal over again, but this time from so much higher. As she wound her legs around his back, he hooked his fingertips, working the inside of her as his palm ground the outside. Trust a doctor to know where the G-spot was—and *just* what to do with it. No fumbling, no guesswork. This was pinpoint, clinical.

And it was working. And she needed to stop thinking about how well it was working and let it happen. She skimmed her fingers over his hair, willing conscious thought to slip away, leaving only the touchpoints of pleasure he was lighting. She had the sensation of separating from her body, floating above, watching his fingers explore, the heel of his palm grind against her, his mouth lave her breast, his teeth tug her nipple. She squeaked as a spark of desire exploded and ping-ponged through her. If that was a taste of things to come then… oh man.

His mouth left her breast and found her lips. They kissed, exploratory and impatient as his fingers maintained their relentless rhythm. Had he studied that at med school?

Shut up, Brain.

She kissed harder, closing her fingers around his neck, and he responded with a groan. His erection pushed into her belly. Oh God, she wanted that, she wanted this—she wanted all of him. Pressure built and coiled as he kissed and circled and thrust, the slide of his fingers telling her how badly she wanted more—as if she didn't already know.

She tipped over the brink, arching and thrashing and crying out. He released her lips and kissed her neck, giving her room to breathe, keeping just the right pressure as her climax detonated and bloomed, racing up and down and out, every limb, every finger, every toe. A sweet frenzied oblivion.

As she returned, she opened her eyes, panting like it was she who'd done all the work. He released her neck and stared down at her, his mouth slightly open, not with the wicked grin of earlier, nor his usual expression of amusement or concern, but something more emotional. Dead serious. Intense. The very look that had scared her off last year, that'd warned her they were skirting dangerously close to the edge of some precipice. The crackle of the fire returned, the smell of burning wood and her own desire. She felt suddenly awkward. That had gone so far beyond her expectations she couldn't recall what she'd expected. Her hands were still implanted in his neck. She couldn't think of a thing to say.

He leaned down and took her in a kiss so gentle and… loving…that something pinged in her chest. Who needed words? Finally, he lowered his body, his skin hot against hers all the way from her neck to her belly.

She broke off. "Shall we move to the bed?" she managed. "And, uh, do you have protection because I didn't even think…?"

The wicked grin again. "Aye, in my wallet. And, aye,

the bed. I want you on top. In control, doing this the way you need it until you come all over me—because I want to see that again. And feel it."

Her belly flipped. A laugh bubbled up—from shock, from embarrassment, from pure freaking joy. Even now, with his need so strong his jeans might well rip, he was empowering her, building her confidence, giving more than he was taking. *So* good for her.

God, he was everything. Everything except available. Everything except hers.

CHAPTER FOURTEEN

JAMIE WOKE TO thick darkness, the air a cold sheet over his exposed skin, one side of Samira's body grazing his. From the living room the clock ticked hollowly. He exhaled and reached for his watch on the bedside table. Pain bolted up his arm. He clutched the elbow and rolled over, picking up the watch with his other hand. Shite— only half an hour since he'd last woken. His mind and body were too overstimulated to stay asleep—pain, vigilance, Samira, the ghosts of this place.

Something about the smell here was so familiar, something undefinable. The trees and plants weren't flowering, so it couldn't be that. Wood smoke, the lingering scent of recent cooking, the stone walls, metallic and earthy. The loch, crisp and decaying at the same time. And the sounds were the same, if deadened by the approaching winter—the haunting cry of a gull, the tiny splash of fish or birds, the cottage creaking like an old man's joints.

When he'd woken here as a boy it was to the promise of a lazy day, the chatter of voices on the water, the slap of an oar—his parents sneaking out fishing, or for a chilly morning dip. His chest twisted. It seemed less like the past and more like a previous life. His father was gone, his mother might as well be, his sister had written him out of her life—understandably. *Every-*

thing's always been about you, hasn't it? she'd hissed, as he'd walked out after the funeral.

He swiveled, planted his feet on the cold floor and adjusted the blankets to cover Samira. His upper arm was hot and painful to the touch. Not a lot he could do about it now.

His parents had been so happy at the loch. Everything was okay when his parents were happy. Every time he topped exam results, won academic prizes and sports trophies, landed scholarships, his first thought would be their faces, that happiness, that pride. Their shoulders would straighten, their eyes would gleam, his mother would clap her hands together, just once, they'd make inane jokes that failed to disguise their delight. *Hope you left something for the other kids! Hope that trophy comes with a bigger house!* In his recollection they were always pleasantly surprised—even though he *always* came top of his class, *always* won everything. They credited genes or sheer talent but in truth he'd worked his skinny arse off—through school, college, med school, the hospital—because he got off on seeing that light in their eyes, that skip in their voices.

That was why he couldn't see them face-to-face after he lost his job and his future, couldn't even call on the phone. He'd posted a letter from Heathrow explaining the whole sorry story. By the time they'd received it, he was in France, incommunicado. No way could he have handled hearing the shock in their voices, seeing that light go out, seeing those shoulders slump. Better they got the news away from him, to save them trying to put up a brave front. For him, imagining their reaction was pain enough. Was still painful.

He pulled on his boxers, awkwardly with his arm a dead weight, padded out to the living room and lit the candles on the plate. The sedative was still sitting on the counter, still loaded. He stared at it until it blurred. He should empty it down the sink, remove the temptation, discard the remaining doses. He would. The fire was down to glowing embers but he could work with that. He drew the bedroom door closed so Samira didn't wake at the sound of ripping paper.

He knelt before the hearth and rubbed his face. Shite, if there was any time he could use sleep, it was now. Or he could use another round with Samira, who was still deliciously naked under the covers. *Jesus, don't go there.* She needed sleep, too. The sex had been almost too good an escape—it made the thumping return of reality harder to bear, like a hangover to make you regret a great night, a reminder of what life could have been.

He dragged the wood basket closer and got started. God, he wanted her—for more than sex, for more than a day or two. But her limbo would end when this crisis passed. His would continue—no thought about the day before or the day beyond. Living for the moment—wasn't that what you were supposed to do? He had nothing to return to the real world for. No possibility of a meaningful job, nowhere else he belonged. Samira—or any woman—would soon learn the meaning of *dour* if she took up with him. Not that she was asking.

He watched over the fire until it was away again and opened the bedroom door. In the flickering light he could just make out the shape of her. He envied her oblivion.

Oblivion. He looked at the syringe, looked back at her. Fuck it. Fuck it all. Just a moderate dose to take the edge off. It'd wear off by morning. If she woke first she'd just think he was a heavy sleeper—which was far from the truth but they wouldn't be together long enough for her to discover that. The last time they'd shared a bed neither of them had thought of sleep. They were safe, for now. If Hyland knew where they'd gone, his goons would be here by now. She needed him rested, sharp. A temporary fix. He'd be back in Corsica soon enough, away from temptation—in all forms.

A few minutes later he climbed into bed, gently pulled her into him so her back skimmed his chest, and wrapped his arms around her. She murmured. He kissed the smooth bump at the top of her spine—her C7 spinous process. He inhaled deeply, momentarily aware of his dimming thoughts, the receding pain.

Oblivion, come and get me.

SAMIRA WOKE TO a buzzing, and a tightening in her heart. Her alarm. Just her alarm. She rolled and grabbed her phone, Jamie's arm slumping off her waist. She swiped and the buzz silenced. She lay back down. Not the *A-Team*. Just time to check progress on the hack.

She listened to the rhythm of Jamie's breath, willing it to calm her. In the low glow from the fire in the living room she could just make out the contours of his face. Peaceful. The joker and flirt had slipped away and let the real Jamie through. As generous and caring in bed as he was out of it. Sex really was the ultimate expression of living for the moment. You couldn't enjoy it if you were worried about the past or the future. You had to let go of fear and doubt.

And yes, her fear and doubt were back but she seemed distanced from them, like they were less an all-consuming fire and more background noise.

It's okay to listen to your fear—just don't let it make all your decisions for you.

She levered herself up and pulled on her clothes. Somehow she'd also managed to let go of any self-consciousness about her body or whether she was doing the right things. Just like last time. But even better.

She leaned over and stroked his cheek. He didn't flinch. "Thank you," she mouthed, dipping to kiss his soft lips. They wouldn't have more than this, but that was okay.

I wish I could, Samira. I really do.

She pushed up from the bed and walked into the living room. She'd been about to ask why he couldn't when he'd kissed her. He might have let down his guard but he was still a multilayered game where you had to work at unlocking the levels to earn new insights.

As she sat down at the table, she touched the computer's mouse pad. The script terminal came up. The screen had stilled. *Successful password detected.*

Holy shit. She pressed her hands over her nose and mouth and sucked in a series of quick breaths. Using as few fingers on the keyboard as possible, she loaded Hyland's Gold Linings server and scrolled to the *Trésor* folder. She extended her right pointer finger, fisted the rest, paused a few seconds, then entered the letters and digits as deliberately and haltingly as a Ouija board. She squeezed her eyes shut a second, opened them and pressed Enter.

The loading screen came up. She was in.

She bounced on the chair and let out a suffocated squeal. Her belly twisted like a pit of snakes. The bedroom remained still and dark. She would let Jamie sleep a little longer. Maybe she'd wake him once she'd transferred the files to Tess, announce that it was all over and slide back into bed for a little…celebration.

A gold screen came up. *Progressing to authentication step two.*

No.

Please input or scan your authentication code.

She smacked her palms on the table, either side of the keyboard. He used two-factor ID for a subfolder? Most people would use two-factor ID for a site log-in, not a single folder. What was important enough to have security within security within security? Which at least backed up the theory that whatever was in the treasure chest was not for public consumption.

She pushed the chair away from the table and pressed her knuckles over her mouth. This wasn't close to being over. "Dammit."

Two-factor ID. *Something you know,* and *something you have.*

She chewed on a knuckle. *Think.* If his first factor was the password—*something you know*—the second—*something you have*—had to be a gadget he carried with him. Gold Linings issued their clients 2FA fobs that created new authentication codes every minute. Whenever the clients logged in, the site would ask for the current code. Hyland could be carrying it on his key ring or belt or watch or some other accessory. A private detective she'd once consulted for had one clipped into her bra.

Samira typed Hyland's name into an image search. And there it was, in photo after photo, clipped to his belt loop—a tiny white rectangular case. She enlarged a high-res photo and zoomed in. The Gold Linings logo.

Nausea pulsed in her stomach. She swallowed. Sixteen hours before the password changed and they lost their one window of opportunity. And the only path into the folder was attached to the waist of her number one enemy. She opened his itinerary. An enemy who was currently sleeping in the Balfour Hotel, surrounded by diplomatic service agents, as well as the personal bodyguards he took everywhere, and hotel security staff, and no doubt a floor full of lackeys and advisers, with maybe a dozen police keeping watch outside.

She flicked back to the image results and scrolled. Was it ever not on his belt? Yes, there—the White House Correspondents' Dinner. A reunion of his Special Forces team. Several inauguration balls.

She blew out her cheeks. What did they have in common?

A tuxedo. He was wearing a tuxedo.

She narrowed the search parameters. Photo after photo of him standing with one or both hands in his pockets and the tuxedo jacket artfully splayed open, like he was an Armani model. No fob. She returned to his Edinburgh itinerary. Meeting, meeting, meeting, photo, working lunch, press conference, meeting, meeting... *cocktail reception*. Dress code: black tie.

She rubbed her clammy face. The fire was dying down. She walked over and started poking at the embers, grabbing a piece of wood. Of course, it was all theoretical information. It wasn't like she could march into Hyland's hotel room and steal the thing while he was out, any more than she could walk up and rip it from his waist.

Her big heroic quest was over. There'd be no celebratory sex. Tess would remain in trouble. Charlotte would remain in danger. And Samira was stuck in the shadows permanently—well, until her "wanted" status changed to "arrested."

Her phone lit up and began a tinny tune. She stared at it, her brain taking a second to compute. *The A-Team*. She pushed out a breath. Probably just someone going to the country house.

At this hour?

She pulled up her monitoring site. Her hand shook

so much it took two attempts to access the camera feed. A white Peugeot.

"Jamie!" she yelled. "Get up! They're coming! We need to leave."

She grabbed the backpack and started shoving things in, her breath short. Their stuff was spread everywhere. What was important? Laptop. Phone. Chargers. Car key—where was the car key?

And what use was it? One road in, one road out. No movement in the bedroom. She yelled again. Warm clothes—they'd have to get out on foot, hide somewhere. Shit. This was why she always kept her belongings packed. She couldn't think and move at the same time.

She shut the laptop. On the kitchen counter, the low-battery light was blinking on Jamie's cell phone. Weird—she'd just charged it. She picked it up. The back of it was hot—the battery had been working overtime. Shit. And the GPS was on. She tried to switch it off but it was stuck. She checked the settings, wincing. It was uploading GPS data to a server in the United States. Hyland's people had to have launched a virus onto the phone, a reverse hack after she'd infiltrated his email using Jamie's Wi-Fi hot spot. Shit.

She opened the fridge door and laid it on a shelf at the back, as carefully as if it were a bomb. If Hyland's goons had control of the phone they could have an audio feed up. Since when? It'd been fine when she'd put it on charge—and the conversation had quickly turned personal after that. They hadn't discussed the hack. And the bandwidth was too low for video, thank God. She closed the door. The damage was already well done but no point in giving their pursuers further clues.

"Jamie!"

What the hell was he doing? She ran into the room, tripped and flew onto the bed, smacking onto some bony body part. Shock rattled through her. He murmured.

"Jamie, wake up!"

She jumped astride him and shook his shoulders. "Come on, Jamie. Please, we have to go."

She grabbed her cell phone, switched on the flashlight app and shone it on his face. His eyelids flickered but stayed shut. Would she have to slap hi—?

The syringe. It was on the bedside table. She grabbed it. Half-empty. It'd been full when he'd left it on the kitchen counter. She reared up and yanked the covers off. He wasn't sleeping; he was sedated. He'd drugged himself.

"Jamie, please, I need you." Her voice shook. "They're coming. We have to get out. I can't do this without you." She was sobbing, panic clutching her chest.

She leaped off the bed, grabbing at chunks of her hair, looking left and right. She couldn't carry him. She'd have to drag him. He was wearing only boxer shorts but frostbite was not the immediate threat. She ran into the living room, pulled her coat and boots on, shoved anything in the backpack she could get her hands on, unlocked the door and dumped it on the grass beyond the steps. Now for Jamie.

Inside, she pulled him into a sitting position, flopped his arms over her back and tried to heave him off the bed. He was too heavy. He skidded onto the floor, his head whacking the bedside table.

"Sorry," she squeaked. She straightened. "No, I'm not sorry. I'm not at all sorry." At this rate, he wouldn't be able to walk after she was finished with him.

The wheelchair. Oh God, the wheelchair in the trunk of the car.

A few minutes later she was bumping the chair down the stone steps onto the grass, Jamie slumped in it. He groaned.

"Oh, I'm not taking complaints from you."

The wheelchair was a bitch to pull over the long, damp grass. Not designed for off-roading. She had to get him to the car, tip him into the back seat. She couldn't drive out the way they came but she might be able to drive it a few hundred meters, hide it between a clump of trees. It was small enough. She sure wouldn't get far heaving the wheelchair.

She got to the car and flung open the back door. The interior light flicked on. The key—where had he put the key? She patted her own pocket, reflexively.

The windowsill. He'd put it on the windowsill. And the gun—was it still on the kitchen counter?

A noise. She stilled. Not a car engine. It was in the sky, getting closer. A helicopter?

Not a helicopter. It was a gnawing buzz, like a whiny lawn-mower engine. A...droning noise.

A drone? In *Scotland*?

She wasn't imagining it. It couldn't be anything else. The fog still hung thickly, so it couldn't be merely a surveillance drone. It had to be operating on GPS, going after the phone coordinates.

Forget the car—too obvious a target. Ditto the shed. Her gaze rested on the overturned dinghy, gleaming like it was trying to tell her something. The car light timed off, leaving the outline of the hull imprinted in her blown vision. She spun the wheelchair and shoved it toward the boat. The buzzing grew louder. Did drones have thermal imaging? It'd have to have something, if it was flying at night. She never did Google them. It whined closer. Shit. She should have thrown Jamie's phone into the loch, as far as she could. Too late now.

She tipped Jamie onto the grass beside the dinghy and dragged it over them, hauling him and curling up to fit between its plank seats. He moaned again.

"Jamie, wake up." How long would he be out for?

The cold from the ground washed through her like she'd dived into a fridge. And she was dressed warmly. He was nearly naked. She grappled for him in the pitch blackness, pulled him on top of her as best she could and wrapped her arms around him. His back was goose pimpled. She clung on as the drone noise became louder, more like a generator. How long until the Peugeot got here? And what would they find—two charred bodies?

All the thought and care she'd put into choosing and securing her safe houses for an entire year, and she'd let Jamie bring her here—a dead-end road. If she'd been thinking straight, thinking about safety rather than screwing him, she'd never have chosen it. She'd put too much trust in him, believed that he could look after her better than she could. What a fool.

Regret, like a tail, comes at the end. Her grandmother's words. A picture came to mind of her grandmother's guest house in Harar, Ethiopia, where Samira and Latif had hidden. It was so remote it'd felt untouchable—until Hyland's goons had killed Latif and flushed her out and forced her on a journey that was likely to end here, now.

The buzz crescendoed. Then, a whooshing sound. Her face prickled. The sound Latif had heard before he'd died?

And here she was, waiting for the end with her arms around another man. A man who had no idea he was about to die.

CHAPTER FIFTEEN

A BOOM STRUCK the ground, bucking it like an earthquake. White light flashed through the gap between the grass and the lip of the boat. Samira held her breath. Thuds, cracks, glass smashing, wood groaning. Something clanged against the hull and the air rang. Jamie flinched and tensed, muttering into her chest like he was fighting to wake. She held tight while debris hammered—clonks of giant hail, then sleet, pattering off to drizzle. The light flared and subsided, leaving a dusty glow. Silence, bar a crackling. A fire? She dared to inhale.

She tipped Jamie to one side, lifted the dinghy and peered out. The skeletal tree burned, flames and smoke swirling with the fog to create an eerie light. The cottage looked like a medieval ruin, the roof and walls caved in on one side, the bedroom flattened. Dust and smoke coated the roof of her mouth.

Jamie groaned. He needed warm clothes—but first she had to get them somewhere safe. Safer. The Peugeot was still coming, and God knew what else. More drones? She hoisted the dinghy aside, crouched over Jamie, threaded her arms under his shoulders and heaved. If she could get him to the car, maybe they'd have time to—

The car. A massive stone had smashed through the back window and the tires were shredded. Her left boot slipped and she crashed butt-first onto the grass, Jamie sprawling on top. He rolled off—by design or gravity, she couldn't tell.

She found the wheelchair embedded in a wild hedge and dragged it out, bringing half the foliage with it. Flattened. Jamie pushed up to hands and knees.

A car engine. Shit.

"Let's get to the water," she said, grabbing the boat. The hull was dented but intact. She could row him better than she could drag him, and if they could get far enough out, fog and darkness would screen them.

He crawled a few feet and collapsed. She half carried, half dragged the boat to the water and ran back. The engine grew louder. As she reached Jamie, he flailed for her like he was blind.

"I'm here," she said. "I'll help you up."

She lifted his arm across her shoulders. He arched, crying out. His bad arm. She changed sides and managed to haul him, staggering, to his feet. They limped and swayed to the water's edge and she tipped him in the boat. Hazy headlight beams tracked around the loch. A few minutes away. She hesitated for a moment, then ran for the backpack. It was dusty but intact. Jamie wouldn't survive long without clothes. She was sweating from exertion but the cold slapped her cheeks.

She shoved the boat out until the water caught it, clambered over Jamie, freed the oars from their clips and bumped down onto the seat, facing the middle of the loch.

No, that wasn't right. Rowing was a thing you did backward. She rearranged herself, angled the oars into the water and pulled. An oar missed its mark, flailing in air. The dinghy spun toward one side. She adjusted and heaved. The hull scraped on stones, and then the boat shuddered clear, tippy but afloat. At the cottage, the burning tree flared like a giant torch. The chimney wobbled and toppled into the front yard with a booming thud. She pulled, finding a rhythm, every frigid inhalation stinging her lungs.

The last time she'd rowed was in Britain, too, when her mother had rented a boat on the Serpentine in Hyde Park. This was a little different.

Jamie heaved himself up, rocking the boat.

"Keep still," she hissed.

He managed to sprawl across the rear plank seat, facedown. A finger of mist curled between the boat and the cottage. The headlights struck the smoking ruins, bumping as the car reached the rutted path. The engine strained. She hauled harder, the oars smacking into the water. Once the car pulled up she'd have to watch the noise but the goons' attention would first be focused on the cottage. Had they heard her yelling to Jamie, over the audio feed? With luck, it'd take a while to figure out whether the two of them were buried under the rubble.

Luck. Like they'd had a lot of that. Not a single thing had gone the way she'd planned. And the man who'd so far got her through all this craziness was currently semiconscious—and snoring. She pushed the toe of her boot into his thigh to shush him.

Beside the cottage, a white blur coasted into view. The engine cut out. Doors opened and closed and four shadowy figures emerged and faded into the fog and smoke. Voices carried on the slight breeze but the words were indistinct. She smoothed her movements, wincing at every plop of the oars. After another minute the misty cloak descended, enclosing her and Jamie in a bubble of fog, the only landmark a diffuse amber glow from the tree. She chanced a glance over her shoulder. Even that wobbled the boat. A yellow fuzz marked the other side of the loch—the country house? They had to have heard the explosion. Could she beg for help?

No. The house would be the first place the goons checked. Not to mention that anyone she asked for help would want to call the authorities—if they hadn't already. Could she steal another car? How would she find the key?

God, how had her life screwed up so badly that car theft seemed like a perfectly reasonable idea?

A clattering noise rose, then a hiss. She caught her breath, checking the sides of the boat. A leak? A sea snake—*loch* snake? Was there such a thing?

No, it was coming from Jamie—his teeth were chattering. How long did hypothermia take? She rowed another few minutes, secured the oars and yanked his clothes from the backpack.

He'd roused enough to at least raise his arms as she pulled layers down over his top half, and help her tug jeans over his hips, once she'd channeled his feet in. His legs felt like refrigerated legs of ham. The boat swung and settled.

"The fuck happened?" he said, too groggy to speak loudly, thank God.

She laid a hand over his mouth, letting go only after he nodded his understanding. He managed to navigate the overcoat. As she dealt with his socks and forced on his shoes, she updated him, so quietly she little more than mouthed the words. Between that and his mental state she had no idea how much he comprehended—until he clutched her hands in his cold ones and whispered, "I'm sorry, Samira. This is what I do. I fuck things up. Can't be trusted with the stuff. Thought I could resist but… I saw it there and… I fucked up."

She frowned. Couldn't be trusted with what?

Oh God, with *drugs*? Was that his big secret? A few hours earlier, his roughening appearance had been sexy—the stubble, the smile lines, the mussed hair—but now he was a disheveled wreck. Drugs. It made complete sense. The talk about addiction. His refusal to take painkillers. His regrets.

Voices drifted from shore—the country house. The lights had brightened. She felt their pull like a lure. Warmth. Civilization. A manager who would take charge, fix this.

But no one could fix it.

"Let me row," Jamie said.

"I don't even know where we're going. Not the country house. They might be there. The police might be there."

Still, she swapped places, momentarily comforted by the touch of his hands on her hips, guiding her. How illogical was that? He wasn't the capable, solid man she'd thought. Stupid thing was, he'd told her he wasn't that man but she hadn't believed it because she'd so desperately wanted a hero. She'd unlocked a level, all right, and found herself in a whole other dimension.

He went to grab the oars, then planted his elbows on his knees and his head in his hands.

"Jamie?"

"Give me a minute."

"I don't think we have a minute." Anger boiled in her belly, rose up her throat. She bit down on it, waited until it settled.

"There's a path over the hills to another loch," he murmured. "I know somebody there who…might help us."

She noted the pause. "Might?"

"There are no certainties in life."

"There certainly are not. Is this another good friend of yours?"

"No."

"Someone who owes you a favor?"

"Definitely not."

"But they'll help."

"Probably."

"Jamie..."

"Definitely. It's definitely probable." He scooped a hand into the water and splashed his face. "Fuck. Maybe we should beach and you go on ahead so I don't slow you down."

"I don't know the way. It's dark."

"It's just over...around the...through the... Fuck, you're right. I'll be okay. I'll come right in a few hours."

"It'll be dawn by then. You know their resources. We've just seen their resources—well, I did. How long until they get a helicopter up here?"

"You're right. You're right." He lurched up, grabbed the oars, took a stroke and hissed.

"Oh God, your arm."

"It's fine."

"*Don't* lie to me anymore. Don't hide things from me. You keep saying you respect me but if that were true you wouldn't shield me. I told you, it's the surprises that make me freak out and panic, not the truth."

"You didn't panic, Samira, just then. Well, no more than the average person would."

"How would you know? You weren't there—well, you were there, but..."

He exhaled heavily. "Okay, you're right. So my shoulder hurts like fuck. Feels like my arm's going to burn right off."

"That's more like it but we should stop speaking.

Move aside." She clambered over and sat heavily next to him. "I'll take one oar."

"I'm sorry, Samira. I really am."

"Eshi."

"Aye, like my arm's *eshi.*"

They settled into silence, finding a rhythm, Samira pulling her oar with both arms, and taking Jamie's lead on the navigation. He angled them to a spot on the shoreline midway between the country house and the cottage—or where she assumed the cottage was, as the burning tree was no longer visible.

They beached the dinghy and Jamie held it steady while Samira stepped out. Icy water seeped into her boots. They stashed the boat among prickly bushes. Jamie opened a hatch and pulled out a plastic bag. "Emergency kit," he said, throwing it to her. "Flares and stuff. Might be useful. Can you put it in the rucksack?"

At least his brain seemed to have been jolted back to normal operating speed. While she packed, he covered the dinghy with ferns and a springy plant.

"This way," he whispered, tightening the straps on the backpack and setting out along the pebbly shore in the direction of the country house.

"How do you know?"

He looked over his shoulder. "Instinct."

Huh. Her instinct had implored her to trust him. Luckily she hadn't left their security completely to him. If she hadn't set that camera trap… She caught up to him, wincing at the crunch under her boots.

"How the hell did Hyland get away with launching a drone in Scotland?" Jamie said. "Isn't that an act of war?"

"He's supposedly supervising a training exercise while he's up here—the US military and the British Army. Maybe something to do with that?"

"Maybe… So this two-factor authentication. Will they change the password now we've been sprung?"

"Possibly, but they can't be aware I'm in their files—they would have locked me out hours ago. They only know I accessed his email, which is separate."

"What about the websites and stuff we've been to—can they track all that now? My comms with Angelito…?"

"Highly unlikely. I used secure software. Nothing's infallible but…"

"So all we're needing is this gadget."

"You make it sound so simple. We can't get it—he carries it with him. *On* him."

"That's about as simple as it gets. Is there any other way we'll end this thing?"

"I'm going to blame the drugs because that's crazy. We can't walk up and steal it from him, right under the eyes of the diplomatic service. We'll get arrested. Or worse. Probably worse."

"You prefer to spend the rest of your short life like this? Waiting for his goons to catch up?"

"No, but—"

"While Tess rots in jail? With Charlotte in danger?"

"What the hell can I do about any of this?"

"We."

"What?"

"What can *we* do. We're still in this together. Despite…" He stopped walking, holding out his arm to stop her, too. "We go up here." He pushed past a weeping willow, then turned. "And Angelito and Holly will be in London by now. They can help. We'll tell them to get to Edinburgh on the first train."

"Great. So instead of two of us against America's

finest diplomatic service agents and Hyland's goons, it'll be four."

"You see?" He resumed walking. "Doubling our chances. And Texas shouldn't be far behind. Tripling our chances."

"An extra three people does not triple our chances."

"Texas is worth two regular people, at least."

She threw up her hands. "Jamie, stop joking. We're talking dozens of people—armed, trained, constantly on alert. Plus the Edinburgh police and possibly Scotland Yard and the British Army and US military. Your friends will take us from zero chance to zero chance."

"There you go, overthinking it again."

"Really."

"Besides, you don't know Angelito like I do. And Holly—she has a secret weapon. She *is* a secret weapon."

"What the hell does that mean?" It was an effort to keep her voice to a whisper. "Can she make herself invisible? Because that's the only thing that might help."

"No, but she is kind of a shape-shifter."

"A what?"

"You know, she can take on other forms. Well, just one other that I'm aware of. But it's the form we're needing."

"You're making no sense." The drugs. Shit, how long had he been under the influence—the whole time they'd been together? Had he taken more than just the sedative? Did that explain his bravado? She wanted to rewind their whole relationship, replay every conversation and every interaction with this new filter. How much of what she'd seen was him and how much some chemical imbalance? Had she fallen for Jamie or for some medically altered version of him?

"I can feel you thinking, Samira."

"There has to be a better way." An easier way. A more passive way. A safer way. The solution was supposed to be so neat and tidy. Online. From a distance.

"Well, you work on that. In the meantime…" He turned, caught her waist and murmured in her ear. "Silence now. I'll fill you in on the details after we lose these goons."

She looked behind, her heart jackhammering. "What goons?"

"Up on the path." He jerked his head as if he expected her to know where it was, took off the backpack and laid it on the ground. "Wait here."

She clutched his elbow. "What are you going to do? You're injured. You have no weapons."

"Ah, but I've had very extensive training. And I have the home advantage." He encircled her waist, yanked her into him and kissed her, hard. She smothered a squeak. "And now I have a wee dram of extra courage. Don't go anywhere."

Courage. Like she had any to spare. She sank to the ground, touching her lips, as he pulled something from the backpack and crept noiselessly away. How could he bounce back to flirty and charming so quickly?

Okay, so his betrayal hadn't chipped at her insane attraction for him. Which was why she was putting her mind back in charge.

He couldn't be serious about going after Hyland. She'd been surrounded by diplomatic security her whole childhood, cushioned by it, flanked by it, driven around by it, tailed by it during her parents' more volatile postings, secure in the knowledge that it was always there. And that was the Ethiopian diplomatic service, which wasn't nearly as comprehensive as its US counterpart.

There was never any mistaking when American diplomats were in town.

A rustling, in the trees above. A thud. She scooted behind a large tree trunk. The thud of a body hitting dirt? She sank to the ground, drew her legs up and hugged them, conscious of her rasping breath. Her eyes had adjusted enough to see strands of mist threading around the trees, like cobwebs from a car-sized spider.

In the distance, multiple car engines strained. Why no sirens? A cottage had just exploded.

Voices, close. A man and a woman. Tooth by tooth, she unzipped the backpack, her throat tightening. There had to be something she could use to defend herself, if she needed to. She would no longer leave everything up to Jamie. A few hours ago she'd thought him a god. A god who was hiding something but who'd seemed as infallible as the security guards that'd protected her as a child.

It was childish indeed to think anyone was infallible. But how could he take a sedative at a time like this? Unforgivable. And yet, that skip in her chest when he kissed her just now...

"Samira Desta." She swiveled, with a gasp. A man stepped out from a stand of trees a few meters away, a handgun pointed at her chest. The blond guy. "It's been quite a trip," he said. "Italy, London, here. But to be honest with you, I don't much like traveling, so if you don't mind, we'll call this your final destination."

She flattened her back against the bag, her arms behind her. "You're Irish." She didn't know what she'd expected—but that wasn't it.

"I always had you figured for a smart woman. You've eluded us awhile—must say I'm impressed. I thought you'd be a far easier target than yer man, Latif. But someone like you can't run from someone like me forever, just like he couldn't." He strolled closer, chatting like they'd known each other for years. "D'you think people will believe it if we put the word about that you were killed in a drone test gone wrong or is that too much of a coincidence? Maybe a gas canister explosion from a barbecue set by squatters. But, hey, these days, the public believe what they want to believe. What their leaders want them to believe. They think they're so well-informed but really they're more gullible than ever. No truth or lies anymore, just differing versions of the same story. But then, no one knows for sure where you are, which makes it very easy for you to disappear. Perhaps we don't need to invent a story at all. Plenty of room in this forest for a double grave. Or that lake looks deep. Two well-weighted bodies could disappear forever."

An echoing crack rang out above them. A gunshot. Oh God. Jamie's gun was…back at the cottage.

He tilted his head. "There's half the problem solved already."

No.

He pulled a phone from a pocket of his dark coat—a satellite phone, which meant a secure line. "You might have to keep me company a little longer, though. The boss'd like a quick word before you…go. He's very curious about you." He pressed a button and held it to his ear. "Oh, and he has a surprise for you."

Her eyes stung. She blinked away the moisture. Jamie couldn't be dead. She wouldn't accept that. He was too…alive. That gunshot…there had to be another explanation.

Denial. The first stage of grief.

No.

"I have her," the guy said, into the phone. He listened a second, then pulled it away from his ear, pretending to be covering the mic. "It's for you!" he said, in a stage whisper.

He threw it to her feet, keeping the gun aimed. The longer she stayed alive, the better, right? She edged a hand out and picked it up, keeping her movements slow.

"Hello?" she said huskily.

"Ms. Desta, at last." Hyland. She'd heard that voice a thousand times but never directed at her. "I'm sorry I'm not able to make your acquaintance in person but it's wonderful to be able to speak on the phone, at last. You've proven quite as problematic as your friend Ms. Newell, but I'm glad we could find a solution to our disagreement. I do apologize that it won't be advantageous to you but I'm sure we could make it work all the same."

He fell silent.

"Ms. Desta, this is when you speak." He overenunciated the *Ms.* like it was an insult.

"I don't know what you're talking about."

"Your parents... I'm told they're a lovely couple. We have a lot of friends in common, you know."

Her cheeks froze.

"You're not much of a talker, are you, Ms. Desta? But that's okay. I am. I'll talk. You'll listen. How 'bout that?"

Her breath shortened. That familiar pinch in her chest. *No.*

"I'll take that as a yes," he continued. "Now, I know and you know and they know that they haven't been involved with your subterfuge—I've had them watched very closely. But once you're revealed as the terrorist you are, it'll be very easy to implicate them."

"A terrorist?"

"Oh, we can label you anything we want—especially

someone who looks like you and comes from your part of the world. And your name sounds foreign enough for people to believe it. A cyber terrorist who got in too deep and took her own life. Oh no, wait—that's how Ms. Liu is going to die. We'll think of something more imaginative for you. We can sort out that after the fact. But there is something we need to talk through now, and that's your parents."

Her nape crawled. *Ms. Liu is going to die.* That meant Charlotte was still alive—for now. But her parents…?

"It's bad enough they're about to lose their beloved only child—something I will make a point of publicly sympathizing with, seeing as I, too, have just one precious child—but we don't want to see them also lose their freedom, do we? Well, to be honest, I don't really care, but I'm sure you do."

Her throat felt like it had closed to the thickness of a toothpick.

He sighed into the phone. "It's not easy to carry on a phone conversation when the other person doesn't say anything. But I'm going to assume you're listening. Sheltering a terrorist—that's a serious charge."

"It's a lie," Samira squeaked.

"Truth and lies are whatever I say they are. I can have your parents picked up whenever I choose. Their government will not want to be seen to be protecting them with such damning evidence on the table. But here's where your dying act of mercy comes in."

Her breath wheezed, like an asthmatic.

"Again, I shall keep on talking. Perhaps you could do me the courtesy of an *uh-huh* every now and then so I know the connection hasn't dropped out." More silence. She couldn't speak if she wanted to. He sighed again. "Maybe a video call would have been better. Then I'd be able to *see* you not talking. So here's the deal I'm prepared to offer. I know about your late fiancé. I know about Ms. Newell and her boyfriend. I know about Ms. Liu. I want the name of the other person you've been communicating with over these leaks."

Samira blinked, repeatedly. "Other person?" she gasped. Jamie? Did that mean he wasn't dead?

"Your other source in Denniston."

"Wh—what?" Her lungs deflated. Not Jamie.

"Don't play a fool. I know how smart you are. I'm a man of my word. Give me the name and I'll leave your parents to their grief."

"Honestly, I don't know who y—" She straightened. The other person in the game?

"A. Name."

"I swear I don't know who you're talking about. You must understand—I was dragged into this. It wasn't of my choosing. I'm not central to any of it."

"You were preparing to testify against me. Yesterday, you hacked into my email. That doesn't sound like someone who is not central."

You hacked into my email. So he *didn't* know about the files? Not that it mattered now.

A rustling came over the phone, as if he were changing ears. "Listen, I have a busy day tomorrow, I'm jet-lagged and I want to get back to sleep. You know what I do when I need an answer quickly?" Silence. "Well, let me tell you. It's an old father trick. I simply count down from ten. If I get to zero and you haven't given me a name, I'm hanging up. At that point, my good friend Fitz there will execute you, and your parents will find themselves in orange jumpsuits with hoods over their heads and shackles on their feet. Your choice. Ten, nine—"

"I'm not lying. I really have no—"

"Eight, seven, six…"

"I don't know who you're talking—"

"Five, four, three…"

"You have to believe me. I don't—"

"Two, one… A name, now."

"I can't! I don't know who—"

The phone beeped. She pulled it from her ear. Call ended, the screen read.

The blond guy—*my friend Fitz*—stepped forward. "Ooh, that didn't sound like it went so well, Samira. Never mind, my dear. I'm about to liberate you from your many worries. Safe travels, now."

He raised the gun.

CHAPTER SIXTEEN

SAMIRA PULLED HER hands from behind her back. She fumbled with the flare in her sweaty grip and yanked the toggle at the tail end, bracing. It cracked and whooshed off, the recoil slamming her spine into the trunk. Fitz stumbled sideways. It arced past him, whacked into a tree and spun, fizzing, into bushes. Damn.

He staggered forward, recovering the hold on his gun. A steely expression rolled down his face as he raised it once more. Samira dived to one side, just as something moved on a low ridge behind him—something *flew*. A man, leaping for Fitz with a guttural roar. As Fitz looked up, the guy smashed an elbow between his eyes. Fitz crumpled.

Samira scrambled back. Jamie landed on the earth in front of her, one side of him lit orange by the flare's pulsing glow. She pressed her hand to her chest. It thumped like a drum. Jamie. She knew it. She knew he wasn't dead.

"Nice move, Samira. Of course, I was a second from taking him out all by myself, but I'll let you share the glory."

"Oh my God, is he dead?"

Jamie nudged Fitz's arm with his shoe. "Just out cold. I did once take a Hippocratic oath in his country, you know. And here's me thinking you'd ask how *I'm* doing rather than the guy who just tried to kill you."

"You knocked him out. I thought that just happened in the movies."

"It's not as easy to do as in the movies. But like I say, I had extensive training."

"I thought you were referring to the military."

"It's handy to have more than one skill set. What's really hard is that Spock Vulcan thing." He pulled a sealed packet from a coat pocket and ripped it open. A syringe. "We spent many a quiet shift at the hospital working on that." He opened another packet—a vial— loaded it into the syringe and strode back to Fitz.

She looked away as he knelt by the prone man. "Is *that* covered by your oath?"

"The oath's really only symbolic. This'll buy us a few hours. The other three have also decided to have a wee nap."

"You took out three men with your bare hands?"

"Don't be sexist. One was a woman." She sensed him standing, and warily looked up. "You see, Samira," he said, scuffling through the undergrowth and stomping on the remains of the flare, "the thing with a narrow path through a forest—it forces a team into single file. And the thing with walking single file along an unfamiliar steep, narrow path at night, without flashlights, while searching for an enemy—it doesn't take much for the last man—or woman—to fall behind. Like, say, getting distracted by a snapping twig. And once the guy at the back disappears, the others come after him, and it rapidly goes downhill in a *Blair Witch* kind of way."

Wow, he'd sure fired up. *Natural* adrenaline, she hoped. "I heard a gunshot."

"It missed."

"I knew you couldn't be dead."

He strode back, pulling two handguns from his coat and examining them. "Listening to your instinct, are you?"

"It wasn't instinct. It was hope." She nodded at the weapons. "Did you take those from the goons? Why didn't you use one on Fitz?"

"Fitz?"

"We had a little time to get acquainted."

"When did you get so bloodthirsty? That was plan B. I didn't want to attract more attention than we already have. They have others out there." He held out a hand and pulled her up. "You okay?"

"Fine."

He held her hand a second longer than necessary. She waited for him to pull her in and kiss her, but he let go, his expression dark.

"It's good being *fine* all the time, isn't it?" he said.

She dusted her coat as he emptied his pockets into the backpack. She really wasn't dressed for trekking through the forest. "I heard other cars," she said.

"Going by the chatter of those three before I sprang them, we can count on another two carloads. Between the gunshot and the flare, we'd better get going. Shall we take his sat phone? I couldn't find any phones on those other goons."

"Too easily tracked. We'll disable it and toss it. Jamie... I spoke to Hyland on that phone."

"Just now? Bloody hell."

"He's going after my parents." She related the details as she stripped the phone.

"Well, then," Jamie said, pulling on the backpack. "We'd better go and get this thingamajig from him before that happens." He started walking, then stopped and turned. "You coming?"

She set her jaw. Tess, Charlotte and now her parents…
What choice did she have?

THEY CLIMBED THE hill behind the loch, emerging from
the misty basin onto bare rocky terrain under stars and
a fat moon. Jamie breathed in cool, dry air. Of all the
corners of the world he'd traveled to, that smell—mossy,
woody, herby—belonged only here. Ahead, just above
the summit's smooth lip, jutted the crumbling battle-
ments and keep of the old castle.

He checked his wrist for the time, but of course, his
watch was back at the cottage, destroyed along with
any remaining self-respect—and Samira's respect. Any
questions he might've had about his ability to withstand
temptation had been emphatically answered. He fisted
and stretched the fingers of his injured arm. Pain pulsed
down to his nail beds.

"Are you okay to jog?" he said to Samira, beside him.
"I'll feel a lot better when we're in the next valley, back
under tree cover."

"Is that where your friend lives?"

"No, we've got to walk a little further, to the next
loch. That okay?"

"Eshi."

He set a steady pace, the rucksack bouncing on his
back. She'd fallen quiet once they'd set out. What was
there to say? Was she so disgusted that she regretted
sleeping with him? But, hey, it was probably healthy
that she saw him for what he was, however much it
hurt his pride.

Of course, now he owed her his life, and was very
nearly responsible for ending hers. Not how this ar-
rangement was meant to work. So much for being addicted to her approval—she sure as shit wouldn't be

looking at him in the way she had before. Aye, like all addictions, it eventually spun round and kicked him in the balls.

A distant thudding rose up. He swore.

"Helicopter?" Samira said, looking around.

"Aye. Run faster. Can you see those ruins up ahead?"

"I see a pile of rocks…?"

"That's them—we'll shelter there and check what it's up to. From there we can sprint up and over the hill and back into the forest." If it was the same high-spec bird that'd chased them through London, he could assume it had thermal.

Its silhouette rose over the hills on the far side of the loch. Yep, the MH-6, a good five miles away, so out of thermal range for now. He grabbed Samira's hand and upped the pace. The crew would be wondering how they'd lost communication with their advance ground team. With the fog, the chopper wouldn't mess around searching the loch and forest. They'd sweep across exposed higher ground.

"They'll have the last GPS coordinates from the sat phone," Samira hissed.

"Aye, that'll be their starting point. An hour or so old but it gives them parameters."

The terrain steepened on approach of the castle. Jamie's eyes and feet worked hard to sidestep strewn rocks. A twisted ankle could prove fatal.

"I can't see much cover in those ruins," Samira said, panting.

"The keep is mostly intact. It's a little obvious but there's enough of a roof to hide us, so long as they don't winch anybody down."

"Or just open fire and bring it down on our heads."

"Well, aye, but let's be optimistic."

They were properly climbing now. They passed a square of foundation stones for a long-extinct outbuilding and clambered over a stone wall. The chopper would be on them in minutes.

He ushered her inside the keep, watching out the archway as the chopper neared. He'd once snogged a girl in here, an English bridesmaid he'd enticed away from a wedding at the country house on the promise of showing her the castle. A different life.

"Is this the keep?"

"Aye," he said, his gaze on the chopper. No searchlight.

"There's no roof."

"What?"

She was right. The damn roof had caved. Not a stone of cover left.

"We could duck down in the corner," she said. "There's a lot of rubble. If we stay still they might not see us."

"They've got thermal."

"Thermal imaging?"

"Without cover, we're pretty much glow-in-the-dark."

"Could we hide under something? Our coats?"

"Fabric will warm up with our body heat." He spun the rucksack off and pulled out the dinghy's emergency kit. Two survival blankets.

"Please tell me they're magic carpets."

He dumped the rucksack in a corner and covered it with flagstones. "Next best thing."

"Invisibility cloaks?"

"Pretty much just two big sheets of tinfoil. But I've heard that these things can hide a heat signature—as long as our bodies aren't warming them up."

"I don't think I have much of a heat signature right now."

"Help me stack these fallen stones. Make a ranger grave. We'll cover it with the blankets. As long as they're not touching us we might be okay."

The chopper's blades thudded, its engine straining. They piled rocks into two parallel rows, leaving a trench just wide enough for two people, just high enough to leave a decent gap between them and the blankets.

"Get in," he shouted over the roaring chopper.

She lay down and he made a roof with the blankets, weighing them with rocks on either side. He slid in next to her, on his side. His shoulder screamed. He was leaning on it but was wedged too tightly to move. He shifted closer to her—if that were possible—but it didn't help. She was also on her side, not a millimeter between them from top to toe. It was smaller than he'd thought. The stone against his back and side was so cold it felt wet, but her warm breath teased his neck. If this was his last moment, he should be kissing her, at the very least. The air shook with the disturbance from the machine. Its thud turned to a whine as it swept overhead. The downdraft lifted a corner of the blanket. Jamie grabbed it. A risk, but better that than the whole thing flying off. His hand was so cold he could hardly feel it.

And he'd thought it risky to lure a bridesmaid from a wedding before the toasts.

The chopper swept away, then back, and hovered right above, pinging pebbles against the walls. Jamie closed his eyes and hoped. Samira's hand rested on his hip. It felt like forgiveness. Or absolution before death.

Would the crew bother identifying their target before they opened fire? What kind of hikers would spend a night up here this time of year, when they could be at the pub at the next loch?

The chopper moved off, its thuds bouncing off the ancient stone walls.

"Do you think it worked?" she whispered, as the sound receded.

"Are you still alive?"

"I think so."

"I think that's an *'awo'* then," he said, mimicking her breathy inhalation.

She laughed, her chest vibrating against his. God, he liked that feeling, that sound. He released the blanket and lowered his hand. For want of options, he rested it on her arm.

"I think we just put the word 'survival' into 'survival blanket,'" he whispered, since that was all the volume that was needed. "But we should stay put a minute in case they come back."

"Sure."

"Talking about survival tools, that was quick thinking back there with the flare. Did you know how to use one?"

"My parents took me sailing around the Greek islands one spring. Using the flares was part of the safety demonstration."

"Trust you to pay attention to the safety demonstration. The Greek islands, huh? We had quite a different upbringing, you and I."

"That cottage must have been special, too."

"I guess."

"Are there bad memories. Is that why you...?"

"The memories are good. It's just...being there drove home the things that have happened since." He screwed up his face. "Samira, I've not thanked you. For getting us out of there, when I...let you down. And I'm sorry."

Silence.

"I'm going to destroy the rest of the drugs."

"Eshi," she said, eventually.

No. It wasn't *eshi*. Nothing was *eshi*. If the memory of their encounter in the cottage wasn't so vivid he'd wonder if it'd happened. Blown from history like the cottage was blown from the map.

Well, seeing as it never should have happened and never would again, that was appropriate. But, damn, he wanted to kiss her right now. Just a little downward shuffle and his lips would be level with hers...

"We should go," he said.

It was still dark more than an hour later when they reached his sister's town house and banged on the door. Samira slipped off a boot and rubbed her toes. The walk had been unrelenting but blessedly uneventful, though his head was pounding hard enough to crack his skull. After a few rounds of knocking, a curtain twitched in the living room. Samira was about to discover that her disappointment in Jamie was nothing next to his family's. A light switched on in the hall and the door arced open.

Nicole pushed her hair—still blue-black but longer—behind her ears, gave him a cursory disapproving look, then studied Samira head to toe and back up. "What the fuck are you doing here? Not you," she added quickly, as Samira flinched. "Him."

Don't give me hell, Nicole. Not today.

"Samira, meet my charming little sister, Nicole," he said. "Nicole, Samira. Uh, Nic, we're needing a lift to Edinburgh."

"What?"

"Edinburgh. It's this city, sixty miles east. A little gothic and gloomy but the tourists seem to like it." The joke was an effort but better that than let his real state of mind loose.

"Three years, Jamie. Three years and you knock on my door at stupid o'clock and there's no, 'Hello, how are you keeping? Sorry for being the world's most useless brother but I'm here for you now.' Just, 'I'm needing a lift,' like I'm fuckin' Uber."

Jamie darted a glance down the street, a curving row of identical dark houses. "We need to get out of here, right away."

"I've got the kids and they've got school."

"Since when did my sister prioritize school? Look, I can't explain and you wouldn't believe me if I did. But we have got to get to Edinburgh, fast. It actually is life or death."

"Your death or the death of someone I might actually care about?" She crossed her arms. "What kind of a mess have you landed in this time?"

"It's a long story but we don't have t—"

"Are the police after you?"

"No... Ah, well, yes, in a sense, but it's not my f—"

"Bloody hell, Jamie."

He fixed her with his most least-bullshit *give-me-a-break* stare. "Nic, I really need this."

She shook her head slowly. Reluctantly defeated. "Am I going to end up in jail?"

"Almost definitely not." He let himself and Samira into the hallway and closed the door.

Nicole stared at him a long minute, then tsked. "I'll go and wake the kids."

"Is there someone you can drop them off to on our way out of town? Best not take them with us." He glanced at Samira. "Just in case."

Another long stare, followed by another shake of the head. He took it as a yes.

"Oh and Nic?"

She flicked her hand through her hair. "I know by the tone of your voice that I don't want to hear what it is you're about to say."

"Is there somewhere else you can stay for the next few days? Just as a precaution."

"No, there's really not."

"I'll give you some money for an inn. You might want to pack a bag. Call it a holiday, on me."

She flipped him the bird.

"Gracious, Nic. And you're welcome."

He and Samira waited silently until Nicole returned, dressed in jeans and shepherding two overgrown urchins, each hauling a schoolbag. Jamie's stomach dropped. Where were the round-faced little kids? He hadn't been gone that long.

"I'll drive," Jamie said, lifting a set of keys from a hook.

Nicole snatched them. "You're on something," she hissed, snatching a wary glance at the kids. "I can see it in your eyes. You're not driving."

"I'm driving."

"You're not, not in that state, not in my car, not with my kids."

"I'm fucking driving."

"Language!" She pushed past him, snatching the keys. He grabbed her bag instead and, after a tug-of-war, won the right to carry it. She was still stubborn as all fuck.

Samira slid into the back of Nicole's Toyota with the kids, forcing Jamie to take the front passenger seat.

"Shite, they grew up," he said to Nicole.

"Language!"

"Oh come on. It's barely *language*." He would have instructed the kids to keep their heads down, just in case, but it wasn't necessary seeing as they were doubled over tablets with headphones on. "Do what I do, not what I say, kids. Kids, meet Samira. Samira, meet... kids."

Nicole clicked her seat belt on. "Their names are Max and Tyler."

"I know their names. I just can't tell which is which."

"One's a boy. One's a girl. You don't need a *medical degree* to figure it out."

Jamie raised his eyebrows at Samira. She looked from kid to kid and shrugged. It was dark and they both had a mop of floppy brown hair and wore jeans, sweatshirts and sneakers. Nicole started the car and it lurched forward.

"Fuck," she said, shoving the gearstick into Neutral.

"Language, Nicole."

"Shut up."

"They're going to learn the words anyway. They might as well learn what they're not supposed to say."

"Because you're *so* experienced at parenting."

Jamie twisted, keeping an eye out the windows as Nicole reversed onto the road. "What she means by that glare, Samira, is that she's having to beg and borrow to get through law school while I—"

"While raising two children," Nicole interjected.

"While raising two childr—"

"Alone."

Jamie took a breath. "While raising two children alone, and meanwhile I—"

"In a shit heap of a house that has so many leaks we need umbrellas indoors."

Jamie waited. "You done?" he said, eventually.

"Just getting started. You can see the bloody car I drive… Samantha, is it?"

"Language, Nicole," Jamie said. "Not that they're listening. And it's Samira. You know tablets can be bad for brain development?"

"I imagine being around you will set them back a few decades."

"I don't think they've noticed I'm here."

Jamie fished the baseball caps from the rucksack and handed one to Samira. Her sunglasses were in the car back at the cottage.

"Are you sure you want to go all the way to Edinburgh?" Nicole said. "I can recommend a sucky bog I can drop you at."

Jamie didn't need light to know Samira's expression was an anxious one. He and Nicole knew their competitive insults were mostly in jest, but Samira wouldn't. "You crack me up, Nic."

Samira cleared her throat. "I don't know if we should be going to Edin—"

"You have eighty minutes to come up with a better plan—seventy, the way Nic drives."

"Sixty, if I can help it," Nicole said. "Sooner I ditch you…"

"And you wonder why I vowed to stay away."

"You didn't vow anything. I made you promise to stay away. But of course you wouldn't remember that because you were so shit-faced at the time. What are you on today?"

Jamie glanced at Samira. *Shut up, Nicole.*

"Oh," Nicole said, pointedly, noting his look. She angled her mirror to take in Samira. "He's not told you, has he, love? If I was you, I'd surrender to whoever's chasing you. You'd be better off."

"Nicole, don't. Seriously." He'd have to have that conversation with Samira at some point—in the unlikely event they stuck together long enough—but not now.

"Who is chasing you, anyway? The police?"

"No." At least, he didn't think so.

"Good. I'd turn around and deliver you to them. So, who?"

"It's a very long story."

"Ooh, let me guess… Somebody trying to get revenge after you screwed up their lives?"

"It's nothing to do with me."

She glanced up at the mirror.

"It's not her fault, either," he said, in an undertone.

"I honestly don't want to know."

"It's best that way. Nic, can I borrow your phone?"

"What for?" Samira said.

"To send word to Angelito and Holly. Don't worry—it'll be secure. And we'll need their help if we're going to…" He glanced at Nicole.

"Say no more," she said, raising a palm. "I don't want to have to testify against you. Because I would."

He took the phone and messaged Angelito. As he waited for a response, he risked the elephant-in-the-room question. "How's Mum?"

Nicole's jaw went rigid. "What do you care?"

"Of course I care. You know I do."

Nicole exhaled. Relenting, slightly. "She's oblivious, thank God. Mostly they have her drugged up enough that she's in her own merry world. Sometimes I envy her that. But then, you'd know all about the magic of modern medication."

For fuck's sake, shut up.

A beep. Angelito. "They're in London," Jamie said to Samira. "They're going to head to King's Cross. I don't think they'd need ID for a ticket to Edinburgh and I can't imagine anybody would be looking for them." Would Holly's name raise flags, given her work history with the senator and Laura? Hyland had no reason to link Holly with Samira or Tess.

"What drugs is Mum on?" he asked Nicole.

Nicole rattled off a list. "The docs say it doesn't improve her dementia but it makes her a happy patient instead of an angry and confused one, so… And they give her something to help her sleep. I can't remember the name."

"You can always email me, you know, if you have questions."

"There's no shortage of doctors to ask."

"That can be part of the problem." He returned the phone to the center console. "How's law school?"

"Great. At this rate I'll graduate about a year after I die of old age."

"Will you ever stop blaming me for everything?"

"Makes me feel better to have somebody to blame."

He shrugged. "As long as I'm making you feel good about yourself… You dating anybody?"

"And how the fuck would I find the time for that?"

"Language, Nicole."

"Screw you, Jamie," Nicole snapped back. But she couldn't help a laugh, of sorts.

That was how it'd always been between them. *An endless game of ping-pong with conkers*, their dad had called it. It was mostly a facade. They had each other's backs when it counted. Like now. He knew she wouldn't refuse to drive them. Well, he was fairly sure. And here they were, so…

"How do you get off level eighteen?" Max/Tyler asked Max/Tyler, leaning over him/her in the back seat, and knocking his/her headset off with a none-too-gentle swipe.

The other kid didn't take his or her eyes off the screen. "Dunno. Not up to there, yet."

"It's fuckin' impossible."

Nicole whacked the steering wheel. "Max!"

"You say it all the time, Mum."

Nicole glanced at Jamie. "Do not."

"Have you tried casting the Spell of Revelation?" Samira said.

In the middle seat, Max was staring at Samira like she was speaking another language.

"On the Orb of Knowing," Samira continued. "Inside the Hall of Shadows. Here, let me show you. It's been a while since I've played but…" She reached over and swiped and tapped. "There, you see?"

"Mint," Max said. "Do you play *Age of Truth*?"

"Used to."

"I'm screwed on that one, too." He—at least Jamie figured he was probably the boy—did some more swiping. "I get this far and them I'm well stuck."

"Can I have a go?" Samira said. "I'll see if I remember. I know I've got up to level thirty. You guys are into old-school games."

"That's because our tablets are shite and Mum's too skint to let us upgrade."

Nicole rolled her eyes at Jamie. He gave what he hoped was a sympathetic look. He'd liked them better when they were shorter and worshipped him. After a few minutes, Samira was playing and chatting away like she was their age, whatever that was. Twelve? Thirteen? He really was a shite uncle. The kids had even unplugged their headphones.

"Maybe that's what I need to do," Nicole whispered, under the volume of the chatter and game music, "rather than trying to force them to play football or Monopoly with me. Admit defeat. I'm always trying to get them off the fuckin' tablets." She glanced at the mirror. "Is she your girlfriend?"

"No."

"Is that a 'No, I'm just screwing her' kind of no, or a 'No, she's married' kind of no, or a 'No, I'm in love with her but she's too sensible to date a schmuck like me' kind of no?"

He laughed. "Mostly just the last one. With a side serving of 'No, I'm not selfish enough to drag anybody down to my level.'"

She raised her eyebrows in a faux-impressed look, like she was surprised at his level of self-awareness.

"Nic, I know I've royally fucked up things." Shite, it really was the day for apologizing for his shortcomings.

She returned her gaze to the road. "I'm glad you've made peace with yourself."

"Wouldn't go that far."

"Good."

"You know I was in no state to stay after the thing in London, and then when Dad died…"

"I wish I'd had the luxury of the choice."

He ran his fingertips through his hair, his shoulder complaining at being raised. The heaviness in his chest suggested he'd well and truly sobered up.

He realized the back seat had fallen quiet. He stole a look. Samira quickly averted her eyes. How much had she heard?

Nicole lapsed into silence, but even after they'd spent

their adult years apart, he could read her thoughts like a book. *When are you going to grow up and come home?*

She was right—he'd gladly left her to take charge when their father died. He'd told himself that sending money to cover his mother's needs was the best way he could help, that Nicole was better at that logistical stuff. She hadn't let on that her marriage was falling apart but he should have noticed, like he should have noticed his father's failing health. If he hadn't been so fucking self-absorbed… And he hadn't known that next time he saw her kids they wouldn't be kids anymore.

Nicole pulled up on a street identical to the one they'd left and knocked on a door almost the same as hers. The woman who opened it looked familiar. An old school friend? Jamie slunk in the seat. He'd warned Nicole not to let on she was with him, but best not take chances. As Nicole shepherded the kids from the car, they pretty much tried to download Samira's brain.

"I used to play so many games with them," Nicole said as she pulled away from the curb again, almost to herself. "Kick a ball, take them places, have fun, but it's been years since I've had time. And now that they're not so little, connecting with them isn't as simple." For a change, she didn't turn it into an accusation against Jamie, which broke his heart a little.

"I can imagine," he said.

"Stupid, huh? They're my number one priority but everything else always comes first—earning an income, looking out for Mum, studying. And on the weekends, when I might have time for more than just being cook and taxi driver and household matron and homework supervisor, they're living it up at their prick of a dad's and I'm catching up on study. No wonder they prefer being with him—he only has to do the fun stuff. And they're always having big gatherings there with grand-parents and aunts and uncles and an ever-expanding bunch of cousins."

Jamie's gut twisted. Had he been so self-obsessed that he'd thought himself the only exile in the family? Somehow Nicole had ended up alone, too. Popular, care-free, easily contented Nicole.

"And then," she continued, "he goes and gives me some 'friendly advice' that I should do more fun stuff with them, too. 'It's a matter of priorities, Nicole.' No fucking idea."

"Sucks, Nic. Seriously."

"Stupid thing is, we split up because I was sick of having an uneven relationship and he was sick of having a grumpy wife. Now it's way more unbalanced and I'm ten times as grumpy while he has a lovely compartmen-talized life—though then he complains he never gets a weekend 'off' like he thinks I do. Sometimes I want to give him full custody so he can see what it's like to have to parent alone 24/7 during the week."

Jamie wanted to say, *I'll make it up to you. I'll make things better.* But he was already sending all the money he could.

"Meanwhile," she continued, "the kids are turning into bigger wee shits by the month. The more I do for them the less grateful they are."

"They'll come right. We were massive wee shits at their age."

"And look how well we turned out. Teen mum and drug addict. So, aye, maybe there's hope."

Jamie winced. *Cheers, sis.* There exploded any re-maining illusions Samira might be under.

"I love them," Nicole added. "I do."

"I know."

He used to envy her uncomplicated life. She'd always seemed content to live well within her comfort zone, within her skill set, to work and marry and breed within a fifty-mile radius of their hometown while he was constantly pushing his boundaries too far, seeking too much, aiming too high.

Now she was at law school, expanding her horizons, while he made sure to operate well within his. He was a trained commando but usually hung back as support. Nobody wanted to risk losing the medic. He was a qualified neurosurgeon but rarely did anything more complicated than dispensing diarrhea remedies.

What an idiot, to let this be the night he slipped. He'd let Samira push him out of his comfort zone, all right—push him to think, to care, to question the path he'd settled for. He'd vowed to stay in the Legion as long as they tolerated him, then retire to the Legion's vineyard in Provence with the others who had no hope of reintegrating to regular life. But the vineyard option was suddenly looking lonely, now that Angelito and Flynn had jumped tracks to regular lives—not that Flynn's was going to plan.

Speaking of which…

He picked up Nicole's phone. First things first. They needed a place to lie low in Edinburgh while they figured out a strategy. The distant future would sort itself out, once he got back to the Legion and banished Samira from his head. But first they had to secure an immediate future, one risk at a time.

CHAPTER SEVENTEEN

JAMIE DIRECTED NICOLE through the Monday morning traffic of the Old Town. She dropped them in a grimy cobblestone lane flanked by the arse-end of blackened stone buildings, roller doors, fire exits and green wheelie bins. He forced a few hundred quid on her and promised to call when it was safe to return home. Hyland probably didn't even know Jamie's identity but it wasn't worth the risk.

He pulled up at a wooden door next to a barred sash window. He'd checked for security cameras on the street view of Nicole's phone map. There was only one, facing the other way.

"This is us," he said to Samira, as Nicole accelerated away, giving the car slightly more gas than necessary.

"Where did you find this?"

"Same accommodation site as the cottage. It's not booked for days and neither are the neighboring apartments. No alarm. Let's hope the key fits." He pulled out Holly's lock-picking kit. He'd studied the streetview photos to figure out the likelihood the door would succumb to his limited skills. "I've told Angelito and Holly to come straight here. We'll lie low until then."

"I can't believe this sort of thing has become my life," she said, keeping watch as he jiggled the lock.

"Don't worry—we've already got housebreaking."

"They're crimes, not collector cards."

"We'll leave it tidy. They'll never know. And you're practically a folk hero—when all this is over the landlords will hike their rack rates on account of the infamy of us having broken in. Bonnie and Clyde indeed." The lock clicked and he opened the door to a flight of stairs. "Don't know why I bother to carry a set of keys."

"Where did Holly get a lock picker? And why?"

"Holly's an interesting person," he said, closing the door behind them. "You'll see."

They climbed several flights and came to another door. As he worked on the lock he could almost feel Samira's blood pressure rising. After several minutes it opened into a modernized low-ceiling one-bedroom flat. He lowered the rucksack next to a pair of sash windows in the living area.

"Bonnie and Clyde couldn't be embalmed—did you know that?" said Samira, walking to the kitchen. "Too many bullet holes."

"Police in Edinburgh don't usually carry guns. Just batons."

She searched a few cupboards and pulled out two glasses. "That makes me feel so much better."

"You're starting to sound like my sister."

"I'm starting to feel like your sister." She filled the glasses from the tap, drank from one and held the other out to him. Suddenly he was parched. "Has she always been that cynical?"

"You noticed?" he said, crossing the wooden floors and downing the water in one. He was hungry as well. "She's had it tough lately. She'll make a cracking good lawyer. She'll not take shit from anybody."

"I'll bet," Samira said, shedding her coat, planting her knuckles in the center of her spine and arching. "We might need a lawyer before the day is done."

"Come here," he said, rounding the kitchen island. He put the glass down. "Let's sort out that back of yours."

She opened her mouth to object, then closed it. The ache had evidently won out. As he coaxed out a drumroll of cracks, she looked resolutely downward. Adamant it wouldn't turn into something more intimate, like last time? What if he ran a finger down her cheek…?

He stepped away and strode to the windows, taking in the view through the net curtains. "Come meet the neighbors."

Across the broad street a champagne-colored neoclassical stone building straddled a whole city block. Or was it technically neo-Renaissance? A white security tent was erected outside, acting as a funnel from a turning bay to the building's entrance.

Samira joined him, reading aloud the name etched across the facade. "'The Balfour'… Jamie, what are we doing? We have no hope of getting through all that security."

Two police officers flanked the tent opening, and two more stood on the turning bay, talking to a trio of security types in suits, lanyards and sunglasses. No visible weapons but they had to be carrying. A fifth officer stood outside a roller car—the hotel's parking garage?

"Just recon, for now," Jamie said. "I'm not suggesting we force our way in."

"What, then? We dig a tunnel under the hotel and come up underneath his room?"

"His room won't be on the ground floor."

She swiped at him.

"Imagine if it worked," he said.

"Imagine if it didn't."

"Look," he said, turning to her, "I'm thinking we'll

find a more diplomatic solution. Just give us a chance to make a plan before you veto it. We have more advantages than you might think."

"You're saying I get right of veto?"

"Samira, there's never going to be a perfect solution and it's never going to be risk-free. We'll all need to weigh it against the bigger risks—that Tess gets convicted, that you have to go back into hiding. And there's your parents, Charlotte…"

She pressed her lips together.

"We need to turn the tables," he continued. "Once Hyland's back in the States he'll be even harder to get to. He doesn't know what we're after. The last thing he'll expect is for us to come to him, here. As far as he knows, we're right now trying to run away from him."

A woman with a little girl approached the tent. An officer spoke to her and she dug around in her bag and showed him a hotel keycard, and some other card—ID? Inside the tent a security screening scanner was visible, like at an airport.

"'When the webs of the spider join they can trap a lion,'" Samira murmured.

"What's that?"

"Something my grandfather used to say."

"Fitting."

"I think we need more than four or five spiders." Samira swiveled and returned to her glass on the kitchen island. "Jamie, tell me what happened, with your family, your career."

He raised his eyebrows, still looking at the tent. She made it sound like a condition of her cooperation. Blackmail. But, hey, no point lying anymore.

"I think you can guess," he said.

"Drugs."

"Aye. Prescription, not street—not that they were prescribed, not for me, anyway."

"Why didn't you tell me?" she asked, her quiet tone ripping into him.

"It was not supposed to become an issue."

"The one thing I wanted from you, the one thing I asked for, was the truth. Trust. No surprises." She spoke slowly, like she was selecting every syllable from a catalog.

He swallowed. "I know."

"'It's rare that somebody we know and trust will betray us.'"

He turned his head. She was examining the water like it was fine wine. "What?"

"Something you said, in the car."

"I talk a lot of bollocks."

She met his gaze, her jaw firm. "Please don't be flippant." She sipped. "Your arm's still giving you trouble."

He'd been cradling it with the other hand. He let go. "It's fine."

"There's that word again—*fine*." Another sip. "So that's why you wouldn't take painkillers—you're an addict. That's what your sister said."

"Aye. I'm an addict." If it was supposed to be healthy to admit that, why did it feel like he was shriveling?

"There must be something we can do for your wound." She strolled up and unbuttoned his coat. Getting bolder—not waiting for an answer. He liked that. He'd like her to undress him for a different reason but...*no*.

"I can probably fix it myself, using the bathroom mirror," he said. "Might need a hand here and there, though."

"Of course."

The bathroom was windowless but had plenty of lights around the mirror. She helped him remove the suture strips and directed the flashlight of her phone onto the wound. He began to excavate. It was as much of a mind-fuck as reversing a trailer—left when you wanted to go right, right to go left.

"You don't need to hide from me," she said, quietly. He got the sense she was studying his face in the mirror. "Or impress me."

"I'm guessing there's no point in either after last night."

"I, for one, am glad we've moved beyond both those things. So? Tell me your story. The full truth, this time."

"It's not something I like to relive."

"You'd rather pretend it didn't happen?"

"Pretend what didn't happen?"

"You know, it's strange." She turned and leaned back against the cabinet, only her back view visible in the mirror. "You come across as so wise and steady. I knew you were hiding something, but this... It doesn't compute with the Jamie I know."

"Well, then, it turns out you don't really know me, do you?"

She straightened a little. "Do you feel like you know me?"

"I see what you're doing there, Samira."

"What?"

He winced as his tweezers closed in on a black speck buried in the pulp. "I'm supposed to say, 'Aye, I feel like I really know you,' so you can turn around and say, 'Then why is it so hard to believe that I could know you, too?'"

"So *do* you?" she said.

"It's a funny thing, Samira. You don't say much—unless you're obsessing about your fears and then, *whoa*—but I get the feeling you're not trying to hide anything from anybody. It's just the way you are. But

me—nobody's ever accused me of being quiet. I talk
a lot but…"

"You don't let people in."

"It's not something I'm comfortable with. Nothing
personal."

"Because you're worried that if they get too close
they might realize you're human and not this kick-ass
doctor-soldier guy?"

"I am a kick-ass doctor-soldier guy."

"You are. But you're also human."

"Human? Don't be ridiculous."

She let out a huff. "And I see what you're doing.
You're making this into a game of joke tennis."

"Joke tennis?"

"Where you lob a comment and I lob a comment
and it feels like we're getting along well and having a
lovely time but when you think back you realize it was
all superficial and just your way of shutting things down
without seeming rude."

He got ahold of the black thing and yanked. "Got
the fucker!" he said, holding up a tiny metal shard. "I
love tennis."

"You see? You just did it."

He looked at her face, shielding his eyes from the
flashlight app. "Jesus, I did, didn't I?"

"Let me guess," she said, raising her chin in that way
she did when she was confident about something. Her
eyes looked smoky beyond the circle of light from her
phone. "When things went wrong in your life, you had
no one to fall back on, no one to turn to, because you
were the guy with a million friends, the most popular
guy in the room, but not one of those people truly knew
you because you were scared to let anyone see that you
had flaws. You were the class clown because people

liked you that way, and you learned to give them what they wanted, and not what they didn't want—what you *thought* they didn't want. The real you."

"Whoa. You might have to write all that down." Blood dribbled down his arm. He wiped it, and peered into the mirror. There had to be more than one sliver of metal, with all that pain. "Anyway, I'm a guy. I don't feel the need to have deep and meaningful conversations with my... What do you call them? My BFFs."

"Everyone needs someone, even just one person. Look, I don't let many people in either but I can say that the truly close friends I've had, including Latif... I let them know the real me and they let me know the real them, flaws and all. And knowing they had insecurities, too, knowing they'd made mistakes, knowing they were fallible, they were imperfect... It didn't ever *lower* my opinion of them—it brought us closer. And it meant I could help them when they were struggling and vice versa. Which brought us still closer." She lowered her voice. "Who helped you when you were struggling, Jamie? Because I'm guessing there was a point in your life that you really struggled. Who did you turn to?"

He swallowed. He'd kept his mouth shut and high-tailed it to France. Plenty of his "friends" had known he was using—people whose best interests were served by keeping quiet. He couldn't talk to his parents about it, obviously. Nicole wouldn't have understood. She was up to her ears in young children and had never know-ingly taken a risk in her life—except unprotected sex as a teenager, obviously. And Samira was right—he hadn't wanted the shame of facing anybody who knew how fucked up he really was.

"I can hear you thinking, Jamie."

He chuckled. "I see what you're doing there."

She turned to him and laid a finger lightly on his lips. "No tennis. Just talk. No matter how this mess turns out, we probably won't see each other again."

We probably won't see each other again. The truth hurt ten times worse than shrapnel.

"But," she continued, "why not get some practice at making a friend—a real friend? Who would I tell?" She lifted her finger.

"You'd better sterilize that again," he said, nodding at her finger. "You don't know where my lips have been. Well, actually, you d—"

The finger went back on, firmer this time, stifling a laugh he didn't feel. He glimpsed a parallel universe in which he pulled it aside, pushed her against the tiled wall, took her in a fierce kiss, stripped her clothes off, got the shower running...

He forced that sliding door to close. It relented with a shove and a rusty shriek.

She hovered her finger an inch off his lips, her eyebrows raised in warning. Ah, what did it matter how much she knew? He couldn't shock or disappoint her any more than he had. And there was already no future for them—she'd said it herself.

"Okay, okay, you win. No tennis." He crossed his foot over his knee. "Which is a shame because I really like it when you play with my—"

The finger, again. He grinned and gently bit it. She pursed her lips, shaking her head.

"Fine," he mumbled, releasing her finger and turning back to the mirror. "There it is, look! The mother lode!" A thick metal fiber, the tip just visible. "Can you hold the wound open while I grab it?"

She met his eye in the mirror. "Only if you talk."

"You're not serious?"

"I'm not serious about withholding my services but I am serious about wanting you to talk." She held his gaze awhile. What happened to her always being the first to turn away? "Jamie, I admire the doctor in you. And I admire the soldier. But the human—that's the part I like best of all."

Okay, so that kind of gutted him. "Fine, you win. I'll talk." He closed in on the fiber with the precision of a drunk trying to walk a straight line. "What do you want to know?"

"The drugs, I guess."

"Where do I start?"

"Try the beginning."

He took a breath. "Okay. I was a med student. A few of us started playing with taking uppers to get through shifts, to cope with the pressure, the lack of sleep. With me they helped a little too much. I became the golden boy."

She was silent awhile. "You *are* going to give me more than that, yes? I had to work very hard to…formulate all those sentences earlier, and put them together in a coherent way."

He closed the tweezers, felt them grip and gently pulled, steadying his breath. No resistance, it just slid out, bringing a whole lot of blood with it. *Jackpot.* "Aye, you were very coherent. You can let go now. I'll clean it, we'll put fresh strips on and that should do me until Corsica."

As he reached for the gauze, her mirror image narrowed its eyes. "So the uppers?"

He sighed, wiping the blood. "Were supposed to be a temporary fix. I thought I could cope with them, quit at any time, because I knew the theory behind it, I understood exactly what they were doing to my brain. I was arrogant enough to think that that put me in control of the drugs. By the time I realized it was the other way around it was too late."

"Go on."

"Jesus, you've missed your calling. You should go and work for Tess's TV station."

"Jamie…" A warning tone, which kind of turned him on.

"It's the classic stupid story. I was supposed to stop before it got to the point where I couldn't operate without them. But I didn't see that point coming until I got way past it. I felt sharper with them, until suddenly I didn't, and by that time I didn't know how to function sober. I needed the drugs to feel normal, whatever that was. And meanwhile I'd started taking sleeping tablets to switch off at night, and then those stopped working so well, so I…"

He closed his eyes. Fuck.

"Go on," she said, gently.

He blinked hard. At least dressing the wound gave him an excuse to avoid her gaze. "I started using more serious drugs, whatever I could get a supply of—amphetamines, opiates… So, aye, a classic vicious cycle—the stronger the drug, the more I needed it. Then my stash of uppers ran out and I couldn't get more. I freaked, fucked up, and a woman nearly died."

"Oh my God, I'm sorry."

"My supervisor stepped in just in time, and no harm came to her. But I would have killed her." He exhaled, heavily. "And she had young kids…" His voice cracked.

"Oh Jamie…"

"The chief exec of the hospital got suspicious and had me drug tested. She wanted to hand me to the cops until she found out just how many of her staff were using drugs—and had stolen them, and bought and sold them. All illegally, of course—and she knew I wasn't bullshitting because she'd had several reports of missing and stolen drugs. In a competitive environment like that, everybody's trying to get an edge."

"I can imagine. God, that must have been awful."

"It was. I thought I was so smart. Kept promising myself that I'd take leave for a month and dry out but it's really bloody hard to do that in such an intense job. I didn't want to miss out on anything, get left behind, be seen as a slacker. In a weird way it was a relief to come clean."

"And the police got involved?"

He shook his head, wincing. "I'd gotten to the point that I was prepared to live with the consequences, no matter what they were. But if they'd pursued criminal charges it wouldn't have ended with just me. There'd have been dozens more arrested, or at least fired. So many promising lives would have been fucked up. They needed treatment, not just punishment. So I suggested to the boss that it wouldn't play out so well in the courts or the media, or bode well for her career or the hospital's funding—once I was under oath I'd have to reveal *everything*. She and the board quietly decided to keep it to internal discipline, and overhaul the hospital's horrendous working conditions, especially for junior doctors. Which didn't make up for anything, but…"

"You blackmailed your bosses."

"Merely laid out the facts and let them make the conclusions. Okay, let's do the suture strips. I'll hold it closed." He gave her instructions, moving aside as she washed her hands again.

"And you were fired?" she said.

"I left before they could. Left the hospital, left medicine, let my license to practice lapse. Figured it was the best way I could 'first do no harm.' After that woman nearly died I couldn't..." He swallowed. It felt like a conker was lodged in his throat. "It came so close to being so much worse. I realized finally the job wasn't all about me and my bloody ambitions. It was about people who trusted me—the patients, most of all. The bosses vowed to make sure I could never work as a doctor again, anywhere. Not that I intended to. And they announced an amnesty and mandatory drug testing, as well as confidential drug counseling for whoever wanted it—which was a lot of people—so it ended well enough."

"For everyone but you. You took the hit for your colleagues." Her mouth puckered as she pressed the strips on. The yellow glow from the bathroom lights painted a sheen on her hair, a warmth on her skin.

"You're being way too generous. I dragged them into it. Like I told you, for whatever reason, people go along with my crazy schemes. But I was relieved that the person worst affected in the end was me. And in a funny way the hospital became a better place for my having been there—just not in the way I'd intended, not in a way I could be proud of."

She pulled another strip off the backing paper. "You couldn't get a job in medicine elsewhere—another country?"

"What's the first thing any employer's going to do? Ring my old bosses, right? Anyway, I didn't trust myself to go back to that environment. I wanted a break from that kind of pressure, from those triggers. I wanted to do an honest day's work. Physical work. Running off to the Legion was my treatment—cheaper than rehab and longer term. Cold turkey. Removed myself from the triggers, became a grunt. Low expectations, low stress. Nobody to impress, nobody to disappoint."

"But you're a commando. A paratrooper. How's that low stress?"

"I worked my way up to it. And mostly I'm in the team for my medical skills. But the thing with the military—it's not like working in a crazy city hospital where it's mental most of the time, where every day you're gambling with people's lives. In the military, it's mostly pretty laid-back. The moments of intense stress are relatively few and usually short-lived. I can cope with that. It was the constant strain of the hospital that got to me."

"Don't you carry drugs as a medic? Morphine?"

"Only small doses, and I have a quiet agreement with my CO to check my supplies every day."

"And that stops you from taking them?"

"The temporary high wouldn't be worth losing his respect or my livelihood. You see? Playing my many flaws off against one another."

She patted down a strip. "How does that look?"

"Perfect," he said, examining it.

"Peeerrrrfect," she murmured. "And last night, at the cottage—how often do lapses like that happen?"

"They don't." He frowned. Except for that one time after the funeral...

"That one did. What was the trigger—stress?"

"More like regret, guilt, insomnia—the usual stuff." *And you.*

He looked her in the eyes. Wide, glazed, beautiful eyes. "Samira, this is why I need the Legion, why I can't have a relationship, why I can't live in the real world. I need those boundaries. I don't want the stress of real life, of free choice, of expectation. I've hurt enough people around me."

"You'd rather have the stress of imminent death and injury?"

"The chances of death are actually pretty low. Worst I've suffered in the military is a sprained ankle and sunburn. And it's not like my previous behavior was without risk."

"So when you set off that trigger next time, what will happen?"

"I'll avoid that happening."

"How?"

He started cleaning up the debris. "Go back to the Legion and stay there."

"Where someone is watching you?"

"And where I can't lose control and break anyone's heart, literally or figuratively."

Silence. *None too subtle, Armstrong.*

"And it gives me healthier ways of releasing stress," he said, barreling on before she could challenge him—if she even wanted to. "I found when I threw myself into the physical side of it, when I trained longer and harder than anybody else, when I reached the point of exhaustion, there was no energy left for guilt or regret—and I no longer had a problem getting to sleep. I no longer needed drugs to keep me going or help me stop. You get the endorphins hitting, and even when I got dog tired— which was a lot in the early days—they gave me enough of a high to ride out the emotional stuff. I was getting through each day, and each day was pretty uncomplicated. And I got lucky enough to eventually get into a team where we're all that physical and focused—and maybe a little obsessive—each for our own reasons."

"You mean Flynn and Angelito."

"Aye, until Angelito retired," he said, clipping the lid on the first-aid kit as he wandered back to the living room. "And Texas. And the others. We're all a little fucked up in our own special ways."

She sat on a bar stool at the kitchen island as he re-packed the kit. "There's a saying in Ethiopia. 'He who conceals his disease cannot expect to be cured.' I'm no psychologist, but aren't you just hiding from the prob-lem and hoping it'll go away? Wouldn't it make more sense to face up to those triggers and try to disconnect them, rather than avoiding them? Because you don't always have a choice when they show up, yes? Like last night."

"Ha," he said, perching on the arm of a sofa. This conversation was getting a little deep, a little personal. *Eject,* caporal. "Like your panic attacks."

"*Awo,* like my panic attacks. If I could live my entire life in a happy bubble, I wouldn't get them. But that's not possible. Problems will always come—not always as dramatically as this craziness—but you can't control what they'll be or when they'll come."

She was dead right, of course. But she'd also given him an opening to wriggle out of the microscope. And he'd take it. He slid down onto the sofa cushions, crossed his legs and planted his feet on the far arm.

"So what are your triggers?" he said.

"No surprises there. Fear."

"And you feel as if you can't breathe, obviously. What else?"

"I get this cold wash of terror sweeping down my body." She shuddered. "My heart's racing. And I get dizzy and shaky and my vision blurs." She held her hand flat in front of her, palm parallel with the floor. "Even half an hour afterward my hand can be still shaking."

"And what do you do to combat it?"

"That's the problem—when it starts I no longer have control. Sometimes it stops again, sometimes it gets really bad, like in the ambulance, but I don't know which way it'll go. There's nothing I can do."

"And what's going through your mind? What are you fearing will happen?"

"That I'm going to flake out. Even die, from lack of oxygen." She jabbed her pointer finger. "But you don't need to tell me it's all in my head. I know that. I tell myself that and it doesn't help."

"Most people's problems are all in their heads."

"Including yours?" she said, archly.

"Definitely mine. But let me tell you this." He swung his feet to the floor and planted his elbows on his knees. "It's very, very, *very* rare for somebody to faint when they're having a panic attack."

She tilted her head. "It is?"

"And nobody dies. Your body flushes with adrenaline, your heart floods with oxygenated blood—that's the very thing paramedics and doctors try to replicate when we…" He winced. "When *they* resuscitate people. Your panic attack is your body's way of keeping you alive when it senses a threat. Okay, your body's reaction is a little over the top and that's the problem, but you're not going to die. So you can let go of that fear."

She chewed her bottom lip.

"And you're not going to pass out, so you can let go of that fear, too."

"It certainly feels like I'm going to."

"And even if you did pass out, it'd probably only last a second and you'd be good again. Your body would be shocked into resetting."

"Really?"

"Aye. So if those are your worst fears, you can let them go."

She stared at the bare wall over his shoulder so intently that he fought the urge to check behind him. "I can't try that until I'm *in* a panic attack. It's easy to solve a hypothetical attack."

"Aye, in the same way you can't test your road crash avoidance skills until you're seconds from death. But one thing you can practice? Breaking the hyperventilation cycle, where you feel like you can't breathe, so you take faster breaths but your breath is too shallow, so you hyperventilate…" He stood, and crossed the space between them. She returned focus to him. "Let's try something." He picked up one of her hands and placed it flat on her chest, and the other across her belly, keeping his hands on top. "Breathe for me, nice and deep, filling your lungs, and then hiss it out until it's completely gone. And I mean empty. Then breathe in again."

He breathed along with her and she followed, her mouth twitching with skepticism.

"Perfect," he said. "Tell you what. Let's do it on the floor."

She double-blinked.

"And by that I mean 'totally relax.' Crumbs, Samira. The places your mind goes to…"

She laughed. He took her hand and led her to a rug in front of the sofa. Shite, now his mind was going to places it shouldn't. *Settle down,* caporal. If he left her with one thing when he returned to the Legion, he wanted it to be this. Not regret.

"Now," he said when they were lying side by side, "do the same hissing thing, but when you've run out of hiss, make no effort at all to breathe in. Instead, totally relax. Don't fight your body, don't instruct it, don't force it to do anything."

"Not even breathe?"

"Not even breathe."

"I hope you have a defibrillator in that first-aid kit."

"I'm a walking defibrillator—and it won't come to that, I promise." He kept a couple of fingers linked with hers. "Follow my lead. After you hiss all your breath out, just become an outside observer, let go of any need to control. Don't force anything but don't stop anything, either."

He audibly breathed in, and she followed. He hissed his breath out and then let his torso expand. This time, after her hiss ran out, she didn't take a panicked gasp.

"So," he said, propping up on his elbow, their fingers still linked. "How was it for you?"

"Okay, I'll give you that. It worked. My lungs filled on their own."

"Automatic, wasn't it? Like a whoopee cushion."

"A what?"

"One of those rubber fart cushions. They inflate automatically after you sit on them."

She shook her head slightly. "I don't understand how this helps me."

"When you're hyperventilating, sometimes the problem is that you're not letting enough breath out, not making space for fresh oxygen. So rather than desperately trying to inhale, maybe focus on exhaling and trust your body to do the rest. Worth a try next time. Or your money back."

"But I can't think clearly when I'm having an attack—that's the problem."

"I know." He threaded his fingers through hers. "When it comes to the human mind and its impulses, Samira, there are no on and off switches, no guarantees."

She smiled, sadly. She knew he wasn't talking just about her panic attacks. Far easier to preach than practice.

"I bet you were a wonderful doctor," she said with a sad smile. Her sincerity stabbed at him.

"Not to be."

Her eyebrows dived together. God, it'd be so easy to lean in and kiss her. As if she read his mind, her gaze dropped to his lips. He felt himself drawing in. Magnets. Before he had time to rationalize it, his lips were on hers, her hand was sliding up his back.

She lurched to a sitting position, almost taking his nose out with her skull, and snatched her hands away. "I need a shower." She pushed up to standing, strode to the rucksack and picked it up. When she reached the bathroom she turned. "Jamie, I can't do this. I'm recovering from one broken heart. I can't risk another. Not when you're going to run away again."

He dropped his focus to the rug, its fibers still carrying her imprint.

I won't break your heart, he wanted to say. *Give me a chance. We can work it out.*

"I understand," he said.

She stayed rigid for a minute. Waiting for something he couldn't give? The bathroom door closed behind her.

CHAPTER EIGHTEEN

BY THE TIME Samira emerged from the bathroom, dressed in jeans and a sweater, Jamie had transformed back into the breezy joker. It was almost a relief when he took his turn in the shower. She didn't have the energy to respond to his quips and she sensed by the dead look in his eyes that his heart wasn't in them. Their mutual rejection had imposed a finality—when this crisis was over, they were over.

She dragged an armchair to the window and opened the laptop, the midmorning sun filtered to a weak haze by the netting. Across the street, the hotel sat like a squat stone cruise ship. In the turning bay three charcoal Land Rovers waited, bookended by two police cars. Cones shut out other vehicles. A man and woman stood with their backs to the convoy, dressed in black trench coats over dark suit trousers, neatly pressed shirts and ties peeping out at the collar. Diplomatic security. Another two agents stood at the tail of the convoy, one wearing black sunglasses. Lanyards carrying ID passes hung from their necks. A police motorbike buzzed up, its rider in a white helmet and high-vis jacket.

Samira brought up the senator's schedule. He was due to meet the Dutch foreign minister at another hotel. Eleven Wi-Fi networks popped up—two for the hotel, others for the shops and offices below her and the surrounding apartments. Four networks still carried the brand name of the Wi-Fi box. If you didn't bother changing your Wi-Fi name, there was a good chance you weren't vigilant about the password, either. She chose one with the brand name of a company that had been defunct for at least nine years—back when "password" or "1234" or your street seemed like totally logical choices, before Wi-Fi boxes came preloaded with passwords like 2u85hjkgs767ds and you were locked out after three attempts. It took a full minute to get online.

In the last hour, Laura had updated her social media with the view from her window. Her room had to be on the other side of the building. It overlooked a grim church with a sharp black steeple, and a castle on a hill, gloomy against a gray sky. Edinburgh Castle, presumably. Samira checked the hotel website's gallery and found the matching view. The two-bedroom Conan Doyle Suite. Had to be on the uppermost of the seven floors, going by the angle of Laura's photo. Laura had also posted the details of that evening's signing, at a bookshop across the city.

A car pulled up to the cones at the far end of the bay and a police officer in shirtsleeves and a chunky black vest strolled up to speak to the driver, while another officer dropped to her knees to check the underside. The driver handed a card and piece of paper through the window and the cop inspected it while his partner checked the trunk and lifted out two suitcases. The first cop waved the car along to a valet parking lectern, where the driver and a passenger climbed out. A porter in a light gray suit, with a kilt instead of trousers, wheeled the suitcases to the security tent, pausing to let the guests go in first. A kilted valet drove the car to the roller door, which slid open, revealing a basement car park.

"That's some serious security."

Samira jumped. Jamie was standing behind her, dressed in the ripped green sweater. His jean legs were splashed with dirt.

"American diplomats always take their security seriously," she said. "And Hyland might not be the only foreign dignitary staying there."

"Whoa." His eyebrows rose, his gaze still across the street.

She turned back. The blond guy—Fitz—had stepped out of the tent with a brunette woman, and was sweeping a narrowed gaze across the scene. Samira shrank into her chair.

"Is that guy a clone?" Jamie said. "He's everywhere at once. The woman he's with—she was the driver of the Peugeot. Both looking fresh after their nap in the forest."

Fitz… She did a partial word search on Hyland's files. A few dozen hits—Fitzpatrick, Fitzgibbon, Fitzsimmon… But it was a Matisse Fitzgerald that seemed most likely. He'd been CCed into memos about the senator's security and was listed on an itinerary of a previous official trip as "head of contract security." A Christmas present list from a few years ago—presumably written by an assistant of Hyland's—listed gifts for a Matisse, Jennifer, Grace and Toby Fitzgerald, and a delivery address in Washington, DC. Hardly damning evidence.

"Bingo," she whispered, as she opened the next file.

"What have you found?" Jamie walked behind the chair.

"Fitz's résumé, with his photo and everything. Matisse Fitzgerald. He's ex-CIA, worked in East Africa the same time as Hyland, after Hyland left the marines and before he started up Denniston. He's been a 'security contractor' ever since."

"A mercenary?"

She frowned up at Jamie. "Isn't that technically what you are?"

"In a sense, but I don't get paid nearly enough. And I don't shoot people for profit and neither does my employer—as far as I know."

Across the road, Fitz approached the nearest pair of diplomatic security agents, who straightened. They exchanged a few words.

Jamie stepped closer to the window. Samira killed an urge to yank him back.

"Does that look tense to you?" he said.

"Diplomatic security would hate that the senator also uses his own security. A senator wouldn't usually get this level of diplomatic protection, but I guess since he's standing in for the secretary of state on an official visit, he's using the secretary's traveling detail."

"It'd be a bad look if somebody sneaked through NATO security."

"And yet you're talking about sneaking through NATO security."

"We're not carrying bombs or AKs. They're screening for terrorists, not petty thieves. They won't check what we carry out, just what we take in."

She shut the laptop and smoothed her hands over the lid. "Are we really going to try this?"

He narrowed his eyes, still watching across the road. "I don't see that we have a choice."

"Maybe Hyland will…trip over and the fob will fall off onto the ground and we can walk past and pick it up."

"Let's hope for that. But we'll plan for something a little more challenging."

"This is crazy. I just don't know where we would start, getting in—"

"Merde." Jamie's jaw dropped.

Several people had stepped out of the tent. Even among the dark suits and coats, a tall, broad man in a dark suit and coat stood out, thick silver hair swept into a boyish style that suggested, in an artful way, he'd just got out of bed with a glamorous woman. Samira stood, and had to dive for the laptop to stop it hitting the floor.

"Oh my God," she said, planting the laptop on the chair. "Hyland."

A dozen people swept in from nowhere—media, holding cameras and recorders. Faint shouts were audible.

"I've never seen him in person," she said.

He strode to the middle Land Rover, flashing his vote-winning smile for the cameras, his suit jacket stretched over broad shoulders that tapered to a narrow waist, the fingers of one hand casually hooked in a trouser pocket. A flash of white on his belt—the fob.

Wow. She'd seen him on video and in photos thousands of times but now she got it. He looked like a film star playing the role of senator. An all-American actor who'd never be cast as anything but a hero.

"That guy tore my life apart and until now I've never laid eyes on him. And look at him. Even I want to believe he's a good guy. That's what we're fighting here."

The senator called out to the media and laughed with all his perfect white teeth. He answered a few questions, an arm slung over the rear door, which was held open by a diplomatic security agent. A camera flashed.

"It looks like an ad for Land Rover," she said. "In *GQ*."

Jamie slipped behind her and placed his hands on her upper arms. "There's a reason they call him Teflon

Tristan. That's why we need that evidence. People aren't going to believe it until he's forced to admit his guilt."

"So we just walk on up and say, 'Hey, Senator, mind if I take a peek at your dongle?'"

"By the look of him, I suspect he gets that kind of talk a lot."

"It wasn't a joke. None of this is a joke."

Jamie squeezed her arms. "I know, Samira," he said, with a quiet seriousness that settled her nerves a touch.

The senator disappeared into the car and the cavalcade moved away, escorted by three police bikes as well as the cars, blue lights flashing from the Land Rover grilles, leaving Fitz, the Peugeot driver and half a dozen police outside the hotel.

The door to the parking basement rolled up and a blue Prius nosed out. Two men in black suits and sunglasses filled the front. Through the windscreen, Samira caught the unmistakable flash of a blond pixie cut in the back seat. The car turned onto the street in the opposite direction from the cavalcade. The rear windows were blacked out.

"That was Laura," she said.

"I would have expected more protection."

"She wouldn't have the same level of protection as a president's daughter. Those would be personal bodyguards—I know Hyland pays for protection for her, too. And there was someone with her in the back, a woman. A social-media manager?"

"Right, then," Jamie said, releasing Samira. "Now's as good a time as any to go and break into his room."

"Oh my God, are you serious? We can't just walk in there and bash our way through the hotel. That place will be crowded with security. And police. And goons. And his staff." She swiveled. "We wouldn't get—"

Jamie was grinning. The bastard.

She brought a hand to her chest. "Another joke."

"Too hard to resist. Lighten up, Samira—it's not like we're about to mug one of the most powerful people in the free world. But, yeah, we'll wait until Angelito and Holly get here in—" he looked at his bare wrist, and hurriedly rubbed it "—at eleven thirty and then we'll come up with a plan that's watertight and one hundred percent safe."

She raised her eyebrows.

"Okay, maybe ninety-nine percent safe and just a little leaky."

He raised his arms, rested his fingers on a ceiling beam and leaned his hips forward. His back cracked. Why did they never come as easily for her? She ached to wrap her arms around his muscular waist, burrow her nose into his sweater.

"Anyway," he said, "nothing we can do until then, so I think my time's best spent in bed."

She stopped breathing.

"Sleeping," he said, his mouth curling. "Unless you have a better idea."

His eyes did that crinkling thing again, which never failed to somersault her belly.

She sat back in the chair, her face heating. Resisting was almost physically painful, but if he wasn't available she was a fool to dig herself in any deeper. "I need to check up on a few things."

Like her parents. God.

Several news outlets reported they were being questioned on Samira's whereabouts, and speculated that the United States was pressuring the Canadian and Ethiopian governments to hand them over on suspicion of "terror-related activities." Samira chewed on her knuck-

les. Her parents were smart and would have good law-
yers, but Ethiopia didn't have a whole lot of clout to
stand up to America. And surely terrorism was an exception to the rule of diplomatic immunity.

In the United States, Tess was still being held by
the FBI, despite legal challenges by her TV network.
Samira was still wanted but Jamie hadn't been identi-
fied.

Samira leaned her head against the wing of the chair.
A dull headache was settling in behind her eyes. She
closed them. How bad would it look for her parents if
she was caught breaking into Hyland's hotel suite? But
what if she wasn't caught? What if she could get access
to the vault and fix everything?

There had to be more she could do to prepare. Virtually explore the hotel layout and security, poke and
prod its systems in the hope there was some useful flaw.
Her eyes stung. *In a minute...*

She was woken by murmuring voices, behind her.
She shot out of the chair, sending the laptop flying
again.

Three people were seated around the dining table—
Jamie, Angelito and an athletic brunette who looked like
she'd fit right into their commando unit.

Jamie stood, scraping the chair back behind him.
"Samira, this is Holly."

The woman gave a sharp, assessing nod. She looked
vaguely familiar.

"Angelito you know," Jamie finished.

Hardly.

"'Rafe,'" Angelito said, in the indiscernible accent
she remembered. Someone who'd moved around a lot,
like her. "I'm just a diving and surfing instructor now."

Was that code for something like *security contractor*

or *assassin*? No amount of surfing would make that guy look like anything but a commando. She finger-combed her hair. As the rush of panic at waking settled, her back began to ache. *No, you can't have another crack.*

"I've just been catching Holly and Angeli—*Rafe* up on the story so far," Jamie said, pulling out the fourth chair for Samira. He was clean-shaven and his face had lost the sunken look. She'd never seen him clean-shaven. He looked less soldier, more doctor—and no less attractive.

She walked behind the kitchen island, found a glass and filled it.

"And we've come up with a plan," he said, leaning back against the wall behind the table, casting a *back-me-up-here* look at Rafe and Holly before returning his gaze to Samira. He folded his arms. "We wait until the senator and his daughter go out tonight—he in the tuxedo to this reception, she to her book launch—and we drive into the car park, go up to the room and get them to let us in."

All sound seemed to mute.

"Well, when I say 'us,' I mean you'll wait here. You're too easily recognized. The three of us will go."

She forced the water down her clamped throat. Relief washed over her at the thought of staying behind, but… "If you think they'll even let you into the hotel, let alone anywhere near his floor, let alone… I've been around diplomats since I was a child. You've seen the security—it's intense. More so these days, with the fear of terrorism. You will need keycards, security clearances, ID—"

"We're hoping there's a notable exception to that."

"What do you mean?"

"Laura, the senator's daughter."

Three pairs of eyes trained on her. "I'm not following. Are you planning to sneak in behind her?"

Rafe frowned up at Jamie, making his permanent glower even more intense. "I don't like that Samira's not getting this."

Holly pulled her hair out of its stumpy ponytail and mussed it up. "It worked before. It will again." An American accent but not one Samira could pinpoint. *She* looked like a watersports instructor, with a freckled face and blond streaks in her hair.

"Last time you only had to pass as her from a distance," Rafe growled.

"I fooled you," Holly said.

"I'd never seen Laura in person."

Samira laid her palms on the kitchen island. "What on earth are you talking about?"

"Holly here is our Trojan horse," Jamie said. "She used to be Laura's body double. That's how she and Angelito met, not that I know the whole story. Someday I'll get the *capitaine* drunk and find out, and I'll tell you everything."

Someday. Again, that suggestion there'd be something between them after this.

Rafe's jaw twitched. Samira guessed he wasn't keen on *someday* coming, either. Was that why Holly looked familiar—she *did* resemble one of the most photographed women in America? The fine bone structure, the athletic body, the honey-colored skin…

"I was paid to act like Laura," Holly said. "I studied her closely. The way she talks, the way she moves, the way she holds herself."

"Maybe with the right clothes and a haircut," Samira said. "And makeup and sunglasses, and…" She pushed the heels of her palms into her eyes. "No, this is crazy."

"It won't fool the senator or anybody else who knows Laura well," Jamie said, "but I'm hoping it'll be enough to get us past security and reception, if we breeze in and out quickly. And you said yourself that these diplomatic security agents wouldn't normally be around her, so..."

Samira released her eyes. Stars actually swam in her vision. "You know that secretaries of state block off an entire secure floor in a hotel when they travel? I've seen it. They set up their own security cameras, sniffer dogs—not to mention the dozens of agents and hordes of local police. Plus there's Hyland's very own goon squad."

"But when Hyland and Laura are out, their personal protection will be with them along with the bulk of diplomatic security. So we'd mostly be dealing with police, hotel security and a handful of diplomatic and support staff."

"And it'll be dinnertime, so most of them would be off the floor, leaving a skeleton security presence," Holly said, swinging back on the chair. "So we fabricate a reason that Laura—well, me—pops back to her room at the hotel to grab some forgotten thing, with her security detail." She nodded at Rafe and Jamie. "And we grab this fob and bring it back. If we don't find it, we leave again pretty damn quick."

"You can't... This is..."

"Ambitious?" Jamie said. "Was that the word you were thinking of? Look, we will consider every eventuality and have it covered—and we'll make sure we have an escape route if things go to hell. We're good at this kind of stuff." His eyes were bright. He *liked* this kind of stuff.

"What if it's in the room safe? What if Fitz is standing right outside the door? Oh my God, I can't believe

I'm taking this seriously enough to point out all the many obvious flaws."

"What do you think we came all the way here for, Samira?" Jamie said. "What did you think we would do?"

"It wasn't my choice to come here. Though maybe I thought I might be able to infiltrate the hotel security systems and... I don't know. Now that I've seen all that security standing around... This just seems all too dangerous."

"Everything in life has risks."

"Maybe in your world. But in the world I live in— *used* to live in, *want* to live in—most people just do ordinary things on ordinary days and have a realistic expectation of not being thrown in jail. Or worse."

Jamie winked at Holly. "You make it sound so dull."

Samira threw up her hands. "Dull? I miss dull. I miss normal. I miss average. How many more laws are we going to break today?"

"By bringing down this arsehole we'll make the world safer for a lot of people. We'll help a lot of people live happily dull and secure lives—including yourself, if that's what you want. You want this guy to continue to be one of the most powerful men on earth? Maybe even US president?"

"Of course not."

"You are in a unique position of being able to prevent it, while securing Tess's freedom and saving Charlotte's neck—and your parents. And then there's you and me." She shut her stinging eyes. He said it like they were an entity. She knew he didn't mean it like that. "And anyway, you'll be waiting here, in safety."

"It's not me I'm worried about." She opened her eyes. He was right. She couldn't let her lack of courage screw things up now. "We're talking about a very short window of opportunity." Her stomach ached like she'd done a hundred sit-ups. "The password is set to expire at eight o'clock. We'd have to get the fob and set the files to copy over before we're locked out."

"How long will they take to upload?"

"That depends on what's there, but it doesn't matter too much. As long as the process *begins* before the password changes, it'll finish the upload."

"So it's going to be tight," Jamie said. "But we have all afternoon to get our plan watertight." He was jumpy, wired. Oh God—*drugged*?

"And if it's not watertight we're not doing it," she said, eyeballing him. How could she tell if he was using? Nicole had seen it in his eyes.

Jamie's gaze flicked momentarily to Rafe. "Sure," he said, unconvincingly.

"And there's one more problem with that plan," Samira said.

Jamie tilted his head, his forehead bunching.

"If I stay here," she continued, "there won't be enough time for you to get back with the fob before the password expires."

She inhaled. God, was she really about to say this?

"I'll have to come with you."

CHAPTER NINETEEN

DARKNESS FELL EARLY, cranking the nerves in Samira's chest, like her body knew what nightfall would bring. It was less of a transition from daylight to sunset to night than a gradual dimming from gray to black. The temperature, which hadn't moved off cold and damp all day, sank along with the light.

Shortly after midday, Laura had posted photos from the West End boutique where she'd bought a dress and coat for the book signing. While Holly bleached her hair and Samira studied YouTube tutorials to figure out how to cut it into something resembling Laura's style, Rafe went shopping for the same dress and coat, and a long list of makeup, to Holly's specifications. He returned grumbling about the price tags and the women he'd had to fight for the clothes.

"Don't worry, *capitaine*," Jamie had said. "You can sell them on eBay for a profit. Unless something happens in the next few hours to, I don't know, ruin Laura Hyland's reputation."

"And don't forget," added Holly, holding the slinky red dress against her. "We're basically using Hyland's money."

"How so?" Jamie said.

"Rafe forced him to pay me hush money after I, uh, *quit* my job, but I always felt too sick about everything to spend it." She gave Samira a sideways look. "I also know some secrets that wouldn't look good for Laura or the senator—but no one would believe them. I'd love to get some dirt on them today."

"Me, too," Samira said, pulling several magnets off the fridge to wipe a keycard Holly had somehow pick-pocketed from a hotel guest in a café that morning. Crime #453.

Still grumbling, Rafe had left again to hire a car the same model and color as Laura's Prius. At least they weren't stealing it. Jamie, meanwhile, visited a suit hire shop and an office supplies store, where he bought a printer and laminator with the last of Samira's savings.

When he returned and pulled on his suit, Samira couldn't help stealing glances. Nothing sexier than a well-cut man in a well-cut suit. Except a well-cut man stripped from his well-cut suit…

With Rafe still out and Holly in the bathroom, Jamie sauntered to the table, where Samira was designing fake security credentials on the laptop, having zoomed in on photos of Laura's bodyguards on the web and enhanced their swing tags, which wasn't easy because they usually kept them flipped over. He stood behind her, his warm presence quickening her breath. On her phone, which he'd set to play loops of her playlist—to give her courage, no doubt—Dionne Warwick was lost in a husky fog. "I'll Never Love This Way Again."

Maybe not, Dionne. But he's not the guy for me.

After a minute he leaned down and gently pushed her hair away from her ear. The skin on her neck tingled and she glanced at the bathroom, her stomach clenching. The back of Holly's newly blond hair was just visible, as she leaned toward the mirror, applying more makeup than Samira would use in a year.

Jamie whispered, "You have a thing for a guy in a suit."

She had a thing for one particular commando doctor in a suit, yeah. Who wouldn't? She zipped up her spine, which only brought Jamie's lips closer to her neck. "Because men in suits don't tend to risk their lives on a daily basis."

He nuzzled her neck. "So, *so* dull."

She pushed away from the table, forcing him to skip sideways to avoid her. "I came up blank on getting into the hotel's systems, though I found a recent video interview in an online industry magazine with their head of security."

"How does that help us?" he said, all business again.

She set the video to play. "He's sitting in front of a bank of hotel security monitors. The interview's ten minutes long, and in that time it cycles through all the camera positions a couple of times. With the help of the photos on their website and internet reviews, and floor plans I found in a heritage architecture magazine online, I've been able to map them."

"Genius."

"Not as cool as rerouting them, but... I also found a little more dirt on Fitz, and I've managed to get into Laura's email, thanks to the virus we planted earlier." She closed the laptop and took a knife to the printer box, sitting on the kitchen island. "It's the password recovery email account for all her social media, which means I can lock her out so she can't post while we're at the hotel, in case anyone there is following her feed. And seeing as she has seven million followers on Twitter alone, that's a high probability. To her, it should just look like a glitch."

"I love it when you talk techie."

As she held the box open, Jamie coaxed the printer out. His arm didn't seem to be hindering him.

"I hoped we might find something revealing in her email," Samira continued, "but she's just like her father—permanently deletes everything."

"Maybe she's more closely involved than we think."

Holly called out from the bathroom. "She's with her father almost all the time, so she'd have to be aware of the shit he's dealing in."

"Isn't she, like, thirty?" Jamie said. "Is this him being overprotective or her being clingy?"

Holly's voice mumbled as she applied something to her lips. "They live in this insular world where they're pretty much all each other has. Works for both of them. She boosts his popularity, he keeps her in the spotlight, which promotes her books and TV programs and things. She's a bit like him—you can't help liking her but you get this nagging sense that there's a hidden agenda to everything she does and says."

"You *like* this guy?"

"I did once," Holly said, standing back and assessing her work. "Everyone does, Doc. You'd get an instant boner, I swear. He's one of these people who connects with everyone—old, young, male, female, rich, poor. He makes you feel like you're the only one in the room—until you look around and realize everyone in the room is under the same spell."

Samira hooked up the printer. A bit like Jamie.

"But I've seen what happens when people get on his bad side," Holly continued, "away from the cameras. It ain't pretty."

"Indeed," Samira said, thinking back to the sat phone conversation in the forest. *Truth and lies are whatever I say they are.* Weird to think that Holly had a personal history with the man who'd for so long been the distant bogeyman in Samira's life.

"These look great," Jamie said a few minutes later as the first of the IDs came off the printer. Holly ducked into the bedroom to dress, closing the door.

Samira stood beside him, watching the next three whir out. "They might not pass scrutiny from someone who knows the system, but I'm hoping it's not those people we'll need to fool, that with 'Laura' with us we'll pass right by the police and hotel staff." She picked up a sheet and scrutinized it. "That's the thing with the VIP life—you don't open doors, doors are opened for you. You don't drive a car, cars are driven for you. You don't carry keys or even a wallet. You just follow the path laid out for you, like a permanent red carpet." She set the paper down. "And, in our case, hope like hell."

Jamie lifted the laminator onto the counter. "Have faith, Samira. It's a good plan and we've done everything we can to ensure it works. We know there will be variables—there always are—but we can handle them. It's what we do, what we're trained to do."

She tore the tape from the top of the laminator box. "Stop making me feel bad about being worried. It's a perfectly reasonable reaction."

"I know it is."

She stopped. He was studying her with a serious face. No wry grin, no twinkling eyes. "You do?"

"I'm not saying you shouldn't be worried. It's a very worrying situation. And I'm certainly not trying to make you feel bad—quite the opposite. I'm saying you need to believe in yourself—and the rest of us. You need to back yourself so you don't end up paralyzed by your anxiety. Yes, you can be worried, you can feel fear. We all do. But don't let that stop you from thinking and acting rationally."

"I wish I had your confidence."

He smiled. "You do."

"Jamie, I'm terrified right now. Look." She held her right hand straight out, palm down. It trembled.

He folded her hand into both of his, coaxing her to face him. His eyes had faded to gray-blue in the gloomy light. "Despite my failures, I have confidence in the skills I've spent much of my adult life working at. Medicine, the military. And so should you. You blow me away with your knowledge and ideas and talents, in things I couldn't begin to understand. Play to those strengths."

Something kicked in her chest. What would it be like to have him around permanently—that reassurance, that smile, that sexy body...

That option wasn't on the table.

He pulled her closer, his chest inches from hers. Why did she always get a flush of guilt over what was happening between them? She was no longer anyone's fiancée.

"You wouldn't expect me to hack into a computer system, and I wouldn't expect you to take someone down in hand-to-hand combat or perform an emergency tracheotomy." With one fingertip, he circled her ear, leaving a trail of goose bumps. "Your strengths are different from mine, and that's a good thing. You don't give yourself enough credit. And, anyway, it's incredibly valuable to know your vulnerabilities and how to manage them. If you're blind to your weaknesses, like a lot of people, you're powerless against them."

"I *don't* know how to manage them. You've seen what happens when I give in to them."

"Well, don't give in."

"It's not that easy. It's not like it's a choice."

"I know it's not easy—but I have immense faith in you. Like you wouldn't believe."

His quiet sincerity was killing her. He traced a finger down her jawline, forcing her to inhale. She should step away. How did they so often end up back here, a breath away from kissing? He leaned in, his open suit jacket brushing her chest. The skin on her face prickled.

She pulled away, a sudden tempest churning in her chest, a storm of emotions she couldn't even define. "Says the man who's too scared to confront his own weakness." She flung up her hands. "You're always trying to fix me. Why don't you fix your damn self?"

The color flushed from his face, leaving an expression she'd seen only once before, on that horrible morning in France.

Hurt.

"Oh God, I'm sorry, Jamie. I just… I can't… I'm too… This is all…"

The doorbell buzzed and the bedroom door flung open. "Rafe's back," said Holly, hopping as she tugged on a stiletto.

"I'll go down and let him in," Jamie said, touching his fist to his mouth as he turned his back.

Shit. What an idiot. Here was Jamie trying to build her confidence, and she went and slayed his, punching him in his weak spot because she was so wrapped up in her own fears. A drowning woman pulling down her rescuer.

"Are you okay, Samira?" Holly said.

"Dehnanay," Samira said, sitting down hard on a dining chair. "Er, fine."

"Is something going on between you and Doc?"

Samira blinked. Holly wore Laura's trademark sooty eye makeup—a few smudges short of two black eyes—but still somehow managed to not look like a zombie. Her irises stood out so bright blue they were difficult to tear focus from. And even harder to lie to.

"It's…got a little complicated, yes. But, no, there's nothing…"

"He's a good guy."

"I know. But he's not available, so…"

"Neither was Rafe when I met him. When this is over, when you can breathe easy again, give him a chance. He deserves a second chance. Everyone does."

Jamie returned, followed by Rafe. Holly smiled at Samira then turned to Rafe, swishing her dress like a flamenco dancer, a matching scarf trailing from her neck, her lips a glossy scarlet. "What do you think?" She clutched a handful of her newly cut hair. "We're waiting for Laura to post a photo so we can style my hair to match. I'm hoping she's going for messy tonight and not sleek."

Samira cringed. Cutting someone's hair had been another first in a long few days of firsts.

"You look amazing, of course." The look in Rafe's eyes, the creak in his voice, made Samira feel like an intruder. Her belly hollowed. She hadn't allowed herself to feel loneliness in so long, but seeing two people so obviously in love… After coming so close yet so far with Jamie…

"There's one problem," Rafe said. "You don't look like Holly anymore."

Holly playfully swatted his shoulder and he grabbed her arm and spun her in a faux fighting move. But he finished by pulling her close, his chest against her back, his hand resting lightly on her belly. She laughed, covering his hand with hers. Samira glanced at Jamie. He was watching them, too, frowning.

"I'm not showing, am I?" Holly said, looking down at their hands. "This dress isn't forgiving."

"Oh my God," Samira said, standing. "You're pregnant?"

Holly fixed her with a tough-girl look that was about as far from Laura as it was possible to get. "I've survived much worse. I can defend myself."

Rafe spun her again, gently, to face him. "You won't be doing anything risky. No ninja moves. I'll be right there the whole time."

"I'm pregnant, not disabled. Tell him, Doc."

"How many weeks?" Jamie said, a happy disbelief in his tone.

"Hardly enough to count. I found out last week."

"Then the baby's well protected," Jamie said. "Still a jelly baby inside a pumpkin."

"I need a nervous pee," Holly said, heading for the bathroom. "Can I blame that on the jelly baby?"

Samira didn't know whether to be relieved that someone else was admitting to nerves, or worried that a woman with Holly's evident confidence was nervous.

I wish I had your confidence.

You do.

"Congrats," Jamie said, holding out his hand to Rafe.

Rafe looked grim—when did he not?—but shook Jamie's hand. He lowered his voice. "I don't care what she says—we're protecting her."

Jamie nodded. *"Oui, capitaine."*

"And don't you dare tell her I said that."

"Oui, capitaine."

AS THE H-HOUR grew nearer, Jamie tried to prop up his energy levels—to fool both Samira and his own brain—but a head-to-toe ache settled into his muscles like he was fighting the flu. He'd spent all the time he was supposed to be napping in a fog of dark temptation and self-loathing. Samira was right—he was a fraud. *You're always trying to fix me. Why don't you fix your damn self?*

In the bad old days, he'd be taking uppers about now—and how good would that feel? He needed to be at his best tonight and he was far from it.

Hyland's convoy left, the senator wearing a thick coat unbuttoned over a tux, talking on a phone. No gadget visible but they couldn't get a clear look. Fitz stayed behind. *Merde.* He was one of a handful of goons who might ID Jamie. Then again, all Fitz would have seen in the forest before he conked out was a disheveled wild man leaping at him in the dark. And he'd have an almighty hangover from the concussion.

Samira fitted and taped covert earpieces, mics and mic packs on each of them, bought by Jamie from an electronics store that morning, after Samira had researched them online. As Holly pulled her hair over her ears to hide hers, Samira taped fake plastic-coated coiled wire onto Rafe's and Jamie's necks, to match Hyland's security agents. Even just having her feathery fingers touching his neck like that...

"I feel like I'm wired up with a bomb," Jamie said, moving away quickly, buttoning his suit jacket.

"Don't even joke about that, after last year," Rafe said.

Jamie shut himself into the bedroom. "Testing, testing," he said, pushing the press-to-talk button disguised as a cuff link.

Three replies, loud and clear, in his ear. Too loud. His head felt stuck in a vise, in danger of caving any second.

"We'll get a little interference," said Samira, her voice clear but distant, "especially when we're on different floors, but it's a powerful and sensitive system, so you should only need to whisper."

Jamie adjusted his earpiece so it sat more comfortably. "Have you used these before, Samira?"

"We used to play around with them at university."

"Of course you did."

"We were fantasists. Never thought I'd be doing something like this for real."

"Heads up," Holly said. "Prius on the move."

Jamie crossed the bedroom, knocking over the rucksack. Through the net curtains he made out the passing car. "Was she in it?"

"Blonde in the back," Holly said.

"She's just posted on social media that she's on her way." Sharp tapping filtered into Jamie's ear—Samira on the keyboard. "With a selfie in the car."

"With a messy hairdo," Holly said, triumphantly. "No need to stake this woman out, is there? She does it all herself."

Jamie exhaled, fluttering the netting. He crouched, stuffing the rucksack's spilled contents back in. He picked up the first-aid kit. Before he knew what he was doing, he'd unclipped the lid. If ever he needed a little help...

"Jamie?"

Feedback squealed in his earpiece. He dived for the mic pack in his pocket. The kit went flying. His fingers fumbled. "How the fuck do you turn this thing off?" Any second his skull would crack.

He ripped the earpiece out, just as Samira burst in. She grabbed the pack from his pocket and flicked a switch. Silence. He squeezed his eyes tight. Thank Christ.

"I'll make some adjust—"

He sensed her freezing, and flicked his eyes open. She crouched and picked up a syringe and vial from the carpet. The contents of the kit had scattered.

"This is the same stuff that was on the bedside table at the cottage." She picked up a blister pack of tabs and then a bottle of pills, reading the labels. "You told me you'd destroy it."

"And I will. They just…fell out of the rucksack." He swept together the drugs and dumped them in the kit. "When have I had time? I can't leave them in a public rubbish bin where any homeless bugger could pick them out."

Her forehead wrinkled. She thought he was lying—and why shouldn't she? *The truth I can deal with. It's lies and deception I have a problem with.*

"Jamie, have you taken any more since the cottage?"

"No."

She dropped eye contact, blinking fast.

"But of course you don't believe me." He clicked the lid back on, shaking his head. "And why should you? That's the problem. That's always going to be the problem. You can't trust me anymore. If I'm jumpy, you'll suspect drugs. If I sleep too heavily, you'll suspect drugs. If I'm too quiet, if I'm on edge, if I'm too chilled, if I'm wired, if I'm tired, if I'm happy, if I go out to meet somebody without telling you every detail, if I spend too long in the bathroom, if my eyes look different… You'll be searching the rubbish and checking my fucking phone log. You see? This is one of the many reasons we could never work, you and I."

"You keep talking as if I'm asking for a relationship,"

she said quietly. "I'm not, okay? I've asked for nothing from you and I'm not going to. I'm not…ready for any of this and neither are you."

He stood, abruptly, his head protesting at the rush of movement. "Shite. I know you're not. I really don't know why I said all of that."

Yes, he did. Because he'd found somebody he'd actually like to go there with but that would mean facing up to things he didn't want to face up to. And he'd screwed everything up before they could get started, anyway. He couldn't be with somebody who didn't trust him any more than she could be with somebody she didn't trust.

She stood, slowly, quickly stepping backward when she realized how close they were. "I have to…disable Laura's social media. We have to…go." She turned away, and froze. "You're not answerable to me, Jamie. Just to yourself."

She left, closing the door behind her. He stared at the box in his hands.

CHAPTER TWENTY

FROM THE HIRED PRIUS, the hotel loomed into the heavy sky like a medieval prison. Hidden downlights cast shadows under its architraves, as if it were frowning down on Samira. *I'm watching you.* Along the road, streetlamps lit silvery blades of rain.

Thank God she'd be waiting out the break-in in the basement, hidden behind the windows Rafe had blacked out to match those of Laura's car. She clutched the laptop. Holly had begged the hotel's Wi-Fi password from the guy she'd stolen the keycard from, pretending to be a fellow guest who'd forgotten it.

They slowed as they passed through the valet parking bay. Holly lowered her window and a parking attendant approached. Beyond him the roller door was guarded by a police officer in a heavy coat. She raised her hand as if to shield her face from the drizzle. Samira opened the laptop with shaking fingers, swiped the mouse pad to bring it out of hibernation and hunkered down over the screen, pulling tendrils of the brown wig over her shoulders, to more closely resemble Laura's brunette assistant.

"Excuse me. I'm so sorry," Holly called to the attendant, in a slightly different accent, loud enough for the cop to hear. "I forgot something. We need to pop back in real quick. Do you mind opening the…?" She gestured at the roller door.

If the attendant or cop thought it odd that Laura was doing the talking and not her staff they said nothing. Samira opened a blank document and furiously typed nonsense, her ears and peripheral vision working overtime. A clunk and rattle. Ahead, the door was lifting. They passed into the gloomy interior, and she practiced exhaling with a whoosh and then letting her chest fill with new oxygen all by itself, as if breathing were a thoroughly normal bodily function. From the driver's seat, Jamie glanced back and gave a somber smile.

She directed him to a security camera black spot in a corner, from where "Laura" and her bodyguard could catch an elevator to the lobby. Rafe would accompany Holly, as he more closely resembled one of Laura's detail, while Jamie stayed with Samira. That too was a comfort, even if the air between them had thickened.

I'm not ready for any of this and neither are you.

A small irrational part of her had hoped he would challenge her, as he had with so many of her fears and doubts, declare that actually he *was* ready. But he'd backed right off. This man who was so willing to fight for what he believed in, for the people he believed in, wasn't prepared to fight for a future for the two of them. But who was she to judge? She wasn't fighting either. Always easier not to take the risk.

Holly grabbed her clutch purse from the seat beside her and, with a wink and grin at Samira, let herself out. Only Rafe seemed to share Samira's doubts, his face steelier by the minute. No need to fake the vigilant glower of a bodyguard. Samira's stomach flip-flopped as she watched them walk to the lift, Holly's head bent over a cell phone in her hand, averting her face from the security camera there. Her new cream coat hung open and a sliver of her red scarf trailed out.

As they disappeared into the elevator, Jamie twisted to face Samira. There'd be no talking about where they'd left things, thank God. They needed to listen to Rafe and Holly's progress over the comms. Rafe had his set to continuous broadcast, for now. Enforced silence—that was something well within Samira's comfort zone. It was bad enough that Rafe and Holly had heard the argument in the bedroom—not that they'd said anything but Samira had noted their sideways glances afterward. She winced at the thought. Jamie frowned, tipping his head in a question. She shook her head.

An elevator bell chimed, through the earpiece. "About to step into the lobby," Rafe murmured. "Wish us luck."

Samira forced her breath to remain even and quiet as Holly's stilettos clicked on the marble floor of the reception atrium. Holly would hang back, in view of the concierge but still apparently absorbed by the phone, while Rafe approached the desk.

"Miss Hyland's keycard has stopped working," Rafe said, in a passable American accent. Samira pictured him raising the wiped card. The connection glitched a moment, and then his voice returned. "...a new card?"

Samira closed her eyes. Rafe was armed with one of the handguns Jamie had stolen from the goons in the forest but that wouldn't get him far. Holly had refused to carry a weapon. A woman's voice filtered in, too distant to make out words. After that, only the slight buzz of white noise, Samira's own quickening breath and an echoing drip, drip, drip from somewhere in the basement.

She opened her eyes. Jamie's eyes were gray again, looking over her shoulder to scan the garage, blinking calmly, his jaw set. Was this Jamie the soldier? He didn't have the jumpiness of earlier, so maybe he wasn't on anything. Or maybe that was why he appeared calm.

That's always going to be the problem. You can't trust me anymore.

True, he wasn't the infallible hero she'd thought him to be, but somehow that made him more attractive, not less. Right now, the attraction was physical—a pull in her gut, a craving to reach out and cup his smooth jaw. It'd been hell to fix his earpiece in place and tape the cords to his neck and back when all she'd wanted was to tiptoe up and kiss him.

Rafe muttered something. Jamie's gaze met hers, his forehead wrinkling. She shrugged. After half a minute the heels clicked again. The ping of an arriving elevator. More clicking. Jamie tapped a hand on the back of his seat.

"All good," Holly whispered, feedback squealing. "That blond guy was in the lobby. Sitting on an armchair, talking to a couple of people. I think he looked my way."

"He did," Rafe added, "but he didn't register a problem."

The elevator chimed. A voice crackled, a Scottish accent. "Are you going down?"

"No, ma'am," Rafe said. "Catch the next one."

A few seconds later, another chime. The top floor? Samira listened for footfalls—but the hallways on the accommodation floors were carpeted. She pictured the scene from the plans and photos, filling in the gaps from her own experience of hotels heaving with diplomats. With Hyland and Laura both out, only a few diplomatic security agents would be on guard in the hall—maybe at the elevators, at the right-hand turn in the corridor, outside the senator's suite… The adjoining rooms would

have been cleared for Hyland's personal staff. A group
of suits wearing lanyards had left the hotel just after
Hyland—going for dinner, maybe—but some might
have stayed back to do paperwork and communica-
tions. Samira rubbed her face with both hands. How
long was the damn hallway? She checked the time on
the car's clock. Less than ninety minutes until the password changed.

"Hey, man, you know the rules." A different American accent in the earpiece. "No men in the suite un-
supervised."

"Yeah, yeah." Rafe, sounding creditably nonchalant.

Samira raised her eyebrows, Jamie mirroring her.
Laura wasn't allowed to be alone with a man in her own
hotel suite? Still, it wasn't much of a setback. Surely
Rafe could wait outside, and it was Holly who had the
safecracking equipment in her clutch—including, curi-
ously, a stethoscope, pen and notebook, in which she'd
drawn a grid. Evidently she hadn't always been a sailing instructor.

"The suite's empty," Holly said, accompanied by
shuffling and slapping noises. She'd switched on her
continuous feed. "No sign of the fob." After a few minutes, a clatter—coat hangers being moved? "The safe
is standard hotel equipment. Shouldn't take long. I'll
have to take out the earpiece for a bit."

A clunk. Holly's breath became audible, joining the
rhythm of the dripping water. Jamie's eyes fixed blindly
into the middle distance behind Samira, as if he were
also conjuring an image of Holly, stethoscope pressed
against the metal door, turning the dial, listening to
whatever it was you listened to when you cracked a safe.
Who knew safecrackers actually used stethoscopes? On
the car clock, three endless minutes flicked by.

"Okay," Holly whispered. "It's a five-digit code."

Jamie refocused on Samira. She widened her eyes. All that time just to figure out how many numbers she had to crack?

Samira's laptop chimed and lit up, making her jump.

"Oh my God," she said to Jamie. "It's the alert I set up for Charlotte. She's online." Hope sparked in her belly, then extinguished. "Or someone else is using her credentials."

"Can you tell the difference?"

Samira tried a few web pages. "Nothing on her public social media, and I don't want to risk logging in to my social media to check her private accounts—not on the hotel's Wi-Fi. I'll check if she's been in the game." She brought up "Cosmos." "Oh God. She hasn't been in here but Erebus has." She clicked into the world where Charlotte had left the message. "There's a new treasure chest, left a couple of hours ago. Damn, I should have checked." She clicked on it. "It's password-protected."

"Shite."

"Hang on. The password is a security question." She clicked through. "Jagger's favorite food. Okay, that's kind of creepy." She typed *kitfo* and hit Enter. "I'm in. This person knew Latif well."

As Samira read, the earpiece crackled. "Good news, for those of you listening at home," Holly said. "I have the fob. Heading back."

Samira looked at Jamie. It worked. It actually worked.

"What's the message?" he said, nodding at the laptop.

"It's a British cell phone number, with the phone provider's website and a PIN. And a note—'This guy has Vespa.'" Samira zeroed in on the number. "That's the phone we stole from the goon at the hospital. We already have access to his information. This doesn't help."

"Are you sure?"

"I remember numbers. It had a lot of sevens in it. It's the same..." Through the earpiece, Holly reported they were safely back in the elevator. "Hold on. No, it's not the same. That number ended in a five. This one's a four. They're sequential—it's one of the phones our goon in the hospital was communicating with. Shit."

"What does that mean?"

"It means that I can log in to the provider website and maybe track the movements of this second phone. If it indeed belongs to someone who's been involved with Charlotte's disappearance, I might be able to triangulate the movements of the two phones with the location she's just logged on from."

"I love it when I have no idea what you're saying."

"It means I might be able to find Charlotte."

"I like that even more."

Her hands shook so hard she couldn't type the web address. She pressed both hands to her chest. Her heart thumped.

"Anything I can help with?" Jamie said.

She shook her head, fighting for breath.

He hopped out of the car, shutting his door behind him. Before she could protest, he'd opened the rear door and slid in beside her. He slipped a hand around her waist. "Breathe with me," he said. "Like we practiced."

Yes, that was one thing he could help with. She lowered her fingers to the keyboard, exhaling, and let her chest fill, without effort. As her breath settled, she began typing. She caught movement outside—Rafe and Holly exiting the elevator, Holly's gaze fixed on the phone.

"If you two are up to something in the back of the car," Rafe murmured, his hand on his cuff link, "now would be a good time to pretend you're not."

Jamie sniggered, reaching his other arm around Samira to activate his mic. "Only virtual excitement in here."

Rafe and Holly opened the front doors and dropped onto the seats. They removed their earpieces and switched off their mics. Jamie did the same.

Holly shook out the contents of her clutch, drew out the fob and held it on her palm. "Too easy."

Samira took it, her hand trembling again. "I can't believe I'm actually holding this." She switched screens. The triangulation would have to wait. Jamie squeezed her waist as she accessed Hyland's server and carefully input the string of numbers on the fob.

Samira swore, as a warning flashed up.

"What's wrong?" Holly said.

"It's telling me this is the wrong number."

"Could you have keyed it in wrong?"

"I swear I didn't but I can try one more time without it locking me out or raising a flag." She waited for the code to refresh. "Okay, Jamie, watch over my shoulder and make sure I get it right."

She input it and pressed Enter.

Incorrect number. You have one more attempt.

"Damn," Samira said. "This must be a fob for something else. Another account, maybe."

Holly slumped. "I knew it was too easy."

Samira ran her hands through her hair. "*Something you have.* What else could it be? What else does he carry—?" She straightened, picturing him walking to his car in his tuxedo. "Oh no."

Jamie tensed. "What?"

"Next best guess? An app on his cell phone. Damn."

"How long until he's due back?" Holly said.

"Thirteen minutes," Samira said. "But we can't walk up and…pickpocket him. It's over."

Holly twisted in her seat. "When he returns to the hotel he'll go up to his room, right? And when you get home at the end of the day, or into your hotel, what's the first thing you do?"

Samira shrugged.

"You empty your pockets, right? Keycard, wallet, phone, whatever."

"What are you suggesting?" Samira's neck goose pimpled.

"I wait in the room for him."

"No." Rafe and Samira spoke together.

"And do what?" Rafe continued. "You might fool a concierge and a few security guards. You won't fool her father."

"I could be lying down in Laura's bedroom with the lights off—I'll call out to say I have a headache. A towel over my eyes. Not quite myself. Tell him I skipped out of the launch early. And then first opportunity I get—he takes a leak, he takes a shower, he goes into his room to get changed—I walk out with the phone."

"What if you don't get an opportunity?" Rafe said.

"I'll come back down and we'll hightail it out of Dodge before Laura returns."

"What if you can't get out? What if he sits by the door the whole time? What if Laura gets back while you're still in there?"

"I'll think of something."

"You'll think of a way to explain why there are suddenly two Lauras? What if he comes in to check on you, bring you some water, realizes you're not her?"

Holly gave a wry smile. "I honestly don't think he pays that much attention to her. He's not the doting type, more the controlling type."

"You're not going back up."

Holly studied Rafe a second, then took in Jamie and Samira. "Anyone got a better plan?"

"We leave," Samira said. "Get out of town, lie low, wait for another break."

"And then what?" Jamie said. "Let Hyland fly out? Leave Tess and your parents and Charlotte to their fates? We're so close—we're unlikely to get a better opportunity."

Samira held up her hands. "I know. I was just... wishful."

Holly grabbed her clutch. "I'm doing it."

"No."

"Rafe, I am doing it." She fitted her earpiece. "I have to get in there before he gets back."

Rafe fisted his hand and knocked it against his thigh with a solid thud. "I won't be able to wait outside the door, this time. As soon as Hyland's personal detail walk up that corridor, they'll know I'm an impostor, which will endanger you."

"Come on. We're running out of time."

As Holly climbed out, Rafe opened his door, slowly shaking his head. "I'll have to wait for you on the floor below. Doc? You coming?"

Jamie removed his arm from Samira's waist. "You'll be okay here?"

She nodded. *No.*

He fixed his earpiece and switched on the mic. "Key is in the ignition if you need it."

"Tell Holly to set her mic to continuous," she said.

They walked to the lifts, while Samira hunkered down and switched screens. Locating Charlotte would take her mind off what was happening above.

As Samira worked, the others remained silent, which didn't help her twisted insides. Other voices filtered through Holly's mic. The invisible drip tap, tap, tapped until it was drumming on Samira's skull.

A thunk, a whir and the roller door rattled upward, headlights behind it. A large car rolled in, followed by another, and another. Land Rovers. Samira pressed her mic button, in her coat pocket. "Hyland's motorcade just came in," she whispered. The cars turned and slotted into parks side by side at the other end of the basement. Samira heard a door open and close. The dark head of a woman appeared over a dozen car roofs. She leaned back, lighting a cigarette. The other doors remained closed. "Looks like it's only the drivers—they must have let the passengers out up top. They seem to be staying with the cars."

"Can we get back without them noticing?" Jamie said, in an undertone.

"No, but hopefully they won't be concerned with us. They'll be local hired help. Their jobs will be to look after the cars, nothing else."

"Okay. Rafe and I are waiting on the stairwell outside the sixth floor. Holly's gone up to the seventh."

Samira chewed her lip. After a minute of murmured voices and clicks, Holly's whisper crackled through. "I'm in. Room's clear. Same guys on the door, so I'm guessing he's not here yet. Wait—a lot of voices outside." Her breath sounded quickened, like she was moving fast.

"No risks, Holly." Rafe.

"When have I ever taken—?"

A man's voice, in the background.

"Hey, Pop," Holly called, sounding like she'd put a towel over her mouth.

Samira strained but couldn't work out the man's words.

"Shit," Holly whispered. "He's on the phone."

"Take your time." Rafe, again. "No risks."

After a silent few minutes, a man's voice murmured again.

"Headache," Holly croaked. "Came home early."

Samira's computer beeped. A news alert. Her mouth dried. "Local radio is reporting that Laura has cut short her signing. She's on her way back."

CHAPTER TWENTY-ONE

A PHONE TRILLED DISTANTLY, in Samira's earpiece. Holly swore. "Hyland's taken another call."

"Get out of there, Holly," Rafe rumbled.

"Couple more minutes."

As they continued a whispered argument, Samira checked an online map. "Guys, Laura will be here within six minutes. We have to get our car out, at the very least. The second the real Prius pulls up outside they'll figure it out and we'll be trapped."

"Can you drive it out?" muttered Rafe.

Samira eyed the key in the transmission. There was nothing she'd rather do. "I have to stay in the hotel to upload these files, if we manage to get this damn phone. We're running out of time."

"I'm going nowhere until Holly is safe." Rafe paused. "That leaves you, Doc."

"Merde," Jamie said.

"Leave me your weapon." Rafe, again. "Park around the corner, out of sight, then come back in through the security tent. You have the pass. Let's hope it works."

"God, this is the last thing I want to do," Jamie said, breathless. "Samira, I'm on my way down. Is there somewhere you can hide?"

She brought up the hotel plans and checked security camera positions. "The gym and pool are at the other end of the basement. I'll go there." She'd have to walk past the drivers but they'd have no reason to be suspicious. The laptop beeped. Her jaw dropped. "Oh my God."

"Samira?" Jamie, again.

"I've found Charlotte."

A door beside the elevators opened. The north stairwell. Jamie strode out, eyeing the Land Rovers, his open suit jacket flapping. He opened the Prius door and landed on the driver's seat.

"Where is she?"

Samira loaded an internet map and input the coordinates. She switched to satellite mode and zoomed in. "A commercial property." She did a web search. "A former paint factory. I don't suppose you have the kind of friends who could rescue a woman from a platoon of armed goons near London?"

"Texas should be in London by now but he couldn't do it alone. We'll have to risk involving the police. I'll call him from a pay phone, while I'm out. He's a resourceful guy. He'll figure it out."

Samira blew out her cheeks and wrote the address on Holly's notepad.

"I'll return as soon as I can," Jamie said.

"We'll be out of comms until you're back."

In the low light his eyes were dull. "I'll come straight to the gym. Stay safe."

"You, too." She gathered the laptop, and retrieved her beanie from her coat pocket and pulled it low, her wig and scarf swallowing most of her face. She was wearing the camel coat, black dress, scarf and boots she'd worn through immigration but they were less recognizable than the blue coat. *Goodbye sanctuary.*

"Webs of the spider, remember?" he said.

She nodded, filled her lungs, took a last look at Jamie, for courage, and opened the door.

Stale cigarette smoke mixed with fresher fumes, garbage and damp. She dared not watch the Prius as Jamie maneuvered it to the roller door, which began to crank open. In her peripheral vision she sensed the smoking driver turning to look—taking the attention away from Samira.

"We're almost out of time." Rafe's voice strained. "Holly, get out now or I swear I'm—"

"He's nearly done with the phone call," Holly whispered.

Samira pushed open a door into a low-lit corridor. She followed a waft of chlorine to the fitness center. A young bearded guy pounded a treadmill, a tinny beat buzzing from his earphones. Behind him a glass wall revealed a few swimmers in an indoor pool. Samira pushed open a door to a changing room. Deserted. She shut herself in a stall, sat on a bench and pressed her hands to her hot cheeks. Jazz played through a speaker. An air-conditioning unit hummed.

She hit the mic button. "I'm in the women's changing rooms at the fitness center."

"Noted." Rafe's voice.

How long before Jamie returned? Would he get back in the building? Would he be arrested? Captured?

She opened the laptop. Nothing she could do about that but there must be more she could do remotely...

After a few minutes, Holly cleared her throat and murmured an "mmm-hmm," like she was replying to Hyland. More talking, then silence. "Okay, he's in the bathroom. I've got the—"

The distant phone trilled again and abruptly silenced. A man's voice.

"No, Pops, that's my phone." Holly sounded like she was shouting through her sleeve. A snap—the phone going into her clutch? "I'm going downstairs for coffee!"

In Samira's earpiece, a door opened, then shut. A change in background noise. More voices. Samira's heart thumped as if she were the one breezing past a crack squad of diplomatic security and goons.

Holly couldn't take the lift down to the lobby or she'd risk walking right into Laura coming up. Samira checked the floor plan. "Holly, get out of the lift at level two and take the stairwell down between rooms 212 and 214."

A squeal. A door opening? The background noise muted. "I'm already on the stairs, heading down." Holly's echoing voice labored, like she was jogging. "Oh shit."

A beat. "Holly?" Rafe's voice, shaking—also on the move. Any second he'd spot Holly.

"Stop!" A man's voice, in the background—of which mic?

Clattering, clunking, heavy breathing. Rafe's or Holly's? Samira clutched her scarf.

"You?" A woman's voice. Not Holly. Oh God, was that…Laura? She'd come up the stairs? "What the hell?"

A war cry from Holly, a hollow smack, a crash, a groan. "My purse," she hissed. "The phone. Behind a plant. Stairs. Sixth floor." She cried out—in pain, this time.

"She's wearing a wire." A man's voice. The connection crackled and died.

"Holly?" Samira whispered. No answer. "Rafe?"

"I can't find her. Holly, if you're there, say something." Silence. "Samira?"

"I'm here."

"I'm on the stairs outside the sixth floor. Holly hasn't come past and she's not above me. She said she was taking the stairs. So where the fuck is she?"

Cold swept over Samira. "I know what's gone wrong. There are two stairwells, one at the end of each floor." The door to the bathroom swished. Two women came in, chatting. Samira lowered her voice. "She must have taken the south stairwell. You're in the north."

"How do I find the south stairwell?" His voice rolled like thunder.

"You're on the restaurant floor. You can cross through the dining area to the other stairwell without a keycard. Set your mic to continuous." Samira reached into her pocket and did the same.

"Putain." With only one connection left, the line was clearer. Rafe's fast footsteps thudded on carpet and then were swallowed by music, the hubbub of raised voices, clinking plates. A heavy door swished open. "I'm in the south stairwell. It's empty. They have to have taken her to Hyland's floor. I'm going up."

"Rafe, no, you can't go alone. Wait for Jamie, at least. And we need that purse."

"You get the purse. I'm not leaving Holly." His ragged breath and a rhythmic thumping suggested he was climbing, fast.

Samira wiped her hands down her coat. Crap, he was right. She couldn't expect him to deliver her the phone, with Holly in danger. But if Samira could sneak up and retrieve it she could bring all this to an end. She stood, before she could talk herself out of it.

"I'm coming up," she said, clutching the laptop to her chest.

Somehow she made her feet move, one step after another. Two minutes later, she pushed open a door to the south stairwell.

"Is that you on the stairs?" Rafe whispered.

"Awo, at basement level."

She climbed, covering her face as she passed the ground-floor security camera, making out she was rubbing her eyes. As she turned onto another flight, she caught a flash of red ahead. She slowed. A piece of fabric was caught in a door stenciled Level Two.

"Rafe, I've found Holly's scarf." Had she dropped it on purpose? "Level two. They must have taken her down, not up."

"What's on level two?"

"Accommodation. The cheaper rooms. Could be where Laura's staff are quartered."

Rafe had already changed course, descending fast, the footsteps in Samira's earpiece falling a microsecond later than the ones above her. He rounded a corner and jogged down to meet her, gun in hand. Cautiously, he tried the door. Locked.

He nodded at a card reader on the handle. "We need a keycard."

Samira pulled out half a dozen from her coat pocket.

"*Merde.* Where did you get those?"

"The changing room." She shuffled through those that were still in their paper folders, the room numbers written on them. "I searched some bags on the way out. Here," she said, shoving one into his hand. "Level two." She climbed past him. "But you should really wait for Jamie. And hide your gun from the cameras. Enough people are after us already—we don't need hotel security joining the chase."

"I'll be discreet. You going for the purse?"

"*Awo.* We need it to finish this."

"Okay," he said, as if it were an everyday kind of thing.

As she climbed, her breath shuddering, she heard the swish of Rafe opening the door below. She braced for

shouts, scuffles—gunshots. Nothing. Her cheeks prickled. Where was Jamie? How much time had passed?

She passed the fifth floor and rounded the stairwell
again, and again. She wiped sweat from her upper lip.
Ahead was the door to the sixth. Beside it, a pot plant
was tipped on its side, the pottery cracked, dirt spilling
across the floor. She pictured Holly cornered, falling
toward it, knocking it over, stashing the clutch.

The purse was wedged between the branches, the
shape of the phone clear within it. Samira retreated
down the stairs, checking her keycards. Time to hide
again, thank God. At level three she pulled a card from
its folder and swiped. A click, and the light went green.
She pushed open the door, hunkering into her scarf and
wig. Another accommodation level. At the far end of
the corridor, a white-haired couple waited for an elevator. The woman smiled at her. She managed to smile
back. The elevator dinged. As they disappeared inside,
Samira strode to the room marked on the keycard and
knocked. No answer. She let herself in. The door clicked
blessedly shut. She leaned against it and yanked off her
beanie, wig and scarf, trying to concentrate on emptying her lungs rather than filling them.

"Rafe?" No answer. "Rafe?" When had she last heard
anything, even ambient sound? "I'm in room 327."

Silence. She pulled the laptop open and perched on
a neatly made bed. A single suitcase lay open in a corner of the room. A woman's clothes. Hopefully a sole
occupant. Hopefully someone who liked long swims.
Through the gauze curtains she could see the sash windows of the apartment building where they'd devised
this ridiculous plan—the safe house where a naive,
slightly younger version of herself thought she'd be sitting this out.

She switched on Hyland's phone. It requested a swipe pattern. No telltale finger marks, this time. Damn. On the laptop, she searched for videos of him using his phone. After the nineteenth video, she'd worked out the shape of the pattern from his hand movements. Two attempts later, she was in. Just a few more minutes and this would be done... The phone beeped and vibrated. Six missed calls—two from Laura. Trying to report Holly's capture?

Samira found the Gold Linings app on the phone, opened the website on the laptop and shakily entered the code. A loading screen popped up. She gave a silent fist pump.

A message beeped on a gold screen. *Progressing to authentication step three.*

Her stomach plummeted. *Another* level of security?

A grunt, through the earpiece—a cry of effort. A thud. Shouts—indistinct, but definitely Rafe's voice.

"Rafe?" she whispered.

A crack, a buzz, then...nothing. Her breath shallowed out.

"Samira." The voice was little more than a crackle—but it wasn't Rafe's.

"Jamie? Oh thank God. Where are you? Are you okay?"

"I'm fine. I'm right outside but I can't..." His voice dissolved. She caught the word *Fitz*.

"I can't hear you." She walked to the window and drew the gauze back a fraction. No sign of him but the hotel's awnings covered much of her view of the pavement. "Jamie?"

"I can't really hear you, Samira, but if you can hear me...stuck outside a bit longer...he's standing...entrance. Hold on. I'll move...corner. Is this any better?"

"Yes, that's better. Can you hear me?"

"Aye, but I'm going to look odd standing here talking to myself. What's the update?"

She quickly filled him in and told him her room number. God, everything was shot to hell. No Rafe, no Holly, an impenetrable vault. From the security tent below, the unmistakable head of Fitz stepped out, a phone to his ear. He looked up, and she shrank back—not that he'd be able to see her.

"Fitz is out there," she said.

"I know. He's patrolling the bloody tent. So what's this step three?"

"Third-factor ID. It's biometric. Not just *something you know* and *something you have* but also *something you are*. This is not the security you use for your vacation photos."

"What is it, a fingerprint?"

She sat at the laptop. "Or an iris scan or a… Oh God, it's asking for a facial scan."

"Can you use a photo of him?"

"It has to be 3-D."

"A 3-D printer?"

"Got one on you?"

"Could we…?" *Crackle.*

"Jamie, I'm losing you." Static. Shit. "Jamie?" The laptop clock ticked over another minute. "Jamie? Rafe?"

Fuck it. They couldn't count on Fitz giving up sentry duty anytime soon, leaving Jamie stranded outside. Rafe and Holly were God knew where. She stared at the clock. In thirty-two minutes they'd all be permanently screwed, along with her parents, Tess and Charlotte. She had to stop waiting for someone else to breeze in and make everything better. *Webs of the spider.* She tapped the laptop casing. How could she make this happen, alone?

She got to work, her hands tap-dancing over the keyboard, conscious of every precious minute that passed. Jamie remained silent.

Finally, she pushed the computer off her lap and rubbed her face, cycling her new plan through her head, probing it for bugs, defects, oversights. She walked to the window.

"Jamie?" Nothing. Fitz was still on his phone, arms crossed, breath puffing out as fog. "Jamie?" Silence. "I wish I had your confidence," she whispered.

You do.

I don't. But I'm doing this anyway.

She walked to the bedside table, picked up the phone and dialed a room number. Her hand shook so much she twice pressed the wrong button and had to start over.

A gruff voice answered. "Yes?"

"Senator Hyland?"

"Yes."

"This is Samira Desta. I believe you are looking for me."

CHAPTER TWENTY-TWO

WHAT DID SAMIRA just say? Jamie hissed her name again but the comms were evidently still only working one way—and patchy at that. What was she doing? He'd heard typing, and then she'd dialed a number on a landline, going by the distant tones.

Merde, she'd called Hyland's room? Fitz or not, Jamie had to get inside.

A tinny, echoing man's voice came through the earpiece. Hyland. She'd put the phone on speaker? "...believe many people are looking for you. Where are you?"

"In your hotel. I want to talk to you and you alone."

"My hotel? Where, exactly?"

"First, I want assurances. You want the name of the person I'm communicating with and you want to stop me testifying against you, and I'm willing to discuss both those things. But you are threatening people who are important to me. I need proof they are safe and will remain so. And I need a new identity and money in exchange for my silence."

Shite. Go, Samira.

"Whoa, whoa," Hyland said. "I have no idea what you're talking about."

"Yes, you do, but I'm sure you'd prefer not to discuss this over the phone."

A stocky man in a black suit charged out of the se-

curity tent, a dark bruise on his temple. The goon Jamie
had sedated in the hospital. Jamie ducked behind a column, hunkering under the baseball cap he'd grabbed
from the car. The earpiece exploded into crackles. When
he peeped out again, the guy was talking to Fitz—
urgent, hushed. Fitz spoke quickly into his phone, pock-
eted it and followed him inside. Going after Samira?

Jamie wandered up to the police guard at the tunnel
entrance, one hand in his trouser pocket. He nodded at
the officer, who waved him in.

"I know you're not alone, Ms. Desta," Hyland was
saying. "Is your companion with you?"

The earpiece squealed with interference, drowning
out her response. The body scanner beeped as Jamie
stepped through. An officer did a paddle scan and let
him pass. A plainclothes woman stood by a computer
with a handheld scanner. She reached for Jamie's lanyard. *Here we go.*

"Early start to winter out there," Jamie said, choosing
an American drawl to match the credentials on his pass.

"Try wearing a kilt," the woman said, jerking her
head toward a hotel doorman.

"No, thank you, ma'am." Never again in his life, if
he could help it.

The scanner beeped. Jamie's face came up on its
screen—the photo Samira had taken a few hours earlier.
Diplomatic Security Special Agent Harrison Roberts Jr.
Top-secret clearance.

Nice work, Samira.

"Thank you, Agent Roberts," the woman said.

In the lobby, Fitz and the driver had disappeared.
Jamie strode toward the lifts, watching the floor indi-
cator. The right-hand elevator passed the second floor
and stopped on the third. *Putain.*

The crackling in his earpiece morphed into Samira's voice. "You have gone after everyone who is close to me. You should know that I am about to do the same, unless you do what I say."

"What do you mean?" Hyland said.

"The carrot and the stick—isn't that how it works, Senator? I have information that will destroy your daughter's reputation, and we both know how much *that* means to her."

"What information?"

Was Samira bluffing? Hyland didn't seem to be buying it.

"I will speak only to you, and only if you come alone," Samira said.

"Ms. Desta, I'm sure you understand that with the level of security—"

A smashing noise. Samira gasped.

"Ah, sounds like my head of security has located you," Hyland said. "He will take it from here. Good talking to you." A click. He'd hung up?

Several clonks, and the earpiece squealed. Jamie upped his pace.

"Lovely to see you again, Ms. Desta." An Irish accent, distant and muffled. Fuck.

Jamie reached the elevators and pressed the call button. It lit up then went dark.

"You have to swipe it with your keycard," a white-haired woman said, walking past. "It's all very involved security around here this week. That senator from America is staying—the handsome one—but I guess you'd know that." Her elderly companion rolled his eyes. "Not that he's *handsome*, I mean. Just that he's here."

In Jamie's ear, Samira cried out faintly, the weak connection making her sound like she was underwater. Shit.

He made a show of patting his pockets. "Oh no, I must have left my card in my room."

"Are you—what's it called—Secret Security Service?" The woman's eyes widened.

"Something like that, ma'am. And, wow, will I be in trouble with the senator for this."

"Oh, we can't have that. Allow me."

She shuffled forward, pulled a keycard from her purse, held it against the scanner and pressed the call button. It lit up—and stayed lit. Jamie held a hand to his ear, cradling his earpiece. Nothing but a faint hum. Seemed like he was the last one standing.

"Appreciate it, ma'am," Jamie said, checking his breath. He'd be the one having a panic attack, in a minute. In what he hoped was a salute befitting the Secret Security Service, he touched two fingertips to his temple. "You two have a nice day."

Once in the elevator, he chose the third floor and hammered the door-close button. What the hell would he do when he got to the room? The doors opened and he peeped out—a quick left and right. The corridor was empty except for a woman in gym gear talking on a phone, her wet hair plastered to her neck. He began walking, checking the room numbers.

"…so embarrassing," the woman was saying as she slotted her card into a lock. "I had to go down to the front desk and get a new key—wet hair, goggle marks, no makeup and this huge zit on my cheek."

Jamie strode faster, counting down the room numbers. He caught up to the woman as she pushed the door open. Room 327.

"Seriously, I look like a zombie with its flesh— Jesus Christ." She held the phone to her chest.

Jamie pulled up behind her. The room looked deserted.

She turned to him. "I think I've been robbed."

He grabbed her shoulders and planted her against the corridor wall. "Wait here." He shouldered open the door as it went to latch, the contact burning into his wound, and reached for a gun that wasn't there. An overturned chair, a spilled suitcase, strewn bedcoverings… Drawers had been pulled out and emptied. The minibar swung open. Jamie crouched and pulled at a corner of dark purple fabric. It snaked out from under a sheet. Samira's scarf.

"Jesus Christ," the woman said again, holding the door open. "Should I report it?" From her phone, a tinny voice squealed.

"No," Jamie said, adopting an authoritative voice. "No, I'll take care of it, ma'am. Go back to the gym and wait there. Speak to nobody."

As she spun, a large figure covered the doorway. She jumped, screeching. The sound echoed in Jamie's ear. Samira's mic had to be still in the room. A guy in a black suit stepped in, holding a Beretta. Laura's security detail. Blood seeped from a wound beside his eye. The woman backed into the room.

"Where is she?" Jamie demanded.

"I swear, man," said the guy, advancing, the woman almost pirouetting in his wake, "I'm not even sure what's going on but your best chance is to come quietly. Your buddy already gave me enough trouble."

The woman tripped and fell backward onto the floor. She scrambled, grabbed a high-heeled boot from a pile of clothing and smashed it into the guy's shin. He flinched. Jamie leaped into a disarming maneuver. The guy swiveled and his fist connected with Jamie's wounded shoulder. Another black-suited goon ran into the room, identical Beretta trained on Jamie's chest.

"Sorry, man," the first guy said. "I did suggest you come quietly."

FITZ SHOVED SAMIRA onto a chair in a windowless meeting room. She didn't even know what floor they were on. The Peugeot driver followed him in and closed the door, Samira's laptop under her arm. They weren't taking her to Hyland?

"I will talk only to the senator," Samira said.

"He's a busy man," Fitz said. "He doesn't deal with minor concerns."

"I am no *minor* concern." Damn her shaky voice. "He wants the name of my contact and he wants my silence. In exchange, I want reassurances. From him, face-to-face."

"I can make you silent anytime I choose."

"But you don't know what information I have or where I've stored it or in whose hands it will end up if something happens to me. Do you think I would have come to you like this without taking precautions?" God, she sounded as desperate as she felt.

He linked his hands behind his back. "If you had any power over the senator you'd have used it by now, you'd have given your intel to the special counsel, the media. You have nothing."

Saliva filled her mouth. She resisted the urge to swallow. "You think I want to put myself in the public eye like that? You think I like all this attention? You think I like living in fear?"

"I know for a fact that you don't."

"Then you know me better than I'd given you credit

for. And you'll understand that I want to come to a solution on the quiet, as I'm sure the senator does."

He waited—stony faced but intrigued enough to find out where she was going with this. Hell, *she* hardly knew where she was going.

"There are three ways this will go away," she said, her words racing along with her pulse. "One, I turn over what I have to the special counsel, which will require me to testify, which will lead to my entire life being dissected in the media, and that attention following me around forever. That's not a win for either of us. Or, two, you buy my intel and my silence—money, a new identity and assurances that the people I love will be protected."

"You said three ways. What's the third?"

"You kill me, and all the dirt I have—on Hyland, on his daughter—will be delivered to the special counsel, the FBI and every major news outlet in America."

"What makes you think we have the power to give you any of these things?"

"I'm not a fool, *Matisse*." His brow flinched. "Oh, did I forget to mention? I have an intriguing dossier of evidence on you among my files. How would Jennifer, Grace and Toby feel if their husband and father was implicated in the LA terror attacks? I have proof of where you were that day—and it wasn't at home on Sixth Street as you claimed, was it?" She eyeballed him, trying to cover for her bluff.

"I will need to see this evidence you claim to have before we enter any negotiations."

She exhaled through her nose. Progress. She flicked her gaze pointedly at the laptop.

"Open it," he said to the woman.

The woman laid it on the table and pulled the cover open. "It's password-protected."

Fitz raised his eyebrows at Samira.

"Some of this material is of a highly…personal nature," Samira said. "I doubt the senator would be comfortable sharing it, even with you."

He strode up to her, grabbed a chunk of her hair and yanked, forcing her head back, pressing her chin into his suit jacket. She gasped, pain shooting over her scalp. He smelled of strong cologne, like he'd sprayed in lieu of showering.

"Don't have a panic attack, Samira," he hissed.

She fought to keep her head from spinning. His outburst had to be a good sign—an attempt to reassert his power because he felt it slipping. She knew all about powerlessness. She breathed out, relaxed and let her lungs fill, breathed out, relaxed. He narrowed his eyes and released her with a shove, toppling her chair backward. Her cheek smacked into a cabinet. She sprawled onto the carpet and scrambled backward, sitting against the wall, drawing in her knees. She touched her palm to her cheek. Hot but not bleeding.

Fitz pulled out a phone and dialed. A second later he met her gaze, eyes wide, jaw dropped. Calling Hyland's cell phone.

She pressed the soles of her feet hard onto the carpet, her back into the wall. "If you're in any doubt about how far I can reach—how far I *have* reached—*that's* just the beginning."

"What is it?" the woman asked Fitz.

He hung up, switched his phone to speaker and called again, eyeballing Samira. It went straight to Hyland's message—his *new* message. Samira's voice scratched out of the phone: "Regrettably, Senator Hyland is presently *detained* and may be for quite some time." She didn't sound nearly as fearful as she'd felt when she'd recorded it, minutes before calling Hyland's room—but then, she'd made three attempts before getting the words straight. His phone was now dismantled, the pieces dropped between the blades of an air vent in the swimmer's room, along with Samira's comms set, hurriedly stashed in the seconds it'd taken Fitz and his goons to push past the set of drawers she'd dragged in front of the door.

"Oh, I can also fix that once I've talked to the senator," Samira said. "Or it might well get switched to something more incriminating, depending on how this next part goes."

He snatched up his phone and walked out, slamming the door behind him. Eyeing Samira, the woman pulled out a chair and sat. She tapped the butt of her gun on the table. *Don't worry, lady. I'm not going anywhere.*

How the hell had Samira got herself into this position? Where was Jamie? Rafe? Holly? Had Charlotte been rescued, at least?

What does your instinct tell you?

She stared at the ceiling. She knew what she wanted to be true—everyone safe, the pressure permanently lifted from her chest, that she could be free to start something with Jamie, that he could be free to give himself to her.

Wow. It turned out she wasn't ready to give up on him. But first she had to convince him to stop giving up on himself.

Well, technically, *first* she had to get out of this alive—get everyone out. *Then* she had to convince him.

Yes. Yes, maybe that was the secret to finding the courage to see this through. She'd lived so long in fear of the future but maybe it was time to look forward to something—the promise of a new day that wouldn't start with waking up alone and empty. Maybe that new day would be tomorrow. A clock ticked. She scanned the walls and found it. Six minutes until the password changed. Or *not* tomorrow.

Footsteps neared. Voices. The door handle moved and the door swished. A heavyset man in a black suit held it open, scanning the room.

Then Hyland strode in, right up to the table. He planted his fists on it, his weight forward, arms straight, like he was commanding a board meeting. Fitz sidled in behind. Samira pushed back into the wall. The senator was way bigger in person.

"Ms. Desta," he said. His tie was gone, his top shirt buttons undone. "How good to meet you after all this time. I apologize that I'm a little rushed—I have several of the world's most powerful people waiting for me—so I'll make this quick. I understand you're attempting a power play. Well, let me school you in power plays because this is what I do best. This…" He waved his security guy forward. "This is what we call a show of strength."

The guy unlocked his phone, strode toward Samira and held it out. The screen showed a photo. A woman lying on a concrete floor, eyes closed, long black hair splayed in a pool of blood. Samira blinked and looked away. No. No.

"You may recognize your friend Ms. Liu. Your *late* friend, Ms. Liu."

Samira's windpipe closed. Her eyes stung.

"I know you thought you'd saved her with your friend's call to the police, in the same deluded, naive way you've convinced yourself you have some kind of power over me. It was quickly dismissed as a hoax. Amateur hour,

Ms. Desta. And this—" he beckoned to Fitz, who opened the door "—is what we call a trump card."

Holly was shoved into the room, hands bound, mouth duct-taped. She squirmed against her captor—one of Laura's guards, a bloody cut smearing his temple. The room tipped. Samira slammed her hands onto the carpet either side of her hips.

"And the other two?" Hyland said, moving aside as Laura's bodyguard fought to force Holly onto a chair. "The men they were with?"

"Dead," the bodyguard said, through clenched teeth.

Samira's chest pinched. The room blurred.

Holly gave a muffled yell as the bodyguard secured her hands to the back of the chair. Hyland's guard tied her ankles to the legs. Her dark makeup was streaked down her face. She looked at Samira with an expression made even more desperate by the makeup and the gag.

Tears escaped Samira's eyes. Her breath scraped.

"Unlike you," Hyland said, shoving his hands in his trouser pockets, "Ms. Ryan here is a genuine threat to me and one I'll be quite happy to be rid of." He nodded at Fitz, who pulled a gun from under his suit jacket, a metal tube on its barrel. A silencer?

Samira's chest felt ready to cave. She pressed her hand to it. Her vision pinpricked.

"Which just leaves the sword of Damocles—in this case, your parents and Tess Newell. The death of Ms. Ryan, right in front of you, along with Ms. Liu and your two male friends, will serve as a warning to you that I mean business. But, as you know, I don't like dealing only in sticks. Leaves a bad taste in the mouth. Your parents and Tess are the carrots that will keep you silent as long as I want to keep you alive—and I haven't yet made a decision on that. Oh, and it's not just their *freedom* that's at stake. No, no. I will have them killed if you don't fully cooperate with me right now, just as I had your traitor fiancé killed." He raised a finger, as if he were making a point of order. "Oh no, wait. That's not a carrot, technically, is it? It's another stick. My mistake. It turns out there are no carrots, here, Ms. Desta. You cannot fight me. You have no power. I have all the power and I always will. Remember that, for as long as you may or may not live."

"Okay," Samira wheezed.

"Speak up, Ms. Desta. I can't hear you." He flicked a finger, and Fitz aimed his gun at Holly, cradling it in both his hands.

"I...I..." She jabbed her pointer finger toward the laptop on the table. "On there," she gasped. "Everything."

Her eyes rolled back. She blinked hard and caught sight of the clock. Two minutes left.

Hyland strolled to the laptop, its screen black. *Hurry up.* He tapped a key. "The password," he said, "before I give instructions to shoot the trump card."

Holly's wide eyes locked on Samira. Samira went to speak but her lungs were sucked hollow. Hyland walked up to her, looking down from his towering height. Then he crouched, eye to eye, and slapped her hard, across her injured cheek.

She gasped, but no air made it in.

You're not going to die... You can let go of that fear.

Sure fucking feels like it, Jamie.

The room darkened. *Let go of the fear. Let go of the effort. Don't fight your body, don't instruct it, don't force it to do anything. Just relax and sit back and watch.*

She closed her eyes, stopped trying to inhale, imagined Jamie's accent rolling over her, his hand on her chest and her belly. The room dived but slowly her lungs inflated. A whoopee cushion finding its normal state. She exhaled again, and then relaxed. After a few breaths she opened her eyes. *Jamie*.

Forget denial. This time she was skipping straight to anger.

"You don't own me," she said, her voice cracking.

"Right now, I think I very much do."

"No." She pointed to the laptop. "It's the password. *You don't own me*. Lowercase, no spaces, no apostrophe."

He studied her a second. *Hurry the fuck up*. Then he ambled back to the table, one hand in his pocket, and tilted the screen. Samira stopped breathing—not with a panic attack, this time. The clock was seconds from running out.

He typed the password, one-fingered, searching for the letters like he was unfamiliar with the layout of a keyboard, and pressed Enter.

"Nothing's happening," he said, after half a minute. "Just a blank screen with an egg timer."

"Oh, there's plenty happening," she said, her voice sounding like it was coming from someone else. "It'll take a while to process."

"How long?"

"That depends how many files you have on your Gold Linings server."

He stared at her. "What are you talking about?"

"I broke into your server."

He scoffed, giving his head a quick shake. "There's nothing you could have found on those servers that would…" He laughed, fleeting and harsh. "Oh man, that's good. That's really good. That's what you think you have on me? Those servers…it's only as much data as my lowliest staff member has access to. Wow, for a minute there, you actually had me worried."

Oh God, was there truly nothing there?

No one put insignificant data behind three-level security. She narrowed her eyes. "I don't think you understand." She damn well hoped he didn't. "I'm not talking just about your cloud server but the *trésor* you hide on there."

For a microsecond his smile wavered. "That's impenetrable."

"Nothing's impenetrable, Senator. You see, Charlotte gave me the password before your goons captured her. That was your first level of security. You may have noticed your cell phone is missing?"

He blinked. Fitz swore.

"That's your second."

"But you—" He looked at the laptop, his forehead wrinkling. "Fuck."

"The second you entered that password, the computer scanned your face, and your files began copying directly from Gold Linings onto twenty newly formed websites—hylandhacks.com, thedirtonhyland.net, teflontristan.co…"

Face reddening, he picked up the laptop and bent the screen back until it snapped. He twisted it into two pieces and smashed his fist onto the keyboard. She felt detached, floating over the scene. She'd won but this was no victory. Charlotte's body, crumpled on a concrete floor. Latif's body, a mess of blood. Rafe. The crinkles at the corners of Jamie's eyes.

A tear rolled down her cheek. She blinked her eyes clear. "Destroying the computer will make no difference. There was nothing at all on it." She felt deflated but…calm. In shock, probably. "Until you entered that password I had nothing on you at all. I don't even know what's in that folder but your level of security told me it was precious to you. It was just an educated guess but I'm thinking I guessed right."

The senator turned to Fitz, who seemed to have shrunk, his face pale and hard. "Find those websites and shut them down."

"It's too late for that, Senator," she said. "Do you know how many social-media followers your daughter has?"

"What the fuck are you talking about now?" His neck seemed to have thickened, purple veins ready to burst.

"Not only did you just hack into your own vault by looking at that webcam, but you triggered a series of scheduled posts to go up on your daughter's social-media accounts directing her followers to my new websites, where they can download every document at their leisure. And she is on pretty much every medium there is. How many million followers? Oh and she's just sent private messages to every major media outlet in America and the UK."

"You're lying."

"You think? Turn on that TV—any international news channel. Let's see how fast news travels."

Hyland stared at her, his jaw tight. He turned to his bodyguard and gave a brusque nod. The guy picked up the remote and clicked. The BBC flickered up. A newscaster. A breaking-news ticker: *Massive hack of Senator Tristan Hyland. More to come.*

"…task has barely begun of sifting through thousands of files but Laura Hyland is claiming on social media that they contain damning evidence that the senator was involved in the deadly Los Angeles atta—"

"Turn it off," Hyland yelled.

The guard flinched and hit the channel button by mistake—switching to footage of Hyland leaving the hotel in his tuxedo, with a voice-over in an American accent: "...including a document that apparently orders the death of a whistle-blower who was killed in Somalia in what was staged to be—"

Hyland strode up to the guard, snatched the remote and hit a red button. The room fell silent. A shout came from the corridor outside. Hyland pinned his gaze on Samira. With a scream of rage, he threw the remote at the wall over her head. It smashed and bounced off. She balled up.

No, this was not a victory. Not without Jamie. She hadn't truly expected this moment to come—and she hadn't expected it to carry such a price. She looked up. Holly's eyes were dry but still wide. "I'm sorry," Samira mouthed, unable to make the words come. Holly had lost her partner, her child's father.

"You can't win this," Hyland said, his teeth clenched. "I'll find a way out. I always do." He turned to the goons. "Kill her," he said, in a low voice. "Kill both of them."

"Allow me," Laura's bodyguard said, stepping in front of Holly. He raised his gun.

"No," Fitz said, striding across the room and shoving him out of the way. "They're mine. This one first." He nodded toward Holly. "So the other bitch gets to see what's coming."

Outside the door, something banged. Holly yelled into her gag, thrashing, the chair hopping on the carpet. Fitz cocked his gun.

CHAPTER TWENTY-THREE

JAMIE WAS DEAD. Latif was dead. Charlotte, Rafe. But Holly, and her baby…

No time to think. No options to assess. Nothing to weigh up. Enough people had died.

Samira launched up and dived at Holly, hazily aware of action around her—the door flying open and banging against the wall, Laura's bodyguard lunging at Fitz, Fitz flying sideways. A hiss and a hollow smack and Samira careered into Holly like something had picked her up and thrown her across the room. She sprawled, her head bouncing on the carpet as the chair thumped them sideways. Her vision filled with the scarlet hue of fresh blood.

Not blood—Holly's dress, hooked over Samira's head. Fitz had missed. But there'd been some explosion, some force had lifted her.

Facedown, tangled, she braced for another gunshot. There were shouts, feet thudding—everything muffled in her blown hearing. That shot had *not* been silent.

A burn, just above her hip. A hot tap at first, then searing pain. She grabbed the spot, twisting, ripping Holly's dress from her face. Her hand found warm liquid, came away coated with…blood. Underneath her, Holly grunted and bucked like she was trying to throw Samira off. Samira went to roll away but her muscles refused to work. The pain…

The room writhed with people—diving, shouting, brawling. Where had they come from? Hyland barked orders that might as well have been in another language. Holly stood in the doorway, hands on hips. No, not Holly—obviously. It was Laura, dressed identically. With a yell that came out a whimper, Samira flopped over and found a wall. A big man in a suit staggered in front of Holly, his back to her and Samira. Samira kicked out weakly, pain bursting through her gut. He caught her leg and then her gaze. Rafe. It was Rafe. It couldn't be. He let go, turned back.

Samira lurched her head up, pain and heat filling her belly. If *Rafe* was here…

Laura's bodyguard had Hyland's goon in a headlock. Another guy—Laura's other security detail—aimed a gun at the Peugeot driver, who slowly put her hands up, still seated, looking baffled.

Jamie. Jamie was wrestling Fitz. Samira scrambled to her feet, clutching her side. He slammed a fist into Fitz's nose with a squelchy crack. In a flash of blurry movements, he wrenched Fitz's arms back, securing him from behind. Laura's bodyguard threw Hyland's goon to the ground and stepped back, aiming a gun at the guy's chest.

"Heads up," Laura's bodyguard shouted. With his free hand, he tossed something to Rafe—a gun, taken from Hyland's goon. Rafe caught it and turned it on Fitz.

"I got him, Doc," Rafe said, scooting to a corner where he could take in everyone.

The room stilled but for multiple pairs of heaving lungs. Adrenaline scented the air, metallic and sharp. Or was that blood? Jamie threw Fitz into the corner Samira had been cowering in minutes ago, stepped back and leveled the gun with the silencer.

The people in the room had split in two. On Samira's side, by the open door, Rafe, Jamie, Holly, Laura and her two bodyguards. Four guns raised. On the other, Fitz and the driver, Hyland's guard and Hyland, looking so fiery he could well begin to smolder. All unarmed.

Rafe sidled over to Holly. "Sorry, *ma chérie*, this may hurt."

Holly muttered. Rafe pulled the tape from her mouth. She yelped.

Samira's legs gave way and she slumped against the wall and slid to the ground.

"Doc, take care of Samira," Rafe said. "We got this."

Jamie's gaze snapped to Samira, his eyes creased. He scanned her body, down and up, and zeroed in on her side. He crossed the room in two strides and knelt before her.

"You got shot?"

She touched the wrinkles beside his eyes. "I love those." Her finger juddered over them. Speed bumps. "They said you were dead."

He gently pulled her hand from the wound. He twisted to glance at Laura's bodyguard, the one who'd brought Holly in. "You were supposed to protect her."

What?

"*And* Holly," Rafe said, darkly.

"Stand down, Rafe," Holly said. "I knew what I was getting into. Trojan horse, remember?"

Laura's bodyguard pulled a phone from his pocket and handed it to his colleague. "Call an ambulance." He glanced at Rafe. "And you were supposed to get here earlier."

"We got a little held up in the hallway, dealing with your colleagues."

The bodyguard scanned the four stunned faces on the other side of the room. "Not my colleagues anymore."

Fitz spit, the phlegm landing on the bodyguard's arm. "You know what happens to traitors in this operation."

The bodyguard shook his head. "You're a traitor to far more than this cluster fuck of a company—ever since you decided to put your loyalty to him above everything else." He jerked his head at Hyland. "You still gonna be his bitch in prison?" He pulled a pocketknife from his suit and handed it to Rafe.

As Rafe freed Holly, Hyland's voice cut through the rest, dark and disbelieving. "Laura? Are you involved in this?"

Laura crossed her arms. "I have been for a long time. I'm over living this lie, *Pops*. I'm over standing beside you, playing the good daughter while you kill and terrorize and blackmail and I don't even know what else. It's finished. I'm out."

"But how—?" Samira flinched as Jamie pressed on her wound.

"Laura was the mystery person in the game," he said, quietly. "She gave us the log-on, the password."

"You naive, selfish piece of shit," the senator spit at Laura, his face beetroot. "You want to destroy your own father, your future, your world?"

Laura's eyes glassed over. "*My* world? I don't even know what that is. All I've ever done is play a role for the cameras. Now maybe I can write the real memoir of my life, not this fiction you forced on me."

"I give you everything and you give me this?"

"You only ever wanted to keep me locked up. Your Rapunzel in a tower. But…" She shook her head, resetting. "This isn't about me. It stopped being about me when Latif discovered your role in the LA attacks."

Hyland advanced on Laura. "If you're talking about the conspiracy theory dreamed up by that idiot—" Her bodyguard stepped between them. Hyland looked ready to strike him.

"Oh my God," Samira whispered to Jamie. "Latif and Charlotte's source in Denniston. It was Laura."

For the first time, Laura met Samira's gaze. "Samira. I'm so sorry for the grief I caused you. I thought I could protect Latif. He was such a good man."

"You knew his favorite food."

"We became friends when he was working at Denniston, when my father was still calling the shots there, training me up to one day take over—before it all went to the dogs, before I found out what was really going on. I grew to trust him, and there have been so few people in my life I've been able to trust." She glanced at her bodyguard, who gave a slight, encouraging smile. "Latif had a contact in military intelligence who put him in touch with Tess Newell. We gathered enough evidence to bring down Denniston and most of those involved in the conspiracy but my father slipped from the net. He'd officially sold the company by then, of course. So my involvement had to remain a carefully guarded secret while I kept digging."

"You little bitch—"

"Shut the fuck up." Laura's bodyguard closed in on Hyland, glowering.

"I'm watched 24/7," Laura continued, lightly touching the bodyguard's arm. He halted, still glaring at Hyland. "My computer is monitored, my phone calls, everything. I once tried to sail around the world to get some freedom but my father found a way to control even that. So Latif worked out a way we could correspond in secret, even after his snooping was detected and the two of you had to go into hiding."

"The game," Samira said. "You communicated through the game. You were Erebus."

Laura's red lips widened into a sad smile. "The god of shadows. Latif named my avatar."

"Why didn't he tell me all this?"

The smile dropped. "He didn't want you to worry."

Samira closed her eyes tightly, for a second. Her side burned but the pain seemed distant, like it was happening to someone else. The entire scene seemed to be happening in another dimension.

"Right before Latif died, he introduced me to Charlotte," Laura continued. "He knew if he didn't…survive, she'd help me track down what we needed. But in the end what we needed was you."

Samira gulped. Latif had trusted Laura and Charlotte but not her. He hadn't thought she could handle it. And maybe she couldn't have, back then. Hell, two hours ago she'd have thought herself incapable of any of this.

"I finally found out where the evidence was kept but Charlotte didn't have the skills to hack in," Laura continued. "We needed you. We just didn't know how to contact you. So she wrote the postcard and I mailed it from Paris. But apparently it got intercepted." She looked at Jamie. "Some of this I've only managed to put together tonight… And then of course Charlotte disappeared and my father bullied his way into a trip to the UK. It didn't take a genius to figure out why."

Hyland advanced on Laura. "Last warning—keep back," her bodyguard said, dark eyes glittering.

"I pay your wages," Hyland hissed. "I hired you."

"You pay me to protect your daughter and that's what

I'm doing. It's what I've always done. You've bullied and used her long enough."

"You fucking trait—"

"Yes, *Pops*. You put people on my detail who are loyal to you but not everyone remains that way, not after they discover what you've done."

"You'll lose everything, you stupid little girl."

Laura's bodyguard met her eye. She held the gaze, like she was downloading strength from him. "Not everything," she said.

"You will regret this," Hyland said to Laura, holding his ground. "If I go down, you're coming, too. I'll wring your pampered neck."

"No, that's not your style. You'd rather pay someone else to." Laura looked at the ceiling, her eyes glossing over. "He wasn't always like this," she said to no one in particular. "They say he was damaged by his time in the marines, the CIA, by Mom's death. He lost his empathy. His black and white was upended."

"You know nothing."

"I know a lot more than you've ever given me credit for, Pops." Laura returned her gaze to Samira. "I was devastated when Latif was killed. I'm so sorry."

Samira's eyes pricked.

"But I'm thankful we got to Charlotte in time."

"Charlotte?" Samira gasped. "Charlotte's dead."

"No." Laura's eyes brightened. "She's fine."

"But the photo... I saw her..."

"A trick. I saw your note in the game, with her location. We already had a team combing the area." Laura exchanged another glance with her bodyguard. The other half of the *we*? "When you gave us the coordinates, we pulled her out quick. One of her guards' phones pinged with a message from Fitz ordering her death, so we faked the photo, to buy us time. Oh, and our team came across a friend of yours trying to extract her single-handedly and unarmed—"

"Texas," Jamie explained.

"Apparently, he'd almost succeeded," Laura's bodyguard added. "He was a little pissed that our guys were crashing his party."

Rafe's lip slightly curved upward.

Footsteps thundered down the hallway. Laura leaned forward to look through the open door, unfolding her arms. "The police commander, at last. I'll go talk to her." She turned. "Pops, I'm still your daughter. Nothing changes that. When the dust clears, when you've let all this go, I'll be the only one standing by you. But I can't be your enabler any longer. It's over. There's no coming back this time." She sniffed.

Hyland sank into a chair, his head in his hands. Suddenly, he looked his age, like the spell of youth had been broken.

"The paramedics are here, too," Laura said, still looking down the hallway. "Shall I send them in, Jamie?"

"I'll take her out," Jamie said, scooping Samira up. "There's enough going on in here."

Laura touched Samira's shoulder as Jamie swept her past. Her cornflower eyes glimmered. "It's an honor to finally meet you." To Jamie she added, "Take care of her—and get her to unlock my social media. I have a few updates of my *own* to post."

"Will do." The beginnings of a grin played on Jamie's face. "And don't worry. She can take care of herself—not that I'm going anywhere." The grin faded. "Not for a while."

Samira's heart clunked as Jamie carried her out, his body warm and solid and lithe. She might not have lost him to death but she would lose him. When? Tomorrow, next week, next month?

She'd had enough of waking up alone. She wanted to wake up to him.

BEFORE SAMIRA EVEN properly woke, the chemical smell clued her in. A hospital. She cracked her eyes open. A small dimmed room, blades of daylight sneaking in either side of a window blind. Distant voices murmured. A pair of sneakers squeaked, approaching and then receding.

She tried to pull herself up but her body wouldn't respond. She patted her hip through a cotton blanket. It was like touching someone else's body. Numbed. Beneath the blanket, beneath a hospital gown, a dressing crackled. An IV line was taped to the back of her hand but it wasn't plugged into anything. She remembered the ambulance ride, lying on a gurney, Jamie holding her hand, breathing through the pain and nausea, waking briefly in a large, busy room—Recovery?

It was over. They'd done it. She exhaled, peace flushing through her veins like a cool anesthetic. They'd won.

And she'd woken alone. The first day of her new life and she'd woken alone. Had Jamie already returned to the Legion? Was this how it would be? Today a hospital, tomorrow maybe a hotel. Beyond that—what? Some apartment she couldn't picture in a city she couldn't picture. She couldn't even picture a country. The world was hers again but she didn't belong anywhere in it.

The door swished open. Jamie stepped in, still wearing his suit—and a smile that turned her insides to syrup. Turned out there was one thing sexier than a well-cut man in a well-cut suit—the same man in the same suit the morning after. Was it even morning?

"You're kidding me," he said. "I spend all night and all day sitting beside your bed and you wake up in the ten minutes it takes me to pop out and say goodbye to Rafe and Holly."

"Wha—?" She coughed. Her throat felt like it had been blasted with a hairdryer.

He crossed to a cabinet beside the bed, poured water into a cup, popped a lid with a straw on it and passed it to her. She drank. Sometimes water tasted so good…

She cleared her throat. "Where are they going?"

"Rafe has a sister he was separated from as a child. He just got word that she's been located, so he and Holly are flying out to meet her. Apparently she has a family of her own. He's pretty stoked—and dare I say, emotional. I swear his eyes glazed for a second."

"Wow."

"They were sorry they couldn't stick around. Holly's looking forward to thanking you personally for saving her life."

"I saved her li—? Oh that…" She touched her hip again.

"'Oh that,' she says, like it's an everyday kind of a something to do."

"I can't believe I did that."

"I can. Though, fuck, hearing that gunshot, seeing the blood on you…" He shuddered. "I think it's going to be one of those recurring nightmares, where I'm looking for you, in room after room, with guns going off."

Her cheek throbbed. She touched it, lightly. It was puffy, tender. Fitz had hit her. And Hyland. "How long have I been asleep?"

"A while. The anesthetic wore off overnight but you were exhausted."

"*Awo.* I remember waking in the night." She'd been

disorientated, tipped out of a shadowy dream. But then Jamie's voice—soothing and deep... She'd drifted off again, with the comforting feeling of being spooned, though he wasn't touching her.

She tried to sit again, and winced, remembering.

"Hey," he said, leaping to the bedside. How did he have so much energy? "Don't lift yourself up. I'll adjust the bed." He fiddled with a control, and the back slowly rose. "You were very lucky that the bullet shied away from your intestine but you have an impressive flesh wound."

"Did you sleep here?"

"Sleep's an exaggeration, but..." He nodded at an armchair. "There was a lot of explaining to do—not nearly as much for me as for Hyland, though. He's on a plane back to the States. Laura talked him into coming clean about everything—seeing as there was no longer any point in denial. It was all in the files you released, clear as day. His links to terrorism, his long history of blackmail and corruption... Tess reckons it could take months before they even figure out how many crimes he's committed—but conspiracy to mass murder is a good start. Honestly, I don't understand half of it, but fortunately, the president does. Apparently he was most especially interested in the photo Hyland had used to blackmail the special counsel into burying evidence in the investigation into him. And Tess is in journalist nirvana, as you can imagine. Flynn reckons she hasn't blinked since the files started uploading."

"She's been released?"

"Aye, and exonerated, along with you and me and your parents. And Charlotte's on her way up to Edinburgh to see you. By outing Hyland you've saved everybody's skins, so the journey's all but over for us." He smoothed her hair back from her forehead. Her scalp tingled. "We just need to get you well."

We. We as in the world, the health system, their little group of rebels—or *we* as in Jamie and Samira?

"When can I go…?" She squeezed her eyes shut.

"Samira?" he said, taking her hand. "You need pain-killers?"

She opened her eyes. He leaned over her, his eyes crinkling. She remembered touching his wrinkles at the hotel, saying something stupid about them. "No. It's just… I was going to say 'When can I go home?' But…"

"You don't have a home."

"Awo."

"You *can* have one, now. You can start rebuilding your life." He hooked his foot around a plastic chair, pulled it up beside her and sat, holding her hand in both of his. "And anyway, you'll not be going anywhere for a few weeks, not while you're recuperating—and there are some immigration matters to be sorted."

"Oh God."

He chuckled. "Nothing to worry about. You've gone from wanted woman to folk hero overnight. The UK authorities have just kindly asked if you can fill out the proper paperwork and present your genuine passport."

She relaxed onto the bed. As she inhaled, her side pinched. "What about you?" she said. "Will you go back to Corsica?"

"I have some recuperating of my own to do. In more ways than one." He tightened his grip on her fingers, shifting his chair closer. "I was thinking, Samira. It's Christmas soon. I know Scotland's not the most pleas-ant of places in winter but it can also be quite…" A grin pulled at his mouth but once again didn't quite erupt. "Romantic."

Her stomach clenched, shooting a bolt of pain deep into her side.

"I'd like to spend some time with Nicole and the kids and see my mother," he continued, dropping focus to their hands. "And I'd love to spend some more time with you."

"Me, too," she squeaked.

"So I'm thinking maybe we could find a wee cottage by a loch—one that hasn't been bombed recently—and hide away for a bit, while we recover, get our heads around everything that's happened. I'm theoretically injured, so getting the leave shouldn't be a problem."

A cottage. With an open fire. And Jamie. And no one shooting or bombing them. Could anything be more appealing? Did it snow in Scotland in December?

"I'd like that," she said.

She wanted to say so much more but the words wouldn't come. Somehow she'd found the courage to confront the man who'd killed her fiancé, and to dive in front of a bullet, but she couldn't find the courage to tell Jamie that there was this big bubble sitting in her chest and it was filled with the magic that was him and she didn't want it to burst.

Or could she?

He rubbed his thumb over the back of her hand. "Before we, you know…return to our lives."

Our lives. Separate lives. Spoken so deliberately, like he'd sensed what she was about to ask—not that even she knew what that was.

"Samira?"

This was exactly what he'd warned her of. *We could never work, you and I. I can't have a relationship. I can't live in the real world.* At the time the real world had seemed so distant. And now here it was, with all its mundane everyday self-doubt. She'd leveled up, all right. Leveled up and bombed out.

"I think... I need to sleep," she said, retrieving her hand. Unable to flip to her side, she turned her head to a beige wall. God, hadn't she told him she wasn't ready for a relationship either? And she'd meant it. But now that her life was no longer in danger, now the people she cared for were safe, she was struggling to remember why.

Regret, like a tail, comes at the end.

He was silent awhile. "Sure," he said. She sensed him leaning in. He pressed a kiss to her temple. "I'll leave you alone." His footsteps padded to the door, then stopped. "I found this for you," he said, quietly, as if not wanting to disturb her from sleep. "Thought you might want it back."

After a few seconds, he padded back over to the bed. She resisted looking. Her eyes would give away too much. A few seconds later, the door whispered open, and hissed closed, leaving the room in thick silence.

She turned. Her scarf was draped over the foot of the bed. *La couleur de minuit.*

She didn't want to be alone anymore.

And it turned out she was the kind of woman who fought for what she wanted.

JAMIE'S BREATH PUFFED out as moonlit fog as he watched Samira unlock their legally rented holiday cottage, after parking their legally hired car. From the loch, a bird cawed. Samira's hair fell softly over her *minuit* scarf as she stepped back and held the door open.

"Next time we're renting a fully insulated twenty-first-century apartment," he said, sweeping past with an armful of firewood and switching on the lights with an elbow. "It's colder inside than out."

"I quite like the eighteenth century now that I'm no longer living in it," she said, hauling in their stash of Christmas presents. "But we'll need to get you a kilt."

"You have a thing for guys in kilts."

"I have a thing for a particular guy in a kilt. At least, I would, if he wore one."

"Nasty, draughty, scratchy things."

"Not very patriotic, Jamie."

As he got started on the fire, she leaned over him to turn on the Christmas tree lights. As she withdrew, she dropped a kiss on his crown. He caught a waft of the perfume he'd given her that morning, which Max and Tyler had helped him choose in a Christmas Eve assault on a mega mall that hadn't existed last time he'd been in Scotland. At first the kids had dragged their clompy feet as if perfume shopping were equivalent to mucking out latrines—but after a few minutes they'd launched into the task with endearing seriousness, wrinkling their noses at anything too floral, or too strong, or too "old lady." In the end the three of them agreed on a perfume that reminded Jamie of running water and jasmine and sunshine. Which would have been far cheaper.

He'd felt a tweak of jealousy that the kids had bonded with Samira so effortlessly when they were still a little standoffish with him, but then, he had a lot of uncle neglect to make up for—and he didn't know where to find the Orb of Glowing or whatever the fuck they were hunting in their latest game. He'd at least figured out which kid was which. He was working on the rest. From now on, he was spending his leave with them, not with medical journals.

As the fire began to take, Samira switched off the overhead light. The pulsing tree lights explored new depths in her softly curling hair—red, green, blue, orange—each color also bringing out a different warmth or coolness in her skin. Her face had lost its strained look in the last month, the sooty circles disappearing from under her eyes.

"Perfect," he said.

"Not quite." She strolled to the butcher's block in the middle of the kitchen, swiping her mobile phone. A familiar intro of piano and strings circled the room. He smiled as a laconic, indecipherable male voice growled the opening to the Pogues' Christmas song. What was it called? "Fairytale of New York"?

Now, *that* was his idea of a Christmas carol, after a day of Nicole's Frank Sinatra on repeat. He'd been content to put up with it during his mother's visit, savoring the look of peace on her face as she swayed in her chair to "Have Yourself a Merry Little Christmas." But by the end of the night even Samira's parents were tactfully dropping hints about changing the music. Their diplomatic skills had been no match for Nicole's determination to create the busy, noisy family Christmas she'd missed out on for so many years—and not even the kids really minded.

"You can bring the music next Christmas," she'd told Samira's parents, with excruciating emphasis. Jamie had looked sideways at Samira, whose gaze had dropped to her lap. They'd hardly talked about the fact that Jamie was due to report to Calvi immediately after the New Year. Only one more week of this borrowed and rented and hired bliss.

Jamie sat back on his haunches. "What, you mean you'll allow a man to sing to you?"

"It's a duet. And at least it's not Sinatra dreaming of a white Christmas for the twentieth time."

"Thank sweet baby Jesus himself for that." Jamie rubbed his hands together as he pushed to his feet. "We'd better do something to warm up while that catches—and by that I mean dance because I know where your dirty mind is going."

She laughed as he swept her into his arms, careful to avoid her injured side. It was healing well but it would trouble her awhile longer. His shoulder was coming right, too. A lot of things had come right in the last month. They swayed together, her new scent wafting in with the wood smoke and wrapping around him. He leaned in for a warm, sweet kiss.

As the drumbeat turned the song from ballad to jig, and the woman singer launched in, Jamie upped the pace, spinning and dipping Samira until she laughed breathlessly, their boots scraping and squeaking across the wooden floor. God, she was beautiful. This was beautiful. The cottage had more comforts than the previous one but it was simple enough that life was dialed back to the small pleasures—not that being with Samira was any *small* pleasure.

They'd wasted quite enough time giving lengthy witness statements to investigators representing more government agencies and crime-fighting forces than he knew existed, juggling medical appointments, and dissecting developments over video calls with Tess and Flynn, Rafe and Holly, Charlotte, and even Laura, whom Hyland had given the credit for forcing him to come clean.

As the song ended, Jamie dipped Samira and kissed her giggling mouth.

"Thank you, *mo ghràidh*." He pulled her up, keeping one arm around her back. She rested her free hand on his chest as the music switched to Roberta Flack's "Killing Me Softly."

"You called me that once. *My friend*, right?"

"No, actually. It means *my love, my darling*. I'd kind of said it then without thinking of the implications, so..."

"You lied. Huh." She pulled back and the skin around her eyes tightened momentarily. "Did you think about the implications just now?"

"Samira," he said, his heart sinking. He didn't want to disappoint her, not on Christmas Day. He shouldn't have used the phrase but it just seemed right. "We need to live in the moment. Appreciate what we've got right now and leave with happy memories. We'll always have the loch." Her lashes flickered down, hiding her eyes. Aye, he was a jerk. They continued swaying gently to the music. "Maybe this isn't the best day for that talk."

Roberta filled the silence. After another verse, Samira stomped one boot on the floor, and pushed his chest. He released her. Damn.

"Screw it," she said, hands fisted by her sides, eyes glittering with reflected flames as if the fire were in them, not the grate. "I've faced down my biggest fears and damn well won. If I'm brave enough to do all that, I'm brave enough to open my mouth and speak my mind."

"You should always feel like you can speak your mind to me." *But don't call it quits on me on Christmas Day. Just one more week...*

"*Always.* You keep on saying things like that—*one day, someday, always...* But you're not open to there being an *always*, or even a *one day* or a *someday*. You only want there to be a *now* because you can't face the past and you refuse to think about the future."

"What future can I offer you, Samira? I fucked up my future and I'm not going to fuck up yours. I used to be a bloody surgeon. *Then* I could have offered you something. I'm nobody now, just a penniless grunt who can't operate in the real world."

"I don't care about what you *did* for a job or what you *do*. I care about who you are. I'm not asking you to give me anything but yourself." She fumbled with the knot on her scarf, yanked it off and tossed it on a chair.

He turned, on the pretense of checking the fire, and chucked another chunk of wood on it. Sparks jumped. "You're asking for something I can't give."

She stepped up to him, took his face in both hands and coaxed him to look at her. "All along I've thought I was the fearful one. But it's you who's afraid. You're stuck in this mind-set that you're defined by your achievements, rather than by the man you are. You're scared to take the risk of just being yourself. You, of all people—scared."

He raised his eyebrows. That struck where it hurt. "Aye, that's…pretty much it. You see right through me."

She slid her hands to his neck, then to his chest, gripping his jumper like she was scared he'd run. "Does that concern you, honestly? And for God's sake, no jokes."

He dropped his hands to her jean-clad hips. "I don't think anybody's ever tried to look that hard. As you say, people like the happy-go-lucky joker, so I guess I stick with that. He's a fun guy to be around and that's all anybody wants."

"And I like that side of you, too. But I like the many other sides. You've given me so much, and I'm not going to let you give up on yourself so easily. Jamie, ever since we met, you've made me feel like this confident woman I thought I wasn't. But now, after everything that's happened, I realize I am that woman. That just because I worry about things, because I feel things deeply, because sometimes my body panics, because I don't have that tough-girl bravado of, say, Tess or Holly, it doesn't mean I'm weak. That I can be reserved and careful, and strong and brave at the same time."

"You can. And so many other things. But I don't want to be the man who ultimately messes that up. You deserve more than I can give."

She flattened her hands onto his chest. "So I finally feel like *I'm* good enough for *you* and—what? Now you think you're not good enough for me?"

Oh why did she have to choose Christmas Day? "Samira, you were always good enough for me. And I was never good enough for you—I'm still not. I just pretended to be what you needed me to be, as long as I could."

"Can I be the judge of that? Because…" She patted his chest. Her tone was forceful but it trembled, like she was exploring a new part of her voice she hadn't yet mastered. "You are *so* good for me. Trust me to know my own mind and make my own decisions."

"Oh I do. I just don't trust my future self. What happens when I fall off the wagon again?"

"Maybe I can help you stop that happening. Maybe you can get some help. Maybe I can be there to pick you up. I don't know. I know nothing about addiction but I can learn. It's a journey we can make together."

He took her hands, clutching them to his chest. "I don't want to disappoint you, Samira. And I will, sooner or later. And that would break both our hearts."

Samira leaned her forehead against their linked hands. The fire popped. After half a minute she pushed away again. "What if I told you that you already have my approval and it's not going to change? What if you didn't have to worry about winning my…?" She looked down a few seconds, her eyes hidden under flickering eyelashes, then up again, jutting her jaw a little. "Okay, I'm going to say it, because I feel it and I don't want to pretend this is all a holiday fling anymore because to me it's not—and I don't think it is to you, either, if you're honest with yourself... What if you didn't have to worry about winning my love, or losing it? What if you just considered it won? How would that change things?"

Her whole body seemed to be fizzing. Her fear had given way to a fight.

Damn, she was fighting for him, for them. And why was *he* fighting this, when he wanted it so bad, wanted her so bad? He swallowed. "You know, when you first started seeing through my jokes, seeing my many flaws, I felt physically sick, physically smaller, even. That night at the cottage, the way I let you down, the disappointment in your eyes..." Nausea bubbled in his stomach at the thought. "But after that passed, it was kind of a relief that you knew the worst, that you understood where I was coming from, even if it meant you lost respect for me."

She opened her mouth to speak.

"And I know you did lose respect, Samira," he said, jumping in. "But somehow that made this thing between us more honest. I've never let anybody this far in. You say I've given you so much? Well, you've given me more, in such a short time. I liked you the minute I met you—you had this quiet strength. And I keep finding more and more things to..." Hell, she'd said the *L* word. So could he. "To love."

She smiled, but she still had a sadness in her eyes. "I'm glad. I feel that way about you, too. More and more things..."

He released her hands, cupped her jaw and leaned in, with a pang of guilt that he wasn't quite giving her what she wanted. Was she right? Could there be someday, a one day—an always? As they kissed, she wound her hands around his back, burrowing under his clothing until she found bare skin. Her hands were cold but he bore down on his muscles to stop from flinching. The kiss was soft and pliant but insistent. A kiss of love, not just passing lust. A kiss with a future in it.

She pulled back, and nestled her head against his neck. "It's all so perfect here," she said, wistfully. "I wish we could stay in this borrowed life."

His stomach coiled tight. He didn't want a borrowed life. He wanted to own his life. He wanted a future he could strive toward, not this effortless rolling away of days. Samira wanted him and he wanted her. She was good for him and he was good for her. So why was he pushing her away? He was fighting himself, which made no sense at all.

He wrapped his arms around her. Maybe he did have a choice here, after all. Maybe all the poor choices he'd made in the past didn't have to determine what happened to him forever.

"Corsica is nice, too," he said, his lips grazing her silky hair, his voice a little shaky. "You'd like it there."

SAMIRA PULLED BACK, her heart thudding. Jamie wore the slightest of frowns.

"What are you saying?" she whispered.

"I'm saying life would be just too dour if I went back without you. The dourest." He didn't come near to pulling off the joke. "But I do need to go back, at least for now. I don't know if I can start over with a totally blank slate. I don't know if it's wise for me to step straight into a vacuum, even with you there. I need boundaries, structure." He swallowed, his Adam's apple moving. "But maybe I can slowly move those boundaries, change those structures. With your help."

She filled her lungs. Pine, smoke, him. Delicious. "Anything," she whispered.

"I can move out of the barracks and we can find a little place to rent—maybe a simple cottage like this one. Except, you know—warmer. Tess has decided to base herself there, as a Europe correspondent for her network, and Rafe and Holly are there. There's a solid group of other wives and partners. Can you do whatever it is you do for a day job from there? I'm sure we could sort out a visa now that I'm eligible for a French passport, if my British one isn't en—"

She laid a finger on his lips. "You don't need to talk me into the logistics of it. I can live anywhere, I can work from anywhere—I just need to figure out what I want to do. But is this really what you want?"

"Oh God, yes." He rubbed her upper arms. "Wow, it's such a relief to say that. I want this. I want you. I want us. Come with me, to Corsica—as a first step in whatever direction this journey might take us. I can't see what the future holds for me—I used to be able to see it so well."

"I know that feeling exactly."

"But I do know I'd like a future with you in it. We're good for each other, you and I."

"We are. And we can both rebuild our lives, together."

He bent slightly, grabbed an end of her scarf from the chair and reeled it in.

"La couleur de minuit," he said, draping it around her shoulders. His voice dropped to a whisper. "I am so thoroughly happy when I'm with you, inside and out. I didn't know I could be properly happy again."

She smiled, her chest expanding at the utter beauty of it all. "Me, too. I don't need four Js. Just the one."

He frowned for a second, then smiled as he figured it out. Outside, a bird called. He looked away, as if expecting to see the creature sitting on the mantelpiece. "And maybe sometimes we can have holidays right here. Because I have some relationships to fix." He turned back with a bone-melting smile. "And one to begin."

"I think it's already well begun, don't you?"

"Oh aye. Come here, *mo ghràidh*."

"I'm already here. Always."

He leaned in, still smiling as their lips touched. Roberta drifted into "Bridge over Troubled Water." Samira wrapped her hands around his neck and he took her waist. As the lyrics floated around the room, the singer taking her slow, delicious time, they settled into a softly swaying dance, Jamie singing along in a low murmur. Samira burrowed under his thick layers of clothing to find his smooth, broad back. His deep, rich voice, the crackle of the fire, the warmth in her cheeks, his arms around her, his face in her hair…

A one day and a someday and an always.

Perfect.

* * * * *

ACKNOWLEDGMENTS

It may be my name alone on the front cover of this book but it takes a village to raise a good story. I'm fortunate that my personal village is populated with so many smart and supportive people.

First and foremost, my reliably perceptive and always charming editor Allison Carroll, and the rest of the talented team at HQN Books.

My agent Nalini Akolekar of Spencerhill Associates. Grateful to have you in my corner.

My technical advisers, beta readers, critique partners and support crew, who are always there when I need feedback, fact-checking, reality checks, talking back down from the cliff, and/or wine, including Mia Kay, Jennifer Brodie, Alexa Rowan, Brad McEvoy, Rosalind Martin, C.A. Speakman, Kari Lemor, Carrie Nichols, M.A. Grant, Stefanie London, Taryn Leigh Taylor, Tanya Wright, Jean Barrett, and my uplifting network of local friends. And my unfailingly wise, supportive and good-humored writing groups, primarily the Dragonflies and Romance Writers of New Zealand.

I am blessed and honored to share this journey with such fine people.

Get 4 FREE REWARDS!

We'll send you 2 FREE Books plus 2 FREE Mystery Gifts.

FREE Value Over **$20**

Both the **Romance** and **Suspense** collections feature compelling novels written by many of today's best-selling authors.

YES! Please send me 2 FREE novels from the Essential Romance or Essential Suspense Collection and my 2 FREE gifts (gifts are worth about $10 retail). After receiving them, if I don't wish to receive any more books, I can return the shipping statement marked "cancel." If I don't cancel, I will receive 4 brand-new novels every month and be billed just $6.74 each in the U.S. or $7.24 each in Canada. That's a savings of at least 16% off the cover price. It's quite a bargain! Shipping and handling is just 50¢ per book in the U.S. and 75¢ per book in Canada*. I understand that accepting the 2 free books and gifts places me under no obligation to buy anything. I can always return a shipment and cancel at any time. The free books and gifts are mine to keep no matter what I decide.

Choose one: ☐ **Essential Romance**
(194/394 MDN GMY7)

☐ **Essential Suspense**
(191/391 MDN GMY7)

Name (please print)

Address   Apt. #

City   State/Province   Zip/Postal Code

Mail to the Reader Service:
IN U.S.A.: P.O. Box 1341, Buffalo, NY 14240-8531
IN CANADA: P.O. Box 603, Fort Erie, Ontario L2A 5X3

Want to try two free books from another series? Call 1-800-873-8635 or visit www.ReaderService.com.

---

*Terms and prices subject to change without notice. Prices do not include applicable taxes. Sales tax applicable in NY. Canadian residents will be charged applicable taxes. Offer not valid in Quebec. This offer is limited to one order per household. Books received may not be as shown. Not valid for current subscribers to the Essential Romance or Essential Suspense Collection. All orders subject to approval. Credit or debit balances in a customer's account(s) may be offset by any other outstanding balance owed by or to the customer. Please allow 4 to 6 weeks for delivery. Offer available while quantities last.

Your Privacy—The Reader Service is committed to protecting your privacy. Our Privacy Policy is available online at www.ReaderService.com or upon request from the Reader Service. We make a portion of our mailing list available to reputable third parties that offer products we believe may interest you. If you prefer that we not exchange your name with third parties, or if you wish to clarify or modify your communication preferences, please visit us at www.ReaderService.com/consumerchoice or write to us at Reader Service Preference Service, P.O. Box 9062, Buffalo, NY 14240-9062. Include your complete name and address.

STRS18